IF IT WEREN'T FOR YOU

DOROTHEA NEAMONITOS

First published in 2018 by Amazon.com, Inc.
Amazon.com
Amazon.co.uk
Kindle Edition: ASIN: B07BSB9H2Z
Paperback Edition: ISBN: 978 1980688877
Map of London from the public domain, no rights reserved.
Cover Design by Irene Lampa, all rights reserved.

For my family ♡

To forgive is to set
a prisoner free and
discover that the
prisoner was you.
– Lewis B. Smedes.

One-punch, two-punch, three.
One for him, one for her, one for me.
Forgive once, forgive twice, try thrice; see.
Purge the memory, and I'll let thee be.
Strike true, strike anew, where mercy cries.
And be there no more anguish, but redemption; rise.
Let the blood fall, and the sweat,
And let it be my paid debt.

PART ONE

Chapter One

Now

My heart gives a sudden, erratic thud, and I backpedal out the door in which I've just stepped through. It slams shut with a *bang!* – a whip to propel my escape faster.

I run…

I am running away… heart pounding as each strangled gasp drives through my straining lungs. I have received an overwhelming shock.

My God! I think. *What's going on?*

My legs pump straight for the Tube. I must get home, I must! This has completely unnerved me. I never expected to see him; not like this!

I am trying to wrap my brain around any logical reason as to why, how, but I am in a tumult, I simply cannot believe it! What was he doing here? Why was he like that? I am stripped of any logical answer. To top it all off, I'm getting flashbacks – a suffusion of long-buried memories crashing to the forefront of my brain, for here is a person I once knew, be something I never thought he would. Knowing the last time I saw him, his life was going in an ascent, rising forth to greatness. Only now, I don't understand it! It holds no resemblance to that advantageous vocation he was destined for. I grieve; where, where is that person?

'James. Who on earth are you?' I whisper, as I wipe away a tear, hands trembling.

I keep running… but I must calm. What is wrong with me? Why am I crying? Why has this affected me so deeply, so that I felt the need to bolt out of there? Jesus, who am I fooling? I know why I am really running. I know the reason why I have such a profound panic. It is him for goodness' sake! And he has brought with him emotions I thought had perished years ago. I shake my head as the recollections hurtle through me. I need lucidity right now, a semblance, a calm – there are too many pictures materialising. I must slow down.

1

I almost fall down the stairs into Warren Street Station, last second, grabbing hold of the banister. With laboured breaths, I rub the stitch at my side, as I wait on platform 1 for my train, and think of home – the tiny place I rent in Hampstead – my refuge. I share the place with Kate, my friend of friends. Kate, bless her: my other sister. I love her but hope she is out now. I want to be alone; consider on what to do with just the echo of my own thoughts. I have to plan. To see. To act. Each machination. I can't just leave it the way it is; it's not who I am…

I see his image again and shake my head. After all these years… Again, I ask myself: How did he end up there? But most importantly, who has he become?

I hear the rumble of the train reverberate through the tunnel and edge closer to the track. The sudden gush of turbulence as the train glides by me, blows back my hair, and my eyes water. The doors slide open and I get on, still shaking with the exertion of the run… and my consternation. There are no seats. London on a Saturday, who am I kidding? I hold onto a rail so as not to fall. I feet faint. I feel sick.

I drift back, as the train trundles out of the station, but not far enough, and smile sadly to myself, remembering how we first met, Kate and I, when I had just begun working at the same shoe shop as her, in my last year of school; Upper VI. Friends for five years, we've been. I stopped working there a couple of months ago, but it feels like I haven't. You can't just efface years of good memories.

Kate and I had been the youngest assistants then. The other ten, or so, were already students. But Kate is a year younger than me. She started at sixteen and me at seventeen, and throughout that first year of getting to know one another, we had formed a bond, authentic in its simplicity, steadfast in its sincerity and hilarious in its stupidity.

She'd slowly started to unravel secrets of her past so intense for one her age that I couldn't refuse her request: to crash at my house, and later the place I rented, whenever life at her home got unbearable. We both needed out – Kate more than I, though. I couldn't turn her down. Things had become so bad with her parents that in her last year home she would rarely sleep there, preferring to commute all the way to where I was lodging, stay the night, then wake up at the crack of dawn to travel all the way northbound to Wembley Park again and go straight to school. I'd always wonder how she had the strength. Not the physical; the mental. How she'd take life by the horns, resolved nothing could stop her. I wasn't like that. I didn't have that grit. She taught me, though. All these years, something rubs off. Worthy of anyone's admiration; she'd finished school with excellent marks and had got into LSE.

It was UCL I had got into, which was as much as a surprise to me as it was to my mother and sister, and probably half the staff at school. It was something I thought would never happen; I was such an academic disappointment. Mum and my sister, Victoria, knew I had the talent, but I'd never shown enough heart. It had been by a last dint of effort, and I'd made it. I left my house, I left my past, and liberated, I soared. I had been the mariner stuck in a windless boat all my life, and when the gale finally blasted through the surf, my sails billowed with exaltation.

Kate and I are in our last year now; few months left of student life. We thought to do a flatshare; see how things fared; test the waters at being "independent women" – cracking up with that stupid phrase. Moreover, we agreed with ease, because the money we made from selling shoes in one of the most prestigious shoe shops in the UK was, to put it bluntly, a lot. Plus, it was a good thing our wages were part on commission; it upped our income enough to tide us over for the whole of the first year (and then some) before we'd even moved in.

And the way we got that commission up?

By selling.

And how did we sell?

By lying.

Lie, after lie, after lie.

We'd made an art of it. We knew how to deliberately con our way into selling products, which half the time the customers didn't really want. But, on the other hand, those *minted* dames loved to be pampered little white lies. We boosted their egos. In fact, I think we did them a service: we totally made their day.

'Yes, madam. That looks amazing on your foot! Why don't you try the other and see how comfortable they are? The leather is so soft, isn't it? There's a matching handbag as well…'

You'd always manoeuvre that last remark in, because selling handbags you got extra bonus *and* it was cash in hand. At the end of the day you were given your dues. Our cashier, Christiane from Paris, who was the quietest girl ever, and who unknowingly made me love the French language again, would count out our change aloud, oblivious to how uncomfortable it was. Everyone could hear your amount; you'd always know who sold the most bags that day.

I had this secret competition going with another salesgirl called Megan. It wasn't hostile competition, and I didn't know we were competing, only I'd seen, or rather, caught her, covertly listening to my wages on many evenings, and how she'd always navigate the conversation towards how many bags I'd sold. Also, we were given these special cards which we were obliged to write down our sales, so each party wouldn't forget what they'd sold. They were handed in at the end of the day for inspection and to be given our handbag cash. So, once, I had been slotting back a box of black, nubuck pumps, which belonged on the shelves behind the wall where we filed our sales cards, when I caught Megan. She hadn't heard me behind her, and I saw through the gap between the shoe boxes that she was checking my card. I recognised my rather babyish, slanted handwriting on the top where my name was. I laughed inwardly at how pedantic she was. It was just a handbag; six bloody quid!

I'd thought then, how some people have too much anxiety, living a life by comparing it to others; too afraid to just get on with theirs. Then I'd bitten my lip, coming to the realisation of how hypocritical I was. I had been like that – too afraid, too apprehensive. Who was I to talk?

The train halts at Hampstead, and I cannot alight fast enough. I am almost home. I feel tears come, heart hammering rapidly. A quick run, down Heath Street, into the smaller side street, and I'll be able to discern the entryway to my flat – my beloved sanctuary.

I slam the flimsy front door behind me, having finally unfumbled the key from my trembling hands, as crusty paint drops to the floor. Kate is nowhere. Good.

I scowl at the door; the place needs work but we never seem to have time. The peephole cap has been snapped off, and anyone can peer through. Not by us – we found it that way when we'd moved in. It's on our never-ending fix-it list, which is surreptitiously wedged underneath the ribbon of our noticeboard, alongside other bits and pieces that need to be done around the place, like a better bolt on our paper-thin door. It's a miracle we've never been robbed.

'The robbers probably came in, looked around, felt sorry for us and left.' Kate had joked. 'I'm surprised they didn't leave us a fiver!'

We had been in stitches.

I see my reflection in the oval, art-nouveau mirror, which is propped up on the wall directly opposite the door. How ghastly I have become. I step closer, as my face becomes convex, and stare into my eyes, the abyss of pitch encircled by pigments of pewter-grey and a trillion flecks of cloudy silver. A thunderstorm sky. Suddenly, my long-term memory ignites, as I am hit with an image. 'Jesus Christ!' I rasp. Satchel and art-tube are dropped to the floor as my shoulders slump, unable to withhold any other weight except for what I have just remembered. I feel heat rise, the force of it bringing my cranium to a blaze. I hear his words: *Your eyes…*

I head straight for the kitchen, pour myself some water and gulp it down. I gasp and almost choke as I tremble. I dab the sheen of sweat off my forehead and take in breaths which catch each time. My heart wrenches again, pain striking at his apparition, now even more forceful on the memory I've recalled. I let out a wail, like an infant just been given a jab – a mournful cry of distress. I feel the remorse. Yes, remorse. The pang of guilt. 'That night,' I whisper to myself. 'What did I do to him! What have I done!'

The memories, the moments, start to emerge as if it were yesterday, as I slowly settle – I'm never able to remember things when I'm fully agitated. I fooled myself in thinking I'd forget him as the years went by, but seeing him today, the way he was, the realisation of what he's become, live before my eyes, jolts an electrifying awakening in my inner consciousness that I have been ignoring for too long. I disgust myself, coward that I am. Liar. Bitch… I did an inexcusable thing to him. What callow, disgraceful behaviour. He has to know what I did. It cannot be left unknown to him, and the only way I'll feel any better with myself, is when I've told him and apologised.

I slip off my parka and sit despondent on my little window seat, looking out onto the misty street. I rest my head on the cold glass, as hard droplets of rain tap incessantly from the other side. It's market day, and I can barely hear the cries. They have been literally drowned out, or venders have probably packed up, finished for the day. I lift the window, damp air enveloping me, and hear car tyres splashing in the streets perpendicular. And there, one faint cry. One producer still perseveres in this rain.

What is *he* doing now? Does he have somewhere warm and dry like me?

I feel a creeping, incipient dread within me. Something. There is something amiss. Perhaps I wasn't told the whole story – something else must have occurred, and it never reached my ears. I don't know. I don't know. I must find out…

He was in his last year of school then. Two years older than me. Just two years; just a boy.

I take in a sharp breath; I am a breezeless boat drifting on the waves of the past…

Back Then

'Bitch, you've gotta help me!'

'I can't… It's weird. I c-can't just go up to a total stranger a-and tell him to be at a certain place at a certain time. W-what am I?' I stammered. I always stammered when I was under stress. In this particular case, being forced to do something against my will. *Will?* I harrumphed bitterly within. *What will?*

My palm was getting slippery with sweat, holding so tight on my phone.

'Don't worry. He'll be curious to know; boys are. They've got massive egos. They always like it if a girl fancies them. Besides, you're just the messenger. He won't take it out on you, El, promise. Lisa told me she had done the same thing to Eddie, and it had worked.'

I really didn't give a shit about Lisa and Eddie, whoever they were. What Bianca was asking of me was to wake up tomorrow morning in time to find a certain Milden boy, whom she knew would be waiting at the bus stop near where I lived. I was to tell him to get off at Mill Hill Broadway Station the following day, which was where she was going to take the bus herself, so she could see him. Bianca's parents usually drove her to school, so I surmised the day after tomorrow they wouldn't be. This Milden boy didn't know her, but she "knew" him from the one time she'd got on the bus and seen him get on about a week ago. She was desperate to see him again, and she thought it would be fun to get him to get off at her stop, just so she could be near him for twenty-odd minutes more, until the next bus came. She wasn't even going to speak to him. Just get me to get him to do this silly thing for her satisfaction. And quite frankly, why would somebody do that? Why get off the bus and wait outside for another twenty minutes in the February freeze? Bianca took it for granted her plan would work. Didn't she think this boy might have a brain and tell me to piss off and get a life? I mean, why would he do me, an ugly cow, the favour? Nonetheless, she was goading me and goading me, like a spoilt brat. She'd already had me on the phone for half an hour, wheedling my ears off. This girl never took no for an answer, and I knew, clenched like her fist had my ratiocination in a death grip, I'd have to give in. I was actually surprised with myself for having put up a fight for that length of time. Lately, whenever Bianca forced me to do something, I would undergo a vacillated, mental arm wrestle. One where my one hand was battling for pluck – to tell her to leave me alone, and the other hand begging not to, because it was too afraid of the consequences.

Milden Public for Boys was half a mile distance from Bianca's and my school: Hilsmond Independent for Girls. And there was only one bus: the two-four-two, which stopped outside Milden, right at the top of the hill, exactly where it started to descend again. Milden was a semi boarding school, boasting to be one of the largest, not only in student body but also in acres, in Greater London. Hilsmond, on the other hand, was a smaller school but with no less worth than Milden on the academic scale. We'd made it into the top ten girl's schools in north London. It was the only thing worth boasting about really.

The bus-stops and the bus itself were places where pupils from both schools met. I dreaded taking that bus; the boisterous ruckus from all the loudmouthed bullies intimidated me. The way they'd abruptly shriek or bellow, lunge suddenly, always made me flinch in fright. In Lower V, Mum'd announced I'd be taking the bus from then on with my sister, Victoria, so I could learn the journey. My sister, being three years older, had finished school that year, and now I was all by myself in Upper V. Alone; left to the wolves in the forest, like a Spartan youngster.

Victoria had passed the entrance exams for Hilsmond, and since Mum wanted us to go to the same school, I only sat for Hilsmond and, thankfully for Mum, passed by the skin of my teeth. I didn't want to go to Hilsmond, but nobody'd asked me. I didn't belong there; I was the epitome of lethargic. What was a private school going to do with me? I never applied myself to my full potential. Just doing absolute minimum, and by this, annoying the shit out of the teachers. 'Eleanora's a bright, young girl, just lazy, Mrs Stephens…' was the standard reply on report-card day. Yes, I was lazy to an extent, but the real reason was: I hated school. The desire to learn flew out of me the first day I had entered my form room in Upper III with my right leg in a cast. I had fractured a tiny bone in my foot that summer, and the sight of me – the stark contrast between the thicknesses of my legs – at the door was so pathetic, it set off a ripple of laughter in the classroom, sealing my fate. There was no empathy for my pain. No shred of guilt, no remorse in tormenting an injured person. Who were these people? What did I do to them? The bullies saw I was weak for not reacting, for not putting up a fight, and after that, there was no stopping them. Why? Why on earth hadn't I reacted? How that one small yet significant act could have changed my future. After being mocked thus, the whole point of school left me with a bitter aftertaste that slowly got worse as the bullying did.

Bianca was indirectly bullying me; I knew her well by now. She was one of those indifferent creatures that would only pretend to like you to get something out of you, and do such a convincing job, cooing and hugging you in the corridor, that you ended up believing her again, trusting her and giving in to her. Once more, gullibly, falling into her trap. Manipulation at its finest.

However, I was weak. I knew she was using me (again) to inflict torment on this Milden boy. But I had no friends, and in a way, I was using her too. I needed her company; without her, I'd be the saddest joke in history.

I sighed and gave in. *Wuss.*

'All right. I'll do it,' I said, feigning defeat. 'But I still think it would be easier if *you* went to his stop.'

'I can't. I told you. My parents would kill me!' I knew this to be a lie. Her parents were perhaps the laxest parents in the world. They say liars must have good memories. She didn't. I could have reminded her of the times she'd done what she wanted, when she wanted, but as usual I played dumb. The real reason was, she just didn't want to get up early. That was it. Queen B wanted her beauty sleep.

'Oh, my God, El!' she squealed down the phone, deafening me. 'He's so hot. I have to see him again!'

No "thank you, Eleanora. You're such a good friend". Nothing. I prayed he wouldn't be there the next day.

She proceeded to give me details. 'OK. He gets on at Edge Lane, the first stop after the bend; three stops after you. Don't ask me how I know this, I just do.'

'I don't doubt it,' I said dryly. Why had *I* never seen him? Perhaps it was because I always had my nose in some book or other, or earbuds stuck in my ears, oblivious, staring out the window. What's more, I always sat bottom deck near the back, whereas all the cool kids went on upstairs to top deck.

'He's about a foot taller than us (Bianca and I had the same height) with blond hair. He's really fit. You can't miss him. Oh, and don't confuse him with other Mildeners. Not that you will; they ain't got nothing on him!' She ended, trying unsuccessfully to put on an American accent. I rolled my eyes. Anthony Hopkins did a better job as Lecter.

'What do I tell him again?' I asked.

'Just say, "Someone you like wants to meet you at Mill Hill Broadway, under the bridge, tomorrow morning at seven thirty". I dunno. Just sell it to him.'

'Eres loca mi amiga,' I told her. She had taught me some Spanish. Her mother was from a small village in Toledo.

Then as an afterthought, 'What's his name?'

'It's James. James Laidlaw.'

Now

I am cold. I feel the chill bite. I give a sudden shiver.

I spot Kate from the street. She's running from the rain, blonde hair sheened. *She* lived through a nightmare. I wonder if James is living in one too. I feel I am about to dive into one myself.

What I did to James probably doesn't compare to what Kate lived through, granted, but that doesn't change the way I feel. It doesn't lighten the burden of wrongdoing. No amount of comparing how much evil one thing is to another can annul the truth in our hearts. I know I am culpable, that I have sinned against another human being – every fibre of my soul accuses me. I had taken matters too far in my indignation, my slighted ego. I shouldn't have. It is right what they say, not to act in anger.

It pains me what I saw today. He isn't meant to be that person. It is so far from the picture I had painted of him in my imagination of the *future James*. It may sound conceited or snobbish, but *I* wasn't the one who had set that bar so high. *He* had been the one. And he was about to pole vault over it with such ease. What went wrong? The pole must have snapped somewhere along the way. But where? When exactly in time did that snap occur, and how? I have to go back, yes; find him. See if he needs any help – I feel so sorry for him. I want to make some recompense, at least, for slandering his name. I've always been too bloody diffident. This time I must talk.

Kate jemmies the key and comes barging in, as if the rain is still chasing her. She sees me and halts.

'What's up?' she says. I look at her. I want to tell her, but nothing comes out. I'd told her that chapter of my life years ago. She probably wouldn't remember it.

'You look like you've seen a ghost,' she says. I harrumph; a quiet breath at the irony. She takes off her raincoat and comes towards me.

'Are you all right?' There's concern etched between her brows.

'No. Not really,' I say.

She scrutinizes me, then says, 'I'll put the kettle on, and then you're talking.'

Kettle? Kettle? I don't want to drink tea! I need to leave. What am I still doing here? I have to go. I walk towards my parka.

'I can't now. I'll talk to you later,' I tell her. I'm at the door and take a brief look at my canvases, all appositionally propped up along the walls, and know I won't be able to get any work done. I know my life is no longer sacrosanct if I don't sort this business with James out first. No exhibition. No dissertation. It is on hold.

'El,' Kate tries.

'Go dry up. You'll catch your death.'

Chapter Two

Back Then

I woke with nausea so strong that I ended up puking, what little I had in my stomach, down the toilet. Today was the day. I was horrendously nervous. It was only logical – I had never spoken to a boy before, other than some childhood friends I'd grown up with and saw only sisterly, and to my cousins. How I was to go through with this message without stumbling on each word and making an utter fool of myself, was anyone's guess.

I had got up earlier than usual, readying myself for Bianca's request, or should I say, demand. It was such a stupid plan in the first place. I mean, why couldn't she just take the bus from the same stop he was waiting at?

9

Stand there nonchalant for as long as she wanted? Look at him for as long as the journey took? It was such a fake excuse about her parents not letting her get the bus from there. Why did I agree to get up at the crack of dawn? I felt like such a sucker. I was so spineless; I couldn't stand up for myself. She was always *Do this! Do that!* Her effing lackey at her behest. How much more could I take? Was it worth it? Did I really need her? I should have said no. Why couldn't I say no? It was brutally ironic how my weaker side always won.

Do not judge me badly – I was no mainstream teenybopper. I never fitted in. I lived in my own secret world of figures and shapes, of which I made colour and light. A mythical dream forged in a mind that could sustain everlasting pictures. Nothing was too inimitable in my mind's eye. No wonder people thought I was weird – always lost in endless sketching. So, when the taunting worsened, I hid that side of me; made myself as weirdless as possible. But alas, I couldn't hide the way I looked, so the bullying continued – almost to the same degree – until Bianca had befriended me. It had been for her own best interest, but I had not known that then. True, I had been rather baffled as to why she had deigned to speak to me in the first place, but soon overcame that surprise when she'd managed to convince me, by some innate thespian mastery, that she was genuine. I thought she really wanted my company. But as the first months went by, the disloyalty started to show. She'd get what she wanted from me, and then days would go by where she'd ignore me; no longer having need of my help. I would think we were on the brink of breaking up, thinking our friendship was through, when she'd come with her coaxing again, pulling me back to her world. And there I was, ignoring how two-faced she was because I had no one else to shield me from some of the worst bullies, relieved she'd done it. Now, there was no illusion as what kind of "friends" we were, but that's what my desperation to fit in did. I didn't want to be taunted any more, harassed, physically harmed. Yes, physically harmed. They'd laid hands on me. I had scars. I'd looked it up once. "Malicious Wounding" or "Grievous Bodily Harm" – that was the technical term. My life had been threatened. Blood had shed.

There was a period, in the early years of Hilsmond, where almost every afternoon I'd get in Mum's car after school in tears.

'What's the matter, darling?' she'd say. I could hear the pain in her voice.

'They made fun of me. Called me an anorexic bitch,' I'd answer, sniffing back my runny nose. The word "anorexic" cut me deep. I was anything but! I loved food. Nevertheless, I was, indeed, very thin, and I knew I could be easily mistaken for one at the threshold of emaciation. Mum would ask me who "they" were, but I'd never say. It didn't matter who they were. I just wanted it to stop.

'They are jealous of you,' was Mum's standard, biased reply, which I could never believe. 'You have a beautiful, slim body, and they don't... and they want it.'

That didn't help.

'Know what?' my sister had interrupted on one of these car talks after school. 'The girls in your year are all, total bitches. The lip we hear from them is outrageous. Lynn and I couldn't believe our ears the other day. What a load of cows! Our year is so much nicer. We don't bully anyone.'

Still no help.

'Well, you are three years older than them,' Mum had interjected. 'You're more mature, Vicky...'

Victoria gave her a dismissive look and said, 'If they bother you again, El, come and get me. Wouldn't mind boxing one of those slags.'

Now that was help.

'Vicky!' Mum had cried. 'That's not mature at all!' Vic had just given her a sage smile and said nothing else.

Sure enough, after about a week, I'd run to fetch my sister. She had come charging into my form room, with her best friend, Lynn, by her side, and gave what for to Amanda. Amanda, who relished the re-enactments of Norman Bates, enjoyed indulging me with her refined, psychotic outbursts. She'd been in her forte that day, having another go at me, shoving me around the room, grabbing my art folder and throwing it out the window. It had been raining all day that day. My water-wash, veritably, got washed. All my work had been destroyed.

I'd watched my sister with awe, telling Amanda that it wasn't fair she bully me; I hadn't done anything to her. Amanda's reply was a slap across my sister's face. Whereupon, Vic, dumbfounded for a second, clenched her fist and punched Amanda with a right hook, squarely on her jaw. She'd picked that up from the boxing match we'd seen the night before with Dad. It sent Amanda careening back to the wall and teetering to the floor. Everyone had burst out laughing. Amanda never touched me again, although she tried. She tried to avenge herself through me, but would always stop, probably reminding herself that that was the reason she was in this fix in the first place. Amanda's family had moved to Bristol the following year – a small mercy... But there were others. My sister's intervention had ebbed the bullying for a while, but the stigma stayed. And when that episode was forgotten, my persecutors came back for more. And as the years rolled by, they got more vicious. I could list all the awesome times I'd been punched, kicked ...and knifed, but that would induce pity, and I didn't want pity. I simply didn't want to be judged for giving in to Bianca.

Now at sixteen, having put on perhaps under two stone since then, but having gone through an insane growth spurt, making matters worse on the beanpole look, I tried my best to, at least, look presentable to this James Laidlaw bloke.

I put on a dab more make up than usual, so that, in the event he got pissed off with what I had to convey to him, he would forgive me more easily if I were pretty. Well, prett*ier*!

Boys are shallow – Vic. I had no reason to disbelieve her.

It was a horrible, late February morning, fog everywhere, and the winter coat for school was a thick, navy-blue duffle, which went down to the knee. I wished it went to the ankle. It was warm enough, but if the blazer fitted underneath that would have been perfect. I wore my thickest tights and my black DM slip-ons. I had awkward big feet that made my legs look even more out of proportion. I never liked showing my legs, especially my calves, but there was nothing I could do. Not even putting on a pair of jeans was plausible, and the pathetic school skirt wasn't long enough. I couldn't walk into school with trousers and take them off in the toilets – it was against school rules, and I'd probably get detention. And taking them off outside school, somewhere on the road, would make everyone look at me, thus giving fuel to even more taunting. Nope. I was stuck with my body and had to learn to live with it. *You're sixteen for crying out loud; suck it up.*

I took one last look at myself in the downstairs mirror. The one next to our front door. The one you instinctively rotated you head towards, to glance at before you left, or upon your return. I halted, a quick check to see I had nothing between my teeth, then I stood for a second, analysing my face.

You're ugly. Just accept it. No amount of makeup is going to change that.

I smoothed down my hair – a long ebony – which always seemed to curl at the sides whenever I didn't want it to. Nothing changed; not even my hair wanted to be pretty. I wanted to punch the mirror. Shatter that image in front of me; never see it again. If only it were that simple… The raven hair contrasted the pale, deathly-white skin even more, giving me this kind of superficial gothic look. What was I going to do with that look? Wear black and pretend I was in the Victorian era? The only black ensemble I had were the clothes I'd worn at Dad's funeral.

I unlatched the door with a sigh.

'You're leaving early,' Mum called from upstairs. 'Everything all right?'

No.

'Yeah… just meeting up with someone,' I called back. It wasn't a lie… was it? That thing about lying by omission kind of rang a bell at that point, but I couldn't tell her. She had enough on her mind, what with being widowed and alone, her world turned upside down. We were about as much as she could handle. She didn't need more worries.

'All right, sweetie pie. Take care.'

"Take care" was all she pretty much said lately.

'Going out, mum!'

'Take care!'

'Staying over at Cousin Nicola's!'

'Take care!'
'Having sex with Tom, Dick and Harry!'
'Take care!'

I needed to get out of there. For good. It was so heartbreakingly morbid. The rooms, the memories of Dad… There was his armchair, vacant, in the living room. There was his place at the table, empty, devoid of his attending ear at mealtimes. There was the hall where we'd always run to kiss him when he came home from work, big smile on his face. I'd never see that face again, live, and I resented having to be reminded of that fact every single day.

I closed the door behind me, about to cry, but held it in. I couldn't afford to smear my face. Not today. I put up my hood, already bracing myself for the bitter cold of the merciless winter that would never seem to thaw. No matter how old I grew, I knew I would never get used to the biting dampness of this otherwise beautiful country.

I lugged my rucksack around one shoulder. Mum used to chide me for not carrying it properly, saying I'd destroy my spine. 'Put it around both shoulders so the weight is distributed evenly, so you won't end up creating a hunch.' Blah, blah… too late. No more chiding now; she was… elsewhere.

I walked briskly down the street, my heart racing to a panic that actually hurt. The thudding constrained my chest, and I had to stop to calm myself. My breaths were quick, condensed puffs of air in the chill of the misty morn. I wanted to chicken out. I prayed and prayed he wouldn't be there. Some unplanned, last-minute appointment. Or the flu. Or he forgot to set his alarm. Christ! I dry-heaved. *Stop, Eleanora! Stop!*

I turned into Edge Lane, and I could just about discern some people huddled around the bus stop in the distance.

My throat was completely dry from panting and the tearing anxiety. No saliva could be found. I rummaged through my bag and felt the ridges of my bottle of water, grabbed it and took a sip. I hadn't had any breakfast that morning, and I felt a pang of hunger strike in my stomach, the knots making the pain worse.

I composed myself as best I could, breathing in through the nose and out through the mouth, saying to myself: *you can do this, you can do this*, and walked slowly towards the huddle.

There were a couple of women and three schoolchildren, who didn't look like they could be anywhere near eighteen. Much younger. One was wearing a Milden uniform. He looked like a thirteen-year-old. Ha! James Laidlaw wasn't there.

I let out a quiet sigh of relief and decided to take the next stop down. Even if he came late to this stop, I could honestly say to Bianca that I never saw him.

I turned, took three steps and stopped dead. A tall, Milden-clad boy in the blacks and greys, with not so much plain blond hair, but more like a sandy blond, came sauntering my way through the silent mist.

He was the most beautiful boy I'd ever seen.

Now

I go back; take the six stops down to Warren Street Station again and jog back to UCL, impervious to the pouring rain. I have to know; it's impossible to continue as normal without an entire unearthing of facts. Leave no stone unturned. It will consume me if I don't learn the truth. It's not only curiosity, nor some altruistic drop of blood flowing in my veins, but it is simply because I feel bad. No. I feel something more, like I am adjunct to this, and … well, perhaps it is also that regard I once had for him.

I saw him sweeping the floors of the Slade building this morning. I usually don't notice the janitorial staff (who does?), but his hair had caught my eye. Hair that I can identify amongst a million. I know the precise colour and texture; it has been branded in my memory long since. And it is longer now – in all its glory. The undulating, sandy waves captured in the beam of light, which burst through the window, right at that point of me opening the door, extenuating that bright opulence, was like a sign from the heavens: Behold, he is here!

Yet, sweeping floors? I picture him again in my mind's eye. The dirty, torn overalls. The weary, meditative face (even seeing him on profile there was no mistake). His hair, ungroomed, and a jaw, unshaven. But the position of employment was what shocked me, what caught me off-guard; made me run, panicked. Run as if I were a criminal…, which I am. I remember something about him applying to Oxford, something about studying engineering; a whole life ahead of him.

I make a swift connection. A dark, veracious factor that seeps its way to my conscience, like *pharmaki* (that's the word Gran had used: a drug, a *poison*). That if he had gone to Oxford, he wouldn't be here sweeping floors. Hence, he never went? I mean, it is a general truth, and of course there are exceptions, but if you don't land a banner job with a degree from one of the top universities in the world, then something is definitely foul.

Saturday. I have no classes, but I made the journey down to do some work and get the art book I borrowed from the library, which I had forgotten in one of the classrooms. Of course, I never got the chance to do either. No sooner had I set one foot in the door, than I'd seen him and run off. I thought it a good opportunity to aim for a better mark – my last spurge of effort in the learning era of my life. It is Easter holidays; time is running out.

I ponder to myself, just then. How much does he know of *that night*? Does he have any suspicion it could have been me? I am prepared for the worst possible reaction, and I will humbly accept it. I even start to recite a speech; prepare myself.

I didn't know, didn't think. I'm sorry…

I enter the hall with trepidation. My heart starting to thud; I can feel it in my throat. I bring my hood – now soaked with the nature's elements – over my head more, in order to conceal my face, and tug on some tufts of hair for extra help, but they're still too short. For some reason, I don't want him to recognise me; not yet. *I* want to be the one to talk first, to explain.

I have changed quite a bit over the last six years – my hair for a start. It's a growing-out pixie cut. Besides, the number of times he happened to look at me back then can be counted on one hand. His eyes were always on the other, pretty girls. The girls who had the exoteric gift of beauty. Except for *that night*… Still, I don't want to take any chances.

I am at the exact same place I saw him earlier, half-expecting him to be there in the exact same position, as if time hasn't passed, but that's ridiculous. I stroll, with bated breath, into the next corridor, through the empty halls; there are few students today. Nothing. I then make my way onto the next corridor, then the next. Seems he's finished for the day. I feel a wave of disappointment plummet in my loins. I stand for a few moments, at a loss for what to do next. Then a thought crosses my mind. I go straight to administration, across the other side of the soggy lawn, head against the torrent.

I clear my throat deliberately. The girl behind the computer looks up through her glasses. Her eyes have magnified doubly.

'Hi,' I say, trying not to stare too much into her pupils like some ophthalmologist conducting a fundoscopy. 'I seem to have lost my, err, (I think quickly – the truth) my jacket.' I lost my leather biker jacket (more like, it was stolen) but it was a while back. I hadn't asked around for it; once something is gone, it is gone, but I have to be convincing it is a recent event. I contort my face into one of anxiety and desperation. 'Did the cleaners bring anything in for the lost and found?'

She raises her brows and blinks.

'No, I don't believe they did,' she says. 'Sorry.'

I tut, 'Oh, no,' feigning to be crestfallen. 'And it was really expensive, ya' know? A proper biker jacket an' all…'

'I'm so sorry,' she says, shaking her head. 'Only a few people hand in lost items, and I haven't seen any leather jackets lately. Hope you find it,' she adds. She knows that's about as likely as a prossy finding her virginity.

'Is there any way I could speak to the cleaner today? Perhaps he may have seen it?' I take in a breath, my heart beats hard with anticipation. Will she help me out? Will she give me his details?

'He? So, you know it was a man, then?' she asks.

'Yes,' I say, blinking, taken aback. Why did I take it for granted the cleaners would be all men? Actually, it couldn't harm if I describe him, I think. 'He was sweeping? Long, blond hair?'

'Yes, that's right.' She checks a list. 'Well, I suppose you could ask him. He'll be in on Monday. Laidlaw's the name. I can't give out any other personal information, though.'

'I understand. So, he'll be cleaning in the same place, then; the Slade?'

'I don't know. That's between the cleaners. Him and another two ladies. I don't know where he'll be and at what time. Where they start and where they finish is up to them, but I have noticed they begin from the top, making their way down. So, it's a matter of a good search, really.'

'I see,' I say, considering. There was nothing else to ask. 'Well, thanks for everyth –' I stop, mid-phrase. There is *one* thing.

'Where do the cleaners exit when they're finished?'

She nods and smiles. 'Ah, yes! They usually leave from here; they drop off the supplies and get their stuff from the staff cloakroom. Around noonish or a little bit later.'

Back Then

I was shit-scared, but I had to do it – the daunting reality hitting me. I had to act fast. I didn't want him to reach the bus stop within earshot of the other commuters. What I had to say, had to be said in private.

I moved in front of his way, knowing I'd obstruct him so that he'd have to stop walking. He did. He stopped short and looked down with a snarl on his face at the person who dared block his path. He flinched, then blinked; there was curiosity in his eyes. I almost went weak in the knees upon seeing those brilliant, striking blues.

All boys are egotistical, self-righteous, arrogant pricks, who think they're God's gift – Bianca.

There was nothing else for it. Now or never. I looked defiantly into those eyes and took an uppity, know-it-all stance I'd seen from a girl at school called Patricia – Trisha – who was renowned for her coolness around boys, having boasted the loss her virginity at thirteen. She'd cock her knee to one side, put weight on the other leg, jutting out her hip, and tip her head slightly to the side.

So, that's what I did. I pretended like I was Trisha, and said to him without a stutter, using the flirtatious whine I'd heard her use on the boys, 'Are you James Laidlaw?'

He instantly arched a brow, interested. His mouth twitched. A lovely, full, pink mouth. He narrowed his eyes, and I felt my cheeks burn.

'Who wants to know?' he said, a bit cockily, playing the game with me. Even his voice was beautiful.

'I have a message for you,' I began. He furrowed his eyebrows, all ears.

'Tomorrow at seven thirty, get off at Mill Hill Broadway under the bridge. There'll be somebody waiting there who you will definitely like to see.' I said it. I couldn't believe it! I said it! I inwardly rejoiced at my non-fumbling and un-awkwardness. It was done, and I was free.

I was about to walk away, having delivered and completed my mission, when he said, 'I'm not doing anything unless you tell me who it is.'

My heart pounded in my ears. I had no idea what to reply. This wasn't in the handbook!

'I…' I began pathetically. 'I can't t-tell you who it is. J-just come and see for yourself!' Shit, my stutter was back.

He blinked and cocked a lip, coming abruptly closer. Then flicked a tuft of hair from his temple, pulling back. 'You're from Hilsmond,' he said, having correctly recognised our shade of blue duffle coat.

'Is it Trisha?' Trisha? Did he know her? She was, somewhat, infamous.

He had a smirk on his face. I took it he liked her. But I didn't want him to think it was her. False assumptions got you into trouble, and I seriously didn't want a confrontation with one of the most popular girls at school. Trisha had to be, categorically, out of the equation.

'No, i-it's not Trisha! It's someone else,' I said to him firmly.

'If you don't tell me, I'm not doing it.' Again, he insisted. I blinked uneasily. What to say? What to say?

'Is it you?' He prodded. He raised his brows and folded his arms, as if he'd found out my secret.

'No!' I almost screeched. This was getting out of hand. I was alarmed. 'No, it isn't me! I-I'm just the messenger!' Then I gave out a nervous laugh. 'W-why would I tell you to get off at Mill Hill when I can see you here?' He blinked and gave me the faintest of nods.

'Just get off at Mill Hill Broadway, a-and you'll see!' I ended, pleading, exasperated. Then I almost ran off, leaving him there. Let him do what he wanted. I certainly wasn't going to force him. My part was over. I didn't want to continue – if anything else was implicated, I'd be responsible.

Chapter Three

Now

It is approaching lunchtime. I haven't eaten anything since this morning and hunger pokes my belly. Paradoxically, I have no appetite to eat, but I'd welcome a cool beer – something to smooth the jagging thoughts.

I turn towards The Crown; I need to dry up. The place is usually packed with patrons of the student kind, and today isn't much different, if you exclude the mass of tourists. I feel sorry for them, what with their backpacks and cameras, all huddled in, out of the rain, probably regretting their decision to come to London in April, but not showing the fact, as a ghost of a smile lingers on their hopeful faces.

The air has a strong fug of wet clothes and lingering cigarette smoke, even though the ban came to force years ago. After decades of jolly smokers, the nicotine scent has stubbornly stuck to the surfaces of the old, cracked wood and baroque-styled wallpaper.

For the past three and a half years, The Crown has claimed a part of my heart. I enter its confines as if I've grown up here, which in a sense I have. Used as a general meeting point, or the go-to spot for a quick, unhealthy yet amazing bite, or even just to sit back and unwind, once The Crown opens its doors, I feel nestled in a welcoming milieu. Whenever I wander in by myself, however, I seek out the section that has closed-off cubicles with benches instead of chairs, so I can hide right in and sketch without obstruction.

I weave my way through the groups of people to get to the bar. I am greeted by some fellow students; quick nods and *hiyas*.

Then, I hear my name being called through the din. It's Sam. He is the only person I know that has this nasty way in rolling out the last syllable – Eleano*rah*. It always makes me cringe to the point of shuddering.

I turn to greet him with a stiff grin on my face. He has a thing for me, still. Even when I shoved him off me last year at a New-Year's-Eve party, when he tried to put his tongue down my throat without my consent, he still didn't get it. No matter what I do to discourage him, he thinks I secretly desire him. He is in denial. When I had told Kate of Sam's *tour de force*, she'd been ecstatic I was making progress with a male. She didn't care what kind, so long as he had a penis. We have had countless arguments on men, some of which have escalated to the art of a polemicist tug of war, and each time having the same outcome – after the desiccation and analysis of these said arguments, we conclude that we agree to disagree. In a nutshell, this particular subject is moot.

'Oh, come on! This is your chance!' she'd said.

'My chance for what?' I'd snapped back. 'Do the single most significant act in my life with someone I abhor?'

She'd tutted and groaned at my insufferableness. 'You've got to try, see how it is… it's not like you're going to marry him! Live it up!'

I had stared at her in disbelief. 'Are you telling me to go with the first person who thrasonically plunges his disgusting tongue in my mouth? Are you seriously telling me to switch off all my feelings just to *try*?'

' "Thrasonically plunges",' she'd tutted under her breath sarcastically. 'Stop throwing those long Greek words at me! And don't be so bloody melodramatic!'

'Sorry, Kate, but I'm not like you. I don't work that way. It's just not my M O!'

It is true, Kate and I are a pitiful antithesis when it comes to comparing the frequency of the *deed*.

'If there were a P H scale for how slutty someone is, then my litmus paper would turn a shocking, acidy red,' she had declared a while back, during another wrangle. 'Yours would be way over on the other side of the scale. A pure, alkali blue.'

'I'm not *that* pure,' I'd protested, a little injured. 'I have had *some* experience.'

'Well, a neutral white, then,' she'd corrected for my wounded ego's sake, not because she believed me. 'Nothing more toxic. Not until you've been deflowered good and proper! God, we are both so pathetic,' she'd ended, looking contemplatively depressed all of a sudden.

I think she may have been mentally tallying the frequency of her regrets…

I felt so sorry for her, and had quietly said, ' "'Tis better to have loved and lost than never to have loved at all." '

She smiled warmly. She knew I knew she was right.

Sam, as I see to my surprise, is sitting with a bunch of good friends of mine in one of the cubicles, and I am happy to see them… and relieved. The stiff grin has turned into a genuine one.

'We missed you today. Where were you?' I am asked by Juliet, my freckled friend, who always frets over things. They had all gone to an optional live-study class. I hadn't wanted to go – I wanted to finish my canvas.

'I wasn't feeling too well,' I say. It isn't a lie. 'Did I miss anything major?'

'Nah, bollocks!' says Aidan, the sharp-witted, laid-back member of the gang. Tall, adorably gangling but with a face you'd proudly introduce your parents to on any given day.

'You can say that again! They were hanging really low this time,' Suze throws in, much peeved, and stretching her hands to the floor to mime cupping invisible balls. Then she finds her black Guinness and takes a doleful swig. Suzanne or Suze, as we call her, is one embarrassingly funny, bubbling brunette, who just so happens to have this mind-boggling knack of knowing when each and every event open to the public is going to take

19

place, even before it's officially announced. She's always in the loop – from the most insignificant underground act to the most widely promoted commercial happening. But what I appreciate most in both her and Aidan is their outdoorsy attitude, and how they charmingly rope the rest of us in to join them on last-minute excursions to wherever. Glorious mountainous peaks; distant historical hamlets; stately homes used on whatever period drama; vineyard harvest fests. Any kind of fun off the beaten track grants a refreshing break from the banalities of routine.

I never thought I'd have such good friends.

'What? Another old bloke?' I ask, trying to focus on the conversation.

'Yeah,' says Aidan. 'Why do you think I'm drowning my sorrows so early in the day? I think it's going to take me years for the nightmares of wrinkly, old men with loose balls to disappear. I'm gonna sue Gibbons for psychological trauma.'

'Now that I see you, you *do* look a bit peaky,' Juliet says, ignoring Aidan. 'Come sit down and dry up.'

'Yeah. Sit here,' Sam says, sliding his arse further in the bench to make room for me, but squashing Juliet in the process. She gives him a side, questioning-look.

'Wish I could but –' I stop mid-sentence, as a colour catches my eye in the distance. A lash of dark gold whips my vision. Hair. Wet hair. But it is *his* hair. It is him that very second, his back to me, exiting the pub.

Gone.

I blink, as though he were a figment of my imagination, still staring at the swinging doors, whooshing to a halt.

'Eherm! Eleanora? Are you OK?' Suze asks. I turn back to them; their perplexed faces.

'I've got to go!' I say in a half-breath, as my heart thrashes into action. There is no time to explain. What can I tell them anyway?

I plunge through the sea of tourists, clogging direct passage to the exit. I twist and turn my body through the throng as fast as I can. Upon reaching the door, I grab the handle, and with a thrust, am freed from the confines of The Crown.

Back Then

'He said what?!' cried Bianca. We were sitting in the cafeteria, eating a lunch of quaggy pizza.

'Yeah. I know!' I said, feigning aghast. We always went for the dramatic. 'I hope I convinced him. He did look curious.'

'Oh, my God!' she screeched excitedly. 'He thought it was Trisha? Then you?'

The "then you" was said in disgust.

'Yep.'

'He knows her. I bet he's going to ring her up tonight and ask her. Shit!'

'Why would he do that?' I asked, puzzled.

'What do you mean?'

'I mean, if they're friends, why would Trisha need to get someone to arrange a meeting with him? Sounds stupid. No, I think he knows it's someone else.'

'Yeah. You're right... Maybe he might ring her to see if she knows anything. Oh, no!' Bianca cried, alarmed.

'What?' I said, getting uneasy.

'Shit! What if he describes you to Trisha and she tells him you hang out with me? Bugger!'

'That could happen,' I said matter of fact, biting at my sagging pizza.

Bianca got up, grabbing her remaining pizza and stormed out the cafeteria. Not even Mrs Smith, who was on lunch duty, was quick enough to reprimand her for taking food out.

I sat by myself, mulling over the whole encounter I had that morning with James. It was like a fantasy –me talking to a boy. Surreal. But I had done it! Yes, I had bloody done it! I felt I had reached a new epoch in my life: the "talking to boys" phase. It elated me. Made me feel like one of the cool girls. Now my little escapade would be known, and I'd become popular. *Get real, El....*

But James. How handsome he was. Beautiful. Now I knew how artists found their muses. How they interpreted their idea of beauty and showed it to the rest of the world, through their depiction of one being. Their stimulus that sparked their inspiration. I brooded on James's eyes. They were a mixture of dreamy blues. There was some brown shade too, next to the pupil. I had been *that* close to him. I would draw them later that night... Oh, but how he'd looked into mine. I could tell he liked them because *his* roamed over them, seeking. The uncommon grey is what captivates people. They find my eyes fascinating. Pity about the rest of me, though...

Did he fancy me? I let myself believe he did. What harm was there in that?

***

A lined piece of paper, crumpled into a ball, fell on my desk, as I sat for the last lesson of the day – French.

We were in class 10, and class 10 was in the old building. And by old, I didn't mean the stately Edwardian structure it should have been, but more like in the decrepit sense of the word. Class 10, in particular, was in desperate need of renovation, since the bellowing wind found its way through the cracks of the window panels, causing the room to be considerably cold. My thumbs were numb, and I had to suck on them to help circulate the blood, for my nails had turned blue. We weren't allowed to wear our coats in class, only our blazers, but the problem with that was, you couldn't wear your blazer under your coat, like I said – it wouldn't fit, so you only had two choices in the morning: either just your blazer or just your coat. And believe you me, the flimsy, sky-blue shirt and royal-blue, V-necked jumper were insufficient for a winter climate in the environs of Hilsmond.

'All that money and they can't fix a bloody window. It's criminal,' Mum had said, after learning from me earlier that school year about class 10 and other such half-in-ruin classrooms.

'I'm going to complain…'

And she was about to, but then Dad passed, and that was that.

I looked to see if Madame Collard had noticed anything suspicious. She was one of the strictest teachers in school, and if she ever caught you so much as whisper for an ink cartridge to your neighbour, she'd spittle a tirade in her accented French, maliciously reducing you as a human being.

'Why iz your 'air so short? I can't pool it! You are lak a boy. I want to pool your 'air!' she had said to Jo once, causing her to almost cry in class. Verbal bullying by a teacher – unsurpassable. Because of her, I hated French.

Collard was oblivious. I uncrumpled the paper slowly under my desk, coughing to hide the noise. It read:

Need to talk. Wait 4 me outside Alice's. B.

Alice's house was on the same road as Hilsmond and Milden. She lived smack dab in between both schools. The good thing about her house was that it hid anyone loitering on its front path from the bus stop.

Bianca didn't want to be seen with me. It was to be expected. If James saw me with her, he'd know it was her who wanted him to get off at Mill Hill Broadway.

Her plan was going awry.

'Qu'est-ce que l'ennui signifie?' Collard's harsh voice clipped, with some saliva ejecting along the way, almost making me jump. *L'ennui* – precisely. I paid attention until bell.

Bianca got up, as soon as the muffled ring sounded, and bolted out the class. She probably had something to do first. I slowly packed my books and found my duffle coat. I put on everything I had to protect me against the freezing cold and reluctantly stepped into the frosty-paved street outside school. I broke into a jog to warm myself up. Icicles could be seen hanging from drainpipes and other ledges, not to mention the surrounding foliage and pavestones cloaked with brittle rime.

I met up with Bianca outside Alice's. Our breaths, misty clouds as we talked.

'So, listen. I told my parents not to come and pick me up. I'm taking the bus, and I don't want you to take this the wrong way, but I can't be seen with you for a while. You understand?'

I nodded. 'Oh, yeah, yeah. Sure…' I agreed immediately. *Wimp.*

'Don't talk to me. Don't stand by me. I don't want him to even think it's me. Not until this all blows over, OK?'

'Yeah. Of course. Don't worry about it…'

'I spoke to Trisha, and she gave me her word she won't say anything to him if he calls her.'

'Cool…' So now Trisha knew…

'Right. I'm going to the stop. Wait five minutes, then come.'

'Five minutes? I might miss the bus,' I tried.

'No, you won't,' she said, and I could swear there was contempt. Then she walked hurriedly to the stop.

No way was I waiting five minutes. We'd already wasted two minutes talking, and the two-four-two was usually on time. I anxiously counted to sixty, then moved.

Now

I swing open the pub doors as they spew me out onto the street. It's as though the rain – which has now developed into a full-on deluge – has washed every soul from sight, leaving only the scent of dirty, wet stone and asphalt.

I look left and right, then across, desperate to find him. Where has he turned? Shit. Shit. Shit.

I catch a glimpse of something. Yes, that's him! He's running out of the rain towards Warren Street Station; his long, sandy hair, drenched, plastered to the back of his black jacket. The jacket is waterproof; that I can tell; the rain doesn't permeate. I follow, but careful; I don't want him to get wind of me, not yet – I want to see, evaluate, judge. Shit, I'm scared. Now that I have the chance, I'm afraid of what his reaction might be. I mean, how does one go about explaining something like that?

I briskly walk, head turned slightly down to avoid the cold splatter of rainfall, which has now probably washed all traces of makeup off my face. Black trickles of mascara are most likely making a statement.

He is already at the entrance amongst a confluence of people all scurrying in, wanting to be rid of the wet. And before I know it, he's disappeared into its depths, being swallowed whole by the horde – out of sight.

He is too fast. I break into a run – stupid, slippery street, sending my left foot skidding, and I topple to the right, last second, using my hand on the mucky ground to save me from not falling flat on my arse. 'Ah!' I cry. I've sprained it. No – something worse!

I feel about for my Oyster card in my pocket, not caring how filthy I've become or how much my wrist hurts, so as I can waste no time in validating myself in at the faregate. I reach the station and see him nowhere, craning my neck, this way and that, over the throng of rushing heads. I swipe my card as the bars fling open, and am off, down the escalator, using the quick lane so as to move as fast as possible, having absolutely no idea where to tread next. Victoria Line or Northern?

I land on the first concourse, heart beating wildly. Where is he? I dash ahead, along with the current of people. I have to search fast – there is no other thing for it – the frequency of the trains give me very little time.

People are dashing towards Victoria Line – the train is coming. Northern Line must be coming too; others are bounding back in the other direction. I'm already at the escalators. Victoria Line, quickly, if he isn't there, I'll continue the search, eliminating each platform one by one.

I hear the reverberation of a train's engine emanating from platform 3 – it has arrived. Heart pounding through me, I scramble down the remaining steps, turning left onto the lower concourse, hopelessly trying to avoid the rush of bodies, who have just alighted, blighting my passage. My wrist stings with every step.

I am in time to watch as the last commuters step onto the impatient train. Its doors shut. Desperately, I search through the carriage windows, the saccade motion – my eyes searching, searching, striving to discern as many faces as possible, before the train picks up speed. Suddenly, I hear the train from the other side.

Sprinting across the concourse, I enter platform 4, just as people are mounting. Others, who have egressed, have flooded the area, and I strain my head, looking up and down the whole expanse. *Beep, beep, beep, beep, beep* – the quick, high-pitched signal, foretelling the carriage doors are about to close, and there! Jesus, there! There he is! I have just caught him, literally last second, climbing in further down. His height and hair, helpful markers. I run in two great bounds, catapulting myself through the doors as they shut. The train pulls forward with a groan, heavily pregnant with all its commuters, and I take in long, pained breaths, heart straining with panic.

As we approach Oxford Circus, I look to see him through the other carriage. He is all the way to the other side, holding on a rail, looking out. I wonder where we are going. This line ends in Brixton. What's in Brixton? The Academy. The prison…

The train slows as it enters Oxford Circus. I watch if he's going to get off. He stays put when the doors open. People get off, then on. Wet shoppers, upset with the rain foiling their shopping day. The doors close, he is still in the same position. We are off again. Green Park.

The rolling stock speeds through, rocking us with every shift of force. As we slow for Green Park, he makes a move. My heart spikes, ready for his next step. Sure enough, he alights and turns right, towards Jubilee Line. I let him pass my doors first, then I alight, right behind him. He is in a hurry. He sidesteps any obstacle with great agility. He is nimble, a grace unexpected for one so large. We are through one of the tunnels, twisting left and out onto the middle concourse. He goes right, onto the escalator which takes us down to Jubilee Line. I know we are going southbound, because if he wanted to go northbound, it would have been easier to get off at Oxford Circus.

I stay hidden behind some people as we wait for the train. He has walked a little further down. I pray he remains undiscerning. My hood has done a lot to disguise me, yet I am aware of such a thing as scopaesthesia – the staring affect. When you "feel" eyes on you. I look down so he doesn't sense me; establish an air of indifference.

It feels wrong to be following him. It's illegal, isn't it? I don't know. *You're not some serial killer*, my mind jests. *That's still no excuse*, my conscience weighs in.

Jubilee Line is fast. We are on within a minute. I am in the carriage next to his again, and watch surreptitiously. Next stop: Westminster. He moves to the doors. We're getting off here? *Westminster?* Why? Perhaps we are taking District or Circle Line? No, that doesn't make sense. If he wanted to get off at Embankment, it would have been easier to get on the Northern Line at Warren Street station, shuttle straight down. And if he wanted to go to St James's Park or Victoria Station, then why change at Green Park? He could have just continued from there! Westminster seems the only reasonable answer. What is he going to do at Westminster? Westminster is purely touristy, unless you're an MP and have work at the Houses of Parliament. Take pictures of Big Ben in the rain, like those who find the romance in it all?

Doors have opened and, sure enough, he is following the route for the exit. I slacken my pace; afraid he might see me. Even if he doesn't remember who I am, the mind remembers shapes, forms and faces through repetition, and my image will be stored in his long-term memory, even if he has seen it through the corner of his eye. So next time he *does* see me, it will spark the synapsis, and then the memory, the recognition. Then curiosity to know who I am will enter his mind, as human beings are accustomed to be curious. It is an unbelievable miracle he hasn't wondered why the same person is following him all this time, but I do believe it has to do with the fact that he has not once looked around him. He has not once interacted with anyone. His body has been taut, rigid. He hasn't relaxed one second.

In short, I think he has something of much importance weighing on his mind, so much so, that he cares little of what is happening around him.

Up we go, not turning for any of the other lines. Up, heading for London's great landmark.

I see the spikes of the neo-gothic masterpiece first, as he walks out in the downpour.

I am out, and I have lost him. I look frantically around. There! He is already jogging down Westminster Bridge, having crossed to the other side. The rain his heavy, double-decker buses and taxis splash by me. I'm losing him. There must be three other people out, braving the weather. At least they have umbrellas. My parka isn't waterproof, and I feel moisture seep through.

I don't move. I see him in the distance. He has stopped and is fumbling for something in his pocket. He turns. I am in his line of vision, but before I can panic, he looks up, he hasn't seen me, but I guess you can't tell someone's face from so far off. The moisture in the air has created a fog, also hindering any clear vision. I'm sure that's a blessing in disguise.

I wait to see what he does. My face has become one with the rain. I am spitting out rainwater. My hood's only use now, is to keep my concealment.

He has something in his hand, too small for me to see, and he is pointing it at Big Ben. What could it be? What is he doing? It doesn't look like a camera, although who knows what kind of technology is out these days. I look at the clock tower – Elizabeth Tower, now named. A deep wash of lineated, sand-coloured brick, surrounded by a delicate mist of pearl greys. It's true, there is a romance and beauty in it… Big Ben is seconds away from striking the hour: 2 o'clock.

James stands for some moments, hand still raised, then suddenly pops whatever it is back in his pocket, and crosses the bridge, dexterously avoiding the big puddle next to the pavement. He runs towards the south bank. I panic. I break into a sprint – I'll lose him! He stops abruptly, and so do I. He takes it out again – that thing in his pocket – and points it, this time, to the London Eye to our left. What on earth is he doing? Five seconds later, he's pocketed it again, and runs full-speed south, between the buildings. He is sprinting so fast; it is as if he has just realised he is getting soaked by the rain. I am too far behind and too slow, but I think I know where he's going. Waterloo? It's a way off, and I waver, tired and hungry, a morsel of energy left. Just then, bells peel from Big Ben, the familiar melody, *DING, DONG, DANG, DONG*… and moments after, two resounding tolls for the hour, reverberating within me. Big Ben has spoken. I press on; out of the remorseless rain.

He has disappeared behind the buildings, turning left. I was right; that's where the entrance is to London Waterloo. I wait for traffic to pass and cross York Road, pacing further through. I think he's already turned left, off Leake Street, not gone under the tunnel. It's quicker to walk parallel, along Waterloo's vast structure, to get to the entrance. And yes, there he is! He's almost reached the corner. I have very little time to close the distance. Once he enters that immense cage, I'll have lost him. There are too many directions to take, too many people; it is a labyrinth of chaos. I have to run now. I must.

I drag my heavy feet, picking up speed. I am out of breath by the time I get to the nearest entrance.

I swing in, finally out of the rain. I hunt, straightaway, for his hair. My heart pumps, a proliferation generating a nervous tremble. Where is he? Where is he? I don't know what to do. He is nowhere to be seen. Not even his height offers as a beacon. *He's probably turned off somewhere*, I think. The Tube? Maybe he's taking the Jubilee Line somewhere further on. I can't come up with a better idea, so I go forth, deeper into the bustling station. I find the escalators indicating Waterloo's underground, and tread onto the first revolving step.

Gran says God always aids us in our decisions whatever we decide to do. I don't know what it is, but my assumption to select the Jubilee Line is correct. For right there, I see him below. I have caught his hair. He is preparing to dismount, he has reached the bottom concourse, and he rushes to his right. Others follow suit. I can only guess it's because a train is coming; they can hear it from down there. But now I know, like a stab in the gut, I will not make it.

I bound down, in spite of it. I don't give up. I turn into the next flight of steps, down, down, as I hear the signal hail the train's departure. The platform's glass screen doors have already slid shut, and the train pulls out. Anguish! I'm too late! But there I see him. He is crammed up against the door, staring out in a detached way, as the train picks up speed. And just then, I must have come into his line of vision because for one second our eyes meet, as he slides out of sight, once more – gone.

Chapter Four

Back Then

I came into view of all the school kids, a mixture of blues, blacks and greys now all a wash of bleak drab from the dark sky.

My eye caught on Bianca; her mouth moving incessantly. She was probably nattering on about the boring minutiae of her life to that poor soul next to her. She resembled an extra on a film set, told to say *rhubarb and custard* a hundred times – her mouth never stopped. As she was doing so, she glanced left and right, artfully eye-flirting with any Mildener that made optical contact with her. I had a funny feeling she wasn't going to let her parents drive her to school for much longer. She was totally in her element with the crowd.

 The distinct sound of the bus revving up the hill could be heard, and I moved closer to the group that was now instinctively in a huddle to push in line to get the good seats on top. I didn't have that inclination and just stood behind everyone. Bianca gave me a conspiratorial squint, and I nodded ever so slightly back to her. It was a game. Everything was a game.

 I couldn't see James Laidlaw anywhere. Was he late? Had he taken an earlier bus? I looked around me to see if he was coming. Nothing.

 I was the last in line, and as I took the high step onto the bus, preparing my card for the card reader, I heard thudding footsteps running up behind me. I didn't look around to see who it was. I saw his reflection on the driver's Perspex protection screen. His close proximity felt like a stampede coming towards me, a rush of excited dread. I held my breath. The fear I'd say or do something stupid made me shake in premature intimidation. I felt the same sickness I had that morning, rise.

 Not daring to look behind me and say *hello*, I moved to the back of the bus amongst the veterans, acting like I hadn't realized he was there. I found a window seat and swung off my rucksack as I sat, ensconced.

 Rear end deposited comfortably, I looked up in front of me. I jumped. James was stood at the foot of the narrow staircase, regarding me. My face set on fire. *Shit*. He suddenly grabbed onto a bar, as the bus's acceleration threw his equilibrium off for a moment. Then he let go, and walked towards me unsteadily while the bus bobbed and bent. And the next thing I knew, he'd plonked himself right down next to me.

Now

 It is a struggle not to break down and cry, right then and there in Waterloo, from all the exertion and consequent failure. I stay, still panting, unable to move, unable to think. I am barely able to feel.

 I close my eyes and see his. His… After six whole years, I see them again. I see them look straight at me, and I shiver, their intensity not having changed one molecule. I have a trove of hues stored in my mind; of all the blues his irises have ever become. It all depends on the shift of light. Today I was given enough time to see the tone – three glorious seconds. I saw they had light; a rich blue, a brightness which only happiness brings. *Is* he happy? I wish to God he is.

He saw me too… I wonder whether he remembers me. Seeing him full-on, it is as if I have fallen through a vortex of time, for I perceived only a slight change. I bring forth his image. It is clear, radiant. Still the same boy, but features more defined, more worldly…

I pace glumly back to Northern Line. I have to get home. I am mentally and physically wrung.

***

I go in through the little side door next to the hairdresser's where I live, and clump upstairs with heavy heart. The stairs creak inside the Victorian-brick building. The façade on top of the white-washed, wooden decor of the shop underneath makes for a sound architectural semblance. We are on a quiet enough road, with only a faint clatter of the far-off train penetrating the air when all is still, and with neighbours keeping themselves to themselves. I'm not dissatisfied with my flat, but I do want a house one day. A garden. Flowers. A pear tree, like my grandparents on my father's side have. Sometimes, I spot a house in the style I want and wish I had the money to buy it. It isn't impossible; it will just take time. It's on my secret wish-list. Victoria is renting a flat in Notting Hill with friends. It's a comfortable, wide-enough space and in a pleasant area, but still; I keep true to my dream. A house, perhaps with a waterway, detached from everything. One day… with someone…

I reach my front door, and I can hear the TV on. We'd bought that TV with the help of Kate's friend, who'd been working in the electronics' shop at the time. The TV had been on display, and he'd told us when it was going to be changed, so we could innocently walk in on that day and buy it on the discount.

I hear Kate's distinct laugh and then someone else's. It is deep. She has some guy over. I roll my eyes to myself. Probably some loser, per usual. She really knows how to pick 'em. I don't know how she can live through every break-up. How could you give your heart to someone every time, only to have it thrown back at you? I think it is something I will never understand.

Her last fling was with a married man. When she introduced me to him, down at our local pub, she had conveniently forgotten to mention he was already wedded to another woman, i.e. taken, *claimed* by another, and even then I thought there was something amiss. He had a restraint in manner, and his laugh was too forced. I told her, later that evening, that he reminded me of me when I was a child and when I had done something bad. Only after that, her body deflated and she confessed he was married. Thinking back on it, it had disturbed me she couldn't respect the importance of wedlock. Did she really want to be the other woman?

'Why didn't you tell me he was married?' I'd asked.

'Because I didn't want you to be influenced negatively by your opinion of him,' she'd retorted, crossing her arms in defence.

I'd harrumphed sarcastically. 'You don't need an opinion on a married man. The fact that he's cheating on his wife is reason enough never to see him again, because he's a cheat!'

She'd started to cry. 'I know…'

Then I had deliberated. 'Actually, that's not a bad tactic.'

She'd raised her brows at my unexpected thought.

'I might do that to you,' I'd mused. 'Get your unbiased opinion on a guy; not tell you a thing about him and see if you like him.'

'You've gotta get the guy first,' she'd said sardonically. Then we'd burst out laughing.

'Yeah but, a bloody married man!' I'd cried. 'I don't care how good looking he is and what he's promised you. You don't do that. Rule number one!'

'All right. I get it.'

Then I continued in a softer voice. 'Why then? Why do you do it?'

'You know why, El. I'm messed up.'

'You're not. Stop saying that. You can do so much better. Your morals were tested in the worst way, and you came out still knowing right from wrong. You've just got your principles all screwed up. It isn't love with this man. It's just sex. There's a difference. You think by having sex he'll fall in love with you and leave his wife for you. Not gonna happen! But let's say he does leave his wife for you, do you know what'll happen? He'll end up cheating on you too. Right now, he is using you and you are using him. It's ephemeral. When he's had enough, he'll dump your arse and go back to his wife. Then what will you have accomplished? Absolute *nada*, that's what!'

I turn my key in the lock with my left hand; it is too painful using my right, and walk in. Kate and someone, whom I vaguely recognise, are seated on the sofa, both heads turned towards me in the last throes of laughter.

'El!' Kate cries. I walk towards them as they get up.

'El? This is Stuart. Stuart? This is Eleanora.' I give him my left. Kate notices.

'You look familiar,' I say to Stuart, with an effort to be sociable.

'Yeah. Stuart was at Jason's party. That's where we first met, but we ran into one another the day before yesterday, and well… here he is!' Kate answers for him, smiling.

'Oh right. Oh yeah,' I say. Of course, I remember his face; my brain never lets me do otherwise. Faces… shapes… shades. A mechanism which lights in cognition to physiognomies and anything else surrounding. Only, I hardly ever remember *where* I've seen them.

Stuart looks pleasant enough, and I return his smile.

'Well, if you'll excuse me. I need to take these wet clothes off,' I say, as I move towards the kitchen, wanting to give Kate her space. In any case, my mind isn't really in any mood for entertaining.

I take off my soaked coat and top, leaving the tee underneath. My jeans look like they've been dipped in a barrel of water. I roll them up with one hand, not bothering to take them off and put on something else. I undo my bootlaces and prop them on our makeshift entryway, which is basically four pallet boxes; two stacked on two, and some hooks at the top for coats. I wash my dirty hands in the bathroom and check my wrist. It is swelling. Puffy, light-red skin. I stutter a silent cry; I don't want to be heard. I bite down on my good arm to muffle the noise, like the time I had done in the girls' toilets at school when I didn't want those bitches to have the satisfaction of knowing what they'd done had hurt. I rummage around for a bandage I know I have somewhere, find it and wrap it as best I can, around my wrist and palm, passing it between thumb and index, just as we were taught in that first-aid seminar at school. I find the hairdryer, and with my left hand again, aim at my head and blow dry all rain from my hair.

I wipe my eyes as I walk out to the kitchen, open the fridge and check my ingredients for the pesto I have to make. Mum's recipe. I have work to do. This is now my income: food. I write a blog and have to update it even when I'm not in the mood. Like now.

I turn to the little island we have and fire up my laptop. It gives a groan and whir of misery, like one who is ailing but forced to rise. That is also on my fix-it list: new PC.

I open the cupboard and find the rigatoni, get out the big pot for pasta and fill it with water, put it on the hob, all the while wincing each spasm of pain in my wrist. Each small bout of agony, a reminder of my day's events.

I turn to my laptop and click onto email.

There is one from Mum, one from Victoria with an attachment (probably a PPS file with sad jokes) and the most recent one, from Melanie, another friend from UCL, also with an attachment. The subject reads: *Official invitation for you and Kate!!!*

I know what it is. Melanie had told me a while back she was getting married, and said she would send me the invite with all the details closer to the date.

'Melanie just sent us the invitation,' I call to Kate. I read the blush-coloured, floral invite. 'The Saturday after next, on the twenty-sixth.'

'Oh, cool!' she replies. 'Melanie's a good friend.' She informs Stuart. 'We need to go shopping!' she adds to me this time.

In the past six months I have been to four weddings; this will be my fifth. I am at the espousal phase of life; surrounded with couples moving in and marrying, having babies, getting on with their lives. Except me. I am a placid onlooker; marriage seems a faraway land for me. One where the ticket to get there has yet to be verified, let alone issued. Shit, I really am pathetic.

I get up and yank a beer out the fridge. I suck urgently, drawing in the cold, crisp bitter, quenching my thirst. Quenching my thoughts.

Back Then

I froze.

He brought a gust of boyish scent with him, mixed with the remnant of aftershave, and...*sniff*... fountain-pen ink. He smelt wonderful. I looked down, not wanting him to see my face redden. I noticed his hands then. He was holding onto the handle of his rucksack, which he had placed in between his thighs, the bottom resting on the floor. What a juxtaposition! My mind went into fantasy mode. I blushed madly. What lovely, long, muscled hands he had, no bitten nail in sight, unlike mine. Mine were in need of a professional manicure, and even then, I didn't think they could be salvaged. I used to bite my nails dreadfully, and it had left slight deformities on some struggling to grow. On top of that, I hadn't got all the oil paint out from under my nails from double Art that day. It looked like I'd been gardening without gloves on. I hid them. I didn't want him to be disgusted by me on top of everything else.

'Why didn't you go upstairs with the rest of Hilsmond?' he asked. No *hello*. There was a tired mellow to his beautiful voice. It was accompanied with a hint of concern. That surprised me. What did he care?

I slowly turned to him, in all likelihood looking as though I had just lost the ability to comprehend English. He looked wan. His eyes bore traces of needing sleep. Working hard for those A Levels, no doubt. He was gazing at me intently, questioningly. How could this wonderful boy, tall, handsome and, I was guessing, popular be giving me the time of day? I was a loser. Surely, he could see that. But, no. Why would he think that after I'd shown such self-confidence that morning? He probably thought I was experienced around boys. I wanted to laugh. I had to speak. I found my voice, albeit, trembling.

'I always sit here u-unless there aren't any seats,' I managed to say.

He raised his eyebrow. 'Why's that? Don't you like the crowd?'

More like the other way round.

'Well,' I began then stopped, as I realised I had absolutely no excuse to give except lie, and I didn't want to lie to this boy. Ever.

I shrugged saying, 'The truth is, i-it's a combination of wanting to be where the silence is, and also that I don't have any good friends on upper deck r-right now.' It was 100% truth. I was glad I told him the truth.

He smiled. I stared at his mouth, which transformed his whole face into brightness.

'Or maybe you mustn't be seen with this mystery person you so avidly said I should meet tomorrow...'

I couldn't help but smile at his clever deduction, and said, 'A-another reason for you to do as I say; see if you're right.' I tinted my voice with a conspiratorial undertone.

He looked at me and rolled his eyes, mock annoyed. That made me giggle. I couldn't help it. He looked so comical. His face smoothed at my laugh, and his lip curved; not like he wanted to laugh, but rather, my laugh amused him. And then I felt strangely at ease with his inviting manner.

'My mate, Nick, said I ought to go for it. He's always going on about me not taking enough chances, like I'm too afraid to step outside my comfort zone... which is utter bullshit. It's just not my M O. He just doesn't get the difference between a harmless risk and a serious one.'

'Well, this one isn't physically dangerous or anything.'

'No. And I suppose I haven't got anything to lose except for some extra sleep. Bus comes every twenty minutes...'

'True...' Then I thought, *doesn't he want to sit with his friend?*

'Is Nick here? Do you want to sit with him?'

'Nah. He lives towards Hendon.' Hendon was in the opposite direction.

We sat in silence for some moments, letting the bus sway us. All the while I was thinking how, at any moment, he was going to get up and leave me. But he didn't. He just kept sitting there, next to me... looking at me... it gave me a bit of a complex, and I panicked. I had to say something. This bus ride must be filled with conversation, else he'd think me a complete fail, with a capital F.

'So, h-how long have you been going to Milden?' I ventured. 'I'd never seen you until this morning. And you speak of Nick like you've known him for years. I'm confused.' I felt my stutter loosen the more I spoke.

He smiled. 'You're right to be confused. Nick and I have been friends for ages. I came to Milden just over a week ago. My old school closed and I thought, why don't I transfer here so I can be with someone I know.'

'And you already know about Trisha?' I said, incredulous.

He chuckled. 'Word like that gets around...'

'She'll be pleased.' It was said matter of fact, but James took it as sarcasm and he laughed out loud. He even had a wonderful laugh and all... and teeth. I grinned back at him.

We were approaching Mill Hill Broadway. A few stops and it was Bianca's turn to get off. If she came down the narrow steps and turned her head to the left, she'd see us at the back of the bus and... it wouldn't look good. She'd misconstrue it as me making a move on James. A betrayal. *Like you'd ever have a chance...*

'You know, you don't have to sit with me if you want to go up and sit with your friends,' I said, suddenly rather panicked.

'Are you trying to get rid of me?' he said, feigning hurt, as the smile still lingered on his face.

'No...' I didn't sound very convincing.

'What then?'

What, exactly. What could I say to persuade him to move? Maybe if I were to tell him I was not who he thought I was, that I was a big, fat zilch, and for the safety of his own popularity he needed to be as far away from me as possible.

'Were you popular at your last school?' I finally said. He looked stunned with my total non-sequitur.

'A bit…'

'You're being modest. Bet you were one of the most popular…'

'Where are you going with this?' His eyebrows furrowed.

'Do you want to remain popular?' I persevered. His eyes suddenly bore into mine, questioning.

'What are you saying?' he said, concern carved his countenance.

'I'm saying that …I'm not exactly popular. I'm not who you think I am. Forget that girl you spoke to this morning. That was just… an act. So… if you don't want to be seen with me, it's OK. I'll understand… I wouldn't like it if they made fun of you, being seen with me.'

He frowned, bemused for some moments, letting it sink in. 'Thanks…' he said.

'For what?'

'Well, for being honest and …for putting me first. Nobody's ever done that.' He considered for a moment, drilling his eyes into mine. 'You could have used this to get popular yourself, but you thought of me… Thanks…' His voice so soft, a seed of solace planted itself somewhere inside me. Bianca's theory on all boys being egotistical pricks flew out the window. James was nothing like them.

'If anyone sees us, there will be talk, only, it'll be bad for you. Me? I've got nothing to lose,' I said quietly. It was the most honest remark I'd ever said. Out loud, at least.

'Come on! I don't believe you're that… unpopular!' he said vehemently.

'You think I'll be… tarnished by association? Pft! I don't care, really, 'cos in three, four months, I'm out of here! Oxford Awaits!' He grinned.

He was right. Such things were petty. Mock exams were over, and now all that was left was the real deal, where every eighteen-year-old would be onto a new, exciting future. Essentially, James was focused on other, more important things.

'Wow, Oxford! That's great!' I said. 'What are you going to study?'

'Anything on the engineering end.'

'Cool!' I said. 'My dad was a civil engineer…' Shit. Why did I say that? Dad was a touchy subject, and I avoided talking about it as much as I could; save myself the pitying looks.

'Was?' he asked tentatively.

'He passed away a few months back.' That's all I said. And even if I wanted to say more I couldn't; the sharp undercurrent of pain halted me. James got the drift. He had been unprepared for such a subject, and merely said, 'I'm sorry.'

We turned the roundabout and onto Mill Hill High Street. My heart started to gallop as we were closing the distance to Bianca's stop. I must have looked tense because James saw the agitation on my face and asked me if I was OK. I smiled weakly at him and nodded. I wanted to throw up. I started to nibble on a nail. My nervous habit.

One more stop and it was Bianca's. I heard her loud mouth calling goodbye to friends. She was coming down, *thud, thud, thud* went her chunky-soled shoes, STOP button already pressed. Then I heard more steps; other kids got off there too. They squeezed passed her, she'd managed to stay on the last step. You could make out part of her arm wrapped around the front of her rucksack, which she had brought to her front. One tiny move forward, and a side glance to the left, and she'd see us. But why should she turn to the left? As far as she knew, James hadn't made it on this bus, unless she wanted to talk to me. But if she wanted to talk to me, she would have done so already.

The bus slowed. My panic rocketed.

My eyes were riveted in front of me, preparing for confrontation. I knew she wouldn't be foolish enough to speak to me and give herself away, but she was capable of slaying you with one look.

The bus stopped and the doors hissed open. The kids disembarked, and Bianca skipped out onto the road in two leaps behind them, none the wiser. Trisha followed. Of course; she lived around there, that's why James had thought it was her.

The doors shut closed with a muffled *thunk,* and I let out a gasp of relief. I didn't know if James understood anything from my tenseness, but he wasn't stupid. He'd had his head turned in the direction I'd had it in. Bianca and Trisha were the only big girls from Hilsmond to exit. It was the closest stop to Mill Hill Broadway Station. He could easily put two and two together since I'd told him it wasn't Trisha. Had I just given the game away with my nail nibbling?

The bus groaned on. We sat quietly for some moments as we trudged up a steep corner, making me lean onto him from the shift in gravity. The length of my arm was up against his, my thigh touching his. He was so incredibly hard, yet soft. I wondered, just then, if he lifted weights. He didn't seem to notice the contact, as he held onto the hand bar in front of him so that he wouldn't flip off his seat. It was as if he was holding on for the both of us. Or at least, I let myself believe so.

I stole a closer look at his clean-shaven jaw. At his downy nape of fine, gold hair. Never, never had I been so close… *a couple more inches and I could kiss him.*

'You shouldn't bite your nails,' he said, as the bus released air with a *tsh* and pulled forward, straightening our bodies. I took my finger out my mouth instantly. Great. Now he was disgusted with me. I turned, wanting to see how he looked when revolted but, to my blinking surprise, he was grinning.

'So, do you live near me?' he asked.

'Define near. Are three stops near?'

'No, probably not,' he said, chuckling. Then, realising something, said, 'Are you telling me this friend of yours got you to walk all that way this morning, just to deliver her message?'

I nodded slowly.

'Jesus. Nice friend,' he said, piqued. 'She must be desperate…'

I laughed. I couldn't help it. Spot on. I wasn't going to dispute it. Bianca's hormones were driving her into nymphomania.

'And what kind of friend does that? Makes you walk three bloody bus stops in the freezing morning? Jesus!' he expanded, almost like he was the one who had been forced to do it. Spot on again. Bianca wasn't a real friend.

'Don't know if I want to wait at Mill Hill tomorrow after that,' he proclaimed.

'What do you mean?' I said, startled, ill at ease at what Bianca's reaction would be if he didn't go. She'd be on my case until she got what she wanted. I wanted this over and done with.

'I mean, she sounds a bit weird,' he stated, getting up and slinging his bag over one shoulder.

No. He had to…

He pressed the STOP button, and I got up, panic-stricken, as he turned and made his way to the doors.

'Please! Please do this, James…' It came out almost anguished, but the anxiety of wanting to explain and knowing time was running out had made my plea even more profound. 'She won't stop… Please. It's just this once!' Some sweet, old, Asian lady turned just then, smiled at me kindly, thinking we'd had a tiff.

James looked at me. He was now standing at the doors, his eyes pent with a frown of deliberation. I was shaking… The bus stopped and the doors opened. He hardly knew me, yet I could see, the way his beautiful eyes softened, he understood how important this was to me.

'James?' It was one last plea. He ground his jaw, weighing the pros and cons for one moment. Then he gave me a nod, *OK*, mind made up, and alighted onto the pavement. The doors shut, the bus pulled forward, and we glanced at each other through the window, as he glided out of sight.

Chapter Five

Now

I get out my Sony A58, focus the aperture, and snap. Upload the el dente pesto dish on the blog, type in the recipe robotically; forcing myself to add the usual witticisms, and it's done. I take another pull on my beer, then another and another. Usually, I love to cook. Usually, the procedure of creating a mouth-watering dish comes to me from an unforeseen, good thought. Ever since I was a child, I'd associate Mum's recipes to a happy day or a wistful moment. Not today. And not since I made my cooking a business. Now, I am forced. Today, I am on autopilot, as I haven't stopped going over calculations in my mind. All I can think is what to do. What to say. The reasons, the excuses… the response…

I cannot alter the past, and that will always be my penance. I have already made up my mind to make redress on whatever I can.

The rain has abated and, by some gracious marvel, clouds have thinned. A timid Helios peeps through the crevices, warming where he touches. I have to go to the specific site; my project beckons. I don't know how many opportunities I'll get.

Stuart senses my quiet, contemplative demeanour and tactfully leaves. I am about to put on my parka; I need to be quick – London weather is fickle, when Kate says, 'Care to tell me what's going on?'

'I need to get out of here,' I tell her, drained. Then I emend, 'I have to see something before it gets dark. Something for my project.'

'I'll come with you.'

She grabs her coat. I am already half-way down the stairs. I open the door and cold, fresh ozone hits me. I breathe in.

'And what on earth is up with your hand?' she asks, vexed, as she closes the door behind us. I pace briskly.

'Bear with me,' I say.

In almost silence I take her to Monument. Northern Line, southbound via Bank. She says nothing as we exit the Tube station. We walk sturdily through the few streets, arriving at St. Dunstan's-in-the-East. We enter in the courtyard, where the benches are, and sit.

The northern hemisphere is passed the March equinox, and days are getting longer as we amble inch by inch towards summer solstice. Thankfully, the clouds remain absent, letting the radiance shoot through the ruins of the gothic-styled windows with shafts of golden, evening light. Vapour rises elegantly from the sward and foliage; a mist almost ethereal, which intertwines itself through the beams. The atmosphere is sharp, and I feel a chill through my bones.

I submit the image to memory and close my eyes… and well up. I hold back a secret lament – I don't know for how long I'll be able to continue; eidetic memories aren't for ever. The ineffable irony in that is not lost on me. I am afraid one day I'll wake up and find myself stripped of every single image. My long-term memory, bare and barren. A void of darkness.

Time is running out…

'Remember that story I told you years ago about a boy?' The words are difficult. I haven't spoken them for so long. Something sticks in my throat.

'No?' she says. She's apologetic but I can hear her strain.

'Do you remember when I told you about saying some lie against a boy?' I open my eyes and see hers lingering off, trying to recall.

'It was years ago. A little while after we'd met at N and L. Do you remember? The party?' I prompt.

'Oh yeah. Yeah. Now I remember,' she says, face lit with dawn. Then she frowns. 'What about it?'

'I saw him today,' I tell her, evoking his aspect to mind.

'You saw him?' she says, not quite seeing the severity of that fact. I nod slowly.

'Well, all right,' she says, composed. 'It couldn't have been all that bad. It just brought back some bad memories, that's all…'

Kate obviously doesn't know *what* I saw exactly. I shake my head, feeling the singe of oncoming tears bristle my nose.

'Kate,' I utter. 'His life is ruined.'

Chapter Six

Back Then

James. He was all I could think about. *JL* was written on the inside of my pencil case so no one, especially Bianca, could see. All wrath would be unleashed if she knew. And rightly so too, I supposed. She'd seen him first. She'd claimed him first. All I could do was dream. Dreams were secret.

But there was something on his part, wasn't there? His pitying eyes, and then when he nodded in acquiescence to my plea? No boy who was indifferent would help out like that, would they?

Conclusion: he either liked me or he felt really sorry for me. But feeling really sorry for someone meant you cared. And caring was tantamount to liking, wasn't it?

That evening at dinner Mum made Italian. Mum hadn't made Italian in ages; not since Dad. Both Victoria and I looked at her dubiously. It had been all hard-as-rock steaks or burnt-to-death broccoli. Now, not only had she made Italian, but she made her most difficult and mouth-watering recipe. Handmade ravioli. Big squares. And filled with just the right amount of spinach and dipped in the creamiest mozzarella sauce you'd ever tasted in your life.

Vic and I were hesitant. It looked good, but it could have been burnt or even undercooked. We didn't trust Mum with food much anymore.

'Dig in!' Mum said smiling. She was in a good mood. 'It's your great-grandma Eleanora's recipe.' As if knowing this piece of news would reassure us of its deliciousness. My great-grandmother Eleanora was my mum's much-loved grandmother, and she had named me after her. Victoria was named after the station – where Dad had first set eyes on Mum. We'd laugh sometimes at this, saying, 'Thank goodness you didn't see her for the first time at Elephant and Castle!'

Vic and I exchanged glances. Then she picked up her knife and fork and cut in. I stared, waiting as if she were the king's taster. Then I felt a nudge under the table. Victoria's foot kicking mine, prompting me to eat. I turned to Mum, smiled, picked up my knife and fork, sliced one ravioli in half, prayed, *I commend my soul...* and opened my mouth. I started to chew with fear, only to be surprised that the ravioli was absolutely *mmm*. The pasta was precisely cooked and seasoned. The spinach was soft and in the perfect ratio to the square ravioli, and the sauce was smooth and textured, giving the taste consistency.

'Mum,' said Victoria. 'It's delicious!'

I nodded in accord, mouth now stuffed. Mum grinned, her eyes glistening.

Later that evening, I went to sleep soundly; satiated. The conversation I had with James and the good meal Mum had made, generated a feeling of contented bliss. Like the whole day was perfectly connected.

I woke up the following morning tranquil. A state of lucid joy embraced me like a silk scarf softly wrapped around my body. For, perhaps the first time in my life, I didn't much care for the Biancas and the Trishas of this world, because merely sitting next to, talking to... *touching* James had filled me to the brim. I didn't much care what the day would hold, and if James met up with Bianca and whatever came next. I didn't much think of anything. Nothing was more intense, more real than our bus ride together. Nothing and no one could ever take that away. Him and me on that bus. That was mine for ever.

Up and ready now, out in the sharp air of the thick, misty morning, as the two-four-two's blustering engine could be heard drawing nearer towards my stop. Out of all the schoolchildren, I was the first on the bus as I lived nearest to the terminus.

I stomped onto the warm, welcoming confines of the double decker, heat instantly wrapping me in its arms.

There were plenty of empty seats to choose from, and I opted for the same one I had sat in the day before, the one where James and I had sat. Soon, I'd find out if he had got up earlier to get the bus and wait at Mill Hill Broadway. I'd either see him at his stop in a matter of minutes or at Mill Hill, getting on with Bianca.

It was funny because I wasn't jealous or anything, well… perhaps a little, but I knew nothing would ever happen between us, so there was no expectation. Things like that never happened to people like me. They happened to people like Bianca and Trisha. All I lived for was news, information that would keep me contented. Let me live in my little pipe dream.

Too nervous to read; we were coming to his stop now. The bus slowed, and I started to gnaw at a hangnail. I peered out of the window as bodies formed a line, cold and peevish. Another day of school. Bo-ring! If he'd been there, I'd have seen him because he was a foot above the rest. But he wasn't amongst them. I took in a breath to calm myself, as my heart was doing overtime, pounding my rib cage.

Good. He went to Mill Hill Broadway. He did it. He did it for me…

I smiled widely behind my old, tattered copy of *Les Mis* – I had forgotten my *Jane*; I knew I had forgotten something. I always got that feeling when something was missing. It pestered me, right in the centre of my solar plexus. What they say about gut feelings is no metaphor for me. But who cared about Jane and Rochester? James had done this inane act because I'd asked him to, and I was dazed with delight.

The bus turned the bend, downwards, beneath the wide span of the steel bridge of Mill Hill Broadway Station. In 100 metres, 90… 80… the stop where he'd be. And Bianca.

Now

'His life is ruined?' Kate repeats. 'What do you mean?'

I wipe a tear, shaking my head. 'He isn't the man I thought he would be. Something must have happened and it has affected his future.'

'What? Is he walking around London naked with an "end is nigh" sign hanging across his goolies, or something?' she says, teasing. I let out a stuttered burst at her unexpected words, snot ejecting from my nose. I fumble for a tissue in my pocket.

Kate isn't insensitive, no; far from it. Her making light of situations by putting an extremity is how she survives. It is her mechanism. She uses it to outweigh the real problem; to reduce the severity of it. And now, she is trying to do it for me.

'No,' I tell her, 'but it looks like things are bloody awful.'

'Like?'

'Like, I remember he was so clever. He was going places, you know? He'd applied to Oxford. *Oxford!* I mean, he isn't what I expected to see after all these years.' I shake my head, as if shaking it will dislodge the image. To no avail. 'His clothes were old and torn,' I continue, my throat thickening. 'It looks like he is… homeless, or close to it. He was sweeping the floors outside one of the classes. I mean, tell me if I'm wrong, but having a degree from a university like Oxford, I think, would give you a better job prospect, wouldn't it? Why on earth is he sweeping floors, tell me?'

I look into Kate's eyes but she is a silent blur.

'His hair is… long and knotted. He's got a short beard, you know… as if he couldn't shave it; not like a fashion choice. He looked like he was in need of a good bath… but he didn't look malnourished.' I stop there, considering that. He was in pretty good shape, actually. He honestly didn't look like he *wasn't* getting a decent meal, but it wasn't only the fact he looked healthy, it was the fact he looked over-nourished, if there were such a thing. He was muscled, beefed up, as though he worked out. I suppose a homeless person wouldn't be able to keep weights…

I look at Kate. That tortured expression of one who knows what it is to be homeless, out on the streets, begging. She had been living anywhere she could find… She'd run away from that troubled house of hers, and has been running since, straight into the arms to whomever gave her a second's notice.

'I ran off and came home as soon as I saw him. That's why you saw me earlier,' I tell her.

She looks at me, perturbed. 'It must have been a great shock,' she says subdued.

'It was,' I answer. 'Because I feel my guilt even more intensified.'

'Oh, El. That was years ago.'

I bite my lip and shake my head, feeling the tears again. 'Do you know, I always wanted an opportunity to speak to him? I owe him an explanation, *and* to get it off my chest. I always said to myself if I ever ran into him again, I'd tell him what I did. But I always thought I'd run into a prosperous, no-need-for-anyone's-pity, well-to-do businessman. The standard of what *he,* himself, had set. Some *made* entrepreneur. Not what I saw today. The confession would be softer if he were all right. It would bounce off him because it would be of no consequence. But now… it would be like kicking a man when he's down. I feel like shit.'

'So, what are you going to do?'

I sigh, numb. 'I want to find out where life went wrong for him… help… then I'll tell him what I did.'

Back Then

The bus slowed and, as it did, I slumped down into my seat placing Hugo's prose even higher so just my eyes could scan the faces that got on. The same old, Asian woman sitting next to me eyed me suspiciously.

Coming to a stop, the doors opened with the familiar hydraulic tug. One by one, passengers filed on, filling most of the bus. Mill Hill usually had the most commuters in one go.

Then I saw them. First Bianca came on, then, after a couple of others, James. They weren't together. I didn't know what that meant and didn't know whether to be happy… or worried. Bianca's expression was as though she had been told to keep a really good secret but was dying to blurt it to the whole world. She had a sly grin and an air of aloofness. She gave me a quick, jerk of her brows as she scuttled up the narrow stairs. James, on the other hand, had disconcerted bewilderment written on his face. I felt so bad. I'd helped Bianca play him. *Oh, God! I'm sorry, James,* my heart cried, *for not telling you that it was just a game…*

He turned fully to where I was sitting, and I put *Les Mis* even higher up; hide my face altogether. He was looking for me… for explanations. I didn't want to confront him. I didn't want to explain; that was Bianca's business. I didn't want to do any more dirty-work for her. Besides, if she came down and saw –

'Hi, Jamie!'

I froze. It was Trisha. That flirtatious *meow*… I lowered my book to see her behind James, in the nick of time, before the bus closed its doors. She was out of breath, rosy-cheeked and fresh, her cork-screw, blonde curls everywhere. He turned to greet her, his back to me, all thoughts of me gone. She gazed up at him deliberately coy, simpered and puckered her lips. I felt like getting up and slapping the pucker off her face. *Leave someone for us, Trisha!* I noticed she'd rolled up her skirt even more. It was a mere slit now, with her thighs on full display. It wasn't flattering; she didn't have great thighs. Did she honestly like looking indecent, I wondered. The skirt didn't even suit her; it looked ludicrous so short. If Mrs Baxter were on duty today, all hell would break lose.

He turned to go upstairs with her. He didn't even turn to see me. That stung. I stared, dejected at the book I was holding, as I felt my heart crush. But it was my doing. I'd been too afraid. Again! What was the matter with me? Where was my tongue when I needed it? Hiding petrified, that's where. I crammed book back in my bag. I didn't think it would hurt me so much. I thought I'd be contented with what we'd said the previous day, but the more I saw of him, the more I craved. Boys, no matter how nice they were, didn't want girls who had their nose in a book, they wanted girls with short skirts. Instantly, I felt for my waist under my jumper. Discreetly, I twisted the skirt band, rolling up, once, twice. I'd never worn a skirt so short, and that rush of daring tingled my senses. Maybe he'd find me more attractive now?

As the two-four-two approached Milden, I got up, happy to see the silly Hilsmond skirt not look too bad on me. I got off first and walked deliberately slow, so I could see him before we all had to part ways to dash to our according schools. I paced towards Alice's as I saw them all get out. He didn't see me; too engrossed in conversation with some fellow pupil, walking towards Milden's entrance. He was neither with Bianca nor with Trisha. I wanted to punch the air like Judd Nelson at the ending scene of The Breakfast Club – *YES!* And then both of the afore-mentioned girls came into my line of vision. Both heads together, both chatting furtively, both walking by me as if I were invisible.

***

'Eleanora! Where are you, you fat slag?'

It was Bianca (who else?) shouting endearments to me in my form room. She thought she was so funny because some girls would laugh at her deliberate lewdness, ostensibly thinking it was cool. Me? I took it with a pinch of salt. As I did with everything Bianca.

It was lunchtime, and I had decided not to eat in the canteen. Mum had packed a sandwich, a very poorly-made sandwich, with a wad of cheese and hardly anything else, but nonetheless, I wanted to honour her effort by eating it.

I rolled my eyes to myself. I hated it when Bianca got like this. I had no moment of peace until some plan of hers had been fully executed to the note. Her coming and finding me in my form room proved she not only needed me, but was in a hurry to get it.

'All right, Bianca?' said Jo to her, stopping her on her way to my desk. I carried on eating my depressing sandwich. I didn't want her to see it because she was the type of person who made fun of sad lunches. She had opinions on everything, and usually they were padded with criticism.

'All right, Jo!' Bianca greeted back. Then they shared a joke, cackling loudly, so the whole class turned to see what was so funny. Bianca basked in that kind of attention. She would sneak glances to see how many people were looking her way. Such a fraud. She adjusted a perfect, theatrical smile to her face, turning gracefully into the best-buddy persona she adopted with me. Sometimes I thought she had a split personality when she did that. It freaked me out. How could someone, so guiltlessly, change who they were? Like a lever existed in her brain and was now shifted to "charming".

'El! Did you see? He came! He came to Mill Hill! Oh, my God!' she squealed, as she came bounding up to my desk and sitting next to me. I munched, trying my best to look enthused. She spied my languishing sandwich in hyperbolic disgust, lip turned up at the side with that *eww* look. I braced for the snide comment.

'What. The fug. Are you eating?'

'Your brain!' I said, surprising myself with this witty rejoinder.

'Looks like saggy dick.' (Everything was dick-related with her). I cringed inwardly.

'You would know!' Again, surprised with myself at this sudden ability to give as good as I got. Who was I? Bianca was momentarily taken aback. She'd never seen me this way. *I'd* never seen me this way! I could see she was trying to find something clever to snap back at me, but my retort was too sophisticated for her. Her mouth hung. The girl was vacuous, no imagination. It made me wonder sometimes how she'd even passed the entrance exams to this place. I gave her a laugh to help her along as things were getting uncomfortable. She burst out laughing, as fake as could be, but she didn't want to admit I'd one-upped her.

She hastily got down to business.

'I wanted to thank you for keeping *shtum* on the bus. I didn't want to make it look like *I* had planned this. He would have put two and two together if he saw we were in cahoots. I kept it cool. I didn't say a word. You should have seen me. I acted like nothing was going on, so innocent.'

He's already put 2 and 2 together, dimwit!

'Why didn't you talk to him?' I asked. I knew that wasn't her objective, but I wanted her to make that step, though. I knew it was the absolute antithesis to what I'd felt earlier, but I'd been thinking about it better. She needed to speak to him. *I* needed her to speak to him. It would appease her insecurity if she ever caught me talking to him. And bonus: if they became friends, then I'd have some extra access to him as well, wouldn't I? My God – the extremity I went to just so I could talk to him, be near him, and not fear Bianca.

'No! You know that wasn't the plan,' she said.

'What are you afraid of? He's just a guy,' I said, trying to make her see how simple it was. She looked at me, stunned once more.

'Well look who's become an expert on boys,' she said sarcastically. It was jealousy.

'I'm just saying what you said to me, remember?' I said, quickly to save. 'Egotistical pricks… and how they like it when a girl fancies them, blah, blah, blah… Come on! It's not as if you've never spoken to boys before. This should be child's play.'

She blinked. 'Yeah…'

'Yeah. If I can do it, you can. Just go up to him and say, "Hi! I'm the nutter who's stalking you", or something.' I laughed. Where was all this temerity coming from? She looked at me peculiarly. I nudged her to show her I was just teasing.

'Screw you!' she said, but laughed too. She knew if she wanted to save face, she'd have to take her own advice.

'All right. I'll say *hi*… Oh, my God!' She said, acting all overheated, flapping her hands about. 'I'm hyperventilating! *Argh*… it's so nerve-racking 'cos he's such a cute guy. I've never spoken to such a cute guy before. Oh, my God!'

'Everything will be fine, B. Don't worry about it. You'll say hi, then he'll say hi, and then next thing, you'll be holding hands…' I had no idea why I said that. I think I was dreaming about myself. Picturing her doing that with James made me want to heave up the saggy-dick sandwich.

'By the way, your skirt doesn't suit you so high up,' she said loudly, so everyone in the class could hear. She got up, strutted some steps towards the door, and turned and shrugged. 'Sorry, but just some friendly advice… Better put it back down. Nobody wants to see your skinny legs.'

Chapter Seven

Now

I stop short in the corridor. My heart makes one gigantic thud and then keeps pounding hard. Stuck in place, I see him slowly sweep the floor, a few yards down, with careful obedience to the job.

He's come! He is here!

I quickly hide behind a corner, just my eyes peek round, silent as a statue. His head, turned towards the floor as his arm moves out, then in, out, then in, bringing whatever is on the ground to the small pan, whose pole he has in his other hand. I watch as he tips the contents into the little bin attached to the cleaner's trolley, and agony coils around my heart and tightens.

He looks up, just then. I catch the look on his face, it is the same as the one I saw on the train. Placidly introspective, absorbed in something …agreeable.

We are officially closed for Easter, but there are still quite a number of people walking around. Two girls giggle to each other as they walk by him, checking him out. No one can deny he is a specimen to be admired. Even through those royal blue overalls, his tall, well-muscled body can be discerned.

He catches their eye, and for a split second, he is the eighteen-year-old I remember. The defiance. The stance. The tinge of cockiness. The expression of the boy who had it all. Self-confident and robust. Then it instantly fades, and he turns away.

What happened to him? The coil squeezes tighter.

Monday. Today is the day… Today is the day I begin to seek the truth; accumulate clues to the insight of his life.

I step onward and out of the building, rubbing my wrist. It still hurts. Physical pain, however, cannot compare, at this moment, to the mental.

Kate and I were up half the night, discussing, then quarrelling, then planning some course of action. We agreed the best method was to gather as much information about him as possible before I acted.

'The sweeping job doesn't necessarily mean he is poor, El,' Kate had conjectured. 'And as for looking homeless, I know plenty of men who have money, but wouldn't know where to stick their deodorant to save their lives! Men are scruffy creatures. If they're not wooing some girl, then they don't much care for personal hygiene.'

This was no easy task, as no search engine showed the *James Laidlaw* we wanted. No pictures, no text, nothing. He had no digital footprint. I also searched public archives in case there were any articles in the papers about that night. The night I articulated my distortion of the truth. My perjury… I had searched every day for weeks, after the event back then, breaking out in a cold sweat every time I clicked on Google or Yahoo – fine-combing every search engine available – but nothing had been written six years ago, and it is the status quo today.

'There's only one thing for it,' I said, resolute. 'I'm going to have to follow him again.'

Kate agreed. I thought once more of the legal implications, but Kate reassured me it wasn't a crime if I wasn't harassing. It's true, bloggers concur, but I am wary.

I also made it clear to Kate that I didn't want to involve her in anything illegal because she already has a record – misdemeanour that it is. But still. Kate can't risk anything mildly illegal, it could initiate an investigation on the LSE board and impinge her degree. I wouldn't be able to forgive myself if I thickened her record.

She'd been caught sleeping under Eyre's Tunnel, on the towpath, whilst she was on the streets. It was the only place she could find to keep out of the rain. The officer that had found her had taken her to the police station – young and over-eager that he was – only to discover that the reason why she hadn't made a run for it was because she'd been burning with fever, drained of all strength and unable to move. 'Two days without so much as a drop of water,' Kate had told me. When undressing her at the police station, they had found someone else's wallet on her; she'd no time or thought to get rid of it. She'd sworn she hadn't stolen it; she'd found it in the street, but of course, they didn't believe her. 'Only *he* believed me. *He* felt sorry for me,' she said of the young officer. But they had put her on record, nonetheless, and it was the day she was sent back home, as she was a minor.

'But what do they call it if a private investigator does it?' I asked Kate in the small hours. 'Isn't that illegal too? They're like glorified stalkers, aren't they?'

'Yeah. I suppose…but I think they are allowed, they have a license or something. Anyway, if you need any help with the computer, I have this friend who could, you know…' she said, nudging her head.

'What?' I asked, with an inkling as to what she meant, but wasn't 100%.

'Oh, El! You're so slow sometimes –'

'Hacking?' I rasped.

'Yes, hacking!' she said, exasperated. 'Sometimes you scare me when you play it dumb.'

'Sorry. I was just making sure. You might have been talking about something else…'

'What else could you do illegally with a computer?' she said rolling her eyes. 'Hit someone over the head with one? Then yes!' She laughed. I tried to.

I walk to the spot.

Back Then

I was still on Bianca's fake blacklist. No engaging in conversation until she enacted her first chat with James. So, we walked up the hill to the stop separately. I stood a distance away from her. Even Laura, the girl I sat next to in form-room, thought it was strange behaviour, as everyone knew Bianca and I were "friends".

'Have you broken up?' she asked. 'Why aren't you speaking?' Laura wasn't a gossip. Well, not much. She did sound concerned.

'We haven't broken up. It's a long story. You'd better ask Bianca because it's not my secret, if you know what I mean,' I said truthfully, glad not to have to explain, being in no mood.

As I was saying these words, my eye caught James emerging from one of the side exits of his school, chatting with some other boy. My heart gave a start. The exit was quite a way off, and I felt relieved he was at a distance. Laura left me then to ask Bianca what was going on, and I was suddenly exposed. I didn't have fantastic eyesight, but I could tell he'd spotted me. I dropped my head, as I felt a wave of heat rushing straight to my face. I fumbled in my bag for dear Valjean, trying to be nonchalant through my tremor. I side-glanced. Yes. He was striding towards me, one hand in pocket. Oh, my God. My eyes fell to his crotch. Shit on sticks! I looked down again, instantly. I'd think about *that* later.

He was coming closer… closer…

His shoes. There were his shoes, not a yard away from mine. I looked straight up to his chest, then to his face. His face; like those painted by the Renaissance greats. Those hues of soft ivory and light pink rose-petal. His eyes, a clearness like light through pale-blue, Grecian glass. His nose, so proportioned it seemed to have been chiselled to perfection. And those lips, abundant and inviting. They curved, now, into a half smile. A smile? The world stopped spinning. There was nothing else but this. Him and me. Him and me. Just him and me. I smiled shyly, all tremor gone, and his face went incandescent. *That will be drawn. Yes, how could it not?*

'Do you know,' he said quietly, 'I don't even know your name?'

I blinked, only realising just then how this was true. All this time, and he never knew what I was called. Somehow, it never seemed important. Shakespeare had been right. But the grin, which was now drawing on my face, wasn't because of that, but because how I found it amusing he never started his conversations with the preliminaries, like a *hello*. I put out my hand, like we were in a business meeting, and with that grin in place, said, 'I'm Eleanora.'

He looked at my hand for a moment, then took it. His was large and perfect and warm, as I expected it to be. Mine was freezing. They were always freezing. He didn't let go. Seemed he wanted to keep it warm. I stayed motionless. *Don't let go. Don't ever let go.*

'Eleanora what?' he asked.

'Stephens.'

'Stephens?'

'Stephens. With a P-H,' I said.

'With a P-H?' he said. Now he was teasing me. I looked down, abashed. He was still holding my hand.

'Is that… paint on your fingers?' he asked, brushing his thumb over my knuckles, sending tingling sensations everywhere, then he gently spread out my palm. I had long, slender fingers, only the nails spoilt the whole look. Thankfully though, the tips were mostly covered in some navy-blue oil paint, which I had no time to clean off properly, per usual.

'Oil,' I told him. 'It's difficult to remove.'

'You're taking Art for GCSE?'

'Yes.'

'So, are you a good artist?' He smirked.

'Well,' I said, giving him a laid-back shrug, trying to evade the question, 'you know…'

I could sense a low buzz of hushed whispers from the kids around us.

'Come on Jamie! Give it some tongue!' a boy called in the distance. I cringed, making to release my hand, but James applied the smallest amount of pressure, expressing silently to me that he didn't want me to let go. I suddenly thought of Bianca. *Oh, no, no, no.*

'You two shagging or what?' came another voice – some Hilsmond bitch joining in with the fun. I bit my lip. James ignored them completely. Then I realised this was the behaviour of a person who had control of his life, not taking schtick from anyone. I was the reverse side to that coin. He could take a situation and mould it just the way he wanted. This was what made you a leader, popular – not just the brawn, but the brain.

'Eleanora. Why not just Eleanor?' he asked. And the taunts stopped so abruptly, it was like he yanked a plug out from a socket, cutting off some irritating, incessant broadcast. I blinked in awe.

'It was my great grandmother's name. She was Greek and, well, Greeks usually put an A at the end of girl's names. In fact, it's pronounced, El-ey-an-or-a,' I said, using a heavy Greek accent to stress each syllable. James stood stock-still. His eyes washed in wonderment. He was about to say something when, 'Oh, El! There you are!' Bianca came out of nowhere and gave me a hug. It was an over-exaggerated display, one just for show, but the movement was so sudden, it severed my hand from James's. Lever switch turned to BFFE. No more fake-blacklist, then. I knew why she'd chosen this moment to make her move. It was perfect timing. She saw the route to get to James, and it was via me. But then she whispered that one, grotesque sentence in my ear, and I almost screamed. 'Watch me play him.' *No! Don't! Don't do that to him!*

Didn't she like him? Didn't she say he was so cute? I thought she was sincere. I honestly thought she wanted to be with him. Why had I forgotten all of this was a game? I should have known her diastrophic mind could never change. I suddenly felt a wave of disgust so acute, I wished I hadn't opened my big mouth and told her to talk to him. I wanted to take it all back. I didn't want him to get hurt – I didn't want him with her! It wasn't because I was Jealous, it was because James didn't deserve that treatment. If Bianca were a sweet girl, I'd bow out gracefully, but now… what could I do? That morning I hadn't wanted to get involved, but after this small exchange, and his warm, beautiful hand, he proved he was a friend, and friends help friends. I couldn't simply stand by and not say something. A warning at most.

I looked at James, as Bianca still had her arms around me. I made no move, no feigned amicability. I did not want to pretend to James. Pretending was lying. *Read it in my eyes, James. Read the truth.*

James's looked at me, then at Bianca, and I could tell he knew exactly who she was – the girl who had set him up.

'Oh! I'm sorry,' Bianca continued, play-acting. 'Was I interrupting something?' I wanted to barf. She turned to me then to James, eyes wide, all innocent-like. The words wouldn't come forth. I opened my mouth, but all I could do was smile uncomfortably.

'Jamie boy!'

Somebody called James out of nowhere and I relaxed, thankful for his interruption. We turned to the person in question. It looked like a schoolmate of his, wearing his Milden uniform rather shabbily, with his tie almost fully undone and his shirt untucked. He was tall and incredibly thin with dark, chestnut-brown hair and skin, rather sallow. However, he had an engaging smile and clever eyes. He trudged up to us, swinging his rucksack over his bony shoulder.

''Sup, mate?' he said to James, slightly out of breath and looking at all three of us one by one.

'All right, Nick. Did the old codger finally let you leave? Didn't you get detention then?' James asked. So, this was Nick.

'Nah. He's a pushover. He just let me off with a warning,' replied Nick, with a naughty wink.

'What? You didn't suck his balls or anything?' said James, smirk on his face. I giggled.

'Nah. Man hasn't got any. I've checked,' said Nick, sniffing hilariously, making us all chuckle. 'Besides, he couldn't prove it was me who hacked the school website… this time.' He wiggled his eyebrows, taking out a packet of cigarettes from his pocket. 'Thought I was going to miss the bus, an' all…' Then he nudged his head towards Bianca and me. 'Care to introduce us?' he said to his friend, still with his welcoming smile. I smiled back.

'This is Eleanora,' James began, hand out to show who I was. 'And this is…' He paused.

'Bianca,' she said on cue, all lovey dovey, grin up to her molars.

'This is Nick. Hacker extraordinaire!'

'At your service,' said Nick. He held out the packet of cigarettes to us, now opened in offering, with a beguiling face. 'And I'm sure my cigarettes will enjoy a good servicing with your lips wrapped around them.' He wiggled his brows. It was all pretend – Nick didn't mean it, but we still cringed at the sad joke.

James shook his head, incredulous. 'Jesus…' he guffawed. He'd reddened.

Bianca took a cigarette without hesitation, just as if it was the most natural thing on earth.

She had started smoking gradually in the past couple of years. When I had first become her friend, she had taken me down to our sports field, right at the edge where an old tree trunk lay across the foliage, rotting. Its circumference was so large, that we were able to crouch behind it and be hidden from the school buildings. She had surreptitiously held out a half-tattered cigarette from her blazer pocket, looking left and right, making sure no one was around, and then a box of matches. She'd lit it up and took in a small breath, inhaling just at the point so that she wouldn't cough. Then she gave it to me. I remember staring at it in disbelief, heart beating frenziedly from what I was about to do. I had held out my two trembling fingers to clasp it, as I'd seen smokers do, and felt that rush of naughty guilt mixed with courageous defiance. I placed it between my lips and drew some of the smoke in my mouth. I didn't dare inhale. I'd spied Bianca, cheeky-grinned, anticipation written on her face for the outcome. I took in the slightest amount of the smoke, still lingering in my mouth, and felt the burn incinerate my throat like a lash of flame. I immediately coughed out the whole thing, spluttering and convulsing to the point of gagging. Bianca had laughed her arse off.

'Thanks,' she said, taking the ciggy carefully out of the box, and not being one to miss a dirty joke added, 'I think my lips can wrap around this one just fine. I'll make sure to… blow hard.' Innuendos galore. *Somebody hand me a bucket…* I smiled uneasily, as did James. We ended up grimacing. Good. Let her make a fool of herself. Nick cracked up. Then he offered a smoke to me. I shook my head politely and said, 'Perhaps another time. Thanks.'

'Jamie?' He then offered to James. 'Oh, whoops,' he said deliberately. 'Jamie here doesn't smoke.'

He gave him a nudge with his elbow, like an apology for taking the mick, and flicked his zippo open, offering the flame to Bianca. She placed one hand around the fire to protect it from the elements. Then Nick did likewise. Two thick, greyish-white clouds of stinky smoke wafted momentarily around their faces and then were gone, leaving their burnt, weedy smell. I looked up at James, just to see if I could read his face. Did he like girls who smoked? Did he like Bianca? I found he was already looking down at me. Something passed unspoken between us – I could sense it.

We could all hear the bus coming from our left, which meant Nick's bus was on its way.

'Shit! Gotta go. See you fine people later,' he said through the cigarette, which was caught precariously between his lips. He gave James a punch on the arm and was off, without so much as a look to see if cars were coming. I froze in fright as he almost got run over, crossing. The car tooted angrily at him as it swerved by, and Nick stuck up his middle finger at it. Most of the kids who saw, laughed.

'He got a death wish?' Bianca asked James.

He harrumphed. 'Probably. Stupid bastard…' he said. I then saw James stoop to look more carefully at Bianca. His face made that imperceptible movement when you find yourself appreciating a beautiful sight in front of you. Yes. Beautiful. Did I forget to mention? Bianca was beautiful. Light brown, curly tresses, skin like she'd sunbathed for a couple of hours. Thick eyelashes and button nose. Her figure was fantastic. The only thing I could claim to have better than her were my breasts. I outdid her on that by far;

she spoke of none. Bet she lit a candle every day to the person who invented the gel bra.

I stared down at my shoe. I didn't want to see the way he looked at her. I wanted to be anywhere but there.

I felt sick.

Where was that bloody bus?

Now

I make my way to a bench; a hidden bench I deem the best lookout. It is out of one's immediate vision when exiting the main building. I sit, cross-legged, taking an art textbook out from my satchel, on the ready to hide my face.

I am disguised as best I can. Inconspicuous clothes, dark, and not emphasizing parts of my body he might remember. Kate practically commanded I wear her wig. A long, strawberry-blonde made from human hair. She'd bought it after a bad experiment with peroxide. When I protested, she reminded me of my physique.

'Have you forgotten how you look? You don't have average height. You don't have average weight. And you don't have average looks. He'll recognise you, first second he glances your way. You were lucky he didn't notice you the first time.'

'No such thing as luck. He just doesn't remember me.'

'I doubt that. All right, I won't call it luck then. I'll call it torrential rain, and that you were at a distance with a hood on. But tomorrow the forecast said no rain, and this time you'll be closer to him. So put bronzer on, those sunglasses you have, 'cos once he sees those dove-greys, he'll know. And the wig. Keep the scarf high; try to cover as much of your face. It will eliminate even the last drop of suspicion.'

'But –'

'Do it!'

Chapter Eight

Back Then

I wished I were her. I wished, again and again, I were her. Her, not me. I was not good enough. My existential being, my mortal body, the form I saw in the mirror, was not good enough. *Of course, he wants her. What were you thinking, you idiot?* Bianca was gorgeous. You know what I was? I was a waste of spacetime.

Bianca was now in full conversation with James. She was winning him over with each smart sentence, each witty reply. All stolen, mind you. It made me shudder; the way she could flip that switch. What character had she embodied now? I retreated slowly, stepping one foot behind the other, reaching Laura. I didn't want to look, didn't want to hear. Alas, I heard. His voice, animated, and it was as if each word, each syllable, was a dagger pushing further and further into my heart.

The bus was heard. Mercy.

'He's a bit of all right!' Laura said, nodding towards James.

'Yeah…' I uttered, as blasé as I could. Then my eyes rebelled, and I looked at him. I jumped as I saw he was already looking straight back at me, Bianca's prattle faintly in the distance, unaware of where his attention really was. His eyes searched, questioned. He seemed bothered, even …pissed off. Shit – I'd pissed him off. Why? He was with *her* now. I saw he liked her – the way she looked, at least. He didn't need me anymore, and besides, he knew I had to do it – leave them to it. He knew Bianca had given me no choice. He turned away, jaw clenched, falling into conversation again with Bianca. She'd asked him something. He couldn't ignore her; he was too good, too polite. That was so woefully rare in a boy. And James was a rare one at that.

We slowly paced to the stop post. Laura was still talking to me, and I could barely keep up with her. I had no idea what the topic was. My ears heard nothing. My eyes saw nothing. I felt them singe with salty drops. I got on the bus and mechanically walked to the back of lower deck. I was about to sit at my usual spot but I observed at the very last second that someone was already sitting there. I looked around me and saw, for perhaps the first time this school year, that lower deck was full.

I turned, there was only one way to go now; upstairs. I had no intention of standing for the whole half hour home, holding onto a handle on lower deck. We had had double hockey, and my necessity to sit overruled my necessity to avoid the J and B show.

James and Bianca were the last in. I waited as Bianca walked towards me at the foot of the stairs. She gave me a wink and the broadest smile – the cat caught its mouse. She scuttled upstairs, and then James came into view. I lowered my eyes. I wanted to warn him, but again I halted. My behaviour would be inconsistent, confusing. First skulk away, leaving them to chat, next tell him to be careful? I was fuddled myself.

'After you,' he said coldly. I blinked startled. He was still pissed off. It was the first time he'd spoken like that to me. I swallowed to hold back the water gathering in my eyes. I couldn't speak; the floodgates would open if I did. I turned, robotically, and ascended the steep steps to upper deck as the bus pulled forward. I almost fell back onto him but caught the metal banister just in time. I could feel his eyes on me as I heard him follow closely behind.

I scanned for Bianca amongst the raucous cacophony emanating from all the mouths surrounding me. Our eyes met and she shook her head, signalling for me not to sit with her – it was for him.

I turned to search for a seat, when I saw a boy from Milden and Clara, in the year above me, start making out in front of everyone. The wolf-whistles and cries resonated through the bus and then everyone clapped. The couple stopped their snog and started laughing. *So, that's how French kissing's done. Much appreciated.*

I found a place to sit. The only free places were in front – reserved for the losers. I trudged over to one, holding onto the bars as the bus pulled forward. I sat myself down, not wanting to see the goings on behind me anymore. They'd be sitting together and flirting, their arms touching. I closed my eyes, wanting the images to go away. They made me suffer.

Life can suck, but that's life! You gotta suck it up and be strong! – Vic. Easier said than done, Sis.

'Oi, Morticia!' It was Sarah's unmistakable, scathing voice. I felt something hard thwack my shoulder blade and ricochet out, spinning to the floor at my feet. A small bottle of water, three-quarters full. That had bloody hurt. A tear fell but not because of any physical pain. Because *he* saw it, and now he'd see for himself an extent of my pathetic life. I wanted to tell Sarah to sod off. What was her problem? But I couldn't. I couldn't stick up for myself. It was like I was shackled, body and mouth, with the bonds of fear.

'Shut the fuck up!' Came a sharp warning. I gasped. That was James's voice! Oh, my God. What was he doing? Did he just tell Sarah to shut the fuck up for *me*?

'All right, Jamie. It's just El –'

'I don't know and don't care who you are, but if you don't shut your trap, I'll throw that bottle right back in your face!'

Silence. One heartbeat, two heartbeats, three… Then the bus continued back to its normal mode of loud noise, as though the whole incident hadn't occurred.

Chapter Nine

Now

It is 12 o'clock. I wait.

I hear someone's footsteps and covertly glance, lifting my head slightly. No. I scan the vicinity just in case. Nothing. I turn down to the book again and look at my watch. 12:14. *Tick. Tick. Tick.* 12:15…

Then, 22 nail-biting minutes later, I hear footfalls on the steps. I look again. *He* is walking at a tangent towards the exit to my right, that familiar saunter, hands in pockets, face pertaining in deep thought.

Blood pulsates throughout my entire body in sudden response at his appearance. A rush of excited panic. I don't move, though; too soon, and it will give the game away. In a few strides he has walked by me, going faster. He is getting dangerously close to the gate.

MOVE! NOW! my brain cries, and I jolt upright, swinging my legs down from the bench, my bag falling and half my material scattering to the ground, the wind blowing my sketchpad open, flicking back each sheet of paper, viciously, like Aeolus suddenly has to inspect my work right then and there. I tremor as I shove each utensil back in clumsily, mentally preparing myself for an act I've never undertaken before in my life, and now, it is a daunting reality, like a slap across the face.

'Move! Move! Move!' I whisper to myself, looking up at that moment to see he's turned right, onto the street. 'You'll lose him!'

Heart pounding, I sling my bag, cross-shoulder and run, perspiration breaking all over me. The man is athletic, long strides and looking like he is in a hurry. I mustn't lose him this time. I mustn't be too far behind. He has his blue overalls on and the same waterproof, black jacket. He is wearing a grey beanie. It is pretty windy today. I use that as a marker because it has some red writing on it, which stands out. That…and the ends of his hair. I can't read what is written on the beanie, though, not from this distance.

He is headed towards Euston Square Station. Will he go in, or will he walk on?

I keep a safe distance of a good 10 yards behind him. I have an opportunity to study him this time. On Saturday I was too panicked, and the rain wasn't much help either. I regard his familiar gait – a reflection of yester years… I smile inwardly, thinking we don't really lose our traits no matter what age we are. The shape and build of his frame; tall, strong and powerful. He has grown at least half a foot since the last time I saw him. I judge him to be roughly at 6'4" now. Broad shoulders… very broad shoulders. He definitely looks like he lifts weights, for there is a more defined muscle on his upper half. At eighteen, there was no doubt he'd grow into a fit man, but he was lean; I don't think his shoulders are shaped thus by a natural development.

Still the most beautiful man I've ever seen… damn it!

I sigh, remembering what had happened to make me act so abominably towards him. What he had said that night at the party. How it had stung. How he had hurt me, so profoundly, that it had felt like a death.

I wonder then, what I would do if he turned around and recognised me. I lower my face in reflex and watch the heels of his trainers walk silently on. If worse comes to worst and he *does* end up recognising me, I'll tell him the truth on the spot, ready for even the direst reaction from him, and I will humbly beg for his forgiveness. But I don't want that to happen… not yet… not yet…

He crosses the street before the entrance to Euston Square Station and is already through the bars by the time I enter the modern glass structure, and I jog so as not to miss where he turns. There is no room for mistakes now. Eastbound or westbound? At least *this* station isn't a labyrinth…

Down the escalators he goes, me, several commuters behind. Alighting on the first concourse, he stops walking and starts to rummage in his pocket for something – his phone. Does he get reception down here? Probably, I think, knowing Euston Square Station is sub-surfaced.

But I'm coming down, closer, closer, the urge to turn back up – against the flow of the escalator – but knowing I can't. *Get a move on, James!* my mind shouts, panicked. If he doesn't start walking, I'll be in limbo; either having to linger, which'll look fishy, or to carry on walking passed him and consequently lose him.

As I am about to alight, just behind him, so close; too close… he moves, I let out a breath of relief. He puts his phone to his ear, all attention on the caller and oblivious to the world around him. Thank God – that was close. He paces at a steady speed. I'm right behind him.

'I told you I'm coming!' I hear him say sharply. His voice arrests me. It hasn't changed in six years. Even though his words are terse, I can still perceive the softness, his own distinct tone, a unique complexion of intonation and annunciation.

'Shit!' he says quietly to himself, ending the call, and shoving the device back in his pocket. It's one of those basic phones with minimal features. Probably without a clock on it, since James juts a hand to read the time on his watch.

What was the last thing he'd said to me? The memory vaults swing open, releasing the words with a breath of life: *Wait for me, yeah?*

'Yeah,' I whisper to myself sardonically.

He turns for platform 2, eastbound. I stride behind, purposefully impassive, catching a whiff of that mundane train smell characteristic to undergrounds – musk and grease.

I lean up against the wall and take out my phone, pretending to search for something on it, as I discretely scan for his trainers, not wanting to fully look up and find him suddenly staring at me. Days are getting warmer. I start to swelter under my woolly hat.

I find his trainers, pacing away from me. That means his back is turned to me. Good. I look up. He takes off his beanie at that moment – no doubt feeling the stifle too – and combs his fingers through his long hair. That hair is mesmerising.

A train sounds its arrival. I move, just my eyes, up at the dot matrix announcement board. It is the Hammersmith & City Line to Barking.

The rumbling, getting more distinct now, as commuters move automatically closer to the yellow line. The platform is almost full; a mob of bodies and heads that screens his. Is this his train also? I covertly search for his trainers again. I cannot see through the sea of feet.

Then the twang of the wheels echoes through the station, as the reverberation of the whole thundering mechanism, appears through the tunnel's mouth, whooshing by us in a turbulent rush, as the brakes screech to a jarring halt. The doors slide open and passengers pour out, obliterating any view I have of him. I've lost his head, his hair; my marker! What if he gets on the train and I don't see? I should have gone closer to him. *Shit!* I crane my neck. Where is he? I should at least see the top of his head!

As the passengers disperse, I catch sight of the familiar gold-sandy tresses, and ease. He'd made his way further down, sat in a chair. The rolling stock trundles out of the station, picking up speed, leaving a gush of wind in its wake, sending my fake hair and other appendages, fluttering up, as it disappears into the tunnel, taking the noise with it.

I try to suppress my shaking body. I have to get closer to him if I am to ensure my not losing sight of him again. I look up. The next train is Circle Line in 2 minutes. I skim the soles of my shoes on the floor and slide, inch by inch, as nearer to him as I can get. Londoners start to fill the platform again. I hide behind them.

Seconds pass and the ominous vibration tremors again. Circle Line is on its way. Something moves out of the corner of my eye. He is approaching the edge of the platform.

The train rushes in with a blast of air and noise. He waits for the passengers to alight and then gets on. As do I.

Back Then

I didn't get it. He confused me. First minute, jaw clenched and cold look, next minute, he's standing up for me. *Boys don't know what they want* – Vic. As much as I didn't want to listen, my ears disobeyed. And my heart. I didn't place earbuds in my ears and get lost in my music. I didn't even want earbuds to muffle out the sound around me. His voice... I caught distinct parts of their conversation as upper deck emptied, person by person, stop by stop. Their voices could be heard more distinctly now.

They were talking about some party that was going to take place right after A Levels were over. I heard Bianca say she'd been told of it, and couldn't wait to go. She hadn't told me of it. I knew she kept things from me. She had other friends, her real friends. But still, it felt like a betrayal. One thing. Just one, tiny thing she could have done for me after all I'd done for her... but, no. She had no feelings for others, no affinity. There was something clinically wrong with her. What a farce my friendship was. We weren't even on the same wavelength anymore, just white noise all over the place.

I got out a floppy, paperback copy of *Persuasion* I had taken from the library, and stared at the lines. I tried very hard to read, but it wasn't happening. I had no appetite to distress over Anne's problems; I had enough of my own. I stuffed it back in my bag and got out my sketchpad and a 2B pencil, flipped to an empty page, and began tracing the first image that popped to mind. A face. I was good with faces. Not his; some other person's I couldn't remember, quite then, where I'd seen. That small fact didn't hinder my memorisation of his features, however, and I swiftly got most of it done. I even added some colour.

The blathering behind me droned on, and I found myself adrift again. I looked at the window, gazing at the droplets of rain on the glass. Then I focused out onto the street passing by. This part of suburbia was so green and spacious, it could easily be mistaken for the country. There were small peaks within the fields, undulating towards the horizon, and with the large oaks and spruces dappled here and there, it easily resembled a pasture or even a valley. Sometimes it was worth sitting on upper deck; you could see beyond the fences and brick walls.

I found myself comparing England with my most recent holiday in Greece. We had gone some weeks after my father's funeral. My mother took us to her grandparents' particular birthplace, a corner of our Earth far different from the mainstream, touristy photos one sees of white-washed, box-shaped houses against a dazzling, blue sea. No. The area where my ancestors hailed from was more like this part of England. *Achilles' hometown* – Gran.

It was Thessaly where the ancient monoliths of Meteora gave way to the soft, green slopes, converging into a basin as far as the eye could see. Hillocks of tall, plush trees – sycamore and weeping willow – resting alongside river banks, whose torrents gurgled through the cluster of villages, where the buildings were of the same stone façades, keeping with the tradition. Our small family of uncles, aunts and cousins. The massive rectangular dinner table we all ate at – salad with feta cheese, a plate with a wedge of *Pastitsio*, watermelon, all savoured in our roughly-paved yard under the pergola of vine leaves, surrounded by basil plants, oregano bushes and olive groves. Those blazing, sanguine sunsets, washing into immaculate, pastel hues – violet, blue, pink. I could understand my mother's need to go. After all, she had grown up going there every year. She loved the place; it was her home too. I remember her face as we stepped off the aeroplane. With closed eyes, she smiled, blissfully, and breathed in deep. So did Vic and I. Greece has its own smell, I remembered thinking, as does England. And each is a welcoming sensation, honing all the memories connected to that redolence. Each a feeling of home.

His voice intermingled with my wandering mind, so much so, that I saw him being there too, watching the glorious sunset with me, weaving his fingers through mine. But as the realisation that it couldn't be so sunk in, I was gradually pulled back down to the here and now. The real.

I heard his voice talk to her in that soft timbre behind me, and I wanted to cry.

'It's at Robert Simmonds' house. Do you know him?' he asked her. I knew him. Well, *of* him. His half-sister and I were taking GCSE Biology and CDT together. Lara was her name, and she had Type-1 diabetes. It was so severe that our whole year was given a two-minute talk on what to do if she had a hypoglycaemic attack. That explained why she was allowed to suck lollies and crack open cola cans in the middle of a lesson. Her natural insulin wasn't working right.

'I know his sister. We're in the same form-room. She's already invited me,' said Bianca. I rolled my eyes.

'Well, Robert told me we could bring along a friend, you know, like a plus one, but since you're already invited, I thought maybe Eleanora could come since we both know her…'

My heart stopped. Bianca's must have done too.

'What do you say?' he said, but it was more a rhetorical question because he then said louder, 'Eleanora?' before Bianca could reply.

I put my sketchbook on my lap and turned slowly, wonderment written on my face, but not from this sudden proposal, but from him baffling me again with his kindness. They were three seats behind me, and I looked straight at him. He was eager to tell me the news. Then my eyes moved to Bianca, and I almost jumped in shock at that look of complete visceral antipathy. I looked straight back at James, knowing my reckoning with Bianca would come soon enough.

'What are you doing on the twenty-eighth of June?' he asked.

I knew exactly what I was doing on the twenty-eighth. 'Nothing,' I said and swallowed. 'Why?'

'Robert Simmonds is having a party.' He paused. It seemed he wanted to phrase his words properly. 'W-would you like to go?' he asked gingerly. There was a restraint, a tenseness, like he was asking me a very difficult question. In a way, he was; he was asking me out. That thought suddenly made me blush. I think my whole face went a perfect crimson. I looked down quickly, trying to hide behind my hair. I took in a breath and looked back at him. His cheeks had gone red too. Bianca was lava. Still waiting for my reply with an expectant smile, I cleared my throat.

'That sounds… great…'

Chapter Ten

Now

We glide in and out of stations. My heart hammering on my sternum, readying for anything instantaneous.

Where am I going?

How far?

What am I doing?

I shouldn't be following him; it's wrong, I know it's wrong. *But how will you know else?* I remind myself.

James has sat down at the first available seat, his long legs taking up most of the floor room in front of him. I got some funny stares from commuters as I stepped on board. I know I look a bit like an idiot, what with the scarf wrapped around my nose and mouth like a cowboy at a stickup, but there is no space in my mind to care about what other people are thinking of me. Just James – it is imperative my disguise keep him from even the smallest iota of suspicion as to who I am.

There are a few free seats to choose from, being nowhere near rush hour. I have found one next to a gentleman with an open newspaper, all that's missing is a bowler hat.

The train makes a judder, and I reflexively hold my bag so it won't fall. My wrist kills from the sudden movement, and I grind back the urge to cry out in pain.

Having passed King's Cross, Farringdon, Barbican, Moorgate and Liverpool Street, I see him make a move.

Sure enough, as the train draws close on upon Tower Hill Station, he gets up. I get up, as furtively as I can, watching as he descends.

It is no surprise to be plunged amongst throngs of tourists at Tower Hill, but the amount today is astounding. I weave in and out of the chaos, reaching a satisfactory distance from the blond head I am following. On his way out, up the escalator with brisk strides, I too, pick up speed; in tandem to the beat of his footsteps, barely registering the medieval landmark to my right.

James strides hurriedly into the Tower Gateway escalator and ascends. I am on it too, some seconds later. Dockland Light Railway? Where on earth are we going? I've never used this terminus before, and I'm not prepared for what I see: virtual emptiness. Apart from three, merrily-chatting station workers, there is hardly anyone else. I half expect tumbleweed to roll by.

With just one way to move; over a narrow path – a bridge – leading out onto the platform where a train is patiently parked to the left, doors open in wait, I hesitate. But I have to move – under the cover of a crowd, or not. When I followed him on Saturday, I was always at a safe distance, never in fear he'd recognise me, but now there is no choice; I have to get close. Even through wig, sunglasses and bronzer, he might recall something. My thin body, my painted hands, my minor intoed gait, the way I hunch slightly… any one of these things can give me away. James has already got on, and the announcement board is too far to read. What if the train is to leave now?

This thought jars me, and I make long strides straight for the bridge, showing to the partially-indifferent train workers my card, since there are no faregates.

I enter the train. I sense him look at me, turning like an iron rod being guided by a magnet. I smell the sweat on me; I am treading on very thin ice. I find a seat with my back to him, not wanting to accidentally meet his eye. Even through the light shade the sunglasses give, he might remember something. *The grey is distinct… he'll know, he'll know…* my hairs bristle.

I am holding my breath, waiting… waiting… Waiting to hear some sudden expostulation be thrown my way. But, no. Only the low murmur of people talking to one another. The disguise did it.

'It's just one stop. This train goes back and forth from Tower Gateway to Shadwell…' I hear a passenger fill in his friend. I thank him, inwardly, for filling me in too.

As preordained, everyone alights at Shadwell. Out goes James, and I, behind him. He stays put on the platform – we will still be in need of DLR.

Beckton 2 mins.

Lewisham 5 mins.

Where to?

He doesn't budge when a train comes. Not Beckton.

The next train looms. A slow, menacing sonance.

Once again, the doors slide open, and I sense him, more than see him, get on. I am one door down, inside now too. The doors shut, and all of a sudden, thoughts ransack my mind of this sheer stupity. My pulse-rate increases, hand in hand with the train's acceleration. What was I thinking?

Office buildings loom into view; London's skyscrapers stretching left and right, as the train dives under the soaring frame structure at Canary Wharf Rail Station. I gaze up at the imposing expanse for a moment, distracted. Out he jumps, and I almost miss him; only that hair caught my eye. Quickly, the doors are about to close, I dart out. Jesus, that was close!

He turns left, I turn left. He goes through revolving doors, I go through revolving doors. I wait for him to notice, any moment now, any moment… but nothing happens. By some wonder, he doesn't turn. By some wonder, he is unaware of me. I ponder this… it is like Saturday – he has something on his mind again, something more important than giving a crap to whoever is behind him. That is why he's in a rush. He has urgent business.

Stepping with haste, down the steps and descending onto the pavement. He walks purposefully, precisely, no pausing to deliberate. He knows exactly where he's going; he's done this before.

He bends into a quiet side street, stopping abruptly, and pulls out his phone. I immediately halt and backpedal quickly, put my back against the wall, leaning flat; out of his vision. My heart is thrashing; he very nearly caught eye of me.

A raindrop finds me on my forehead and I look up. Granite sky and there – I hear a distant thunderclap. What did Kate say about the weather forecast? I tut.

I have to look. I need a visual. Something. Make sure he is still there.

Extremely carefully, I walk to the wall's edge, body placed firmly to the brick, and prepare my phone. I manoeuvre it horizontally, letting just as far as the lens peek out from the edge of the wall, and tap. The fake shutter sound is heard, ever so faintly. A quick look to ascertain he's still standing there, and I see that he is. He's waiting.

My gut clutches. Now what? Keep taking photos until he starts moving? It is all I can do under the circumstances.

I take another five or six snaps, with about a ten-second interval between them, as I gradually become soaked with the falling rain. How much longer?

The engine is loud, louder than a regular car's. It startles me and I look, inherently, in the direction it is coming. It is getting closer – the great grille expanding as it approaches. Then it soars by me and turns into the street where James is. Malign with its windows tinted in a sinister, pristine black – the windscreen wipers pounding to and fro, to and fro. It parks right in front of James, blocking any view I have of him it is so large. The vehicle loiters for a bit. I see it is a Chevrolet Tahoe. I still have my phone in camera mode and, call it curiosity, or even a hankering to have a picture of it on my phone, but I take a snap. Then the car – if you can call it that – revs hard, shrieking as the tyre makes a wheel-spin on the wet tarmac, and is off.

James is nowhere to be seen.

Back Then

I wanted to run and hug him, thank him, kiss him…

The bus was nearing Mill Hill Broadway, and a herd of kids grouped towards the stairs. Trisha could be heard amongst them. Bianca too. I could just hear Bianca's thoughts on my reply to James's invite: *that bitch* and other such epithets in my honour. I knew I was going to hear it at some point.

After saying a flirtatious, 'Bye, Jamie. See you tomorrow,' she turned to me, feigning a voice in something akin to nice. 'See you tomorrow, El.' And slit her eyes in sharp acerbity before turning to descend. Yes, I was definitely going to hear it.

The bus stopped, the doors opened with a *pshh*, and made small swaying motions as each kid clumped out. Suddenly, I saw James get up from the corner of my eye, walk awkwardly down the narrow passage between the rows of seats, and make himself comfortable on the empty seat next to mine, which was a difficult feat because of his long legs. The doors closed and we were off again.

He sat there, and I could sense he was just staring at me. What was he thinking? What was he feeling? Whatever it was, I ought to thank him for putting Sarah in her place, and for the invite …and then explain the Bianca situation.

I was about to speak when, 'Why did you walk away?'

I blinked, startled with the faint hurt apparent in his tone, but his eyes were calm. Was that why he was pissed off earlier, because I'd walked away?

'I thought…' I stopped. What had I thought?

'Thought what?'

I looked out, ahead. I was tired. Tired of Bianca and the slipshod way she took advantage of me. How she could hijack my feelings. How I let her get to me. She didn't care about the affect it could have on others. I wanted it to stop. STOP.

'I don't know, James. I really don't know. I'm sorry,' I said, worn out.

He sat quietly for some moments, his eyes trying to interpret my expression. 'Don't apologise,' he said, finally. 'I'm just …tired. I haven't been sleeping well. It's a free world, Eleanora. You can walk away whenever you want.'

I stared at him with only one thought prevailing the rest: he hadn't wanted me to walk away. He had wanted me beside him.

'Same goes for you,' I said to him, raising a brow so he'd know I was talking about Bianca. He curled one side of his lips up. He got the message.

The bus made a stop, and I remembered I wanted to thank him. 'By the way, thank you for helping me out with Sarah…' I shrugged, embarrassed he would always have that sad image of me.

James blinked momentarily, like coming out of a trance, then, 'No problem.' His mind was on something else.

'What is it?' I asked.

'That,' he said, nodding to my lap. I had completely forgotten about the sketch. 'That's yesterday's bus driver, isn't it?'

I sat, gobsmacked. Now *that* was a good memory.

'Did you draw that from memory?' he asked, awed. I said nothing again. 'But that's a stupid question,' he continued. 'Of course you did. He wasn't up here modelling all this time, was he?'

I tried to guffaw at his wit, but it came out more like a, 'Hhuh.' I swallowed. I didn't like it when I had to tell, no, admit my secret. I didn't even make a big song and dance out of it to the closest people in my life. I sat biting my lip, debating whether I should tell him this… "gift" of mine. In the end, there was no need because he said, 'So, do you have an eidetic memory?' and my heart jolted. I whipped my head to him and stared right into his eyes. I couldn't believe what I'd just heard. Everyone called it a photographic memory, but that was more for numbers and words. They didn't know the real term for remembering images was "eidetic". James seemed to be more erudite than your average Joe.

I embedded that cerulean, the soft baby blue and the flecks of midday sky. The tiny amount of sandstone around his pupils, all soft, all coalescing to form that organ of the soul. *Yes, I have an eidetic memory,* I wanted to tell him… *I could draw your eye to the tenth of a millimetre in accuracy, and even after a year's time the outcome would be the same.*

I shook my head. Call it modesty, call it fear he think me weird; I didn't want to go into it. 'Nah,' I said offhand. 'I'm just a good drawer. No big deal…' And flipped shut my pad, closing, as it were, the subject. He knew I was hiding the truth, I could see it in the gleam of his eye. He said nothing. I guessed he respected my discomfiture on the matter.

'Thanks for inviting me to the party,' I said, quickly changing the subject.

'No problem. You deserve to go.'

I blinked, moved. 'I do?'

'Definitely. I mean, after all you did for What's-Her-Face,' he said. Was there light hostility there? 'And I'm guessing that wasn't the first time you've helped her.' I looked down at a loss at what to say with his correct assumption about Bianca and her scheming. My silence; an admittance he was right. I had no need to warn him of her, no need to explain; he was figuring things out by himself, bit by bit.

'It was the least she could have done, you know? Invite you. Jesus!' he said, ticked off. Yes. Yes, he got it.

'I suppose… I don't know. I don't really hang with that crowd so it doesn't really make a difference whether I go or not.' I said.

'That doesn't matter. It's a good opportunity to get out and have a nice time. That's how I see it. I don't know Robert that well, I've only been here two weeks remember, but I accepted his invitation straight away.'

'Hello?' I said dryly. '*You* are popular. *I* am not. Whether IRL or online, we are total, social opposites. May I remind you of Sarah's bottle-toss?'

'That's bullshit,' he said. 'I don't understand why you're unpopular, or you think you are. What happened? Because as far as I can tell, you're… you're not some *weirdo*…' He stopped. I saw he was trying to find the right words.

'Thank you for that but… it's not like that. You don't know what happens to me in my school. What they do to me. What they say. You only got the tip of the iceberg today.' I shook my head, biting back the tears.

'What do they do to you?' he asked, almost afraid to hear the answer. Disquietude filled the air. I looked outside the front window, not able to look him in the eye. The road roving, shifting. No. What was that we'd learnt in physics about displacement and motion? The road wasn't moving, *we* were. I saw a parallax.

'Eleanora?' James said, impatient, snapping me out of it. 'What do they do to you?'

I closed my eyes. How to explain? What to say? List every malicious taunt, every physical strike?

'Nothing…' I muttered.

'Not nothing!' he cried. 'Tell me!' He sounded truly concerned, distressed even. I turned to him in disbelief, reading his eyes. They were sincere. Then I shrugged and looked out the window again, feeling the tears build once more.

'Eleanora…' He whispered so gently.

'Anything…' I said finally, giving in to his soft whisper tipping me over the edge. 'They do anything they can find t-to reduce me as a human being. My body. My face. My hair. I am ridiculed. I try to fight back but i-it's not really fair when you're ganged up on. Five against one? No chance…'

Silence. Just the whir of the bus.

I wiped a tear off my cheek.

'The bullies find me an easy target. I suppose I am… and I suppose that's why everyone else avoids me.' I took in a breath and said it. 'I'm a loser. It's as simple as that.'

I looked up at him. He shook his head slowly. 'They have to stop. This has to stop. Eleanora, you have to try… Don't let them carry on. Take matters into your own hands.'

I shook my head violently. 'I'm not like you. I could never… What you did earlier outside Milden, how you handled their taunts… I don't have that. I don't have your courage.'

He stared at me wildly, and then said quietly, yet acridly. 'Do you think that's courage? That's not courage. That's just …resilience.'

I blinked. 'What do you mean?'

'I mean I don't have courage. I've simply learnt not to let mediocrity get to me. When you've lived with someone like my father, you tend to find other things rather less significant in comparison,' he exclaimed, with a strange intensity I'd never seen on anyone before. I couldn't move. What was he telling me? What was his father doing to make other situations less significant? James saw the agitation on my face and hastily reassured me. 'He's a good man, don't get me wrong. He's just who he is, and I…' He paused. I gazed at him, waited for his words.

'What I'm saying is, it's good to measure what's important and what' not. Don't let stupid things get to you. Know what's worth your time, worth your pain, worth your joy. Learn to be resilient… like me. Then slowly, they'll stop.'

His reasoning resonated into the abyss of my soul. Never had a human being touched me so compassionately than the way he did that day. Even if I didn't believe what he said would happen, the ardour, the integrity in which he believed in *me* was enough to give me hope, some foothold through this drudgery called school life.

'I don't think they're bullying you because you're an easy target,' he said decisively, after some thought.

'No?'

'No.'

'Why then?'

He smiled evasively. 'I'll tell you some other time. Right now, I've got to get off. This is my stop.'

Had we arrived so soon? Where had time gone? He reached out for the STOP button and the faint *ding* was heard.

'Well, don't keep me in the dark for long. If I know the problem, then I can fix it. Right?' I said, as he prepared to descend. He slung his rucksack over his shoulder and sighed.

'You can't fix it … and it isn't a problem.'

Chapter Eleven

Now

I blink in disbelief, staring at empty space.

The cold rain splashes my face, as I pull down the stupid scarf from my mouth and whip off the annoying sunglasses, sharp pain in my wrist, bewildered and peeved at losing him. After all I went through. 'Oh, no!' I cry. 'No!'

Who are these people with their bloody tank for an SUV? I can't explain what I just saw. It was surreal; like something out of a cheap film. An SUV from nowhere, picking him up. What is on earth is going on?

The rain is unrelenting, and I run to find shelter; think on what to do. I see people disappear through a glass door and follow. An underground shopping centre. Off to the ladies, I relieve my bladder and take off my wig at the mirrors, my hair matted with damp. A girl dabbing on lipstick, pauses for a second, giving me a side look through the mirror. I want to say something as an excuse just to see her reaction, like, I'm following my boyfriend to catch him cheating and I'm in disguise, but leave it – let her think what she wants. I give her conspiratorial smirk. She raises her brows and smirks back. Then she adjusts her sleek, spiralling locks and leaves.

I feel the heat evaporate from my scalp, the encumbrance lifting, and I splash some water on my face, cooling but not calming; I seem to be trembling all over. I draw in a big breath and let it out too quickly making myself cough. I cram wig, woolly and scarf in my satchel, and go grab a coffee. I haven't eaten since breakfast, and I can't wait to put the rim of the cup to my lips, smell the aroma and taste the warm bitter sweetness.

I sit at a window in the café, lift my cup and gulp with vigour, like a half-starved babe who is just given its bottle and voraciously sucks. I look out at the shoppers passing by my window and rack my brain. What shall I do? Wait? Leave? What if he gets on the underground and not DLR? Everything is a possibility – he could leave by car, by bus. In fact, who was to say he would leave at all? He could be staying… all night. Did he live here? God! *No, no, calm down, El.* I have a feeling the Tahoe wasn't a chauffeur taking him to his mansion. Whoever picked James up, will probably drop him off again.

I walk hurriedly towards the entrance to DLR, scanning stealthily for the beanie, for the hair… anything. Nothing.

Under a bridge, back up the steps and through the glass doors, safely out of the rain, I wait for him. I stand there like some stationery, head-rotating statue, all the while checking outside and inside, back and forth, back and forth, back and forth. Every resonant engine. Every footstep.

The sun has reached its zenith and is now on a descent, changing the clouds into a bleak hue in the east. I grow weary and slink down in a corner. Even the rain has had enough and dissipates. I wait… I wait… Looking at my watch – 6:16 – I decide to leave. I've been there for approximately four hours.

He isn't coming.

Gathering my bag and slinging it over my shoulder in resolute, sombre defeat, I haggardly tread out into the cold, crisp evening air, the residue of ozone hitting my nostrils. Off to the Tube station which will get me home faster.

Jubilee Line, crossing at London Bridge for Northern Line and up, up, home. Home to cry...

It is as I'm regarding the fine, steel structure at Canary Wharf Tube Station, descending the escalator, when it happens. It is quick and I almost don't register it, I am so immersed. Resigned I've lost him, it takes my brain a moment to realise *he* has brushed by me, fast, on my left. I look down, responding to the touch and that flash of blond, and freeze. Then my heart pounds with adrenaline, suddenly pulled back to life, as I watch him land on the polished slabs of concrete and continue walking briskly to the long row of faregates.

Jesus Christ! My senses ignite and I clamour down the rest of the escalator, not letting my eyes off him, as I hear a train come dimly through the platform's glass-screened doors. I need to get closer to him. The need to hold him; never let go. Never lose him again. Joy this day isn't over is so overwhelming; a tear trickles down my cheek.

I beep through the faregate and hurriedly walk further towards him – head down, but I have no scarf, no wig. I pull scarf out of my satchel and wind it round my neck, over my nose, legs not losing momentum. There is no time to put on the wig. *Your eyes...* I tug out the sunglasses, almost snapping them, and they are on my face before I reach his vicinity.

The train comes calmly yet swiftly, aligns its doors with the platform doors, and both open in sync. He gets closer, waiting his turn to board. The mass rolls out, leaving the carriage relatively empty. This is short lived, as it seems half of London's populous starts packing itself on board. I am rendered to a corner and can barely see where he is standing.

The doors hiss shut and the burdened train moves slowly, gradually gathering some speed, as it rocks us onto its next stop.

Where is he? Where?

There!

James has been squashed in a corner close to the door, wedged slightly to the side so as not to bump his head.

I am screened by a plethora of bodies so I can't be seen directly, but I can see his face through a gap created by a shoulder and head. I have the comfort to study him for the while it takes to get to the next stop. He still wears that meditative look. Not once does he look up and casually check his surroundings, as one usually does when entering the train. Nothing. A contemplative, sedate stillness. Eyes riveted down; brows heavy with concentration. He didn't have that look earlier. OK, sure, he looked like he had something on his mind, but now, it looks more serious. What has intervened?

First stop: Canada Water. He doesn't move. Second stop: Bermondsey. Nothing. As we approach London Bridge, he looks up. I prepare.

Sure enough, he murmurs an, 'Excuse me' to someone so as to pass and egress.

Within seconds, we enter the blue and grey cylindrical station, as the train decelerates.

The doors open and, since I am closest to the door, I am the first one out. That means he won't be in front of me and I'll have to stall to see where he goes. And that means, I'll need to devise a quick plan not to look obvious. The only thing I can come up with, at such short notice, is to simply pretend to have a problem with my boot, and I walk to a bench where I act like I'm tying the laces up. The one thing I love about Londoners is how they mind their own business, not giving a second's notice to what someone does. They all shuffle by me, concerned to get to their destinations. As does James. And I am right behind him.

There are two choices: either he is to take the Northern Line or none. I don't know if he's going home or if he's simply making another stop before going home. He could be having another rendezvous with another Tahoe, for all I know. For some reason, I don't think he lives in the London Bridge area, unless it is actually under the bridge... in a box. I wince at the thought.

We are on the move. He turns – Northern Line. It is getting difficult to follow him this time, as rush hour is upon us, people in a hurry, barging in front of me, reducing my field of vision. A busker can be heard strumming his guitar, infiltrating the underground's monotonous hubbub with a joyful tune, the propagation of sound refracting as I walk by, drowning out the melody.

I panic as, at that moment, I lose sight of him. My heart beats fast, pounding all the way to my throat. I rush in front of others, afraid I'll lose him altogether, finding his beanie.

We come out onto the northbound platform. I smile to myself. *Bet he's going home.* He turns to walk down a little further to the left, I turned to the right. I am in the thick of a crowd.

High Barnet 2 mins.

Edgware 4 mins. Edgware. I haven't been home in ages. After Victoria and I had moved out, Gran and Granddad moved in with Mum. It's economical that way. They can't maintain two houses on two measly pensions and a widow's pension.

I need to see them. Victoria goes every Sunday without fail. I have become a bit more of the prodigal daughter. Easter Sunday – that's when.

The High Barnet train's screech reverberates through the tunnel as it comes clattering through. I hurriedly look up. Where is he? I can't see him now, as everyone is a great horde of limbs, heads and torsos all huddling one step before the gap. Where is he? No beanie! No hair! Gone! I only looked away for a second! One accursed second!

I feel the stomach-wrenching, pain of panic hit me. My eyes moisten. It is too much!

The train stops and doors open. People get off then others start to get on. The last beeps signal the doors are closing and just then, I spot the ends of his hair, inside.

I dive in at the very last second, inches away from getting caught between the two sliding doors shutting.

Off we go.

Chapter Twelve

Back Then

My phone buzzed. I was glad for the interruption. Bloody maths. I had been quizzing over an equation for too long and was in need of a break.

Bianca. Come to think of it, I wasn't *that* glad for the interruption. Shit. Here goes…

'Hi, Bianca,' I said, as nice as I could. My sister walked by my door just then, and mimed the image of a hanged man, tongue hanging out. Her opinion of Bianca. I was too tense to smile back.

'El? Listen.' Bianca's voice was curt; the orgulous inflection she used when pissed off.

'W-what's up?' I braced.

'I've got a bone to pick with you,' she snapped. My heart pounded.

'What is it?' I swallowed. Nothing but dryness.

'I'll get to that later. First, I want to know what you and James said on the bus when I got off.'

No! That was my business, not hers.

'Nothing,' I answered.

'Are you telling me you didn't say one word to him?'

'Umm… well, I thanked him for inviting me to the party…'

'And that's the other thing!' she said, not hiding her rage. 'Why did you say yes, you little bitch?'

'What do –'

'Do you understand you're not helping me?' She cried. 'I saw him first, El! It's not nice, you butting in. Friends don't do that. So just stay, the fug, away.'

What was she saying? Like I'd have any chance! Besides: 'I thought you wanted to play him,' I reminded her.

'Yeah, me, not you! What I do with him is none of your business,' she bit. I couldn't put thoughts together right then and merely said mechanically, 'Oh…'

'Butt out!' she yelled, and shut the phone in my face. I stared at it, befuddled. My mind felt like it was whisking in a blender. What on earth was I to do? I wiped a tear. Not from Bianca's request as such, but from what it meant. It meant I wasn't to speak to him again. Not to have any contact. *Deprive me of air, while you're at it.* No. No, she couldn't do that. It was James's choice too…

Too distracted to continue with the equation, I tapped the browser on my phone. I typed *Milden Public London,* and the website loaded little by little. Hilsmond published student achievements – even exam results – and I wanted to see if Milden did it too. If they did, there might be a chance James was on there. I could know, at least, how he was doing on a scholarly level. I was in luck: there was a box with *Our Students* written on it. I tapped it and it took me to the achievement page. I skimmed through. There was nothing on James. *It is early days yet,* I reminded myself. *He's only been there two weeks…*

'What's crawled up Bianca's fundament *this* time?' Victoria's head peeped through my bedroom door. I stared at her. I didn't know what she saw in my eyes, but she sighed, 'I seriously don't understand why you put up with that two-faced user.'

I shrugged. 'I don't know why either…'

Victoria tutted, aggravated. 'Jesus. What's the matter?'

'Nothing. It's OK.'

Victoria wasn't buying it. She folded her arms and waited.

'She likes this guy,' I said quietly. 'And she got me to take a message to him –'

'You're always doing her dirty work.'

'Yeah, well… We… the guy, James, and I have kind of become friends and –'

'What?!' Victoria cried, pleased but incredulous. 'Oh, my God. Finally! I'm so happy for you. Is he hot?'

'Vic…'

'What? I just want to ascertain if it's worth your time to worry over.'

'So, if he's ugly, I shouldn't care? What if he has a nice character?'

'Nice character is good, but excuse me if I'm totally superficial and want pure sexiness for my sister as well. Besides, we've been over what kind of characters boys have.'

I rolled my eyes.

'So, is he?'

'What?'

'Hot?'

I paused. 'Very.' I bit my lip, suppressing a smile.

'Knew it!' She grinned. 'Describe him to me. Better still, sketch him.' She got up and found my sketchpad and a pencil and shoved them into my hands, and sweetly demanded, 'Draw!'

'I've –'

'Do it! I want to see what he looks like. Indulge me, sis.'

I flipped the pages in my block and stopped at a specific page.

'That's him.' I said to Vic, holding out a detailed portrayal of James's head I had done the night before.

Vic's mouth went slack.

'Wow!' she mouthed, eyes popping out. 'I can see what all the fuss is about. Actually, what is all the fuss about? No, no. Let me guess. She doesn't want you anywhere near him, right?'

I nodded. 'She asked me to not talk to him anymore. More like demanded…'

'You're competition,' she stated. 'She feels threatened by you.'

'Me?' I burst. 'Me a threat? Don't make me laugh. James wouldn't look twice at a girl like me.'

'Bull. Shit!' she cried. 'And what is wrong with you, might I ask? Look at that face,' she said, turning my head to my dressing-table mirror. 'Excuse me, but *you* are gorgeous. The hair, the eyes, the skin. Who's got skin like yours, tell me? You've got juicier lips than me, and your nose is nice and straight. Not like mine – all thin with a knob on it. No. Sorry. Bianca is jealous!'

'My body, Vic. My legs… they're awful!'

'Some boys like the Twiggy look, you never know…' Poor Vic; ever the encourager of oneself.

'Listen, don't worry about Bianca and her squad. It's a classic case of the green-eyed monster if you ask me,' Victoria said decisively. 'I say continue the way you were with him. Don't become something you're not, just because someone tells you to act a certain way. Bianca is a selfish cow, and quite frankly, she doesn't deserve him… or you.'

Then Vic came close. 'And if a boy really likes a girl and wants to be with her, nothing, and I mean *nothing*, will get in his way. If this James honestly likes you and wants to be with you, then she, or anyone else, shouldn't be a problem.'

'But what if she starts to get really bitchy and does something? You know how devious she gets.'

Victoria looked deeply in my eyes, her navy-blue irises reflecting my depressed face.

'Listen to me,' she said firmly. 'Stop being afraid of her. What's the worst she can do, blow her top off? Hide your stuff? Let her! But I want you to learn to be above that, do you know what I mean? Like, no matter what she does, it won't affect you. You will always have shitty circumstances in your life, Ellie. What are you going to do, just run away? Live in the shadows?' I shook my head. 'Learn to distinguish between what you want and what other people want from you, so long as it's for you own good. Surpass anything that will bring you down. And above all, learn to walk away from all the bull-shitters with you head held high.'

I looked at her as a tear dropped. It is what James had meant. Then she added with a wry smile, 'And if you ever need me to impersonate you over the phone and tell her to get lost for you, then I will.'

She wiped the tear from my face and left the room.

Now

It takes me several seconds to calm my shaking body, drawing in deep breaths. *Calm! Calm!*

Did I make a show? Did he notice my gaffe? Did he see me, see who it is? I keep my face down and away – motionless. Please, no, I think… pray. I am perspiring all over. Everyone is taking up the air. I hold on tightly to a bar as the train clatters and clangs on – rightfully being dubbed the loudest Tube line of all. I need to sit; too exhausted to stand. *My kingdom for a seat.* The train slows, and I check to see if he moves. Nothing.

At Bank, the other half of London gets on, forcing me to be shoved rigid against the side of the door. I can only see his arm and part of his torso now – that thick, black jacket.

Passing Moorgate onto Old Street, James stays put. The train gives a sudden jerk and he makes a quick movement with his hand, like saving something from dropping out from under his jacket. He looks up to see if anyone has noticed, and I spasmodically twist my head the opposite direction so he doesn't catch my eye. He's hiding something. Something worth being extremely cautious about. Has that got something to do with him being so tense?

Angel, King's Cross, Euston… no movement. I start to wonder what he could possibly have hidden under that jacket. What mustn't we see?

Just as the train is in its last yards to Camden Town's platform, he turns. I can see his chest expand, like he's taking a long breath. A sigh.

He alights and I also, one step behind, one door down. He doesn't make for Edgware branch (I was wrong), he strides towards the exit. Up the escalator, the gusts of wind blustering around us, the turbulence so fierce, my face is hit by the force, coat flying up at the corners. I look in front of me and see James's hair become a whirling, golden abundance.

Out to the right, onto the main street, and down the road where all the uniquely decorated shops are, we pace. Through the thoroughfare, through stalls and street-artists. We pass that shop where Vic and I had gone once to buy a leather jacket. She was going through a heavy metal phase, and

Camden was the place! A sales guy had tried to convince us that the jacket was a perfect fit, when in reality it was made for a heavyweight champion. 'This would be too big for both Eubank senior and junior put together!' Vic had retorted, flapping the too-long sleeves in the process. The guy had a lot to learn. I had reached that level of lie at the N&L – I could sell hot red, five-inch, satin pumps to a nun. In the end, Vic had found the biker jacket of her dreams in the goth shop next door. I grin to myself upon looking at the eerie façade now; the recollection of the salesgirl who had thought I was a goth-in-the-making, and the look of horror when I had told her my features were natural. To this day I wonder whether that were a compliment or not. 'She was right jealous of you!' Vic had declared as soon as we stepped out and onto the street. 'She probably has to cake on a ton of Titanium-white foundation and go through ten bottles of blue-black hair dye to get to the way she looks…'

The streets are pitch black with a blurry moon hidden behind the clouds, and unbelievably freezing, like shards of ice prickling my skin. I pull my hood up and do my scarf up tighter.

I softly jog forward, careful not to tread heavily on the pavement. I can't afford to make noise – he'll look back. He moves in and out of street lamps, his breath a white wisp of air.

A yawn escapes me. I'm half-dead. How much longer? Are we to walk the streets of London all night?

He turns a corner, beyond the Lock. I get to it and peek around first. He's still walking quickly down the side street, hands in pockets, then he turns another corner, passed a park, and I quietly stride, my heartbeat accompanying his steps. Another peek; still en route to wherever he is going. I am around that corner too. He isn't there any longer, but I don't panic because I can still hear the rhythm of his soft-soled footsteps and the faint susurrus of his jacket and overalls – that's how silent our surroundings are; just the low, monotonous hum of far-off traffic. I walk quietly, ears ready to snag any new auditory emission. His pace gets dimmer until I can hear it no more.

A faint jingling of what sounds like keys is heard. My eyes automatically look in the direction. The sound seems to be coming from behind a brick wall perpendicular to the street I am in, giving the appearance of reaching a dead-end. Too tall for me to see what is behind, and too long for me to see where it begins and ends from where I am standing, I wait in the hushed night.

Then, an ear-splitting screech of grating metal scraping on metal rips the air, scaring the wits out of me, and I jump. There is a pause, then the cacophony is heard again – an unoiled, metallic scratch – *SLAM!*

Silence.

The only sound, my heart thrashing.

In the abeyance of silence, I linger. I stay rooted to the ground, staring at the brick wall and the cars parked alongside it, breathing heavily. Silence loiters with me in the dark, eerie street. From what I can tell, he has entered somewhere using keys. Is he home?

I tread, one foot after the other, ever so cautiously, towards the brick wall readying for anything unforeseen. A blasting toot from a passing car startles me, and I turn instantly in the direction. I notice a road at a tangent to the right of the wall. There is an opening between the row of terraced houses. A narrow path which gives access to the street, and to whatever is behind the wall. A streetlamp is too far off to help with its light. Perhaps it's for the best; remain undercover.

I reach the wall and turn to my right, making my way to the edge. I put my back to the brick and, very circumspect, turn my head into an alley.

All is still.

My eyes have got used to the dark, having dilated to big, black pools, and I make out a couple of rubbish bins up against the wall, some litter scattered here and there, partially soaking in puddles. Opposite, three heavy, corrugated-iron garage doors stare back at me. They are built in, on what looks like, the back of a big, one-storey building.

A rustle of leaves stirred by the wind, stirs me too. I take a step and turn fully into the alley, careful I stay a shadow in the dark.

Suddenly, a dim light emanates through a small, murky window in between two of the garage doors, and I instantly crouch. I blink, mouth agape. Is he in there? From what I can see, there is some makeshift curtain draped over most of the window, leaving a small wedge on the bottom right corner uncovered.

I tread fast to the side where the garages are, a mere five, six strides, and plaster my back against the wall, drawing in deep breaths. Jesus, what am I doing? Anyone looking out into the street would be able to detect the condensation in the air from my exhalations, even through my scarf.

I see the iron doors are thick and rusty. They are propped on rails and slide open and shut. That explains the clanging. Two of the garage doors are padlocked; one isn't. That one is next to the small window. There is no doubt about it in my mind, he is in there.

I side-step quietly, until I reach the window, heart continuing to pound like a fist striking on my chest. I am hot despite the chill. This is it – if I get caught, not only could I be charged with trespassing or snooping, but he'll resent me for the rest of his life.

I can't look through the window; it's too much of a risk. What if he is to look out the moment I put my eyes to it?

Phone.

Totally illegal, I know, but I have to do it. I have to know, come hell or high water, whether James Laidlaw is living in insalubrious circumstances. There must be undeniable, conclusive fact. I never thought I'd become a bloody peeping tom… *You're not a voyeur, here to see him naked or anything*, I rationalise, hence giving myself permission. I prepare mobile to camera mode, making sure the automatic flash is off and all sounds mute, and crouch under the window. With trembling hand, I lift it so as the lens comes level to the window, calculating where the gap in the curtain is. And tap. I take a look; see if anything is caught.

There, in front of my eyes, is a not so blurry, slightly lop-sided, shot of the place. Yes. It may not be great but objects are distinguishable. James can be seen sitting with his back to me at a desk with a light shining on front of him. A laptop. He isn't in blue overalls anymore. He is wearing a white, long-sleeved vest, hair down and spread on his incredibly muscled shoulders; undulations of said muscle rippling under the vest. *My God, he is toned!* The back of the chair hides everything else from his shoulder blades and down.

I risk it and take more pictures, each time checking the images are OK. I'll take a better look at them as soon as I get home.

I don't know how long I am out there for, but I start to shiver, my body temperature dropping caused from immobility and lack of food. Time to go home; I have found out where he lives and… *how* he lives. The first step in my own private investigation is accomplished. I feel awful I was right. His sunken circumstances sets off bitter self-loathing within me. What cruel misfortune befell him, turning his life upside down?

As I move away from the window, I hear the high pitch of a phone ring through the flimsy glass.

'Hello?' comes his muffled voice. There's a pause.

'Who is this?' he says loudly, angrily. There's another pause.

'Hello? Are you there? Hello?' he demands. There is anger.

Silence.

'Shit!' he hiss-shouts. 'Dammit!'

Someone with a wrong number and has hung up on him? Personally, I wouldn't have become so upset about it, unless they were pestering me. Perhaps that is what is going on here?

Still crouching, I walk quietly along the side of the garage wall, and as soon as I hit the end, make a dash for the wall, round it, and break into a sprint, up the narrow street.

I run back to the station. Reaching it, I swerve in, swipe my card and hasten down the escalators.

I have to know; my next step. I have to look into why he is living in a garage, suddenly full of agonizing curiosity.

Perhaps Kate's friend can help?

Chapter Thirteen

Back Then

Tactics needed to avoid contact with James:

Number one: Get on an earlier bus so he won't see me. (Plausible).

Number two: Get on the bus late after school. Again, so he won't see me. (Plausible).

Number three: Disguise myself. (Stupid).

Number four: Discourage him. How? Behave like a bitch to him. (Couldn't do that).

Number five: Get Mum to drive me to and from school. (Difficult).

Number six: Talk to Bianca. Get her advice. After all, she's the one who wants this. (Yes).

Number seven: If he approaches, tell him you have a contagious disease. (Won't fall for it).

Number eight…

Number eight…

I had no other ideas.

Being the exploitable, sad idiot that I was, I couldn't put in motion my sister's advice, nor James's for that matter, and just go about my day pretending Bianca didn't exist. No. I still didn't have the balls. I was still too much of a pussy.

I'll start with getting on an earlier bus, I pondered. *And why is female genitalia considered weak, and male genitalia considered strong?* My thoughts wondered. I shook my head. I couldn't think of the political correctness of derogatory terms right now; I had more pressing issues. I'd have to have a talk with Her Highness at school. See if I could suggest an amendment to last night's decree, and modify that ban on James. Then there was the weekend ahead of us. I'd let her mull it over and hopefully, come Monday, she'd be more rational. *Fat chance,* my intuition harrumphed sardonically. Who was I kidding? I needed to get a life. I needed to free myself from Bianca's yoke. No – I needed to free myself from my incapability to be brave.

Be careful in what decisions you make. You may think they only affect you, but they don't. They affect everyone around you – Gran.

'What's going on, sweetie-pie? Why so early?' asked Mum's croaky morning-voice. I must have woken her up.

'Nothing, Mum. I just want to get to school early…'

I waited for her "why" but nothing came. *Ask me, Mum! Ask me! Don't give up so easily on me! Prod me like you used to! Give a shit!*

I opened the front door, one of those old Tudor-styled ones, made of solid oak with the same galvanised bolts and latch from when the house was first built, and reluctantly left those warm confines once more.

The fog was even thicker at this time of the morning, enfolding me in an eerie, vapoured silence. The towering Ash whose bare, scraggly branches awoke as a chill breeze whispered its way through them, then leaving a bitter, icy kiss on my face. The shrill chatter from a magpie suddenly broke the silence, leaving me with a chill up my spine.

I made my way to my stop. The bus came almost immediately. Ten seconds' delay and I'd've missed it. I climbed in eagerly, grateful to be out of the stinging, wintry chill.

Upon sitting, I thought how he wouldn't see me today and probably wonder why. Then I thought, *no he won't. Get real, Eleanora.*

I got to school just as it was opening for the day. Some students were already there, waiting outside for the teacher in charge to come with his or her keys and open the place. Now the main entrance was unlocked and doors wide open to gobble us in.

The day advanced steadily and, at first break, off I went to find Bianca. I had twenty minutes. I took an apple and ate as I searched the school grounds.

I sought for her in all her usual haunts. The toilets; the locker rooms; the back of the gym; a corner in the library she hid in. She wasn't anywhere to be found. I proceeded to her form room to see if she had come in today. A couple of girls told me she had. Did they know where she was? No, was their answer.

I was about to leave the form room when one of the girls, Lucy, came up to me at the door and said, 'She told us not to tell you she's hiding from you, but I don't give a shit what she wants, the pretentious cow.'

I felt the usual disappointment of having fallen for it again. I had been used and now she had no use for me and was avoiding me.

'She didn't tell us where she was going but she walked in the direction of the main building. I hope that helps. Probably with Trisha's lot.'

'Thanks, Lucy…' I said gratefully.

'Tell her to kiss my arse, would you?'

'Yeah…' I harrumphed.

I knew where she was.

I entered the old, Edwardian building and went up the squeaky, wooden stairs, passing the huge, polished plaques with all the names of each and every girl that had attended the school, gilded on them. Glorious. Whenever I passed those foreboding plaques, I always wondered if even the unworthy girls deserved to be on that list. The idle, unapplied ones, like me.

I turned on the landing, through the double doors of old wood with distorted glass rectangles, and found the classroom I was looking for. The door was ajar, and in one corner, there stood Bianca, her back to me, surrounded by Trisha's cronies; a squad I did not want to mess with. There was Henrietta; always quoting Martin Luther King, and how everyone on earth is equal. She had the pleasure of punching me in the stomach because, as she'd said, she'd "felt like it". Obviously, she'd skipped the part where it said Martin Luther's methods were nonviolent. I remembered the pain seething through me like a hot iron skewing my guts, as I had doubled over, clutching my belly, unable to breathe. My abdomen tightened reflexively whenever I saw her.

And there was Sarah; with a face like she had constant constipation and limbs like she pumped iron. She had pulled my hair once. Yanked it so hard, it sent me sprawling to the ground. To this day, I have no idea why. I guessed it made her feel more confident when she put me down. Then I remembered James; what he told her the day before, and bit my lip… *If you don't shut your trap…* I stifled a giggle.

With only a few minutes left till bell, I stepped in, heart pounding.

'Oi, B. Your stinky, little biotch,' said Sarah to Bianca, motioning in my direction. I met Sarah's eye, and she flinched unperceptively, and something shifted in that heartbeat. Something small but full of potential I had never felt before. Guts?

Bianca turned and tutted disdainfully, shaking her head like I'd been a bad girl. That look of repulsion. Switch turned to "bitchy mode".

She strode towards me, 'How dare you come here?' she hissed, and pushed me back, out of the class, 'Bugger off!' and slammed the door in my face.

Laughter from inside was heard, and there were a couple of titters from others who had witnessed the scene from the corridor. I wiped off a renegade tear, disgusted with myself for showing weakness.

Fine. See if I do what you say, I thought. If James wants to talk to me, I'll let him.

Chapter Fourteen

Now

I enter an empty flat. Kate is nowhere, but I know, straight away, where she is: over at Stuart's. I don't think 24 hours pass in a new relationship, before she's in bed with whomever.

And as if I've called her spirit, I instantly receive a text from her.

Tomorrow. 10. Oxford Circus. Wedding shopping.

I forgot. She said she was arranging a shopping spree for the wedding with the girls.
I text back,

Need help with hitting someone over the head.

On it, she replies, *Tell u details mañana.*

I fire up my PC, and while waiting for the programs to fill the screen, I get undressed. Exhaustion tugs, and my eyes water, needing rest. My body depletes as all the tension in my muscles kink. It feels like I've swum the whole of the Thames estuary.
I bring my laptop to my bed, yawning, eyes now drooping, but I keep at it – any information as to help.
I double click on the first picture. It is my blurry face, distorted to fisheye extent. I hate selfies; they never turn out the way you want. I click on to get to the picture of the Tahoe, and find it. It was taken to the side so the back licence plate is slanted, but it's not difficult to make out the letters with the help of the zoom. A *G, S* and a *Y.* It is a personalised plate. My eyes rove over the rest of the car, in case I've missed anything. I spot a sticker and zoom in a little more. Some kind of obscure design I can't make out.
I peruse the rest of the pictures, taking my time.
Click.
His back still to me, slightly curved in that writing position, at his PC. I look at the surroundings carefully, now I have time on my hands – little as that is, as I'm half-asleep. It is difficult to make out the rest of his place as the top left corner of the picture is a blur of curtain. I can discern a brick wall with some posters and notes stuck to it, and something that looks like the side of a bed. Yes; it is a mattress.
Click.
Click.
The next two pictures aren't much different. I took as many angles of the place as I could, twisting my hand this way and that. Things do look rather frugal.
Click.
Now I see a different angle, and inspect. The bed comes into better view. It is one of those fold-out beds with, what looks like, a good mattress. He must have swapped the thin, uncomfortable one for a proper one. There's an open book to the side of the desk, and his head is tilted like he's reading it while still having his hands on the keyboard. There's no way I can make out what book it is though, only that it's thick; text book like, or an encyclopedia.

Click.

The same scene, roughly.

Click.

Now he's stretching his arms, placing his hands behind his head. I take long seconds to admire his upper body. No, I study it. Long, hard limbs, yet a tenderness like a force lying in wait.

Click.

Now he's up. I see from his chest, down to his knees at a three-quarter turn, walking left. My left. The picture's a little bit blurry, as he is captured on the move, but I am still able to make out how low his black trousers are hanging. Looking carefully, I realise they are tracksuit bottoms and they are either undone or very loose. So loose, I can see that deep indentation of his love handle, guiding my eyes down... Omg! My body pulsates instantaneously, the throbbing reaching down between my legs.

'Fwah,' I whisper, then shake my head. 'You *are* a bloody peeping tom, El...'

My eyes rest on red writing on the side of the tracksuit. It reminds me of something – a familiar brand of clothing? I look at it harder. Then I recognise it. It's the same logo as was on his beanie. Initials. An *M*, a *C*, an *A* and a *T*, all capitalised except for the C.

Click.

The next picture is my blurry face again. I have come to the beginning of the photos; no more left of James.

I pull up the browser, swearing at my internet connection through a yawn, then as soon as it is up, I type the initials, printed on his beanie and track suit, in the search engine. *Enter.* I nibble my nail.

McAT. Nothing I can see relevant comes up. I click "images" and scroll. And there I see the same red logo a little further down. I click on the image and then click on the *Visit Site* box. McAdam's Training is the result. Aha! So, he *does* work out. I sift through the website. McAdam's is situated on the first floor of a brick-walled warehouse somewhere off Angel Station in Islington, specialising in boxing. Boxing? Something shoots to memory, the illustration of it projecting before my eyes. James in a boxer's stance. Where did I see that? Of course – at the party.

I lie, mulling over my infraction of the law by taking these photographs. An encroachment of James's privacy that I have grossly invaded; stripped him of that liberty and moral right as a human being. I did something illegal back then too. Is it good to fight fire with fire? Does the cause always justify the means?

Yes, I think. *Yes! For his good, for his welfare, anything is justified.*

Back Then

There they were; the pack of them. They were encircling him like a wake of vultures. *Nip, nip, nip.* Trisha, Bianca and a couple of other girls known for their "reputation". Not Sarah; she'd been ousted after James had shown his dislike for her.

I had reached the bus stop a little late, as I couldn't find my Art portfolio where I had left it. *Someone* had placed it on one of the shelves in the adjoining room in the Art building. Bianca. She was starting to show her fangs, one named Devious and the other, Spiteful, and this trickery told me she wanted me to miss the bus, for obvious reasons. I supposed I had to be grateful she hadn't tossed my folio over someone's garden fence.

Luckily, I could run. Being one of the fastest in my year, I wasted no time and ran all the way up the hill, reducing speed upon seeing kids still there, thank goodness. I stopped walking altogether, when I made out who they were.

They weren't giving him any room to breathe, inundated with the sudden spotlight. Since he was tall and towered over them, I could see his face clearly. He had a smile, but it was an uncomfortable one. He seemed bewildered at all this sudden attention, but he played it cool, as was his disposition.

Nick made an appearance, coming up to his friend's side, lightening the atmosphere with his wit. James seemed more at ease now.

Bianca saw me. And my folio. I looked away, calmly enough, although I was quavering uncontrollably. I'd had enough of her… Blow after blow after humiliating blow. I hadn't recognised it then, but in hindsight, that must have been the day the pound of flesh had tilted the scale.

I could hear her talk loudly on purpose, prattling away about some crap. I turned and watched James, and without realising, I smiled. He didn't see me but I didn't care – just being near him was…

We all heard the bus groan up the hill, and James's head looked up in its direction. I just so happened to be still standing in the same spot, which was in his line of vision, and his eyes cut to mine, catching me with my goofy grin. He gave me a wink and then the cutest smile in the history of smiles. My pulse leaped, and I felt the burning blush hit my face as the bus whooshed by me, already hitting the brakes. Everything was him. All the rest was a blur.

Then he was suddenly in the force of the mob, being coerced into getting on top deck with the "in" crowd. I lingered last in line and found my place with the old biddies on lower deck. There was that little old, Asian woman again. She gave me a smile. She reminded me of Gran. OK, the women weren't the same ethnicity and didn't look anything alike, but there was something similar in both their eyes. An inscrutable depth you knew held the wisdom of the world.

The bus's whirring engine lulled me into a trance. I dreamt of the upcoming party. What I would wear, how I would look, what I would say. Christ. I didn't know what girls my age wore at parties – never having been to one. Pathetic. What attire was suitable? Vic could help...

The bus came to a halt at Mill Hill Broadway, and the thump, thump, thump of shoes coming down the steps, reverberated through the bus. Down came Bianca and following her, Trisha and, to my shock, James, followed by Nick. *Nick?* When did he get on our bus? and two other girls in Trisha's squad. Gabs and what was the other girl's name? Oh, yeah – Natasha.

It was Friday. Bianca had probably invited them to her house. She'd have it to herself until after eight; then her parents got home. Jealousy rampaged through me.

Out they hopped into the whipping wind, all grinning to one another, as their hair blustered around them. Bianca could be heard above all of them, saying something to James about getting to her house so they wouldn't freeze to death. She put her arm through the nook of his elbow and, catching sight of me staring feebly out the window, narrowed her eyes contemptuously, and, behind James's back, stuck her middle finger up rigidly at me, mouthing, 'In your face!' Then turned, skipping off with James in her clutches. She really *did* think I was competition.

The weekend went by morbidly.

On Monday morning, I got up at my usual time. I didn't set my watch earlier just to accommodate Bianca's caprice. I was going to see James. I sat on the seat closest to the staircase for upper deck. He'd see me there. I had done extra-nice make up and toned my lips a little more pinkish, "for added irresistibility" (Vic's words) and, for once, my hair was looking good. Long, wavy raven tresses all the way down my back.

His stop was seconds away. I prepared, sitting up straight and adjusting my hair, bringing some to the front.

The doors opened, and on he stepped. He validated his card, and then walked to the stairs, facing me. His uniform fit him so well. Those long, proportioned legs were a sight to be revered. His torso, lean, and glorious – Da Vinci's Golden Ratio didn't compare. His head – a Pre-Raphaelite knight. That head, now drooped, looking weary. That wasn't like him. *Look up! look up!* He froze as his eyes caught my face. His cheeks fired for an instant, checking me out, but there was something off about his expression. It was as if he was afraid to smile.

'Hi,' I said softly, eagerly. He stood for a moment. Was he actually deliberating whether to speak to me? I felt the slap of distress strike viciously. What had happened on Friday? What had Bianca said about me? What did they tell him? Poisoned him against me, I'd bet.

'Hi,' he said, and failed to smile. It was a different James. I felt my heart plummet. Then, not daring to look me in the eye, he walked up the stairs.

Cutting me with a serrated blade would have hurt less. I wiped away a bothersome tear while my throat constricted.

Bianca got on a few stops after at Mill Hill. She gave the most indiscreet jerk of the head when she saw me. Her way of pretending she never saw me. I gave her a stiff look and averted my eyes.

On stepped Trisha also, and her two friends, jabbering away loudly, their body spray wafted over filling the air with some sickly, overdone aloe vera.

'Come on! James is upstairs…'

'Oh, my God, he was so cute Saturday night.'

'Totally fit. He's such a sexy MF!'

' "You sexy motherfuckerrr",' they sang. Then they burst out laughing, snorts and grunts. They thought they were so funny.

As soon as we reached the stop outside Milden, I ran off down the hill so they wouldn't see me. I didn't want them to see my face. I didn't want to give Bianca the satisfaction that it got to me.

So, they had gone out Saturday night? It wasn't just a one-off on Friday. Now they were all *tight*. A *posse*. A *crew*. *BFFE*s or whateverthefuck. If that were the case, then chances of me ever speaking to him again were zero; I was already excluded, disregarded like a piece of garbage by Bianca. I could grovel back to her… Jesus. That was pitiful. But… I would lose him if I didn't… He had given me one dry *hi* that morning, already showing signs he was pulling away from me. Was his company worth losing all my self-respect?

Chapter Fifteen

Now

'I think you should go for the ditsy tea dress. The sleeves are so cute.'

No.

'I like that dark-crimson, bodycon midi. It suits your colouring. Plus, you're the only person I know that can pull off something that tight.'

I am barely awake. I barely hear what my friends say. My mind is on the dream that woke me so horribly this morning. Opening my eyes to the light of dawn washing my room in a spectral, pale yellow. I wasn't able to get back to sleep. How can one? Such a nightmare would make you rethink going under, the prospect in seeing *that* again…

'You! You have done this to me!' he'd shouted, enraged, with an accusatory finger pointed my way. Those blue eyes, piercing, embittered, hurt. Wind was blowing around us, and I was on a precipice. I took a step back, about to fall, when I awoke with a ripping gasp, crying. It wrung everything out of me. It has now evoked an incipient fear, I try to ignore.

'I always told her, she could be a model,' Kate says. 'I swear, those bullies at your school really killed your self-esteem.'

Juliet, Suze and Kate all look at me. I blink. 'What?'

'Bullying… you know, when you were at school?' Kate prompts.

'It's true, yeah…' I concur, trying to get into the conversation. Kate knows my story but the other two, no. I give them a summary of my wonder years, both are shocked when I show them the scars for proof. 'So that's why I… I'm hesitant in wearing anything that emphasizes my… skinniness.' I shrug in conclusion. 'But I'd try the bodycon… looks nice.'

'What is this girl talking about?' cries Suze to Juliet and Kate, pointing her thumb at me. Some shoppers turn. Then, turning to me says, 'You're not a skinny sixteen-year-old anymore. You've got a figure people would die for, including me!'

'Don't be stupid,' I say weakly. I always take compliment difficultly. The truth is, for the past year, I have been working out a little, going to a gym, trying to amend the body I was born with. It's been a slow process. Perhaps that's why nobody can tell – there's hardly a difference. Still, I plod on. I've never disclosed the fact to anyone because I don't want to tell them the reason why. Even Kate had been in the dark for a while. It was only when I came home one evening in my gym gear, having forgotten my change of clothing at home, when she found out. I hadn't kept it a secret from her intentionally. I suppose we both have so much on our minds, what with finals and dissertations overshadowing our every move, that we've become half-estranged; stuck in a limbo of cramming, frustrated painting and the anxiety of what our futures hold after our degrees. There is a certain amount of stress. Today is a breather, however. West-End shopping with the girls has been long overdue. After the dream, I was close to cancelling, but I didn't want to let the girls down – it's so seldom we meet up for a day out nowadays. How our lives are changing, right before our eyes.

'I think,' I say, 'I'll get the bodycon.'

'Yeah!' squeals Kate.

'Woohoo baby!' Suze howls.

'You guys are so embarrassing,' Juliet says peremptorily.

Suddenly, I give out a massive yawn.

'El, you look shattered. Why don't you go upstairs, get us a table and wait for us? We'll buy the stuff for you,' offers Juliet.

'Yeah, what's up with you? You've been yawning all day. Late night last night? Wink, wink, nudge, nudge,' says Suze, feigning a pun. 'Seriously, please tell me there's a man in your life.'

I harrumph, then cough. 'No,' I say. *Not in the sense* you *mean…* 'I wish there were…' and glance at Kate.

'Yeah,' she says. 'I'm afraid hell hasn't frozen over yet.' It was sarcasm with a large pinch of truth. But she is right; four years a student and still a desert isle. Except for that one time two years ago. But that wasn't a relationship; that was stupidity.

'Honestly, I'd like to think you can do better than Sam,' Suze utters.

'Agreed,' murmurs Kate.

'Sam?!' Juliet exclaims. 'You're with Sam?' she asks me.

'Please don't insult me,' I tell her, shaking my head vehemently. 'He had a thing for me, that's all… I turned him down ages ago.'

'Oh,' Juliet says faintly.

'I tell her there are so many guys out there who want her, but she doesn't even try –'

'Thank you, Katie, dearest!' I interrupt her before she starts disseminating examples of just *how* I don't try. 'Can we stop talking about it?' I yawn again.

'El, go upstairs and find us a table. Gimme your stuff,' Juliet says, holding out her hands to take my clothes.

'Cheers, Jules.' I hand her the bodycon and some money.

'I'll come with you,' says Kate to me. 'Make sure you don't drop off and someone steals your purse, or something.' She gives me a "time to talk" look.

We are elevated to the top floor: the restaurant. A table is about to be vacated near the window, overlooking the rooftops of London, and Kate and I run for it.

'You have to know a couple of things before you get in touch with Sophie,' Kate says, slotting herself opposite me.

'I'm all ears.'

'No contact via mobile, unless you have a burner.'

'Burner? Where on earth am I going to get a burner?'

'El, shut up and listen before the girls come.'

I nod. Why is my heart thudding so?

'OK, this is how you'll communicate with her since you don't have a burner. You will be sending each other emails but not sending them technically. Let me explain,' she says after seeing my confused expression. 'You will share an email account, address and password. Emails are traced when you hit the *send* button but you won't hit the button – you'll just be saving them to drafts for each other to read when you sign in alternately. Sophie will read them and write back to you in the drafts. Whatever you do, don't press *send*. Do you get it?'

'Yeah, but where am I going to get the email? Who's creating it?'

'She sent it to me last night, in code. It's on here.' Kate hands me a small piece of paper, with an email and password on it. 'It would be best if you can memorise it – not that you have a problem with that – and then throw it away, or burn it…'

'That's rather OTT, isn't it?' I say. 'And I don't have a photographic memory, I have an *eidetic* memory, remember?'

'Nothing is OTT with Sophie. What she does is a felony at best. You can go straight to jail for shit like this. Make sure nobody finds this piece of paper or the email. And I was thinking of synaesthesia. Sorry.'

'Well, synaesthesia or not, I don't think *frankly-my-dear-I-don't-give-a-damn* is a difficult username to remember.'

'True. Oh, and don't write your name or other personal details; nothing which the police might use against you.'

'Got it.'

'So, tell me,' her voice has taken a lower pitch. 'Did you find anything else… of use?'

I look out at the skyline. The sun peeps through a slow cloud. 'Yes…'

'What?'

'He's living in indigence,' I rasp, as a lump swells in my larynx. 'I feel…'

'What?' she asks tentatively.

'Like…' I bite my lip.

'Like?'

'Like I might have had a hand in it…'

She raises her brows. 'What makes you say that?'

'I don't know… I… I just have a horrible feeling…'

***

I type GSY in the search engine.

Golden Sea Yachts.

A yachting company? I click onto the site, and a page loads with a short video of an elegant yacht slicing through the deep blue, sails at full mast. I skip it and enter the site. There is that usual boastful text on what a top-quality yachting agency they are, and so on and so forth. I click on *About* and see a location. Main offices, Canary Wharf. I click on *People* and the page shows a couple of photos of employees and their managerial positions. Further down is a list of more employees and their various jobs, '…in making Golden Sea Yachts number one in customer service'. These aren't accompanied with photos. I scan each name, hoping there might be something or someone I know. It is a long shot, so when nothing rings a bell, I'm not greatly discouraged.

I suck at my nail, thinking on my next move.

What to do? Find information on the garage; speak to the owners of the house attached to his. Learn what is really going on with his living conditions. Does he own the place? Does he use the garage as a den, and his house is the building behind? Is it some pied-à-terre? Doubtful, yes, but I'll never know if I don't ask. All must be made known before I confront him; know exactly what to do and what to say.

I get dressed, putting on my usual garb, no need for disguises now. Jeans, boots and a jumper and jacket. Mobile, keys, money, all in the pockets (I hate handbags) and I'm off.

One, two, three… four stops – Camden Town Station. I turn into the high street and plunge directly into the vibe of the buzzing atmosphere. There are more people around than I would have expected on a Tuesday evening. Probably some cool event is happening in the confines of a building, which looks nothing like it seems…

Like that time I was taken to a goth-punk club, somewhere around there. You wouldn't have thought it such a place, in fact, you'd have walked right by it, unaware of what was going on inside. I flash back to that sexy punk with his amazing Mohican. He'd asked me out… the memory makes me twinge in shame. Not even then had I said yes. Why? What was I waiting for? What was wrong with me?

I transverse through the same streets as the night before, and hit the brick wall. Heart thumping, I turn into the alley, holding my breath. There is no sound, no movement from inside. The window is dark, the padlock on the outside; he isn't home. I let out a breath.

I look to the street through the pathway, walk out to the row of houses and stop at the cross section. At better inspection, I see the garages are detached from the back of the terraced houses. That means there is no adjoining entrance to the house itself. Are they on different property?

I'll ask – just an innocent inquiry. There isn't any harm in that, is there?

I estimate which house is directly behind James's garage and step up the short path to the doorbell.

A sudden gush of nerves hits me with a thousand "what if's".

What if *he* is in there?

What if no one is home?

What if no one answers, afraid of such a late caller?

What if some crazy person is living there?

Too late now. I hear footsteps and someone ask from the other side, 'Who is it?' It is a woman's voice. It is hushed.

'Um… Sorry to bother you,' I say, apologetic. 'Really, really sorry for the time…' I continue.

The door cracks open on a chain. Two round, hazel eyes look through. I give her a smile of reassurance I'm not some nutcase. She unlatches the door; I see highlighted hair up in a messy bun and a taxed face. I put her to be around thirty. She gives me a drained smile. 'What can I do for you?'

'I'm sorry for the hour,' I say again. 'But I just wanted to ask you a quick question if I may?'

'It's OK. I was just tucking son in for the night. I didn't want the doorbell to wake him,' she explains.

'Oh, goodness! I hope I didn't wake him.'

'No. He's OK.' She waits for my question. How to word it?

'I… wanted to know about the garages behind you.'

'Yeah?'

'Do they belong to your property?'

'No,' she says, shaking her head. 'Lots of people get that confused. They aren't even attached to our house.'

'So, basically, you own this house and someone else owns the garages behind you?'

'Yeah. That's right,' she said. 'They aren't exactly garages. They are more like storerooms.'

'Oh, I see,' I say. 'You wouldn't happen to know who the one behind you belongs to, by any chance?' I ask. The million-dollar question. 'I'm interested in acquiring one.' I have no idea why I put that in. Perhaps to sound less dodgy.

'I'm not sure.' She shakes her head. Then something amuses her and she smiles widely. 'Sorry…'

'Oh, please don't apologise,' I say. 'I'm the one who should be apologising for bothering you at this time of night…'

'Oh, that's no problem.' She shoos her hand, pursing her lips together so she can stop smiling. Do I look that ridiculous? Can she see through my façade?

'Well, thanks for everything,' I say, dismayed. 'So sorry again for the… intrusion.' I turn and make to leave when she says, 'You know, you could always look it up on Land Registry Services.'

I gawk at her for a second like a child unable to comprehend an abstruse meaning.

'I am such an idiot…' I say.

Here she stifles a laugh. 'Sorry you came all this way…'

'Oh, that's all right. I needed to get out…'

She sizes me up then, like she's deliberating something. 'FYI,' she says, 'the person who lives there rents it, as far as I know.' Is she telling me indirectly that she knows James?

'Oh,' I nod, intrigued. 'Really?'

We pause uncomfortably. Clearly, she is savvier about James's situation than she is letting on; I can sense a reluctance to disclose further information, though, like she wants to help but is bound to secrecy not to. I am a stranger, after all. I'd probably do the same thing in her place.

'Well, I can't thank you enough for your help,' I say, seeing her lips firmly sealed.

'Sure, no problem. Take care now.' It is affably said.
'Goodnight,' I bid her, and walk off. I hear her front door shut as I turn the corner.

Chapter Sixteen

Back Then

The locker-room door shut in my face, an inch from bashing me on the nose. The message was loud and clear; a bullhorn at my ear couldn't have made it clearer. I had been contemplating whether to grovel to Bianca for James's sake, or keep the last shred of dignity I had in this world and leave things be.

In the end, I chose James. I said to myself, one more try, and if Bianca was still set on ignoring me, then I'd leave it… for good. It would be up to James now, if he ever wanted to speak to me again.

It was her who had kicked the door shut. The resounding *BAM!* hit me straight though. The shuddering repercussion of this final statement was indisputably received. In a way I was glad because I never wanted to stoop that low; I didn't want to be enslaved to someone so undeserving.

I stood outside the locker room, eye fixed on some deliberate scrape of paint, leaving the wood showing underneath. *Underneath…* I thought, then, that we know little of people; what's truly hidden beneath the surface. Even James. What was all that crap about him leaving in three months and couldn't care less what popularity meant to him? I shook my head, turning to the library so I could hide for a bit. Perhaps make head and tail of it. No matter what, I would never know the truth unless he told me what was really going on. I was convinced he was ignoring me for some reason other than his own. He wasn't a Bianca with an inner lever. It had to be something else. *If a boy really likes a girl and wants to be with her, nothing, and I mean nothing, will get in his way…*

I found that fat book on the history of art, and opened to one of my favourite paintings. Waterhouse's *Ophelia*. I loved that dress. I loved the way Siddal's face was painted, the inevitability of her character's future in that expression of pure despair. So concise. But *I* didn't want to look like that; feel that despair. I didn't want to let a man do that to me. I didn't want anyone to affect me so detrimentally.

Walk away with your head held high… I heeded my sister's words. Bianca; I wanted to be rid of her once and for all, be the one to finally snap any remaining link between us. She'd blatantly stuck her finger up at me, now it was my turn; my way. Both parties have to say goodbye for whatever relationship between them to be dissolved permanently. She had always been the one who commanded and ordered – called all the shots. One second friend, next second foe. I had never instigated that behaviour to her, to anyone. I wasn't insecure in that respect. I'd never dragged someone on a whim of pure selfishness just to satisfy my ego. I could forgive. I easily put water in my wine, as Greeks say.

Putting water into wine is good, agape mou (my love)— *we must forgive. But it also means you fill your cup to the brim quicker, and it will overflow* – Gran's wisdom.

I knew what my grandmother meant now. You forgive, but some people aren't ready to be better beings, and they keep on doing the crap they do, which just ends up giving you grief. All well and good Gran, but then again, I reflected, was it fair to ascribe attributes to someone who didn't possess them, and foolishly expected them be someone they weren't? It wasn't Bianca's fault; me expecting her to be nice and humane. She was who she was. No. It was purely my foolishness for being so trusting, again and again and again. Whatever the case, the Bianca-cup had long since sprung a damaging leak.

So now… now things were different. It would be me – for the first time in my life – to pull the plug on this pathetic, so-called friendship. No more pretence. No more lies and feigned probity. James. James had to come into my life for me to see that. His belief in me, his presence alone, had been able to imbue a faith in myself. Warm and remedial. Whether I never spoke to him again, he would be that axis, the one who'd turned me in the right direction.

First things first: Victoria.

On coming home that evening, I bolted upstairs to Vic's room, calling her name as I did so.

'WHAT?' she called out. I opened her door and found her writing at her desk, as usual. Ever the swot.

'I want you to make that phone call to Bianca,' I said, mind set. Vic stared at me for a heartbeat, pen still held upright, then she smiled broadly. 'About bloody time!'

We prepped on the exact words Vic should say. Words to make it crystal clear, no ambiguity whatsoever, it was over for good. She then did some mimicking of me to get the right expression in her voice, annotation and pitch. She was ready. I gave her my phone, contact ready for dial.

'She's home alone right now, so you'll have her undivided attention. She usually lies on the phone when her parents are there, acting like the perfect daughter. So just say, "Bianca? It's Eleanora. Listen, I don't want you to talk to me anymore". Those had been her words to me once,' I explained to Vic. She had a sly smile and eager face.

'That's good; hit her back with her own words!'

I told her some other niceties Bianca had said to me throughout the years, and she scribbled them down to use them too. Seriously – she was taking notes!

'I don't know what happened between you two, but I'm glad you finally came to your senses and not taking her bullshit anymore,' she said to me.

'It's about that boy I told you,' I said and paused to see her reaction. Her eyes met mine, and she raised an inquisitive eyebrow. 'I'll tell you about it after the call. First, I want you to get her out my life.'

Vic turned on the screen and tapped the dial icon. My heart started to gear up. My nail was wedged in my mouth with anticipation.

Vic cleared her throat and tapped on speaker. The ringing tone was heard and then that cold, 'What do you want, El?' She didn't have to pick up, but I knew how her curiosity-itch had to be scratched. She couldn't *not* know why I was calling. Curiosity was going to kill the cat.

'Bianca? Listen,' my sister began. I suddenly stared at her in in awe. We had the same voice, yes, but not the same drawl or cadence. Victoria impersonated my voice to a T. I slapped my hands across my mouth, stifling a giggle. Vic stared at me to shut up. 'I don't want you to t-talk to me anymore –' she continued in a perfect portrayal of me.

'El, look,' Bianca said, cutting my sister off in her usual hoity-toity way. 'I don't want to take this the wrong –'

'Listen to me, Bianca!' Vic said slicing Bianca's words off. I had never cut her off. She was taken by surprise. Then Vic laid it on her with a vengeance, relishing each moment. 'Don't interrupt me! Stop thinking about yourself all the time.' Silence. 'I called to say, it was… sort of nice knowing you, and the b-backstabbing shit you've done to me over the years, but this is where it ends. I've had enough of your crap. Being friends with t-two-faced bitches is not my style. I gave you so many chances, and you used me like I was a piece of shit. So this is my goodbye. Don't come up to me tomorrow. Don't ever act like you're my friend. I-I won't condescend to speak to you. Got it?'

'Ell!' said Bianca, affright. 'I didn't mean to ignore you today –'

'You still don't get it. I'm. Moving. On,' said Vic, spelling it to her. 'Goodbye!' And she tapped the "call off" icon.

Vic and I said nothing. We both stared, motionless at the phone, like it was going to spew Bianca out. Then we looked at each other, and burst out laughing.

'Condescend?' I said through the giggles. 'I don't talk like that!'

'Yes, you do! Still, she'll probably know it was me and not you…'

'You know what? I don't give a shit. You have officially broken us up for good.'

Bianca never took anything lying down. She hit back with a vengeance the following day. Of course, being Miss Unoriginal, she'd somehow managed to hide my duffle coat instead of my portfolio this time. It was missing from its hook, and I found it thrown on the floor of the last cubicle in the science-department toilets. It was the end of the day, and a hundred girls must have used that toilet. The reek of dank piss was indescribable.

Off I ran, up that blasted hill, heart hammering, just to see the two-four-two shut all doors and pull out, packed with kids. I stood to catch my breath as a trickle of blood escaped from my left nostril – the one with the delicate capillary. I held my waist, now feeling the muscle cramp, as I tried to catch my breath. I looked up on the back window of top deck and saw *him* looking at me. His eyes wide with… what? Pity for me? Remorse? I wanted to scowl at his pity. I hated pity. He'd made his choice. But it didn't bother me, as such, as to *why* he was doing this. It bothered me that *I* wasn't enough for him not to. So why feel bad about me? Why care? Right then, the aching ran through me, and I began to cry. *I'm not good enough…*

***

For the next weeks, I paid no attention to James, and glad of Easter holidays – a small reprieve from all the pain of rejection. After that, I waded through the rest of the school year, circumventing my way under a charade of indifference. Perhaps this was the resilience he was talking about. Perhaps this was what Vic was talking about – learning to distinguish…

All I saw was the outline of him, getting on and getting off the bus, like his body was there but his spirit was far away. He never sat down beside me ever again, but he never forgot to acknowledge my presence, nevertheless, which was perplexing. Even Nick would approach me now and again, ask how I was doing, try to initiate a conversation. I wasn't moody by nature, and would try to be nice, even with short answers. But he wasn't his friend. And as for James, I could see he didn't want to cut me off entirely. He would always catch my eye and give me a small nod. But never spoke. *Speak to me, James! Speak! Give a shit!* I would turn and face the window most times, headphones in, acting as though *I* didn't give a shit. His vagary was arduous, and my heart couldn't stand it.

Know when to leave with you head held high. My sister's words infiltrated in my mind again. The time had come to stop pining and being such a sad cow. I had to focus on my GCSEs; the future, because the present held nothing.

There were two months left to really put an effort, a last-minute dint. So that's what I did. I swotted up – crammed my mind with Shakespeare, Ancient Greece and Rome, Algebraic theorems, conjugations of French verbs and the anatomy of organisms. I stuffed my Art portfolio with additional works for the examiners to see, begged Mrs Wiles, with tears I might add, to let me rewrite my *Catcher in the Rye* essay in English Lit I'd got a D in, so that the new one could be handed in instead; the deadline was in two days. I went home, locked myself in my room and worked on it all night. Mrs Wiles found me two days after and intimated with a smile that she'd given me an A-. I'd cried.

Time went by in a half-daze of mental submersion, drowning myself in intellect, and before I knew it, it was May, and the jolt back to reality, and… exams.

Now

The moonbeam hits the edge of my mattress as I wait. I have left my curtains open, always preferring natural light in whatever shape or form.

In just a few clicks I am to receive the information I need.

I'd carefully typed the address, full location, postcode, and whatever else they wanted to know, in all the desired fields. And with a nominal amount, all the information is to be emailed to me from Her Majesty's Land Registry Services.

I open my mail some minutes later, and there it is.

The storeroom is owned by a certain Tom Garner. Name of which means nothing to me. I strum my fingers on the laptop, frustrated. Who's Garner? What's his relationship with James? Is he merely just a landlord or…?

Oh, Crap! Perhaps I should ask Sophie to help me out on this. *No,* I think. *I can do this.* No need to break more laws… yet.

I search his name with James's; see if they are connected. Nothing. I do, however, find an ancestry site – Garner's family tree. The search has struck out the word *Laidlaw.*

Again, I scan each name. Tom Garner is in his 60's and his remaining family are siblings, children, and nephews and nieces.

I let out big yawn, my eyes getting bleary and heavy, thwarting visibility, mental and physical. I don't want to sleep; I'm afraid. I don't want to see those hurt eyes again, but the deprivation is severe; it's impossible to continue. My eyes close…

Chapter Seventeen

Back Then

It was almost 8:30 on a Thursday morning in mid-June, and all who were sitting for the History of Art exam were waiting outside the gym, subdued from the severity of the situation. None of us laughed or cracked jokes. None of us could barely talk. I, for one, felt the nausea whirl in my stomach.

Not a lot of girls had the talent to draw, so there were only a few of us who had selected Art as a subject.

'Who can tell me something on Munch? I've totally blanked out. Shit!' said Padma. I looked alarmed at her. She was one of the brightest pupils, and she was freaking me out.

'What do you mean, you've blanked out?' I said.

She was about to cry. 'Oh, God! Help me, Eleanora!'

'All right, girls! Everybody in, please,' said Mrs Greene, a Chemistry teacher in charge of us that day.

Padma looked at me imploringly. Padma had always been a presence on the periphery of my school life, and I'd never really given her much thought. Since I cut ties with Bianca, however, Padma and I had formed a contented friendship. In that split second, I recalled the times she'd quietly helped me when I missed a lesson, filling me in, and how, one another time, she'd told me where to find the new tempera paint-bottles hidden in the cupboard of the Art department. Little things, but considerate. Throughout the last two months of school, we had become …friends.

'Norwegian. Impressionist. Symbolist. Death. Pain. The Scream. Breakdown,' I whispered hastily to her as we entered the gym.

She gave me an agitated smile.

'No talking now!' barked Mrs Greene.

We sat at our appointed places, propping our transparent pencil cases on the A2 sheet of paper, which lined our desks. I instantly settled, jitters gone. Feeling that relaxation in my stomach muscles. *It will all be over in two hours,* I mused happily.

I thought of summer just around the corner. Our village and loud relatives. I thought how I'd sprawl out on the sofa and watch TV all day. I thought how I'd finally get to finish playing Broken Sword and then play it all over again.

I wrote well. If it wasn't a B, I'd be surprised. It was a pass, and 40% of the final mark. The other 60 was my coursework throughout the two years, in which I had replenished, so I was sure I'd do well on the whole.

'Ten more minutes, girls,' said Mrs Greene. 'Start finishing up, please.'

Ten more minutes to freedom. I had finished already, and was reading through for any mistakes.

'Two minutes, girls!'

Two! I counted down inwardly, *120, 119, 118, 117, 116, 115…*

'All right, girls. Please put your pens down now and check all your papers have been marked and numbered properly…' Her voice faded away in my mind. The ordeal was over. Bliss.

I handed my papers in and left the gym. I took a sombre look around the school grounds – I wouldn't see them for another two months. Filled with a sweet elation, I made my way to my locker and inspected it in case I had left anything. Apart from an old, cracked ruler and some tattered notes, there was nothing else. I took my padlock off, put it in my bag, and walked to the main building to say goodbye to some of my teachers and wish them a nice summer. I was received with smiles and luck for good marks. They had hopes for me yet.

Mum had offered to pick me up, but I had insisted on taking the bus. I wanted to be alone for as long as possible.

The late morning was a sky of blue calm, soft psithurism through the leaves and distant chirping. The day, wistful, filled with silent yearning – a pledge of good things to come.

Thwack! Something crashed into my back, hitting my shoulder blade. I didn't hurt, but it startled the shit out of me. There was a laugh, then another hit.

'Ouch!' I looked to see the cracked, raw egg-white and yolk dribble down my arm. Another laugh. It was Laura, ready to fling me with some flour.

'Oh, my God!' I screamed in excited fright, running a second too late as a powdery cloud burst on the side of my face. The egg and flour fight. I had totally forgotten.

Laura laughed her arse off, and suddenly out of nowhere, other girls came out and started throwing more eggs at us. She squealed and I did too. It was full attack, and I didn't have ammo.

'Give me an egg!' I shouted to Laura. She handed me the rest of the box, and I hurled the last three at the girls charging towards us, as they threw back at us. One landed on my shoe and one on the front of my summer uniform. Not that I minded for that one-piece gingham dress which I'd grown out of, but still, I was mirthfully miffed. Just then more girls poured out from behind us, egg and flour mixed in their hair and clothes, propelling a white turbulence in our direction. Laura and I were stuck in the middle, and seeing we were going to get pelted, I made a run for it, breaking into a sprint for the top of the hill.

I approached the bus stop outside Milden gasping and laughing at the same time. I stood to catch my breath catching sight of a group of boys in the distance in non-uniform, when two arms came around me from behind, squeezing. I stopped as the wind was taken out of me.

'Oh, El! Thank you so much!' Padma cried from behind me. I turned and her full-smiling face was gazing up at me. It looked like she hadn't escaped the egg and flour fight either.

'Thank you, thank you, thank you!' she cried. 'You saved my life! I think I wrote really well. It all came back to me after what you said. OMG, I was freaking out like mad… I thought I was going to fail and my parents would kill me!'

'You're welcome, seriously. It was nothing!' I said, returning her hug.

'What was nothing?'

His voice was jovial. I hadn't heard it in so long. My heart sped up at the warm cadence. I turned to him, somewhat incredulous – was he really talking to me? He started, obviously not expecting to see my floury face, and then bit his lower lip, chuckling. I shared his chuckle, although completely annoyed with myself at how easily he affected me. There had been a chasm between us for so long, and yet I was immediately susceptible to his charm. What was wrong with me? Was I incapable of resisting him? Or was it maybe because he'd never actually stopped acknowledging my presence all this while that made me succumb to his warmth so easily now.

My eyes hovered on him. It was the first time I'd seen him in anything other than his uniform. He wore jeans, which hung a little, and a white T-shirt that was a fraction too tight over his deltoids. I marvelled at the sight of him. *Anything would suit that body,* I thought to myself. But why was he talking to me now? I had lost all train of thought in the short, uncomfortable silence.

'Eleanora helped me in our Art History exam today,' blurted Padma, seeing the silence was getting awkward, bless her.

'Yeah?' said James. He smiled at her. 'Well, you're a good friend, I'm sure.'

'El's a darling!' Padma said decisively. 'Nobody else gave a shit. They were all staring at me like I'd gone mad. Not 'er!' she said, thumbing my way.

'Padma, it was nothing, seriously,' I said again.

'No, Eleanora. Padma's right.' James became serious. 'When it comes to exams, it's kill or be killed. We're talking about one of the most competitive situations we're given in life. It *is* something serious. It was very generous of you to help.'

'I suppose…' I mumbled. It felt weird speaking to him after such a long time, and the way he was looking at me…

'Generous is an understatement!' Padma told him. 'She practically spelled Munch's life out for me, and it got the gears working. I would have failed today if it weren't for her,'

We heard the bus climb the hill in the distance. 'Shit. Gotta go!' she said. She hugged me tight. I reciprocated.

'We'll talk, yeah? Will you be going to Greece this year?' she asked, as she crossed the street.

'Hope so.'

'I'll call you! We'll be going to Thessalonica first, then down to Athens…'

'Cool!' I called. 'Email me!'

She nodded. Then said, 'Nice meeting you, James!' having reached the pavement and waving to him.

'Likewise!' he called back, lifting a hand, as the bus's red bulk came and hid her from sight.

I looked on as the bus left.

Quiet.

James hadn't moved. I could feel his heat.

'Eleanora?' His voice, soft in the still air. It was imploring and contrite. I looked at him, baffled. I said nothing.

'How have you been?'

'Fine…' I was defensive. It wasn't to be severe with him for not speaking to me for months, but as armour because he was confusing me again.

He looked at me solemnly. 'I finished yesterday. I have officially finished school.' He couldn't contain his happiness. His eyes were dancing, bright and celadon blue. 'I came in today to get some stuff and say goodbye, you know…'

I wanted to say, *what do you want, a medal?* But the way he beamed, so sweetly, all I felt was the need to put my palm on his soft cheek and kiss his lips.

'Congratulations, James. I hope you get in to Oxford,' I said quietly. I was happy for him, I was. But I still felt the bruises.

'Thank you, Eleanora. I hope you do well too.' He paused. He was holding something back.

'Thanks. As my grandmother says, "From your mouth to God's ear!" ' I said it with her Greek lilt, not meaning for it to be so funny, but James laughed so loud, it made me giggle too.

'I've got to meet your grandmother one day, seriously. She sounds cool!' he said, shaking his head still on a chuckle.

'Yeah. She makes a pretty mean souvlaki as well…' I said playfully. Then the jesting died down and we were silent for a breath. I wondered again what brought on his sudden change of heart. Why was he speaking to me? And where was his "sorry"?

'So… I hope you haven't forgotten about the party this Saturday?' he said expectantly. I had. I had completely forgotten about it.

'You forgot, didn't you?' he said incredulous, catching my unmistakable expression.

'Yeah. Oh, my goodness. Is it this Saturday? It slipped my mind entirely. Thanks for reminding me,' I said. A sudden smack of nervous excitement hit me – I was going to go to my first real party. None of that childish stuff where you went to your friend's house with your parents and shit. No – *this* was what it was all about.

'Where does.' I paused briefly to remember our host's name. It came to me. 'Robert live?' I asked. 'I never got to find out.' More like, Bianca deliberately never told me.

James was about to say something but stopped himself. I could see he was probably going to ask why Bianca hadn't told me, and then probably realised we weren't talking. After all this time hanging out with her and the rest of that crowd, he should have known all the ins and outs of my relationship with her.

So, he said, 'He lives in Finchley. I saw it on the map, and it's not too far off from the Finchley Central. It's at two hundred and eight, Saint Peter's Lane. It'd be good if you got someone to take you. Nick's taking me and a couple of other mates, but I'm not returning with him; I have to get home early. Dad needs my sister and I Sunday morning… Nick's father is giving him the car for the night, so…'

So? What? Was he apologising for not being able to take me? Had he been considering it? I blushed, thankfully hidden behind the flour. He *had* been the one to ask me to the party…

'Oh! Oh, I'll be all right. I'm sure my mum will help me out,' I said. *In another life,* I added to myself. His face smoothed ever so faintly. Was he worried for my safety? I wasn't sure. It could have been my imagination. All in all, his whole behaviour left me confounded.

'Good…' he said, and smiled. There was another uncomfortable pause. I looked beyond his shoulder, unable to find anything else to say to him, rubbing off some of the flour from my eyelash that was beginning to irritate me.

'Eleanora?' he said hesitantly. My eyes darted straight to his, shocked he'd said my name the proper way. He used all the syllables, El-ey-an-o-ra. No one, except for my family, had ever pronounced my name like that. No one. No teacher, no friend… no one.

His white cheeks dappled in light, became that rose-petal pink. I stood there, admiring his countenance, questioning those startling blue oculi of his, now glinting in the sun. He was about to continue when we heard Nick's distinct yell call to him from beyond.

'Oi! Jamie! We've got to get cracking, mate!' Nick was unlocking a much-used, old-model BMW, parked outside Milden. He waved at me. 'All right, gorgeous?!' he called. 'That look's wicked on ya!'

'Thought you'd like it!' I retorted.

'Yeah. I'm all for the powdered look!' He smirked wickedly, making me tee-hee. 'We'll see you at the party, yeah?' he said.

'Yeah.'

'I've got to go,' James said apologetically, brushing his hand through his hair. It was getting long. 'I'll see you there.'

'Yeah… See you there.'

Chapter Eighteen

Now

 I awake with a jolt, gasping like I have just immersed from too long under water, strenuous panting seizing my chest. I breathe hard. Reality kicks in. Relief… None of it was real. It was just a figment of my imagination again… yet, how it hurt.
 I've always been prone to bad dreams. When I was younger, I'd seek out my parents' bed in the middle of the night to mitigate the terror and help sooth me back to sleep. Now, after all that's happening, bad dreams are intensifying. I utter a short prayer, banishing the malevolent torment for the time being.
 I've woken before my alarm and fumble to switch it off, having no appetite to hear the shrill fanfare it makes. My alarm sounds have to be annoying to get me up and out of bed. If they're tranquil sounds of water trickling down a brook, or some such nonsense, I fall right back to sleep again.
 I lie in bed in that state of morning torpor with a thought lingering from my dream. The scene spears at my conscience. That instant in time I conceived my shallow deed. That is where I must begin. I must take it from that point in the past and let events fold out sequentially. Because as far as I know, his plans were untampered with, the last time I saw him. The police would know. After all, they had been summoned there that night.
 There was also something else bothering me from the day before. What was it? It can't have been a picture, my LTM wouldn't have let me forget that, unless I was agitated when I saw it. Text? Possibly. I must have seen it more than once, though, for it to cause my brain to wonder. I'll have to meticulously look through all my online history again, for right now I am on a voyage of scrupulous enlightenment. The vanguard on his vessel to unknown spheres. Determined; I must persevere, even if I am afraid of what I might find.
 I get up and stomp to the window. I open a small-enough gap to see the street outside. A foggy, early Wednesday dawn. The whole world seems to be asleep, except for me.
 I tread lightly to the bathroom, not to wake Kate. Kate? Hang on! Is she home? I don't recall hearing her coming in last night. I usually stir when she tries to be quiet, coming in from a long night out. It didn't happen last night.
 I see light through her door, and I know her curtains aren't closed, meaning she was never here to pull them shut.

I open her door to an empty bed. Did she leave me a message? I go back to my bedside table and check my phone while going to the bathroom. There's a text from her.

Won't be home tonight, it reads, with two winking smileys.

'When am I gonna get me some?' I say to my reflection in the bathroom mirror. A vivid memory comes to mind just then. Embarrassment floods my face. I can never undo that mortifying experience – such things are scarred for ever.

It was at a wedding, and I had consumed a considerable amount of alcohol, just over two years ago. The wedding had been held in a vast, Victorian estate, with plenty of secret nooks to hide in. I barely remember his name, let alone the deed. Something beginning with K. Kevin? Kieran? I remembered laughing a lot; we were both totally smashed off our heads. How he had coerced me into following him to some small storeroom, was a mystery. I don't remember much when I drink. There had been a lot of snogging and rummaging. It felt… good. But when he had penetrated, ever so slightly – *that* I do remember – I had suddenly cried, 'STOP!'

'Stupid, stupid girl!' I say, bashing my forehead on the bathroom mirror. It was not the way I wanted it to be, especially for my first time. I had apologised feebly and ran out, making some excuse about him not having gloved himself and me not being on the pill… The only consolation was, he wasn't in any circles of mine, therefore, the likelihood of meeting him again was null. I cringe whenever I think of it. I think how reckless I was; how it hadn't even crossed my mind he could have been carrying an STD. Foolish! Foolish! How panicked I had been when it came to me as I was driving home, sobering up into clarity. That sudden lurid realisation spreading over me, like a reaper's shadow, that I could be carrying some kind of life-threatening disease. I'd gone, first thing, to the GP the following day. Thankfully, all the tests had come out negative. I'd been bloody fortunate, so bloody fortunate. I learnt my lesson; I've never made the same mistake since. Kate would say I was sowing my wild oats, and I'd look back on this one day and laugh. I'm NOT laughing.

'Done enough stupid things in my life. Time to make amends,' I declare aloud, to the mirror. I glare into my eyes.

I get undressed and step in the shower. The warm water sooths my heart and mind. A much-appreciated *catharsis*, even if it only is for five minutes.

I air-dry my hair as I get dressed. Jeans and a light grey, cashmere-knit jumper Mum bought me for my birthday last September, 'To match your eyes'. Nice and soft.

I make myself breakfast but hardly touch it. Nerves tighten my abdomen. There's no way any more food will go down.

I need to get out of this tiny space. Gym? No. *His* gym! Yes! I could phone the police from somewhere there. I want to make a formal apology, but since I had broken the law, I wanted to ask hypotheticals first, learn what the worst-case scenario would be for me – my penalty for lying. But not from my mobile; from a discreet telephone box, harboured in anonymity. I don't want them to find out my name through my mobile number (I heard they could do things like that), then I'll take it from there.

McAdam's. Where abouts was it?

I get my aged laptop going and wait for it to decide whether it wants to cooperate with me or not.

The laptop grinds and, after a bit, the browser comes up. I type *McAdam's Training* in the search engine again, and get to the website. Location. Find it. Click it. Opening hours are at seven a.m. Excellent.

Then my eyes wander to an announcement about a competition I hadn't noticed the day before. I click on it. Another tab pops up and the picture loads.

A flyer, showing a boxer in his gloves and shorts in a southpaw stance, is depicted. And underneath, a program of dates and times, announcing a tournament for amateur boxing of all the weight divisions from super heavyweight, all the way down to light flyweight. It's being organised by various boxing clubs in London and Greater London. And it starts this Saturday, a day before Easter, in order of ascending weights, namely starting with the lightest categories and ending with the heaviest, on the third and last Saturday.

I always liked watching matches on TV with Dad; he loved the sport – invariably switching to events, engrossed with the action. He would always call for me and Vic to come watch with him. I ended up learning the terminology for various throws and body stances and even got to the point in recognising when the referee had to call for a stop. And the fearful rush I'd get when some player was about to get his arse handed to him, all bloody-faced, sweat trickling all over his body, and dizzy from all the punching he had endured, collapsing to the floor. Some may think brutal and macabre, but I think empowerment. The skill and dedication, all something to be admired. Of course, that was professional boxing where you don't wear head gear. This McAdam's place is for Olympic-style, amateur. Or is it? Maybe they do both.

I leave for Angel. Six stops, Northern Line, on the eastern corollary, via Bank.

The train rolls into Angel Station, doors open and I alight, wondering just then, if James might be there at the gym. What convincing excuse could I give to make it seem coincidental? I comb through some ideas. All sound utterly stupid…

Exiting the station, I jog through the streets, whereupon I find myself opposite the entrance to the boxing club. On street level there are shops.

On top, the overbearing stone façade, I'd seen on the website – fitting for a place like this. I look ahead of me at the entrance. A royal-blue, painted door with a frosted window and large handle. It is shut. I look up again. There are three arched windows with some metal mesh on the inside protecting the glass, no doubt. I can't see any movement or shadow from within. They are too high up.

I come face to face with the door and place my palm to it. I push and it springs open.

'Ha,' I utter, as a rush of excitement speeds through me. I've never been in a boxing club and am eager to taste.

I enter a small landing at the foot of a staircase, leading up to an entry on the left.

'Come on, faster! One, two, one, two!' I hear shouting and swearing bouncing off the walls around me, a man's gruff voice. I take the first few steps up, the voices becoming more distinct. I continue up and up, my heart accelerating with every step.

'Don't punch like a schoolgirl! Use your back! That's right,' another voice growls. I harrumph to myself as I remember my punching encounters with "schoolgirls". Thinking girls can't fight is an urban myth.

Those familiar dull pounding sounds on a punch bag like you see in films are heard. Am I going to enter a scene from *Rocky* or something?

I get to the top of the stairs and peep my head around the doorway. My jaw drops as I am struck with awe at what I see: a boxer's paradise, spacious and fully equipped.

There are punch bags to one side with a guy jabbing away at one, back arched and focused. There is weight-lifting equipment to another, some other guy arranging weights on the bar, buffed to the extreme. Further down are those smaller hanging punch bags I know are called speed bags, thanks to Dad. Various paraphernalia is on the walls with the familiar red McAdam's logo emblazoned on them, alongside some of their sponsors' logos. But the pièce de résistance is the boxing ring itself, predominant and imperious, situated right in the centre of it all. It is impossible not to revere it.

Two men are in the ring. The boxer and his coach. The boxer, small in height but extremely muscled, wears his protective head gear and gloves. The trainer, mitts on and protection on his head and thorax, shouts commands with each movement his protégé makes.

They are in the middle of a session… no, bout. They are *sparring* – that's the word! I haven't uttered them in almost a decade. The only time I heard the word "boxing" recently was when I was told the Ancient Greeks had it as an Olympic sport by my proud, Greek cousin… two summers ago, when we were actually watching the London Olympics.

Nobody has noticed me, their full attention is on the job. James is nowhere – a fact I apprehended the first second I looked. Isn't he training for the upcoming event? Perhaps he isn't competing. His absence makes me ease a bit – no need to hide and sneak about. No need for a lame excuse.

I carry on looking at the two men in the ring, wide-eyed. Bewitched. I can almost hear my father say to me, 'Now, the boxer is in an orthodox stance, El. Now he's going to throw a right jab. He's an outside fighter, strategically thinking over his next move. See?' I feel something stir. A memory. Something about my father and boxing. What –

'More force!' the coach shouts, breaking my thoughts.

I turn slowly and place my body in full-view now, just as a beam of light bursts through the windows, bathing the room in a heavenly, soft glow. Continuing to gawk in astonishment at the place and the people, now in this new light, I capture the intensity, the vigour, the literal strength alone in those ardent bodies. Each manoeuvre with each calculated step-punch-step, exudes a sense of sublime coherence. I see a harmony and grace unlike any other. The composition of motion, strength and introspection. The boxers have to endure and the coaches have to teach that endurance. I admire the homogeneity between them all. They belong. They are united for a beautiful cause – to win the fight. Here is where the soul is debunked. Here lies the truth; do you have what it takes? I close my eyes. I encapsulate it, and pray there is time to limn on canvas.

I think I have found my excuse to be there, and it isn't a lie.

'Can I help you?'

I jump, startled at the girl's unexpected voice. She comes out from behind a computer screen and makes her way towards me. She's around my age and very pretty, with platinum-blonde hair and kind eyes. Shame about the acne scars, though. She is a little shorter than me, and covered, from head to foot, in Lycra with a hoodie on top.

'Um… I'm so sorry to disturb you,' I say, apologetic. She studies me, then smiles.

'You're not disturbing,' she says in a heavy Estuary. 'What can we do for you?'

'I was walking by and thought maybe I could get some information,' I say.

'Sure! Would you like to join?' she asks. I am about to answer in the affirmative, when she starts to take off her hoodie to reveal a much-toned upper body, all ripped and bulging in places I never knew us women had. Short or not, she could probably spin me around with one hand, like twirling a baton stick.

'Well,' I say, trying not to stare at her biceps, nor be intimidated by them. 'I'm interested in boxing, and I wanted some information.'

The girl peers at my thin frame sceptically. Our bodies are polar opposites. 'I see… well,' she says, smiling broadly, 'we've got five other girls, around your age here, including me. Training is any time between seven in the morning till ten at night, Mondays to Saturdays. I have a leaflet here with the details.' She hands me a printed piece of paper, crammed with writing.

'The leaflet will tell you what items of clothing you'll need and footwear, hours and fees but you don't have to worry about the fees for now. You're welcome to come and try first, see if you like it and –'

'WHERE THE FUCK IS JAMIE?' Someone suddenly shouts, cutting Biceps off. I jump. 'SOMEONE GET 'IM ON THE PHONE! 'E'S LATE. AGAIN!'

Pause.

'SIOBHAN!' he barks. Biceps turns. So do I. A tall, hugely-muscular bloke with an afro fade, good square jaw and slightly bandy legs, marches up to us. He stops and eyes me for a second or two, making me smile uncomfortably. He gives me a quick nod, trying to suppress his frustration and the acrimonious look.

Jamie? Was he talking about James?

'Siobhan, do me a favour and get Laidlaw on the phone,' he says in a resigned manner. My stomach dips; confirmed.

''Scuse me,' Siobhan says to me, and makes her way to the desk.

'By all means,' I mumble. She pauses, looks at me again and smiles, then dials his number. I notice she knows it off by heart. Jealousy smacks.

'Jamie? Hi. It's Siobhan –' she says, reminding me bit of how Trisha used to talk to boys. She is quiet, listening to the other end, then she puts the phone down.

'He's on his way, Brian,' she says, obviously reciting James's words. 'He got in late last night.'

It takes me precisely one heartbeat to realise that at any moment James is going to walk right through that door and he'll see me.

'Well, I have to get going,' I say, as I take some steps back towards the exit. 'Thanks for everything.' I smile awkwardly.

'No problem,' Siobhan says, both her and Brian looking at me like I'm off my rocker.

I'm down the stairs as fast as I can go without breaking a leg. *Quick, quick, quick!* I swing the door open, check if he's coming, and seeing the coast is clear, walk briskly to the curb. I wait for cars to pass, and jog to the island, covertly looking to see if he's anywhere near. No. I cross the rest of the road. When I get to the other side, I turn towards the building I was in but seconds ago. I loiter outside a café perpendicular to the gym.

There he is, not even a minute later, hastily making his way to the entrance. He has black, cotton tracksuit bottoms on and his big, thick jacket. A gym bag slung over his shoulder. His hair is tied back and he has shaven; no more beard. His eyes are down, still holding deep contemplation between his brows. Not even that statue of Atlas I'd seen, wore that look while holding the weight of the world.

He disappears through the blue door, and I sigh. I wish I knew what it was; what was bothering him. He'd been happy the other day, now what was going on?

I'm not making much progress, and feel every step I take, I make two steps back.

I jog to find a telephone box.

Chapter Nineteen

Back Then

It was Saturday. It was 8 o'clock. And I was still home, staring at my dressing-table mirror. I was dressed, made up, hair washed and buoyant. Mum's Burberry spritzed on and antiperspirant spread nice and thick. I was ready to go but sat rooted to the seat because, truth was, I was shit-scared. I'd never been to a party of this calibre before, and it completely terrified me. I was in worse anxiety than I had been for my exams.

I can't… I can't… But I knew I had to do it. *Pull yourself together!* I must find that courage, so far hidden within me, and haul it out. Force myself to be braver. And of course, if I didn't go, I wouldn't see James.

I needed Victoria. She had to help me…

Outside her closed door, I heard her caterwauling an ear-piercing rendition of the song she had on from within. I knocked, or more like thumped, so she could hear me over the din. The CD went silent.

'Can I come in?' I asked to the door. She opened it in such a rush that she crashed into me.

'Oh, my God! I'm late!' she cried. And in a fury of glitter, leather and suffocatingly-rich perfume, was running down the stairs and to the car. I ran out shouting for her to take me as far as the station at least. Then she saw how I was dressed and blinked, surprised. And of course she was surprised, because it was the first time she'd ever seen me dressed like that.

'Where are *you* going?' she cried.

'To a party…'

'To a party?! *Yeah, right!* Does Mum know?' She turned the ignition. I held my palms up in panic. 'Wait!' I called. 'Please, Vic! I have to go!'

She let out a resigned sigh. We both knew it had become her job to take care of me, not Mum's. 'All right. Get in!'

I did. As soon as she reversed out onto the street and put first gear, she said, 'Listen, you are to have your mobile on at all times, and I want you to call me the moment you get to this party. Are we clear?' I nodded.

'Don't you dare let that phone go to voicemail if I call, otherwise I'll get really pissed off. If you need anything, whenever for whatever, don't hesitate for one second to call me, you hear?!'

'Yeah…'

'Promise!'

'I promise…'

I had never seen Victoria so distraught over me. It was the first time, admittedly, I'd laid something like this on her. Sprung her with it last moment, and it was understandable; that added pressure of responsibility. But she needn't have been so fraught with worry – I was almost seventeen.

'El, next time, tell me a day before that you're going out…' she chided.

'Sorry, Vic. I didn't think it through properly. Don't worry, though, I'm old enough. You were going out my age.'

'I was, but I was going out with friends by my side. Not all alone to who knew where.' She paused. 'So, where is this party and whose is it?'

'Finchley…'

'Finchley? Jesus!'

'And Lara's half-brother is having it. You know Lara? The girl with diabetes in my year?'

She nodded.

She turned into Edgware Station and pulled the handbrake.

'Listen. The only reason I'm letting you go is that it's still light outside and you'll get there before it gets dark. But there is no way I'm going to let you come home by yourself. You're not going to get raped and murdered walking home in the dead of night on my shift! So, you're going to text me the address, and I'll come and pick you up. And since Mum didn't give you a curfew, I'll let you stay till midnight. No later! If you want to leave earlier, call.'

'I don't want to wreck your night…'

'Don't even think that. You are to call no matter what. They'll be plenty of other nights for me, don't you worry. Now go, or you'll miss your bus.'

'Thanks, Vic. And sorry…'

'It's all right…' she softened. 'Have a lovely time.'

It must have been the most nerve-wracking bus-ride of my life. My heart couldn't hush throughout the whole journey, as one poor fingertip after another became a victim to my compulsive teeth. By the time the bus had reached Finchley Central, I'd become a pile of quavering bones. Thank God I'd laid that anti-perspirant on thick.

I was doing this. I was actually doing this. I was going to this effing party whether it killed me or not. Enough of the guarded skittishness. Enough on how I reacted when confronted with new and difficult situations. I despised that side of me, the constant fear of the unknown. I had to learn to survive. I had to grow up and, simultaneously, grow a spine.

Even if nobody talked to me all night, it wouldn't matter. It would be nice, for sure, if James said *hi* and chatted with me, but if he didn't, I'd accept that. It was what he'd said that rang true: it's a good chance to get out and have a good time. Yes. It was high time.

I walked on, closer, closer to my destiny. My ear caught the faintest beat of some hip-hop tune dispersing through the smooth evening air. It got louder as I approached, guiding me to the right house. 208.

An Edwardian detached of mansion-like proportions, assuming and hoity, dared me to enter. It wasn't enough that the guests were intimidating, the bloody house was too. Kids my age and older hung around the whole building in different groups, talking, drinking and some, dancing.

The front door was wide open, letting people come and go freely. No one gave me a second's notice. That was cool. Better to be ignored than to be made fun of.

I walked to the open front door and stepped in, as all of a sudden, my eardrums were assaulted with the blaring *BOOM, BOOM, BOOM* of the track. The house was jam-packed with people, all a reticulation of laughing, singing, shouting. Some girls had made a part of the living room into a dancefloor, as a DJ spun vinyl on a turntable. I didn't know anyone here. A small ball of panic began to germinate, threatening to grow. *Keep it together, El!* I looked to my right, partially into the kitchen, but still, no one. The house was vast; there could be someone I knew further in.

Careful not to squash the droplets of disregarded pizza scattered on the floor, I warily paced my way into the depths, passing toppled beer cans, plastic cups and other party paraphernalia. The unmistakable smell of cigarette smoke started to get to my lungs and throat, and something else, a more pungent, dry, sweetish waft, stagnant in the atmosphere. Weed. At this rate, I'd get high just by inhaling the air.

And then I saw her. Bianca. Dressed in short shorts, about to run up the stairs with a bottle of gin, she stopped in her tracks upon seeing me. The drunken smile disappeared and her usual sneer took over. She looked me up and down, not hiding her revulsion. I straightened my back, and jutted out my chin boldly, challenging her to dare do or say anything. The climate was torrid, a miasma of tense, foul heat that would take one fraction of a degree to ignite. She didn't move, however, and in that fraction of a second, that same feeling I'd had four months back, when I'd seen something pass over Sarah's eyes, came over me again.

'I believe *this* belongs to you,' I said in deliberate menacing tone, and stuck up my middle finger at her. She slurped some cliché about my weight, and I held up my palm in front of her face.

'Save it,' I spat. 'I've heard it all before. You have no originality, you sad, little cow. Go back to your cesspit, because nothing you say will ever harm me again.' And I turned, almost running with the exhilaration of what those words truly meant. They meant change was here. This was more than the *Sarah effect. This* was a whole new leaf.

I finally found a familiar face. Lara. She was in the kitchen talking to some friends of hers, a couple of whom I knew. They were all drinking beer from cans. Lara was the host, as well as her brother, and I felt I had to say some verbal thanks for being at her party. It was viable my presence would come as a surprise to her, knowing my status at school, but I prayed it wouldn't be a distasteful surprise. Lara was cool, in general. She maintained a neutrality to my bullying, so I laid my bet that she'd be OK with me being there.

She turned and stared at me, then the other three of her group turned. All four faces gawked, unmoving. I smiled and put up a hand and waved awkwardly. They made no answer. I wanted to disappear as I felt their criticising eyes scanning my attire. Not having asked Vic's advice on what to wear, I put on the only items of clothing I thought best for this night. Namely, black, dressy trousers and a ditsy, chiffon blouse. Did I look that bad? I felt the heat rise to my face, and I had no idea what to do or say.

Then Lara said with a chortle, 'Eleanora! Hi! I didn't know you were invited! Why didn't you say?'

I instantly let out a secret breath of relief and smiled again, full-toothed.

'Yeah… I was invited a while back but I had totally forgotten about it what with exams, then I was reminded of it on Thursday again… I came to say thank you for the invitation.'

'You forgot!' she said incredulous.

'Yeah, I know,' I said rolling my eyes, 'silly me!'

They tittered. It wasn't that funny. Then I realised they were a bit tipsy.

'You look really pretty, El!' said Sally, a girl in my English Lit class.

'Yeah,' said Lara. 'I like what you've done to your hair, and your eyes are so gorgeous!'

And before I knew it, I was being offered a beer and included in their conversation. What world had I just stepped into?

'Cheers!' said Jo, lifting her can. 'May we all pass our GCSEs with flying colours and never have to lay eyes on Madame Collard again!'

'Hear, hear!'

'I'll drink to that,' I said, and we all chinked our cans and gulped some bitter down. Lara burped vulgarly, sending us into laughter and grunts.

I turned then, and caught sight of a familiar shape way in the distance. It was him. He was outside in the garden, laughing about something with some friends. He had dark jeans on and a short-sleeved shirt, which left me breathless. He made a sudden movement, flaring an arm and squatting. My breath hitched. That… where had I seen that? Karate? No. He did it again, this time he had his fists clenched and was fake-punching some boy. The other boy was following suit. Then it came to me: boxing. My mind skimmed the times I'd watched those matches on TV with Dad. How I'd wanted to learn too. I'd begun in secret. Nobody knew. Taught myself styles and manoeuvres in the seclusion of my bedroom. It had been short lived, unfortunately.

James and the other boy were play-boxing, going through some techniques, as two other boys watched on, commenting and laughing. Then one of them said something, and they all started to make their way towards the house. James wore a face of complete contentedness. His laugh, his demeanour, his genuine happiness. It was summer; freedom, then off to Oxford. Off to a life of exciting, unknown latitudes.

If a person is beautiful from within, it shows on the outside – Gran. James was the quintessence of that, right then.

The girls' babble registered lightly through my musings, and my ears picked up a sentence.

'What was that about Bianca?' I asked Lara.

'She won't be at Hilsmond next year. She's going to do her A Levels at Chapel.'

I smiled. Excellent news. 'Thought you'd like that piece of information!' she grinned.

'Good riddance!' said Sally. 'I always hated it when she'd twist up her skirt and then lean forward, showing us her knickers on purpose! What was that?'

'Yeah, like, "look at my awesome groin"'! Talk about insecurity problem, right?' said Lara. 'Daddy issues?'

I shrugged. My days of trying to figure out Bianca's aberrant, idiosyncratic behaviour were over, and it looked like for good.

I looked in James's direction again.

'That boy is too gorgeous for his own good,' said the girl, whose name I didn't know, to me. She was looking directly at James.

'I don't know. Beauty is in the eye of the beer-holder!' Jo said.

'I kind of like his funny friend. I have a soft spot for skinny boys,' said Lara.

I was starting to get that woozy feeling. Muscles relaxing and brain reflexes slowing, when just then, Lara cried, 'Oh! I love this song!' and she grabbed my hand and started to make her way to the other room where people were dancing. A part of me wanted to wrench my hand from her grip and run. Not give fuel to the flame of taunt and jeer at my ridiculous moves on the dancefloor. But there was another part that spurred me on, to go for it. And I knew that part was in the right.

It was dark, the only light was from the three dance-floor lights flickering to the beat of the song – some club anthem. The uplifting tune helped me yield my dread, and I let myself go, shedding my fear bit by bit, as I felt the verve enter my senses. Lara was pounding the air, a freefall of ecstasy. Jo and Sally were holding hands and doing an exaggerated version of ring-a-ring-o-roses. Then I found myself singing along to the refrain. It was simple enough, and kept on repeating itself.

I was moving my head this way and that, when I spotted him walk in. He met my eye. I didn't cease dancing. How could I? I was having – for the first time in my life – fun. That, and perhaps the alcohol making me brave.

He bit his lip then smiled. It was coy and, dare I say it, sexy. I'd never seen him make that gesture before. His eyes drifted up and down my swaying body, and I couldn't stop my face from burning red hot, as my heart thudded hard, all self-conscious. I wanted him to take me away from there and kiss me. Bodies, hearts and lips touching. Explain to me why he had avoided me for so long, and how sorry he was for doing so…

He strode up to the little crowd of girls I was in, and held out his hand. I stared at it in momentary disbelief – I was being allowed to touch it? It had been months since the last time, and a gush of nervousness took hold. Nevertheless, I placed my trembling hand on his palm, as he closed his fingers around mine, then gently pulled me out of the crowd.

'I have to leave soon,' he said. 'I wanted…' He paused. 'Come…' he adjured.

Still holding my hand, he led me out into the garden, without a word. I was a pace behind, and my eyes were riveted to the back of his body. Those broad shoulders and lean waist. Then lower… what a perfect backside! He stopped under some ivy that was partially clinging to the exterior of the house with sprigs of it drooping down like a fairy curtain. A secret nook. Dusk was fading into dark, as he looked imploringly into my eyes. The faint glimmer of light from within the house, lined his features and glinted in his soft, blue irises. Coming closer, his face down, my face up, our bodies on the brink of touching. I could smell the sweet scent of something other than beer on his breath. Rum? Whiskey? He lifted his free hand and stroked the side of my face, sending me into shivers.

'Your eyes,' he said gently. 'Never seen anything like them.' Then he threaded his fingers through my hair, almost combing it, all the way down. His hand lingered on my back. An embrace. Our bodies touched. Both my breasts pushing into his firm, warm chest. He let in a breath. A burst of emotion unlike anything I'd ever felt collided through me; every nerve-ending stimulated my whole body.

He flicked his hair back slightly, and beheld me with eyes so tender, a look which whispered a thousand words. His face came closer. This was it. He had barely touched his lips to mine when, 'There you are, Jamie boy!'

We pulled away instantly, awkwardly. It was Nick. A thoroughly smashed Nick, cigarette in hand and a glass of something amber in the other. He was slurring something as he came swerving up to us.

'I'm sorry, Jamie… I was told to come and fetch you… so sorry…' Nick articulated with difficulty.

''S all right,' James answered, but the expression on his face showed otherwise. 'Who told you to come and get me?' He left my side to put Nick's arm over his shoulder, steadying him.

'The girls. They said they wanted to talk to you right away. They told me to run. Come… come…'

'But I'm leaving in half an hour, tops. I told you… My parents have something planned for my sister and I tomorrow morning. What do they want?' Nick was so plastered he didn't even answer James. James sighed and looked back at me apologetically. 'I'm sorry. I need to take him inside… see what's going on.'

'It's OK,' I reassured. I was in a blissful daze, still trying to get a grip on what was about to happen before Nick interrupted.

'I'm really sorry, Eleanora,' Nick said, turning back to me, in a half stupor. 'Forgive me…'

'It's OK, Nick…' I said, wondering why he wanted forgiveness, then just putting it down to him being wasted.

'Wait for me, yeah?' James asked, anxious I'd leave. I nodded and smiled shyly. His eyes lingered on mine for one more second, and then they were gone.

Gone…

Chapter Twenty

Now

'Police. How may I help you?' Her voice is upbeat.

I hesitate for a second, looking out of the classic, red K6 telephone box I found on the A1, to the church spire opposite. I haven't prepared what to say.

'Hi,' I say, heart racing. 'I… um… I have a question.'

'Yes?'

'What would be the penalty if someone gave false information on a crime?' There is a pause.

'It depends on the crime and when it happened.' Comes the answer.

Back then

I mused happily to myself, still lost in the trance of rapture. I giggled and bit my lip, just as he had done. *He wanted to kiss me. Our lips touched.* I waited for him to come. He knew I'd be waiting…

The garden was still. I couldn't see anyone else close by. The sound of a deep R&B tune flowed towards me. It was slow and soothing. Mariah conveying, we belonged together…

I propped myself on the ledge, and sat under the ivy, half shadowed by it.

Suddenly, a pained scream ripped through the stillness of the garden. It startled me for a second, but then I relaxed, thinking it was probably someone larking about. But then I heard it again; a shout, like someone's yelling coming from the end of the garden. I couldn't make out if it was a girl or a boy; the music was too close to my ear.

I shot up, off the ledge, still obscured by the ivy, not knowing what to do. Was it real or not? Was someone playing a game, or were they in genuine distress? Should I go and see, or would I be accosted for interfering?

Within seconds, however, I saw a movement emerge from the shadows. For a beat I thought it was a dog or a fox, just like our back garden was frequented by them at night, but soon enough, a male figure rushed out from behind the last shrubs, heading straight for the kitchen. He disappeared through them without having noticed me.

What was that all about? My heart had sped up, somewhat, on alert. Where was James? I was starting to get nervous. I didn't want to be outside alone. I waited one more minute, then made up my mind and went in.

I searched around the house. First on the ground floor, then I tried the stairs which led to the basement. I popped my head in. It was a recreational room, all carpeted and sound proof, with a big-screen TV. There were gamers playing on the Play Station and others gathered around the computer. A snooker table was situated a little way off, and there stood a sober bunch watching the players hit the ball with silent precision. He wasn't in there, but I thought I recognised the boy from the garden. His face was flushed and he was gulping down some beer, hands shaking. What had he been doing there? Why had he screamed?

He burped. 'Right! My turn bitches!' he hollered, and then he adjusted his crotch. I hated it when men did that, thinking nobody notices it. Everybody did.

'Just because it's your house, doesn't mean you can stop our game, mate!' said one of the guys, clicking on a joypad with vigour, not taking his eyes off the screen.

His house? So, *he* was Robert.

I left. I went upstairs with the beginnings of what seemed worriment. It was the only place I hadn't searched. James would have to be there. I got to the landing; the lights were off. A single, dimmed lamp shone weakly from a room creating an obscure shifting of shadows. I recognised the shaded shapes of heads, shoulders, arms moving quietly within the dark corners, touching close; some kids had found the opportunity to take advantage of their surroundings and were making out.

I looked down the landing, squinting. The music was muffled up here, and, at the very least, I could hear myself think. Things were getting weird. Where was he?

Suddenly, I caught Bianca drunkenly strutting from the bathroom to one of the rooms diagonal, her back to me. She disappeared inside. I remembered Nick telling James that the girls wanted him, and instantly I felt my heart give a pained beat. *Of course, you idiot. He was talking about* these *girls.*

I treaded slowly up to the door, my back rigid against the wall. I didn't want to be seen spying.

The door was partly open, but I couldn't see anyone. They all must have been sitting behind the wall I was up against. That thick, burnt smell of marijuana drifted through the crevice of the door. Great.

There was whispering and hushed talking, then a burst of laughter. That was Bianca's snort. I waited. A zippo lid opening… then closing. *Clink!* I didn't like what I was feeling. That lingering queasiness stuck to my stomach like I'd swallowed tar.

'How is it?' I heard Trisha say in a slow, intoxicated modulation. 'Is it good? Do you feel it?'

Feel what? My God! What were they doing? I peeked through the crack of the door where the hinges were. I could only discern a head. Nick's probably, judging from the colour and length of hair… and vapour swirling around.

'Jamie boy has finally popped his spliff cherry!' Nick slurred. 'Ha, ha, ha!' he laughed coarsely.

What?

'So, what were you doing out there with Eleanora? Ugh! I feel I have to rinse my mouth out after saying her name. Hope you were finally telling her the sad truth about herself.' *What? Me?* It was Bianca. A vindictive Bianca. Typical. I clenched my teeth.

'She's such a loser,' she continued. 'I mean, I bet she didn't even catch on, right?' *Catch on?*

'How long did you have to string her along before you told her to fug off?' *String me along?* What did Trisha mean? And why was she being so malicious? What did I ever do to *her*?

'Didn't take me long.'

My heart stopped. It was James. Then I heard him snort. *Snort!* 'That fucking ugly, anorexic bitch fell right for it! What… what an absolute, gullible… fucking loser!'

My ears rang. I couldn't draw breath. Everything stopped. No…No… He didn't say that! It was a joke. He was just joking…

Laughter broke out. Cackling. Mocking.

'She's so disgustingly skinny! All bony… Ugh! Wouldn't want to touch that, might catch something,' he continued, revulsion in his tone. My ears rang anew, the reverberation of each cruel syllable – his fist crushing my heart, squeezing the blood out. I stood paralysed, then the gasps escaped from my lips. I put my hand over my mouth to stifle a cry, as the tears flowed from my eyes.

'And her hair is like, creepy long, like a witch's…'

More contemptuous cackling, pungent with scorn. I made an anguished sound, but it was obliterated by their cachinnations.

'Looks like we saved you from her clutches just in time,' Bianca said. 'What a fugly cow! I hate her!'

'Fugly!' chimed in Trisha. 'Hahaha! Fugly El-the-smell!'

'El-the-smell!' Bianca squealed malevolently. 'Wait, wait. I've got one. El-what-the-hell!'

I wrapped my arms around my waist. My body ached. I actually swayed, my knees almost giving way, I had to take a step back not to fall. I held onto the wall. I crouched down, my diaphragm contracted, leaving me gasping. I was handed a heavy blow. One I didn't see coming, and it struck deep.

I took some steps back, away from the caustic words, the lies, the deceit. Away from him. I couldn't go in and confront him, damn it! I wanted to. I wanted to tell them all to go fuck themselves, but as usual, Eleanora was too weak. Eleanora couldn't face all of them. Eleanora couldn't face *him*!

I should have known. I should have known he was the same as the rest of them. No, he was worse; because *he* had led me on. He carried on like he cared, making me believe he liked me. A sycophant. A fraud. A liar.

I had been thoroughly disillusioned. Right from the start. Of course. Why would he like a loser?

I hid around a corner and cried. It didn't come out the usual way. It was the cry of a five-year-old. The short, cut off breaths of a victimized kid. I was pathetic. Bloody pathetic.

I drew a long, stuttered breath accompanied with a runny sniff. I needed to get out of there.

Just as I was about to descend, two girls were hurriedly climbing the stairs. One was holding the other girl up and guiding her footing. *Probably drunk,* I thought. Then, as she got closer, I noticed her face had scratches on it and her blouse was open. Ripped. She had been crying, as the mascara marks showed trickling down her cheeks. Her hair was in a state, and there were leaves in it. *Leaves?*

I gasped as I realised what I was witnessing. Leaves. The garden had leaves. The scream. It wasn't Robert screaming. It was this girl's scream.

The crying girl was muttering about how she just wanted to go home, how she didn't want to be in this house anymore. I seconded that feeling, and was about to leave, when the other girl said to her that she had to call the police. The crying girl shook her head. 'No... I don't want anyone to know...' She let out a wail that mirrored my pain.

'You must. He can't get away with it,' urged the other.

He can't get away with it, I thought. *He can't...*

And a revelation, an idea came to me so abruptly, I was already half-way down the stairs.

I found the land phone. There was a cordless charging in its slot in the kitchen. I swiped it and quickly exited a side door next to the fridge. It was less noisy outside, and I needed to be heard.

999, I pressed on the digits. In 2 seconds flat, the operator said, 'Emergency. Which service?'

'Police,' I said. I was connected and, in a fraction of a second, the officer on the other end answered.

'Police. What is your emergency?'

'There's been a rape. Please come quickly,' I said through the tears.

'We will need an address.'

'Two O eight, Saint Peter's Street.'

'Finchley?'

'Yes.'

'And you are, Miss?'

That wasn't important. All he needed to know was, 'It was James Laidlaw! James Laidlaw did it!'

Now

'It was a rape charge,' I say to the officer, as shame burns me.

'Are you saying the rape didn't happen?' she asks.

'No. I'm saying the person named for it, wasn't really the rapist.'

There is a pause.

'I see,' she says slowly. I guess she doesn't take these type of phone calls every day.

'When was the false information given?' she asks.

'Six years ago.'

Back Then

It was to get my own back. Just a little scare. I knew he wouldn't be charged because, firstly, he didn't do it, so there was no evidence. Secondly,

116

he had Nick, Bianca, and Trisha for alibis and thirdly, the girl herself knew who her real assaulter was. At least, that's what I told myself.

I fled the party like a thief as soon as I hung up, and ran down the street to the corner, whereupon I texted Vic to come and get me. I didn't know who would come first; the police or my sister. I had no idea how fast a response each would have or from what distance they would be coming.

It felt like a lifetime had passed until I saw the flashing-blue light from down the street come brighter and brighter. I was crouched behind a rubbish bin, shaded by a tree trunk and its branches, as they sped by me. They had no warning sirens on – their surprise tactic, I surmised. Only when they'd slowed outside the house did they blare their arrival to the partygoers. I heard terrified shouts and screams, and my body stiffened. The deep bass of the music suddenly ceased, like someone just cut the power. Some kids actually made their escape, as I saw fast bodies run between the shadows of the street.

I felt a gnawing sense of guilt, rapidly realising the police would find drugs and some kids would be in deep shit. James too. Perhaps the police would run drug tests on them? The thought made me cry out, 'Oh, shit! Shit!' I hadn't thought it through properly. What had I done?

Now

'What is the worst-case scenario if someone gives false information?' I ask.

'False information constitutes a fine. But the statute of limitations is over in this case, whereas for rape there are no limitations. We strongly advise you to come to the station and help with any information you can. The case might be unsolved.'

I swallow. 'I just want to clear his name,' I tell her. I don't want to get involved in a rape case.

'Clearing someone's name is done with a written statement,' she tells me. 'You'll have to go to the station in charge of the area the rape was committed so they can see the file and tell you there what needs to be done.'

'I see,' I say. 'Thank you…'

'No problem. But I strongly urge you to discuss it with an officer as soon as possible.'

Chapter Twenty-One

Back Then

Victoria came and got me near the A1, some 10 minutes later; oblivious to what was half a mile further east. She stank of cigarette smoke and booze, a stifling odour which made me want to convulse. But I couldn't attest if she was drunk; no other senses registered. I was deadened, apathetic.

She made a U-turn and left the way she came.

'That was quick! Weren't you having a good time, then?' she asked.

I didn't answer. I couldn't. I started to shiver.

'Aww,' she teased. 'Shame!'

Silence.

Vic caught my tenor and didn't say anything else. She dropped me off at home then left to continue her night out. It was barely 11 o'clock. I opened the door and went upstairs. Mum called out something about it being me, and I muttered, 'Yeah…'

I went to my room and bawled in my pillow.

'You idiot. You stupid, fucking idiot…'

Now

I get back home, load every single tab from my browser history from the past few days, and read again. Names. People. Places. Numbers. Pictures.

'Come on! What is it? Where are you hiding?'

It isn't a picture. Definitely not. Number? Apart from the address numbers, nothing. The addresses… the places. Canary Wharf. The storeroom. What connected James with Tom Garner and Canary Wharf? I click on the ancestral page and study the names one by one, fastidiously. The people? Then I run the list of employees at GSY, and there… there it is!

A name. *The* name.

Back Then

The sharp ring shot through the sleeping house, jolting me awake. Mum's footsteps ran frantically to pick up the phone. I gasped. I had fallen asleep. What time was it? I glanced at my alarm clock. 03:21.

'Hello?' Mum's shrill voice sounded. A pause.

'Oh, my goodness! What happened?' she yelled. My heart seized. I scrambled out of bed to where she was, afraid of what I might hear. What fearful news lay ahead? Vic. Vic wasn't home.

'An accident? Jesus Christ! Yes. Yes. I'm on my way. Thank you.' Mum turned to me, ashen, hand on her heart and trembling violently. I had started to cry. 'WHAT? WHAT?' I screamed, frenzied, knees bucking, falling to the floor.

'She's... she's in surgery...'

That's all I wanted to hear. I released my terror with a heavy gasp. Surgery was good. Surgery meant she was alive. Alive, not dead. My sister was still alive.

We called a cab, too shaken to drive, and went to the hospital, terrified something bad was going to happen before we got there. Vic wasn't out of the woods yet. Mum was praying, tears streaming down her face, clutching me tight. The cab driver worried for us, silently driving. The first hints of dawn, in the horizon, painting the sky in a dark, white veil.

Please, God. Not Vic. Not my sister... Not her too...

We entered the hospital, running to the first medic we saw.

'Victoria Stephens!' Mum cried. 'Any news on Victoria Stephens?'

The nurse called for a doctor.

Victoria would be fine, the doctor said. I cried anew. The relief, the ache of fear released into a flow of joyful tears. That was all that mattered. Vic was alive and she was going to make it.

Everything else didn't seem that important anymore.

***

Eight o'clock in the morning, Mum and I came home, leaving Victoria to recuperate under the aid of professionals. Mum prepared a small suitcase, and told me she was going back to the hospital, and that I should get some rest.

She left.

I went to the bathroom upstairs. I walked to the sink, looked in the mirror, stared at my blotched, pale face, and spat. I despised myself, because there was my poor sister, lying in a hospital bed, and I had the gall, the audacity, to think my petty problem was the worst thing on earth. I recalled his words, how they had torn through me. I remembered what Gran had said to Vic after her first breakup: *If he doesn't want you once, then you don't want him ten times.*

I closed my eyes and gave him no more tears. I didn't want anything else to remind me of him. I got under the shower, washing off, washing his touch off. Enough... enough of him. Enough of that boy who didn't deserve my tears.

I got out, water dripping from my naked body to the floor, opened the medical cabinet, and took out a pair of sharp scissors. I turned to the mirror again, grabbed a fistful of all my hair close to my scalp – hair he had touched. I angled the scissors and cut, cut him off, extricating myself with each falling tress.

Chapter Twenty-Two

Now

Nicholas Barton.

I don't know who he is, but his name is on both Garner's family tree and the GSY employee list. Apparently, he is a nephew of Garner's; his sister, Sadie's, son, aged 24. She was married to a Henry Barton and together they had produced two sons. Frederick and Nicholas. Nicholas being the youngest.

The only Nicholas I know James knew, is Nick – Nick... Nick what? I pause, realising I have no idea what his surname is. Could it be him? The age fits. I type on the browser for Milden's archives; a slim chance they'd publicise the names of former pupils. The page is filled with platitudes of their notable alumni but no record to download, no file to click onto. 'The School will be happy to answer any enquiries,' it says. I dial the contact number the site has to offer, but no one answers except for a machine, informing me the school is closed for Easter. I don't believe *nobody* is there, the place *is* a semi-boarding school. There has to be someone in charge of the boys who haven't gone home, surely.

I hasten to the Tube, one stop up to Golders Green, and then the two-four-two ...for the first time in years. 4 to be precise. What a singular sensation that conjures; Milden revisited. Jesus.

I mount the two-four-two, the surroundings bring forth an innate revival of my formative years riding this bus. I sit in that same place by the window, as instinctive as I had done back then, and as the journey takes me closer to familiar tacks, it evokes narratives of my past. Instances, both wonderful and depressing.

A little after passing Middlesex University, the bus stops. Its doors open, and a petite figure steps on. I take in an incredulous breath. I almost laugh. There she is – the old, Asian woman, not having changed a jot. She quickly hovers to a seat, and as she is about to turn to sit, one hand on the rail so the bus's tug won't fling her light body to the floor, she involuntarily tilts her head to the side, and spots me staring at her. I am already smiling. It takes her half a tick to remember who I am, then her wise face is lucent, returning the smile.

***

The creamy-white stone of the Greco-Roman edifice overshadows most of the road, as the bus rolls to its stop. The doors fling open and, for a heartbeat, I hesitate. At once my mind is filled with a bluster of images of bygone days. Pupils clustered together, others in little groups, all shivering, waiting to go home, but happy the day is over. Of course, now, the Milden pathway is devoid of pupils. Just one quondam individual. Me.
 'You gonna get off, love?' calls the bus driver. How long have I been standing there?
 'Oh, yeah. Sorry.' I quickly jump off and walk straight to the main entrance, as I hear the grinding whirr of the engine pull out.
 Milden is ginormous. All is quiet; just a sonance of life dimly vibrating further in. A sign says "Office", and I turn in the direction it offers.
Through a long corridor, I find two ladies behind computers having a chat.
 'Good morning,' I say. They look at me and jump, like they've been caught red handed. They were gossiping about something saucy, I suspect.
 'Good morning,' one says, then clears her throat. The other nods a *hello* and turns to her computer.
 'How may we help you?' Number One asks. I proceed, straight to the point.
 'I'd like to know whether Nicholas Barton graduated from this school in two thousand eight.'
 'Barton,' she says, narrowing her eyes in thought. 'That rings a bell…'
 'Oh, come on,' interrupts Number Two. 'The arrest! Who can forget that?'
 'Oh, yes!' Number One says, as her face dawns. 'Yes. Well, he had officially finished school before he got arrested, so typically and formally, he is an alumnus… You *do* know about his arrest?' She looks at me, worried she might have said a bit too much.
 'No…'

Back Then

121

As soon as Victoria was well enough, we left for Greece. 'Nothing like some good rest for all of us,' Mum had said, and she'd booked tickets for practically the whole summer.

Padma and I had managed to meet up in Athens as arranged. We usually stayed for a week in our grandparents' cramped flat before we left for London. Soak up some of the ancient history in our neck of the woods, which basically meant taking goofy photos in front of the Parthenon.

There was no word, no details on what had happened at the party, and I was dying to know if Padma had heard anything. I'd searched online, day after day, typing keywords that might cache an answer, but to no avail. I didn't know everyone at the party, and was sure something of the tragic outcome would have been referred to in someone's social media account. So I typed the names of the people I did know, who had been there, and to my surprise, Bianca's, Trisha's and Lara's accounts were all deactivated. Gone. Nick had said he never put personal details on the World Wide Web, being against the mass roundup of stored, profiled information. Being a hacker, he knew! And James? I knew he didn't have an account, long since. I'd checked. I, too, had never gone to the trouble of creating one. Get cyber bullied on top of normal bullying? Forget *that*.

Padma had heard the police had come to the party but nothing more. She hadn't been there, and none of her friends either, apart from me...   •

'I suppose we'll find out when we get back,' she said, sucking the straw of her frappe. 'Mind you, most of that lot won't be there. Trisha and Bianca would have got expelled, but they'd already applied to other schools, so Mrs Lake didn't have to lift a finger. Good riddance, I say...'

***

I was now a Sixth-former. Two more years and school would be over. A-level subjects chosen: Classical Civilisation (easy A), Art with Art History (... easy A), English Literature (not so easy A) and AS Ancient Greek (I'd be lucky if I passed). Goodbye, Mathematics – our relationship didn't work out.

September and autumn. The fall, as they say in America. The falling of leaves, the renewal of life. Out with the old, in with the new. Nature's cycle was beginning again, and so was mine.

The street I lived on was filled with deciduous trees, all turning a rusty colour and sprinkling the road with their first moulting. Within days the whole road through would be a golden-red tunnel. A magical pathway, where I'd daydream of knights in shining armour and ardent trysts, hidden amongst the luring tree trunks and low-hanging branches. My easel was out, and painting the life out of every canvas. A superabundance, like Monet did with his *Grainstacks*, capturing the different light, each changing harmony of colour. I loved autumn.

***

One week in of school, and there were the first rumours circulating about the tragic party. I was hesitant to ask and find out what happened; too afraid of what I might hear. Only whispers and occasional glances fell my way, but nothing was directed straight at me. People knew I had been at the party but nothing more. Nobody had seen me call the police, and I hadn't left a name. They were scrounging for gossip. There was only one girl, I knew, who would know. Lara. I'd learnt from Padma, she and Robert had been grounded so severely, they weren't even allowed to speak to her friends all through summer, and any online accounts were suspended.

I found her sitting by herself in the cafeteria, one relatively warm afternoon.

I came up to her table and stopped. She turned and looked to see who it was, and her munching halted.

'Can I sit down?' I asked. She nodded and gave me a sad smile, then swallowed the rest of her food down as if it was made of sandpaper.

'Can we talk?' I asked tentatively. She looked down. 'I know you're not allowed to, but I need to know. I'd left early that night, and I never found out what happened.'

She didn't open her mouth.

'Look,' I said, 'you don't have to tell me details, just tell me what happened to… someone in particular… Please, Lara. I have to know. I can't find anything online, and everybody who was there has left –'

'Who do you want to know about?' she asked, defensive.

'James.'

'James?' She looked uncertain she knew him.

'James? James Laidlaw? The guy who'd taken me from the dancefloor? You said you liked his skinny friend, remember?'

'Oh… yeah… Sorry, El. I don't remember much. I was shitfaced. He was Rob's friend, right? I don't know what happened to him… I was in the loo, being sick.'

I rubbed my temples. 'Shit…' I uttered.

'El, you have to know.' Lara grabbed my hand. Her eyes watery. 'It was very likely he got arrested; lots of kids did, but they got off with a warning, or paid on-the-spot fines. Some of the lucky ones made a run for it as soon as they heard sirens. But I don't know about James… My parents had come and taken me home after I'd thrown my guts up. Dad stayed to help Rob… it was a mess. The police said there had been two phone calls from the house, both claiming there'd been a rape. I mean, who'd say such a thing?'

'Maybe the girl who'd been raped?' I said, indignant, trying to hide my disgust in her brother. So, the assaulted girl and her friend had rung the police too?

Lara hung her head and sobbed. 'I don't want to talk about it anymore…'

I put my arm over her shoulder. If her brother really raped that girl, then she had plenty of hardships ahead of her. 'Oh, Lara… I'm so sorry…' *Sorry for everything…*

A fortnight later, Lara left Hilsmond. Apparently, she wanted to leave because of all the hassle the girls were giving her over the party. She wanted to go somewhere where nobody knew her or of that night. Rumour had it, she had slit her wrists to get her point across. It'd done the job.

So, I never got to hear any more news on the matter. I believed all was settled. There had been a kerfuffle at a wild party, and now it was over. The boys and girls continued their lives, as did I.

I felt my mind ease from the tumult and the self-loathing weighing in the depths of my conscience. I was guilty, responsible for getting all those kids into trouble, but they were all right now, continuing their lives as normal. I suppose a good lesson learnt – for me in particular. Thus, time went by, and all tempestuous thoughts from that night ebbed into a ripple of distant memory.

A year went by without any shock-worthy events, the placid flow of time chaperoning me to adulthood.

I felt a restlessness, a yearning to do something more. A job, perhaps.

I applied to various shops but no one replied. Then after about a month of job-hunting, Mum decided to remember that she knew someone who knew someone who was a manager in one of the largest shoe-shops in one of the largest shopping centres in North London. And after finally landing an interview, I was hired, part-time, working on Friday afternoons and all day Saturday, at N&L Shoes and Leather Goods.

Now

'Oh, dear,' the secretary says, plainly distraught. I see her move uncomfortably behind her computer. She put herself in a precarious position, but I lied, partially. I knew there had been arrests but not specific names. I made like I didn't know anything about the party in the hope of her elaborating.

'I never really found out what precisely happened. Could you tell me, perhaps, what you know of that night?'

She shakes her head. 'All I know is the police had turned up, and there had been quite a number of arrests. Some boys who were over eighteen had been questioned and given on-the-spot fines. I can't remember specifically.

But the good thing was, it happened after school was over. I remember we were all thankful Milden wasn't tainted.'

'The school kept it hush hush, so did the parents. And as luck would have it, there was no report of it in the papers either,' put in the other woman. 'That was a good thing, I can tell you.'

'But you remember Barton, specifically. Why is that?' I ask them.

'Oh, well, because he was in possession, wasn't he?' She says it like I ought to have known. 'It didn't come as a surprise, mind you. He was always getting into trouble about something or other. I don't think a full week went by without hearing Nick Barton's name being talked of amongst the faculty. It was him and another lad. What was his name?' She turns to her colleague. Her colleague shakes her head, not being able to remember.

'Can't remember that one. He hadn't been with us for long. He was a new boy. Don't think I heard his name before that night.'

'Was it James Laidlaw by any chance?' I ask, and hold my breath.

'You know, I think that's it!' she crows. My psyche experiences the complete opposite quality. I inwardly berate myself. Why hadn't I thought of that contingency? Why hadn't I stopped myself acting in the heat of the moment? I was rash, unthinking. Stupid. Possession of drugs is, indeed, a more serious charge, but could it have been the cause of his present-day situation – a repercussion of that night?

I take my leave of the two women, too wrought with guilt at my calumny for any further discourse. They don't know much else, at any rate.

I jog to Mill Hill East. I'm not going to go home. I can't. I'm going to go to Camden. I must speak to him. Now that I know he was arrested specifically, I need to apologise. I feel guilt drown me.

I exit Camden Town Tube. I go up the escalator, up and up. I feel that expectant, sharp chill nip my cheeks and nape, sending its frigid fingers down the span of my spine.

I sit near the Lock, waiting. He isn't home – I've already checked; padlock on the outside.

So, I wait and stare at the road he'll need to turn into to get home.

It is starting to get dark.

Chapter Twenty-Three

Now

A hand juts in front of me unexpectedly. I look down at it, notice a one-pound coin in it, and look up at the person offering it to me. Male, with a kind smile, smooth on his dark-skinned face, and serious dreadlocks under a knitted hat with the colours of Jamaica. He thinks I'm homeless. Do I look that wretched?

'I'm not homeless,' I say. He lowers his hand. I smile uncomfortably. 'Thank you, anyway,' I say.

He starts to walk away. 'You'd better get home,' he says with a strong, Jamaican accent. 'This is not a place for a pretty girl to be alone at night.'

I stare after him. He's right; it's time I left.

I have been going over the latest information again and again. My brain has gone numb. Nick must have offered his uncle's storeroom to James. Apparently, they are still friends. But if Nick had been arrested as well as James, then how come Nick has a super position in a company and James... doesn't? The police must hold the key to that, or better yet, his family?

I put my hood up, shivering reflexively. I make one step towards the station and then freeze, taking in a sharp breath of air. He's startled me. He's just turned into the street I am in, walking swiftly, head down against the coolness of the night, brows drawn together, thinking, thinking, thinking. His gym-bag straps are over one shoulder as the rest of the bag bulges from behind him, hands stuffed in his jacket pockets. The light strands of hair flowing down from his shoulders under his beanie. They almost look white in the street lamplight against the stygian backdrop. Chiaroscuro – a Caravaggio.

My pulse comes alive as he makes his way closer and closer to me. I suddenly panic. I can't! I can't go through with it. I hide beneath my hood, letting the lamplight shade my face. He rushes into the side street, his jacket brushing mine by mere millimetres – a blessed miss.

I breathe hard, calming myself, as his retreating form disappears around a corner. I don't know why I lack the courage. Didn't I say I would speak to him? Why am I hiding? Why am I so afraid? I'm not the sixteen-year-old Eleanora anymore. Get a grip!

I move, determined, towards him. I stride to the last stretch where I can discern the wall in the distance. I pace one step in the silent, static night.

'AGHH!' A sharp cry rips into the night air, and my heart leaps. What was that? It came from behind the wall. James! The adrenaline surges through me, and I run.

'AGHH!' comes another pained shout. I hear swearing, and sounds of punching and ripping of material. Something whams into a rubbish bin, and the loud clatter of it toppling over to the ground reverberates through the alley. I halt, dead still. *What's going –*

''Ad enough?' says a gruff voice. I do not breathe. Who is that? I stare at the wall, my mind going wild with what might be on the other side. I am one step away. I carefully move my feet in silence. I reach the edge – heart thrashing – and look slowly around the side. It takes me three seconds to see two large men over James's sprawled body, as he is gasping for air, half-conscious. He can barely move. I can't see his whole face, just his crown, hair spread on the filthy ground. One of the men's leg hides the majority of it. *What is going on?* I want to stop them, but I fear them. I am no match… they'll probably render me to the ground too.

'Get on wiv i'!' says one of them, deep cockney. Then I hear a quick, sharp, metallic sound— *clink, clink,* and my heart stops. Do they have some kind of weapon? A gun?

'No!' the other one hisses. 'Nothing that can be traced.'

Traced?

They want to kill him? I turn back, I don't see; only hear the thwack across the face. The sound is horrendous; whipping flesh on bone. I run to a parked car on the other end of the wall, expensive and I hope equipped with a blaring alarm. I heave, all the force of my arms and body, and sway it in hope the alarm will start, tugging on the door handle. *PLEASE!*

It does. The high-pitched wail tears through my ears, startling me and hopefully those men.

I run for my life, turn and bolt back to the street, my phone open as I dial 999, praying dear God, I have stopped more harm being done to James.

'Ambulance! Please… he needs an ambulance!' I am shaking badly. 'Come quickly!' I check behind me, feeling a sudden dread they are coming. A voice from dispatch is saying something, but I have no time to hear.

'I can't speak, I'm afraid… Please come for him…'

I duck into an adjoining street and run again, distancing myself from those men. I am closer to the main street now. That's good – the sounds will muffle my screaming down the phone to the woman on the other end.

She asks me for the address, and I give the name of the street behind the garage where the blond-highlighted mother lives, explaining where about the alleyway is and how they'll have better access from there.

'Come quickly! Please come quickly! Please!' I hang up, trembling.

I wipe my eyes again and again.

I want to be near him. He is lying in the street, cold – maybe dead! *No, no… No, God, please!*

Have those men gone? Blood pounds, my mind saying not to go back – it isn't safe, my heart not listening as my feet obey my heart, and I steadily walk back; internal debate is over.

I take a few steps and almost stop dead in my tracks, as I see the two incredibly tall, muscle-bound men stride up the road towards me. I turn back, run and duck into the entryway of a house, fast. I kneel down in the darkness and dare not breathe. I am scared, yes, but I am sanguine. Sanguine, because deep within, I am rejoicing. I've seen them. I've seen their faces. I've seen their stature. I have seen their everything.

127

'Did you get the stuff?' says one, low voiced; probably thinking he can't be heard. With a deep baritone like that, who was he fooling?

'Yeah. Let's get da fuck out,' answers the other, not bothering to keep his voice down.

They cross the road to a parked vehicle, some SUV make I've never seen before, with the same darkly-tinted windows as the Tahoe at Canary Wharf. They rev the engine and drive away.

I bolt.

I turn to the alley, half-insane with worry, and see he is motionless, still lying on his back.

'Oh, my God! Oh, my God!' I gasp, as I kneel down next to his head, now more able to see the full extent of damage. A weak emission of condensed air escapes his mouth – his nose is one, bloody mess. But he is alive. He is alive.

His coat has been ripped open, and his sweatshirt has soaked up blood like ink to blotting paper. I lift a shaking hand and touch him for the first time …after so long. I put my hand on his heart, strong, rhythmical beats. I touch his hand, it is gelid. He's lost too much blood, and him lying on the cold, wet ground isn't helping. Quickly, I take off my jacket and then my jumper, and with my good hand, lift his head and quickly place the jumper under it with my bad hand, bunched up like a pillow. The strain strikes through my wrist but I ignore it. I place my jacket on him for warmth, shivering from my sudden lack of clothes, left only with my vest and bra. I smooth a strand of his hair back, careful not to touch his open wounds lest I infect them. There's a deep cut on the bottom of his right jaw line. His eyes are swelling, and blood has stopped trickling from his nose. There is blood and saliva dripping from his lips. I put my arm around the crown of his head, half cradling, like a saint's halo in a Byzantine icon, and remain there until I hear the sirens come in the distance.

'Mhmm…' he murmurs. He moves his head slightly, without opening an eye – he can't, even if he wants to.

'Don't move, James,' I whisper to him, tears anew streaming down my face, happy tears, as anxiety is subdued in seeing him responsive. 'The ambulance is coming. You're safe now…'

I look around me; his gym bag has been thrown further down. I bring it closer to him, so the paramedics can take it and not be stolen.

The glow from the ambulance's lights douse the houses in blue flickers. They are here.

But this is where I leave him, picking up just my coat, and I run.

A crime has been committed, I think with sudden clear-headedness, as I run passed the Lock. I, too, may have committed a crime by following him, stalking him. The police; they'll want to know. They'll want to know how I came to be there. I am not prepared. I am scared. I don't want to tell them the reason I was there, not until I know how serious following someone without their knowledge is. Kate had reassured me, but I want solid proof. But most of all, I don't want James to find out I followed him before I am prepared to tell all.

He is in good hands now, in any case. Whether I stay or not, it is of little difference to his current, physical well-being.

PART TWO

Chapter Twenty-Four

Back Then

'Hello, everyone. How are we all doing today? Just a couple of things before we open. First, I'd like to introduce you to Eleanora Stephens, who will be working for us on Fridays and Saturdays. Everybody say hi.'

'Hi,' said everybody drowsily. I was being introduced by Roselyn, the Shop Supervisor at N&L Shoes, to the rest of the employees, bright and early, before the shopfront shutters were fully open.

'Tell us a little bit about yourself.'

Everyone, dressed in an awful uniform – boys in unstimulating blues and girls in light blues with a long, tight skirt –, was sitting on the long, comfy sofa to one side of the shop, looking up at me with assorted expressions on their faces. The three boys were smiling and a couple of the girls. The other ten or so were either seriously unimpressed or just plain bored. One was even playing with her split ends.

'Hi!' I said back to them, forcing myself to speak as the nerves were predominant. My first day, and I wanted to make a good impression. I took in a big breath.

'Well, um, you can call me El. I'm finishing off my A Levels. I've never worked before, so I hope I do well here…' I said, without any self-confidence. There was a second's awkward silence.

'Lovely,' said Roselyn in her curt, professional way. 'You'll get to learn everyone's names today, as you work, but we are a bit pressed for time, so take a seat on the sofa now, El, while I quickly go over today's goal.'

I had no idea what she was talking about, but obediently walked over to the sofa, which had hardly any space for me to sit, unless I placed half my arse on one of the boy's lap. He saw me quiz over the small space and budged up a little more for me to sit, smiling in the process. He couldn't have been older than me – he still had that young, babyish face and unmuscular boyish lank. But his smile was dead sexy, what with that dimple, and he knew it. I sat, trying not to touch my thigh to his. Failed.

'All right,' began Roselyn. 'Today's goal is twenty-two thousand, guys…'

Twenty-two thousand? Twenty-two thousand *Pounds*? Did she mean we were to sell twenty-two-thousand-pounds worth of goods for today alone? I could feel myself gape in disbelief at the astronomical sum. How were we to pull that off?

'And as for the sundries, please try to sell some, otherwise they'll expire, and it'll be a waste. Tell them how important it is to take care of their new, two-hundred-and-fifty-quid shoe by protecting the sensitive leather, and stress it even more for nubuck or suede, all right guys?'

Everyone bobbed their heads in consent.

'And I want to see you all bring out at least two bags whenever you serve a customer. And boys, don't underestimate the power of your compliments to the women. They'll buy the shoe much quicker if they think a guy likes it on them. The same goes for you girls with the men.'

For the most part, it was all Greek to me. There was, however, one point I did comprehend. When Roselyn said "compliments" she meant "fibs".

There was a low buzz of commenting from among the employees. Just then, our manager, Mr Millard, trod into the centre of the shop with a peremptory flair, hands behind his back, eyeing all of us. He was short and straightened his back as high as it would take him. Those extra millimetres making no difference whatsoever. From the quick five-minute interview I'd had with him, I gathered he was harbouring some kind of grudge against women. He spoke abruptly to me and put on an air of condescension, almost recoiling, whenever I answered his questions. I wasn't a good judge of character, and may have been wrong, but that was what I had felt. Later, I would discover he had absolutely no sense of humour.

'So,' Roslyn said, after finishing her update to everyone, 'let's make it a good day, people!'

130

This must have been the signal for "time to work", as all the assistants got up lethargically from the sofa, and went towards a narrow opening in the wall, which took them to the area behind the shop, where stacks upon stacks, row upon row, of shoeboxes were stored. I was shown a small bathroom and a kitchenette hidden within where we could sit and have a rushed break for lunch.

'El, you'll be with Kate Ward today,' Roselyn informed me. I looked at her, confused. Kate? Be with Kate? What did that mean?

'Kate!' Roselyn called to her side at a bunch of girls.

'Coming!' cried one of the girls, making her way towards us.

'OK, Kate. El is going to shadow you today. Show her the ropes,' Roselyn declared. 'I'll leave you to it then!' And she was off, leaving Kate and I looking awkwardly at one another. The first thing I noticed was her completely bare face. She hadn't an ounce of makeup anywhere. No soft eyeliner. No light mascara. No hint of lippy. Nothing. The other girls looked like they'd caked it on with a spatula, from what I saw earlier. Kate, however, didn't really need it, granted. Her skin was clear, no blemish in sight. She might not have had the most striking visage in the world but it was dainty enough. I smiled. She had her eyebrows raised, discreetly measuring me up, just as I was doing to her. Then, a big smile broke out and she said, 'Come on, then!' with a jerk of the head, and off we went.

And show me the ropes, she did. I tailed her everywhere. She expounded knowhow on finding a specific pair of shoes amidst the thousands stacked in the stockroom, in under thirty seconds. How each were labelled and their taxonomy. She demonstrated a tactic on how to pull out the lowest shoebox from a pile without the other boxes on top falling to the floor. She executed the sale of a pair of patent, riding boots to a particularly fussy customer, but clinched it when I had mumbled feebly to the customer on how if worse came to worst, they could always return them. Kate had given me a high-five as soon as the customer left the shop with her boots. Then she went inside the stockroom, pulled out my sales card, and wrote my first sell on it. I had protested, telling her it was *her* customer, but she wouldn't hear of it.

'I was about to lose the sale; I could see it in her face. If it weren't for you, I wouldn't have sold it.'

At the end of the day, I calculated a rough estimate. Each of the assistants had sold an average of 15 shoes and 4 bags, ranging from £40 - £195. The mean of which was £117 and 50p. So, 19 times 117.5 made 2,232.5. Then, I punched in the last multiplication on my phone, of the 14 sales assistants, not including me, and was gobsmacked at the sum. Needless to say, Roselyn got what she wanted …with extra cream.

'Jesus Christ! What happened?' Kate's voice startles me; I wasn't expecting her to be home. 'You look like death itself.'

I squint at her, my eyes hurt from the incessant tears. I drop on the sofa; all energy has been pumped out of me.

'Why are you covered in blood? Where's your jumper? El?' She is alarmed, scared.

I blink up at her, then down at my hands. Bloodied and trembling from the aftermath.

'They were going to kill him,' I utter.

'What?' she cries. 'What do you mean? Who? Kill who?'

'James…'

'El? You're scaring me. Tell me what happened. Everything. From beginning till end.'

I tell her. I tell all of what transpired in the alley. She doesn't move, just silently sobs and holds both her hands in mine, shaking her head, aggrieved. 'I can't believe it,' she whispers, when I finish my horrifying account. 'Sounds like they were lying in wait.'

'Yeah. And they knew what they were after.' We sit in quiet thought for a second, then Kate spells what I am thinking.

'Drugs?' she asks.

I shrug. 'God, I hope not.' I sob as the battered image of him comes so vividly to mind. 'He almost… died…' The last word comes out almost inaudibly.

'He'll be fine, you'll see,' she says, trying her best to soothe, her voice filled with sadness for him. For me.

'I… I stopped them in time… I stopped them from killing him…' I burst into tears, grateful tears, trembling still. I cannot calm. I cannot calm.

'Oh, El!' Kate wipes an eye and puts her arm around me. 'You did… you did… he is safe now.'

I lay my head down on the sofa with a strange apprehension making its way through the crevices of my thoughts. I have no idea what bothers me and sheer weariness makes it impossible to pursue it any further. And for once, I fall asleep right away. A dense, uninterrupted repose with no cataclysm of fret and harrowing thought. How rare, yet there it was.

I wake the next day in the same place, covered with a thick, fleece blanket and the scent of coffee.

'Kate?' I say croakily.

'Hey,' she says softly. 'You up?'

'Yeah…'

'How are you feeling?'

'I'm aching everywhere,' I tell her as I sit up, stretching gradually, rubbing at my nape. I pace heavily to my laptop. By the time I finish in the bathroom, it will be on the ready.

'El?' I turn to her. 'Don't get a shock when you see your face in the mirror… I wanted to wake you but…'

My face has crusty patches of his blood. I wiped my blood-stained hands across my nose last night, and there are marks left. That's why I got strange looks on the Tube home. I was in shock; last night was a surreal, invidious nightmare. Little heed did I give to my appearance. My mind was only on him.

I remember him now, as an anguished cry escapes my lips. His face, his body; the way he looked. Helpless, harmed, fallen to the ground, beaten within an inch of his life.

Why? Why? What was it all about? Who were those men? What had he done? Who is he?

I undress and get in the bath, and let the torrent of hot water wash over me, the scathing pain in my wrist is nothing compared to my inner torment. Where is the catharsis now? Nowhere, because I am not worthy of it. If it weren't for me and that bloody phone call, he wouldn't have been arrested. None of them would have been arrested. But why was he in possession, though? It sounds so out of character. He had such deep morals… I think now on what that thug said, about him getting *the stuff*. Could James really be consorting in drugs? Was this another means for sustaining his life? Were things that bad?

I pull on my jeans and an unironed top. I don't care – no one'll see it under my parka, anyway.

'Coffee?' Kate calls, as I get to my PC.

'I can't. I feel like shit.'

'You'll feel better after a sip. I promise,' she urges. I take one sip, not feeling much different but trying not to show it.

'Kate? I shouldn't have told you anything last night…I'm sorry… The police might ask you questions –'

She cuts me off. 'El? Are you kidding?' She has a peculiar grin.

'No. Why?'

'It's a whole new ball game now. Don't you see?'

'No…'

'You have become an eye witness to a crime. That's leverage!'

'Leverage for what?'

'Anything you bloody well want!'

I know I have to go to the police. I am an eye witness. I am *the* eye witness. I should. But I don't. Despite the importance, I'm set to finish what I've started. If anything, I feel the need to clear his name, in the eyes of the police, even more pronounced after this. My injustice put right. I'm going to go to the police station that was in charge that night.

I type in the search engine to see if James's parents are listed. I find only one Laidlaw in Edgware. The house is close to where James used to take the bus. I know where it is. I know that area like the back of my hand. After the police, I'm going to them. I want to apologise, to explain my place in getting their son arrested. And beg for their forgiveness. No… not then. There is one more person who could shed light. Nick. I need the whole story.

Bringing up another tab, I search for anything I can on the legalities of following a person. I don't get to read much; my head is throbbing.

'I'll be out tonight,' Kate announces.

I nod unenthusiastically. 'Stuart?'

'Yeah. We're going to try that new Korean place near Marble Arch.'

'It looks good,' I say quietly.

'You're welcome to come, if you want,' she tells me. 'Come and unwind.'

'I don't think Korean will quite cut it.'

'Tomorrow, then? You, me and some margaritas.' She's trying, bless her.

'Lovely offer.' I sigh. 'But I need to sort this business out first. You know me: no stone unturned.'

'OK. I'm off… shit!' she says, looking at the time. 'Take care, and keep me updated.'

Bam! goes the door behind her, and with it half the crusty paint. I sigh and get out the pan and brush.

***

I spot the Victorian-style, blue lamppost – an augury awaiting. I only realise then, every police station has one. It's strange what you don't really take heed in – truly notice – only when it becomes part of your life.

I enter a muggy front area, humidity so stagnant, I want to strip. It's full of notices of missing people and have-you-seen-this-man pictures with ugly mugshots of criminals. People around are either sitting, waiting, or making inquiries to uniformed officers, in hushed voices.

I get to the desk sergeant and awkwardly explain the reason I'm there. I wait for some look, some judgmental brow, but nothing. He just takes my name and begs me wait.

As I sit, I reflect. How strange I am here; something I never thought would happen in my life, especially not in the capacity I am today. I'm about to execute one of the most difficult moves on the chessboard that is my life. Not in a million years did I think I'd end up having to give such a condemning account of my contemptible behaviour. It never passed my mind there could have been this day – my day of judgment. I am to admit I lied to these people, perhaps even the very same from that night. To openly say that I deliberately fooled them, the law. I do have a choice, though – I can skip this part and go onto helping James in other ways, but I know, deep down in the core of my conscience, that even something as small as my past perjury will haunt me for ever, now that I know it had provoked harm. I need to put as many things right as is within my power – not only for James but for me.

I wait for over ten minutes, cradling my hurt wrist. It's bad – the blood pumps around, swelling. I think it must be broken; fractured.

And that feeling I had last night? What was it?

'Miss Stephens?'

I look up at the desk sergeant. 'Chief Inspector Daley will see you now.'

I am shown to an office deep in the confines of the station. The door is ajar but I can't see all the way inside. I tap.

'Come in!' says an authoritative female voice. Why did I think Daley was male for some reason? My stereotypical small-mindedness, I suppose. I'm pleased she isn't.

I enter, and see a woman in her late forties, still in great shape, with neat uniform, holding out her hand to me from over her desk.

'Good morning,' she says, on a sage smile. I give her my left hand, explaining that my right is sprained.

'I see,' she says. 'Please. Take a seat.' I do, and my pulse gets louder in my ears. The hot seat.

'So, Ms Stephens. What can I do for you?'

I swallow. 'I don't know how to explain this,' I begin. I take in a deep breath and sigh. 'Six years ago, I called the police claiming a… certain boy had r-raped a girl.' My stutter is back. Shit.

CI Daley pulls forward in her desk and rests clutched hands in front of her, anticipative. She says nothing, not wanting to interrupt my confession undoubtedly.

In for a penny.

'Y-you see, I had falsely accused him.' I stop, my oesophagus closing as I feel a lump, rendering me unable to talk with an even flow. I swallow again, remembering images from the night before. CI Daley's eyes are fixed on mine, concern lining her brow.

'It's a long story, a-and I was young and stupid, and he'd broken my heart, and in my fury, I thought I'd give him a scare,' I explain. 'He didn't do anything…' My eyes sting.

She nods encouragingly. I wet my lips; they have suddenly gone dry.

'I want to know what happened that night b-because I never really found out – not properly. I know he was arrested, but I'd like to know how far his punishment went. And I would like to take it back. Admit I lied, and apologise.'

CI Daley nods again. 'Well, the statute of limitations on malicious falsehood is one year, so whether or not you gave false information, you won't be charged for it now.' *Malicious falsehood.* It sounds so brutal, so wicked. I am stricken.

135

'Now, here's the thing. In the UK, there is no statute of limitations of serious sexual crimes. And if this boy was charged and went to court and the information you gave us incriminated him, then yes, we'd need a statement saying it was false information.'

I feel sick.

'I should have done it years ago. I-I always thought everything had been all right. There was no news, none about him, at least. None of my friends told me anything bad, they'd said the police had come but no one was taken to the station. So, I carried on life thinking, "Oh, the police hadn't taken me seriously, thank goodness." Now you're saying he could have gone to court? Prison?'

'Rape cases usually do,' she says. I sit, dismal. How had I been so indurate, so insensitive, so down-right stupid?

'Can you tell me? Can you check and see if he went to court, to p-prison?' I beg.

'We'll see… Before we do, tell me why the worry now after all these years? Has something happened?' I stare at her, startled for a moment she might know of last-night's events. Her face doesn't seem to be hiding something.

'I saw him a few days ago and things… didn't look right.' I stop there, not knowing how to phrase. The answer is inadequate. I give her a little bit more.

'He was on his way to great things. Good university, good job… But from what I saw, well, let's just say, he didn't look like someone who has a BA from Oxford. I know that sounds horribly double-standard, but the gulf between how he looked and how he ought to have looked is what made me wonder what went wrong.'

She is sympathetic, understanding. 'OK then. Let's have a look,' she says, clicking on the mouse on the side of her desk. 'What's his name?'

'James Laidlaw.'

'And the date of the alleged crime?'

I give her the date and she begins to type. One final louder click for the "enter" button. I hold my breath, my index finger finding a cracked nail and toying with it. I have a thought just then, if there is a report from last night's assault. If his name is up on some main police database. Shit! How'll I explain that coincidence to her?

'Here we are,' she says, eyes glued to the monitor. 'Hmm,' she utters, devouring the information on her screen. 'Well, this is interesting.'

I am suddenly alert, the beating inside me heightening.

'It seems there were two phone calls made that night. Let me see… the first at eleven, forty-three, officers had been dispatched, then as they were on their way, they heard dispatch mention the address again. The call had come in at twelve, O-one,' she mumbles, almost to herself. I wonder: if I hadn't called, would James have had enough time to leave before the second call had dispatched the officers? Jesus!

'The first caller was me,' I tell her, mulling over my theory and feeling nausea.

'Aha. Yes… Oh! There *was* an alleged rape,' She takes her eyes off the monitor, pointing them at me. 'They ended up retracting. Shame… Did you know there had been an assault?'

I have no immediate answer; her question is unexpected, and I feel uneasy the way the conversation is turning. I don't want to talk about the alleged rape. I want to officially apologise to James. I flush, frustrated. But now, forced to remember, the images come to mind, flickering like an old TV screen. Her sobbing face. Her downtrodden walk. The sudden recollection of how the whole idea of getting back at James had been contrived.

In for a pound.

I shake my head and sigh. 'There could have been. Now that I recall, that's where I got my idea to say it was rape.'

Daley stares. 'Oh?'

'I saw a girl that night. It looked like she had been beaten. Assaulted. She was crying and her shirt was torn. I didn't see… what happened, I wasn't a witness to… it, but I overheard the girl with her friend. They were discussing something about calling the police. That's where I got the idea of calling you, myself.'

Daley is all ears, incredulous. 'It doesn't say anything here about torn clothes. She might have changed so it wouldn't look like she was assaulted…' She pauses, waiting for something. Does she want my theory?

'Possibly,' I say. 'I think I remember her saying she didn't want anybody to know. Her friend must have been the one who called.'

'Tell me, Ms Stephens. Tell me of that night.'

I rub my eyes, I don't want to; I'm wasting time, but there is no way out of this; only through.

'I… I had heard a scream while I was in the garden… I saw a boy run into the house. I-I didn't know what it meant at the time. I didn't want to get involved. I was young. All I had on m-my mind was to be with James. I didn't care about anything else. I later learnt he had been leading me on, James, that is, and it hurt… it hurt me deeply.' I stop to wipe my nose with the old, crumpled tissue in my pocket. 'So, after I saw the girl, I thought I'd ring the police, n-not only for her but for revenge on James.'

The word resounds in my ears and it sticks in my mouth like bile. *Revenge.* It is the first time I've admitted it to myself. It *was* revenge. I'd acted spitefully, maliciously. It had been vengeance. Pure vengeance. I had stooped that low. I had become a Bianca.

'I want to take it all back. I want to clear his name.'

Daley is nibbling on her bottom lip. 'Well, Ms Stephens, you'll be glad to know the case was never indicted.'

I let that sink in. Never indicted… 'That's… that's great…'

'For James, yes. Apparently, the girl never pressed charges. As I said, she had denied everything, even knowing who James Laidlaw was. Which was true in this case. He had been taken in for questioning, though. Officers can't turn a blind eye if a certain name has been mentioned. They have to be thorough.'

I remember having thought he wouldn't be charged. I had been right. But he was brought in… like a common criminal. *Just a little scare… You stupid, stupid idiot.*

'Lots of girls think the court won't believe them, so they say nothing, not wanting to go through the whole humiliating process,' CI Daley continues. 'They'd rather stay silent and try to forget about the whole thing, rather than exposing what they went through. But if I got in contact with her and told her there was hope she could win the case, would you be willing to give us a statement? As for Mr Laidlaw, you don't need to apologise. You don't need to make a statement since there was no case.'

My breath catches. I think of that poor girl. Her scream of terror. 'Of course,' I say. 'Anything she wants…'

Daley smiles. 'Good.'

I don't get it. If he hadn't been charged, why is he in such a state? Maybe the one thing has absolutely nothing to do with the other. Maybe his impoverished position was formulated by his own devise; not from my phone call. He could have gone to Oxford, but maybe didn't do well or something, and had left.

Perhaps the fact of being picked up by the police isn't exactly a fantastic landmark in one's life either. Other people find it degrading, shameful. Something that could stigmatise you. Something that would be in the records and smudge your name for life. Any number of possibilities.

'Chief Inspector?'

'Yes?'

'Is it on record, the arrest?'

'Yes, of course.'

'So, that means people will get to see it, like when he gets hired for work. His employer?'

'Well, yes…'

'I don't understand. That's unfair. He didn't do it! Why blemish his name for no reason?' I raise my voice.

'Well, that's how the system is. He had been arrested for two things but charged for one. He was over eighteen. That's what the employers get to see.'

'Charged? For what?' I cry.

The woman hesitates. 'Weren't you there? Weren't you at the party?'

'Yes…'

'Didn't you see? Didn't you smell the weed everywhere?'

'He got arrested and charged for *that*? My God! This is all my fault…'

'It's not your fault if he was taking drugs.'

'Yes, but it's my fault he got caught…'

'If you hadn't called, there was the other phone call. He would have been caught one way or another.'

'No. No, he wouldn't have,' I say, as I hold back the tears. 'He was going to leave. He'd told me he was going home early. Eighteen minutes. Eighteen more minutes!'

Daley purses her lips. 'Well, that's a hypothetical,' she says. *True*. 'But, the good thing is, he was given an absolute discharge by the magistrate. He wasn't punished in the least.'

That's good. I know that's good, but I shake my head, still feeling the error of my ways. 'His record is his punishment. It will follow him for the rest of his life.'

She shrugs, resolute. 'He did break the law…'

She is right. Damn it, she is right. 'I feel awful… I just wanted to apologise…'

'Miss Stephens, the best apologies, the ones that won't make you feel awful, are those said directly to the person of interest.' Right again.

'Yes,' I utter quietly, 'I know…'

She gets up and so do I, disheartened from what I've just heard, when she says, 'You know, I was there that night.'

My mind halts.

'I didn't remember right away, but after reading the report, it came back to me. That's why I asked you if you smelt the weed. You could smell it a mile off.'

What is she saying? What does she know that isn't in the report? What am I missing? Because one's life doesn't get blown to smithereens by a flimsy cannabis charge. There has to be something else more detrimental, more life-changing. I need Daley to tell me what she knows.

'Chief Inspector? Was there anything… anything you found strange? Something that isn't written in the report?'

She deliberates. 'Well, no. Nothing strange. Nothing you wouldn't see in a case like this. There was a lot of crying and panicking and anger; parents were furious. Some didn't even come to help their children out. Told them to spend the night in jail; teach them a lesson. Of course, we didn't take anyone in. We let them pay on-the-spot fines –'

'Except for James!'

She sighs. 'Yes. Except for James.'

'Because I named him.'

'Because you named him…'

One heartbeat, two heartbeats, three… I feel the tremble on my lips. I take one step to leave, but stop, inert.

'Are you all right, Eleanora?' She's said my first name. I blink, pulling myself together. I have one more crucial question.

'Chief Inspector, is it a crime to follow someone?' I need the answer from the horse's mouth, as I were, before I open mine. She drags her lips down and blinks at the non sequitur.

'I know, it's irrelevant, but I need to know from the proper source, not just from some site where a blogger gives his opinion,' I tell her. *Or Kate's take.*

'If you're stalking, it's a crime. Stalking includes following.'

'What if there is no harassment in any way? What if they follow someone for a couple of hours, no interaction whatsoever, and the person who is being followed is none the wiser?'

'That's a very fine line. They could sue if they find out. Then the courts can decide. It all depends on intent, however. Why. What the reason was for following, and so on.'

'I see…' I move towards the door, thanking her for all her help.

'By the way,' she says, 'do you know who the alleged rapist was?'

There is stillness for a second. Then I inhale, filling my lungs with life. It feels like I've been holding my breath for six years. 'Yes, I believe I do.'

She waits. Her pupils dilating, a fraction, over her hazel eyes.

'The party host. Robert. Robert Simmonds.'

Chapter Twenty-Five

Back Then

'Ciggy?'

A packet of B&H was thrust under my nose, as I was sitting on one of the benches outside N&L Shoes. I looked who was offering me. Kate. I took one out of the packet but I didn't feel much like smoking it.

'Thanks,' I said, and let her light it nonetheless. Then she lit hers, and drew in a long drag.

'Know what?' she said, blowing out half the cigarette she'd already sucked in.

'What?'

'You get paid a whole fifty P more than me, per hour. Even if I have been working here longer than you.'

I raised my brows. 'I do?'

'Yep.'

'How do you know that?' I asked, wondering how she obtained that information. That shit was private, wasn't it?

'I know everything when it comes to money.' She winked.

I looked up reflectively. 'Must be all those hand jobs I've been giving Millard,' I said, so matter of fact, that she spluttered out smoke and burst into a coughing laughter. I gave her a thump on the back.

'Jesus!' she said, with a scratchy voice. I smirked wickedly. She wiped her eyes. 'I seriously was not expecting that reply!'

'What did you expect me to say? "Go and complain to the government"?'

'Yeah, something like that!'

'Why?' I asked, incredulous. 'Do you take me for some highfalutin intellect, skilled in the art of left-wing politics?'

She lingered for a moment, on what to reply. I must have overwhelmed her with that answer. 'Well yeah, but not about being skilled in left-wing politics, but about being clever. Actually, it's your accent that's a dead giveaway,' she stated.

'A dead giveaway for what?' Now I was utterly confused.

'That you've got muchas pasetas.'

'Excuse me?!'

'Yeah. Posh, RP, private-school accent. You've had an excellent education. That's why I was expecting a more intellectual reply.'

I stared at her, with an are-you-shitting-me look. 'Receiving an excellent education has nothing to do with intellect. Or with your sense of humour. I know plenty of stupid doctors, for example.'

'Agreed…' She smiled. 'Which brings me to my next query.'

I sighed. 'Fire away!'

'Why do you need to work if you have money?'

I harrumphed. 'I like the way you deduce my bank account just by the way I speak.'

'You know what I mean…'

'Yes. I know what you mean, but I don't like thinking that way. I wasn't brought up taking my family's money for granted. I'm almost eighteen, and I don't have a quid to my name. The private school was paid by my mum, which I'm grateful for, but now I want to be more independent. I don't want her to pay for my shit anymore. Simple as that.'

'I hear you. You could say that's why I'm working too. More independence…'

'And, by the way, *your* accent isn't exactly rivalling Michael Caine's!' I stated. She huffed. 'You've got a salt-of-the-earth London accent. A refined Estuary. It's lovely!'

She pondered that, her eyes narrowing through the smoke. Then a broad smile broke out.

'Oh,' I said. 'And talking about language, please don't talk Spanish to me. It reminds me of a cow I once knew.'

She put out her cigarette in the ashtray bin beside her, and said, 'You know,' blowing out the last of her smoke, 'the best way to stop identifying one bad thing to another, is by associating it to something else. Give a new, nicer, better identification. Spanish is lovely. You shouldn't condemn it or banish it from your life just because you had a bad experience with someone who spoke it.'

'You're right,' I said, deliberating. 'Perhaps I should listen to someone else speak it.'

'Yeah. Good idea. Antonio Banderas!' she said, doing a smoulder look.

'Nah! Not my type…'

'Antonio is not your type?' she said, shocked.

'Nope. He's too baby-face for me. I like a more masculine, rougher face.'

'Antonio is not your type?' she repeated deliberately.

'No!'

'I think you're the only person I know who doesn't find him attractive.'

'So, we have different taste in men.' I shrugged. 'Think of it as something positive. We won't ever fight over the same guy.'

She blinked then grinned. 'I think this the beginning of a beautiful friendship…'

Chapter Twenty-Six

Now

Father, I've lied. I ruined someone's life. Through my lie, he has suffered.

Child, through confession, God can absolve the sin of lying, but you will not be truly free unless you come clean, come face to face with the man you have done this harm to. Until then, let me bless you, now, with the remission of your sin.

No, Father. I cannot. The slate can never be wiped clean; there will always be an irremovable stain. Not until I have told him. Not until I have done whatever I can to make recompense. Only then will I let God remit my sin.

The burning tears of rage fall. I gasp, lamenting, as my conscience plunges in a viscous of damning truths. What I had done to James was base and unforgivable. I think of all the things I could have had a hand in depriving him of throughout these past six years, had I not opened my stupid mouth. Potential employers turning him down after learning he'd been booked. I don't know! And I am still under the conviction James never went to his intended university the year he was supposed to go, nor the following years. How serious a crime must one commit in order for a university not to accept you? I mean, hash? That can't be the case, surely, otherwise half the kids in England wouldn't be matriculating into higher education. And even Kate was accepted after her misdemeanour. But if rape comes into the equation? I got him into trouble with the law, and that must have triggered a series of events which ruined his life. Kate will say I'm jumping to conclusions. True, I don't have proof, but I can feel it. I can feel it is all my fault. Because, fact was, thanks to me, he had a record. Thanks to me, he went to court. And, thanks to me, James's current state of affairs has my signature scored onto it.

I cannot live with this treachery. I am a rotten human being.

***

My phone vibrates as I walk towards my flat. Withheld number. I ignore it – I am in no mood for some eager salesperson offering me a free, no-strings-attached trip to Hawaii.

I go passed my front-door mirror; I dare not meet my eyes. I am a Judas – he whose gaze had averted deliberately from the eyes of his once-loved teacher, as his lips touched the innocent cheek.

'Forgive me, James. Forgive me…' I am crying. I haven't cried like this since Vic's accident.

I have to see him… I have reached a mental point where I can no longer pursue my task until I know he's doing OK. The only problem is, I have no idea which hospital he's been taken to.

I browse on the laptop. Hospitals. Time to find his hospital. But before I do, I search, questioning how severe would a crime have to be for an applicant not to be accepted in tertiary education. There are varying results, but most universities say they would generally accept students depending on the crime. Apparently, they do accept you if you have a record. It's judged by a committee. That puts a weight off my chest.

I pull up another tab. With the help of an online map, I see a radius of hospitals closest to where James was picked up from, and begin the search. I ring the first. They claim they aren't an emergency hospital, and there is no one under his name. I try another; they don't have his name. The third hospital suggests I ought to try the neighbouring hospital as they are a better candidate for the specific area, and they have A&E. So, I do.

'I'm afraid we don't seem to have his name here,' a girl in administration says. 'When did he come in?'

'Last night. It must have been around nineish,' I tell her, starting to get worried I'll never find him. 'He's tall, well-built, long, blond hair? He had been beaten up quite badly…'

'Oh, yes, yes. We have a man fitting that description who came in last night with no identity,' she informs me. She sounds happy I called. 'I was told to have my ears peeled if someone phoned. Would you be able to come in and identify him? He had been mugged, so there was nothing on him. No official papers with his name on them. We would be obliged.'

'Yes. Yes, of course.'

No identity? They took his wallet? Well, that explains why nothing came up on CI Daley's database: they had no name to enter.

I hang up, grab my stuff and am out the door.

Critical Care Ward is where I am at. It is restricted access, and I look down the waxy corridor as nurses and doctors move about their duties. I reach the nurses' station where some nurses are chatting while moving around paperwork.

One looks my way. Fifties, medium height and buxom – the type of person you want to hug just because they look comfortable. Her highlighted afro pulled back in various twists and tiny plats giving her face a welcome openness. The nurse, or Faith Weston as her nametag states, says, 'Can I help you?'

'Yes, please. I have been asked to identify a patient of yours. He came in last night, unconscious, no ID on him.'

'Oh, yes!' she says, suddenly moving around to the opening of the counter. Then she spies someone behind me.

'Doctor Wright!' she cries. A tall, thin, swarthy-skinned woman in a white doctor's jacket, stethoscope dangling around her neck, stops in her tracks and turns to us. Tired, solemn face.

'The young lady here says she can identify our Joe Bloggs from last night.'

'Oh wonderful!' Dr Wright says. Then her brows deepen. 'How did you know he was here? Are you family?'

'No, I… I know him… He's an old friend of mine. I was the one who found him and called the ambulance, but I didn't… h-have the chance to speak with the paramedics, so I didn't know where he'd be taken. And I also didn't know he had no ID on him. I phoned some hospitals asking if they had him, describing him, and well… here I am.'

There is a leak in my story, and Dr Wright knows it. Why hadn't I accompanied him to the hospital? Why didn't I stick around and talk to the paramedics? Why had I fled the scene? But she says nothing. It *is* my prerogative, after all.

144

'I see,' she says, contented with my answer, nonetheless. 'Where on earth are the police?' she asks Nurse Faith. Nurse Faith shrugs her shoulders.

'Well, we're in a predicament,' says Dr Wright, now turning back to me. 'You see, the police asked us to tell them if anyone comes to identify him… but… oh, well, we can't wait now, and I have a job to do! If they're outside smoking, it's their loss. I'm not their mother. Come with me!'

I walk behind her, trying to subdue my thrashing heart at mention of the police, and in a few short steps, we are at an open doorway. A vestiary of some sort.

'OK, then. Nurse? I'll leave you to it,' the doctor says, and leaves me with Nurse Faith.

'Right! Well then… before you enter the ICU, you have to put a robe on, tied at the back, and a mask, and shoe covers. Scrub your hands with the disinfectant hand-wash over at the basin. Try not to touch anything afterwards. OK?'

'OK.'

'I'll be waiting outside to take you to his room.' She leaves me to it.

I put on a thin-fibered, semi-transparent robe, light as a feather and made to be disposable after one use. I find the shelf with tons of disposable masks, and take one. I place the shoe covers over my shoes, walk to the basin and scrub. I check my face in the mirror. I look ridiculous.

Nurse Faith is waiting for me, mask on. *She* doesn't look any better.

We pass large chambers, three or four cots in each, with patients hooked up to bleeping machines and tubes of all sizes. I only catch a glimpse, but it is enough to know why this floor is called "critical".

Dr Wright, masked up, is waiting outside one of the rooms. *His*, I surmise. My heart speeds up as each step brings me closer.

'You have one minute to confirm it's him, all right?' Dr Wright tells me. My eyes give something away and she adds, 'We can't risk infection.' I nod.

The room is small. It has two cots. One is empty. The other, lies James.

I pace and pause, taken off-guard by the unceremonious state he is in. Motionless. Naked under the sheet; the vulnerability is stark. It seizes my sensibility. I am almost embarrassed to look at him. There he lies, bare, forsaken, abandoned.

I gather my wits and move closer to him. I have one minute to be with him, and I have already wasted precious seconds.

He looks like he is sleeping in pain, as there is a soft groove between his eyebrows. Is he dreaming of something bad?

His wounds have been tended to with neat, little bandages to show for it, on his face and neck. And there is a bigger, thicker gauze where he was cut along the jaw. Both eyes are puffy and purple, bruised and, I pray, not harmed. I can't see the rest of him; the sheet is up to his shoulders. There are tubes and wires leading out, tethered onto a machine measuring heart, pulse and temperature. There is no tube coming out of his mouth, so he isn't on any life support. That is a good sign. The drip leading into his bloodstream is a saline, and there is another smaller IV, being administrated, with *HYD* written on it. Morphine.

'James…' I whisper, finally losing composure. A tear makes its way down my cheek, only to be absorbed on the rim of my mask. 'Get better soon. You hear me?'

He doesn't move; fast asleep, but the groove disappears.

'So, you can confirm who it is?' asks Dr Wright, behind me.

'Yes. His name is J-James Laidlaw,' I say, articulating each word with difficulty for the lump in my throat has swollen, my eyes unwavering from James's face.

'I see. James… Laid…law,' she spells out, and I hear her click a pen. 'Well, that is about as much as I'm allowed to let you stay. Only one member of the family is allowed to enter at this point, you know, but I made an exception for you because the police requested it. There is to be an inquiry, and I can't obstruct the law now, can I?'

'I understand,' I say. I part my eyes from him, and we walk to the corridor. 'Is he all right, at least? I see he isn't hooked up to any support. That's good, isn't it?'

'I'm not permitted to say, as you aren't a member of his family. I cannot disclose any test results,' she tells me, almost brusque. She is tired, I understand. But so, *my dear*, am I.

'Doctor,' I say, pulling down my mask. 'If it weren't for me, he wouldn't be here in the first place!' She has no idea by what other context I allude to secretly, but I press on. 'I'm the one who called the ambulance, remember? I'm the one who found him lying half-dead on the ground. I'm the one who just identified him! I don't see his family anywhere. Do you?'

She takes off her mask. She has her lips pressed together, measuring what I just said. Then she lets out a breath. 'All I can tell you is that he isn't in any danger.'

***

In the small changing room, my phone rings.

'Hi, Mum,' I say despondently, as I take off the shoe covers.

'El!' she cries frantically. 'What's going on? I just got a visit from the police. They were looking for you.'

'What?' I say, dazed. 'What did you tell them?'

'The truth. I told them you didn't live here anymore, and I gave them your address. What's going on, love?'

'It's nothing, Mum. Don't worry about it. I'll tell you later, OK? Don't worry, seriously…' It is all I can say to keep her calm. The woman has been through enough scares in her life.

So, the police are already looking for me? My phone was traced, and they have the number associated with my old address – the one that was recorded when I had applied for my phone's SIM. Literally, my life is at their fingertips. I didn't expect it to be so fast. They will be on their way to my flat, no doubt. Why didn't they just call me? Or maybe that was them, with the withheld number? I am suddenly very afraid – not for the police, as such, but for the stark simplicity at how they found me, and my train of thought drifts to those men that beat James. If they ever find out I was the one who rang for the ambulance, then they might think I saw something. A witness. They can find me. I don't think they'd have any qualms over hacking. But then again, they'd need to know the precise time I called, find my number then, in turn, my name. I think of my old house. The police thought I was there. What if the criminals do too? Mum…

I descend to A&E, and am about to exit, when a sign catches my eye. "Outpatients".

It has just occurred to me that I could get my wrist checked and bandaged properly here, so I make my way down to trauma. I stare in disbelief at the mountain of people waiting, and leave, knowing there is no chance of me being attended to within the hour. I go to the pharmacy. No sooner do I put the wrist brace on, my pain eases. I've been under too much dull pain, and the secure hold is just what I need. One less thing to worry about.

Euston Station, Northern Line via Bank and onto DLR. It's time I have a talk with Nick.

Chapter Twenty-Seven

Back Then

'So, what A Levels are you taking then?' asked Kate, as she drew in her last drag from the cigarette she wanted to finish before we rounded the pub. She blew out the last puff into the black night air and dropped the butt on the slab of wet pavement, metres away from the warmly lit doors, not bothering to snub the last ember out with her boot – the sleet would do that.

'A Levels?' I said, teeth chatting, as I swung open the door, shivering from the winter breeze. Immediately, the heat welcomed us, and without a word, Kate and I walked straight to the bar, ordered our beers and found a table.

I sipped on my draught, letting the cool slake me. 'Ahh,' I sighed. 'I needed that!' We were in the nearest pub we could find for a beer. Some of the others we worked with said they might pop in later. But for now, Kate and I were alone, sitting at a small, round, wooden table. It was Friday, and the place would be packed before we knew it.

'What university do you want to go to?' she asked. I shrugged. 'I've applied to most in London for a BA. I'm going to do my foundation course in the summer, so I get that over and done with. You? What do you want to be when you grow up?' I teased.

'Me?' she harrumphed. 'I'll be lucky if I even finish school.'

'Why do you say that?'

''Cos I want to leave. I want to continue working full-time and find a place far away from my parents' house.'

'Really? Don't you want to go to university?'

'Not as much as I want to leave home,' she said, taking a long gulp of beer. I stared inquisitively, nibbling my lower lip. What was up with that answer? Full of enigmas, this girl.

'Is it that bad?' I asked tentatively. She didn't hide her inner deliberation – hesitant, whether or not to confide something.

'I ran away from home a while back. I lived on the streets for three months.' She paused deliberately to interpret my reaction. My eyes went wide. She nodded.

'Wow,' was all I said, in astonishment. I didn't ask why – it was none of my business. I wasn't the probing type, in general.

'And I would have stayed on the streets if I hadn't been about to die,' she added.

I blinked, not knowing how to respond. She rubbed her eyes, exhausted.

'Some people, out walking their dog, found me under Eyre's Tunnel. One of the tunnels on Regent's Canal in Saint John's Wood. Ever heard of it? There's a little towpath you can hide under; keep you dry from the rain. Anyway, they called the police, and this young officer – raring to do his job well – took me to the police station. They found a wallet on me, which wasn't mine. They thought I'd stolen it, but I hadn't – I found it in the street. Anyway, they didn't believe me except for the young officer, and booked me with a misdemeanour, then took me home. I didn't want to go home, but I was half delirious… He, the young officer, coaxed me for my address and I gave it to him. I remember, he'd been so nice… and he had the greenest eyes you just couldn't refuse… Besides, I didn't want to die.'

I just gawked at her, unable to grasp this arrant fact of her life. And also, not quite understanding why she divulged something so intimate to me, whom she only knew but weeks. I had never met anyone who had run away from home, and I had to admit, I was curious. She took another sip of beer, and was about to say more, when suddenly we were surrounded with the rest of the N&L gang.

Light-hearted conversation ensued, and Kate and I were thrown into other topics of discussion. Her wrought face smoothed as she tried her hardest to emerge from the torment I saw in her eyes. Not even seventeen, and it seemed she'd lived through ten lifetimes.

I felt for her. I hardly knew her, yet her genuine heart had won me instantly. What you saw was what you got. She was no Bianca.

Now

There is no reception underground, so when I find some, surfacing from the bowels of London, on my way to get on Docklands Light Railway at Bank, I see I have three missed calls. One is from Kate, the other is from our landlord, Mr Jones, and the third is undisclosed.

Although I want to know their reasons for calling, all I feel is the urgency in getting to Nick. All my focus, all my attention is centred on this. I have to know what it was. What had caused James to end up like this.

I find the high-rise building, placed between skyscrapers, ride the elevator to the desired floor, and finally, push open a heavy, glass door – gateway to the Golden Sea.

A receptionist behind a shiny, mahogany desk, mechanically smiles up at me – something, I suppose, she was asked to do to everyone. A receptionist is the face of the company. The first thing you see. There has to be subjective beauty as a qualification. In this case, startling blue-green eyes and great skin.

I ask her if I can see Nicholas Barton.

'I'm afraid he is on sick leave,' is her answer. The smile has disappeared, and in its place, a glumness. 'Unfortunately, Nick was involved in a car accident. He's in pretty bad shape, in fact, he's critical.'

Something creeps up my spine. 'A car accident?' I blurt. 'Seriously?'

'Yes. We've all been shocked by it. He is in a coma.'

'Christ!' I gasp. 'This can't be…'

It is too much of a coincidence. I look, bewildered, through the glass wall, beyond the dark, khaki waters of the Thames. Looking but not observing, as I try to assimilate – my mind a maelstrom of disbelief and, yes, fear.

'W-what happened?' I ask. She tries a friendly face. I must look completely wired.

'Some vehicle came out of nowhere and slammed right into his car, leaving him wounded. The driver just drove off, bloody bastard. The police are looking into it.'

'A hit and run?' She nods. 'Poor Nick.' I remember that sly, comical face of his. How he always went out of his way to talk to me. My head thuds.

'You wouldn't happen to know which hospital he's at?'

'No, sorry… All I know it happened close to his house in north London… Hendon, if I'm not mistaken.'

I leave Golden Sea Yachts none the wiser. I want to scream. When am I to get the answer? That missing piece in this chronological puzzle? Nick would know everything, I am sure of that, but now, oh, dear Lord… what's happened to him? Dear Nick in a coma.

I call Mr Jones. He calls me so rarely; it can't be about anything trivial.

'The police were around, looking for you,' he says, deep concern. My heart makes a hard pump, blood reaching to my temples.

There is one more place I have to go before speaking to the police. It is my last resort.

Back Then

'I've never made up anyone before. This could be a complete failure,' I forewarned, as I sharpened the lip-liner.

'I want to see how it looks on me. I'm shit with make-up. I think Sean will like it,' Kate said, preparing her lips.

'OK, then. I'll fard your lips. Consider yourself warned…'

'Do *what* to my lips?!' she said, affright.

I snickered. 'Hold still!'

I tried my best. I did. But no matter how great a painter I was, I was no make-up artist.

'I think I just made you Robert Smith's doppelganger…' I said, cringing. She grabbed the little face mirror, and burst out laughing.

'Shite! You're crap!' she said, through the giggling.

The front door slammed shut downstairs, and her giggle ceased with a gasp. I looked at her, puzzled, and saw all the jocose rosiness in her cheeks drain out, making her go whiter than I'd ever seen her before.

'Kate?'

'Oh, no. He's here…'

Chapter Twenty-Eight

Now

There is nothing now, just an inflexible perseverance within my core. I am reaching the end of my tether. I need to fill in that space that will give me the proof I seek, so that I know where I stand, when the time comes to confront him, and say, here! Here's what I did. Now you know everything. Now you may castigate me and vindicate yourself…

The street is familiar. If I remember correctly, his old stop is nearby.

I find myself walking along the same path I had done all those years ago, retracing each step, which I can still see in my mind's eye, the very first time I saw him. One step, the Laburnum tree, whose roots have displaced the pavement. Another step, the same Bostock-styled, wrought-iron gate. There is mist. A thick mist biting its way through my flesh. The sharp, damp of the morning; a pungent smell of ozone lingering in the dense air. One more step, there! There is the bus-stop post. The red rondel with the line through it. Now I turn into the road adjacent. There he walks. There he is. I see him materialise through the misty vapour. The boy… no, the man. He is striding straight towards me, and I continue in his direction, closer… closer. We are an inch apart and… he is gone. A wisp of air. An apparition.

'My God!' I gasp. The image of him intense, so intense, that it could pass for real. 'James… I'm so sorry…' A whisper to his ear.

By the time I reach his house, or I should say, his parents' house, my mind is in an upheaval. The tumult taking hold, leaves it confused and flustered, therefore, I have not devised some monologue in preparation to this visit – some humble excuse. I don't know what I'll say, nor am I sure if there'll be niceties, the way I feel. In short, I am a notch away from breaking point.

The hard truth. Facts. That is what I want now.

The house is a Tudor-revival detached, much like mine, or rather, Mum's.

Along a short gravel path, with some kind of failed rockery arranged on the two patches of grass on either side, I tread. Some early spring flowers are trying to bud, tiny blue and white petals, sparsely scattered. But a beautiful cherry tree in full bloom, is stood gloriously on the front, giving the house all its beauty.

Under the front-door archway, a small, tiled shelter before you enter, I halt. There are some wellington boots and an umbrella-stand to the right. The door has one of those rectangular windows with distorted glass in the middle.

I find the doorbell and press hard, determined. The distinct chime can be heard from within.

Then, silence. They could very well have gone to the hospital already. I push the doorbell again. Again, silence. Those first tinges of disappointment disperse within me, like ink in water. Blackening. I heave a breath, and it takes all of me not to cry.

I ring one more time. 'Please,' I teethe, reproachfully, to the door. And there, I hear thudding. Yes, there are footfalls coming down a flight of stairs.

'Who is it?' a trembling voice says. She, for indeed it is a girl's voice, can be seen, blotched and blurry through the glass, as I am sure it is how she can see me. I wonder who she is. Perhaps James's parents don't live here anymore. Then my anamnesis sparks: *Dad needs my sister and I Sunday morning.*

'Y-you don't know me, but I know your brother,' I say, as clearly and as friendly as I can.

Suddenly she cries out, 'Jamie!' and she unlocks the door.

I see a dark-blonde teenager, wide, blue eyes now red, alongside mottled features from crying. She is wearing a black, sequenced mini skirt, and party top. She is trembling, distraught.

'Are you all right?' I ask, straightaway, taking a step forward and putting my hand on her arm, trying to give comfort.

She sniffs. 'I'm sorry, it's just that Jamie is in hospital. I just got the message from Mum now. I came straight over.'

'Yes. I know,' I say. She looks up at me expectantly. 'The doctor said he'll be fine,' I add quickly; ease her mind. 'Don't worry –' I want to say her name but I don't know it. I never learnt what it was.

'I-I know,' she says, still trembling. 'Mum said, but still… poor Jamie… beaten up and in hospital, and me out partying! I only switched on my phone an hour ago!' She lets out another sob. I pat her arm.

'Mum asked me to bring some stuff to the hospital for him… they left right away, as soon as they got the call… someone …they said someone had just identified him… he'd been there all night without us beside him!' She lets out another sob. I take her straight in my arms, not only to comfort her but also to comfort myself. 'But I don't know what to take; what clothes, I mean, He hasn't lived here for years, and only some of his old clothes are here. They don't fit him anymore.'

'Let me help you,' I say. She holds back, only just realising I'm a total stranger.

I give her a sympathetic smile. 'I was the one who called the ambulance. I only found out this morning he had no ID on him. I went straightaway to tell the doctors. Your brother and I… we've known one another for six years.'

She gasps and hugs me tight. 'It was you? Thank you so much.'

I am led into a small foyer, soft, grey carpet under my feet, with a slim table to the right side and a mirror on top. To the other side is a little entryway, coats and shoes all neatly placed. The staircase ahead, and through the hall, I discern a spacious kitchen. Bright, as the setting sunlight hits the big bay window, balloon curtains pulled all the way up, and beyond, the garden. I surmise the living room is through two large, wooden-panel doors to my right. All in all, the house has a very elegant feel to it. No kitsch decor in sight. Good taste.

James's sister goes up the stairs, and I follow.

We reach the landing. I take a discreet moment to look around where James grew up. I imagine a little boy running up and down the hall, getting up to mischief, then an older version of the boy, with school uniform on, getting ready for the day. Then I imagine the eighteen-year-old version. Tall, handsome, fine, in the blacks and greys of Milden, bracing his bag over his shoulder and trotting, languidly, downstairs for breakfast.

'I'm going to change,' his sister says, walking to one of the doors. Her room obviously. 'What should I take for Jamie?' she asks me.

'Perhaps you could pack something from your father's clothes. Some underclothes and something comfortable to rest in.'

She shakes her head. 'I don't think he'll want anything from Dad,' she says equivocally. 'They haven't spoken since –' She stops suddenly. That! I knew that *that* had something to do with it. Something had happened between him and his father.

'Oh?' I say, feigning wonder, and trying to keep the excitement out of my voice. I am onto something. I can feel it. All the key words are there; I just have to decipher them.

'What? James never told you?' she asks. She takes it for granted I know, since James and I are "friends".

'About him and his father?' I venture.

'Yeah.'

Thank God! Now I am getting somewhere. 'No. He never got the chance… but I gather it has to do with his arrest six years ago, right?'

She nods and tears came down her face again. I can't help it; I take her in my arms again and let her weep on me. Apparently, it is a painful memory.

'Shhh… it's all right –' again, stopping short, not knowing her name. 'Everything will be OK, I promise.'

The clues are falling into place. An angry father. Bad blood? He left home? But it still doesn't explain why he never went to Oxford, or any other place. My train of thought comes to a sudden halt there. Why am I so adamant he hasn't studied? Who is to say? He could have gone somewhere else. *Then why is he so poor?* my mind asks back. *He could still be studying,* I answer myself. Whatever it is, I'll have to investigate it somehow. Ask his sister? That'll look strange; me knowing him for six years and, yet, not knowing if he were studying.

'Go and get ready. Your brother will be waiting for you. Just point me in the right direction. Maybe there's something that can fit him.'

She points at a door opposite the bathroom. 'That's his room. I think there are some of his old Tees in there, although I doubt they'll fit.'

She turns to her room and opens the door. I see her dressing table. An array of knick-knacks, make up and perfume is displayed before me, and right on top of the mirror, a bunting in pastel colours, spells in large capitals. ELIZAB –

Elizabeth.

I reach the bathroom. There is a navy-blue school blazer chucked in the floor, pleated skirt and grey jumper. A uniform whose colours I know not which school they belong to. I place my hand on the door to the room that once was his, and creak it open.

It is in shades of grey and blue. All the furniture is there but untouched for so long. His bed has no quilt on it, just a light-grey blanket. The walls have some rectangular patches where the light hadn't worn out the paint, leaving the imprint of what used to be pictures or posters. The curtains are open, washing-down the place with a sub fusc monotone. The space is miserable. Empty. Hollow.

I turn to the closet. I open one of the sliding panels. It feels wrong, like I'm invading his privacy, but I need to find clothes for him. It's almost bare, save some jumpers and T shirts on a side shelf. I take one T-shirt, plain white, and unfolded it. I hold it up for size – there is no way that is going to fit him!

I slide open the other panel, and it is as if I have just been kicked in the stomach. There hangs his Milden school blazer. Just the blazer, the badge patched onto the left breast pocket. *VERITAS LUX MEA* the motto written in capitals, stark against the black. *The truth enlightens me.*

I take a benumbed breath, now thoroughly subdued.

My phone vibrates suddenly, and I jump, the resonance more enhanced in the silence. I check the display. It is the withheld number…

'Hello?' I answer.

'Good afternoon. May I speak with Eleanora Stephens?' It is a rigid voice, authoritative, male.

'Speaking,' I say, and prepare.

'This is Detective Inspector William Archer from the Metropolitan Police.'

My heart thumps uncontrollably. 'Good afternoon, Detective Inspector.'

My voice remains staid, notwithstanding my heart.

'Ms Stephens, we have been trying to locate you all morning, concerning a phone call, placed by your number, to nine, nine, nine last night. Were you the one who made the call?' Strong, decisive, professional.

'Yes.'

'Well, we would like some information about last night, whether you saw anything, how you found the victim. We understand you identified him today?' Rhetorical question. He's spoken to Dr Wright and/or Nurse Faith.

'Yes. I didn't know he was without identification until this morning. I was meaning to get in touch with you, in any case.'

There is a short pause. 'I see,' he says. 'We will be needing your cooperation on this. You weren't with the victim last night, when we arrived. Assault is a serious crime, Ms Stephens…'

Ah. So, the police were there too last night. I was right to leave. I wasn't prepared. Not that I am prepared now. All I can do is help. Dispense all my knowledge on this vicious attack on James. And prepare for the consequences.

'Yes, I know.'

'It is imperative you give a statement as quickly as possible. Can you come to the station?' He tells me where they are situated. I give him a rough estimate of the time it'll take me. We say a formal goodbye and hang up.

All is still. Had Elizabeth been listening in? She probably had. Then I hear a swish of footsteps.

'Was that the police?'

'Yeah,' I say. I turn; she is ready, cleaned up – jeans, top and coat.

'What did they want?'

What can I tell her? That the police were looking for me because they didn't find me the night before because I had abandoned her brother before they got there?

'They need some information… don't worry about it… let's figure out what we're going to do about clothes,' I tell her. Then I hold up the T-shirt and say, '*This* is never going to fit him!'

She harrumphs, and I grin back. The tee is pretty pathetic.

'All his clothes are at his place. Jamie won't accept anything from Dad. Not that he doesn't love him – he just doesn't want to cause him any more pain. So, I can't take any of Dad's.'

'So, what do you suggest we do?' I ask.

'I need to go to his place. I'm getting the Tube, anyway, to get to the hospital, so I'll make a stop there first.'

There is no way I am letting her travel by herself in the state she is and at this time of night, for night it will be by the time she gets there. And there is no way I am going to take another Tube ride. I have exceeded my underground quota for today.

'No, you're not. I'm driving us,' I say.

Back Then

My heart sped up in alarm at Kate's words. What did she mean "He's here"? Who? Who was here?

Her parents were out, and her brother was in Liverpool somewhere, studying. Did someone else have a key to the place?

'Who?' I whispered, as I turned to the closed door, half expecting whoever it was to pounce on me at any moment. We could hear the thudding footfalls on the staircase.

'Shhh!' she hissed, rubbing off the lip-liner with a tissue. 'My brother.' Her voice was panicked. I turned to her with an interrogative eye. What was wrong with her brother?

'Kate!' Came a deep, male shout. 'You here?' Then the door swung open. In one second, all three of us stood motionless. I met her brother's gaze, and upon seeing me, he was out again, slamming the door behind him. But I had caught it; the savageness in his eye. And my mind just paralyzed.

Chapter Twenty-Nine

Now

Within 20 minutes, Elizabeth and I turn into the North Circular, southbound.

I've borrowed Mum's car. A second-hand silver XJ6, which is a few years away from being officially vintage, and costs more money to maintain, what with its 4.2 litre engine, than what it's actually worth. Vic is constantly telling her to sell it (the only practical opinion that ever escaped her lips), and buy something more economical, but Mum can't bring herself to part with it. And secretly, neither can I. It has all the comfort and efficiency bestowed upon every Jaguar. To wit, it's bloody fast.

Elizabeth protested when I told her I would take her. I threw something about her brother getting upset if he found out she'd roamed London by herself in the state she was, and she promptly suppressed any further objection.

I swing through some lights, vaulting to Camden quicker. The Jag is automatic, and there is no direct need to use my injured hand, thank goodness.

I glance at Elizabeth. She's shivering. I turn the heating up.

'Have you eaten?' I ask.

'No. I've lost my appetite,' she tells me, gazing out the windscreen, on edge.

'We'll get some tea at the hospital…' I trail off. She makes a facial expression that reminds me of James. They aren't so very similar. You can take both of them for siblings, yes, but other than colouring, I perceive those subtle differences, which makes one sibling look more like one parent more, and the other, look more like the other parent. She's tall; a couple of inches shorter than me, but she's got a long way ahead of her. She has a slightly larger frame than I do. Not surprising, that!

The only way you'll put on a bit of weight is when you get pregnant! – Vic. She's probably right. Vic has normal weight and is curvaceous. Mum's side of the family. I take after the thin Stephenses.

We drive a little way in silence, just the purr of the hydraulics serenading us.

I slow as we reach the first roundabout that expedites us onto Hendon Way, as it starts to drizzle. I turn the wipers on, and wind through and down, having the right of way. It's relatively empty, and I press on gas to the limit.

'Thank you for doing this,' Elizabeth says. 'Jamie is really lucky to have you as a friend.'

I swallow, and I feel my cheeks burn. Her words are kind. Too kind. I smile. She opens her mouth to say something, then closes it. Then says, 'What's your name? Jamie never mentioned.'

'Oh, I never said, did I? It's El. Eleanora. You can call me El.'

'El?!' she cries. 'Seriously?'

'Yeah. Why?' She's spiked my curiosity.

'It's nothing, just, it's funny because Jamie used to call me El…'

I don't know what to make of that.

'What a coincidence, eh?' she says. I'm starting to hate that word.

'Yeah…'

'He used to call me Lizzy when I was young, then at one point he changed it to El, just a few weeks before he left home. But now it's back to Lizzy, mostly.'

'Lizzy is nice,' is all I can say. My mind boggles over that piece of fact. Had he named his sister after me? He hated me – that had been clear enough. His past verbal laceration indicated exactly how he saw me.

But then, why was he so tender minutes earlier? Had he really been leading me on? It didn't feel like it, even to this day. The touch of his fingers through my hair felt like a spark of life, no… a fire, igniting from within. That electrifying sensation had felt so genuine. But then, why? WHY?

ASK! my mind shouts to me. Ask him. *No! Ask her! Elizabeth. Get the information you need.*

'Elizabeth?' I begin tentatively. 'Both of your parents are at the hospital, right?'

'Right.'

'And your father? You said there was a rift?'

'Yeah.'

'From back then? From the arrest?'

'Yes,' she says, and folds her arms, clamming up. Immured. It obviously upsets her, my questioning. She is in the defence position. She's closed the walls around her. There is no way to pursue the subject now.

We are about ten minutes away from Camden, and traffic is gathering. I decide to change the subject; alleviate that grey cloud lingering over her head.

'So, what school do you go to?'

She unfolds her arms and scratches her head. 'Hilsmond. Do you know it?' she asks.

'Do I know it?' I say, incredulous. 'I used to go there!'

'No shit!' Her face is animated, the veil of gloom lifted.

'No shit! Have they changed the uniform, then?' I remember the school had been discussing uniform change one year shy of me leaving.

'Yeah. Two years ago. Apparently, we're sharing with a couple of other schools to be more *economical*...' She says the word "economical" with air quotes.

'Hope they've fixed that swimming pool...' I utter.

'Yeah...They are starting on it next month... should be finished by twenty, twenty!'

'Hah!'

'Fond memories?'

'Oh, yeah... Best years of my life! Including the bullying.'

'No! You were bullied? I don't believe it.'

Her words and mannerisms strike a chord. *Just like him.* He also had a theory, I recall. A theory I never learnt.

'But you're so beautiful. How could that be?' Elizabeth says.

I guffaw sarcastically. 'No, I'm not!'

'I know why,' she says, ignoring me, brows raised in divining etiology. 'They were jealous.'

They're jealous – Mum.

It's not a problem, and you can't fix it – Him. I take in a sharp breath. Had that been his theory too?

I shrug. 'Probably...' I say. 'Whatever the reason, I suppose it made me more resilient.' Resilient. Resilient... Jesus. *He* had said that too. He had told me, taught me how to handle my situation, how to cope, and I only just realised it. My memory shoots back, and I see it now. I see myself in sixth form. How I'd gradually started to surpass all my inhibitions because

158

I'd done what he had advised. How I'd found that part of me that could manage the bullies, and how… finally, they'd stopped.

My eyes have watered, but I continue.

'Do you see that?' I show her a small scar I have on my hairline, lifting up some of my fringe.

'Yeah,' she says, interested.

'That's where I was bashed up against the brick wall outside the gym by a very sweet person called Tamara. She broke my front tooth, and left me with a bleeding nose and lip, and a threat against my life.' Elizabeth's face contorts in shock.

'Got it fixed,' I say. 'My tooth, I mean. You can't really tell – the dentist did a good job.'

'What a bitch!' Elizabeth exclaims. 'I would have kicked her face in!'

'I would have too, but her posse was there. I couldn't move a muscle unless I had a death wish.'

Elizabeth is speechless.

I lift up my sleeve on my left arm to partially reveal a vertical, silverish scar, just above my dorsal radial carpal. 'What's that?' she gasps.

'Tamara had got out her knife.'

'Jesus Christ!'

'The doctor said I was lucky. Any further in, and I would have bled to death before the ambulance came.'

'Those bitches!'

I smile. 'Don't worry, I got my own back, per say.'

'Yeah?' She is all ears. 'What did you do?'

'I ignored them.'

'What?!' She sounds disappointed with my answer.

'Yeah. They taunted me, called me names. They even slapped me around in the corridor to stop me ignoring them, but I didn't want to antagonise them. In hindsight, it was your brother's advice. He'd told me to measure what's important, what's worth my time, my pain, my joy…' I drift off, as I relive the scene. The urgency, the vehemence. With what zeal. His countenance so genuine. And, oh, the soft succour he'd given me, like a pillow to fall on, in those dark hours.

'Sounds like Jamie.' Elizabeth interrupts my thoughts. 'But what? You ignored them until you finished school?'

'No. Tamara got expelled, not too long later, actually. She'd been caught smoking some hash down in the fields. She got picked up!'

'Oh, my God! What an idiot!'

Then realising what we've just said, turn silent. The windscreen wipers thudding away, once, twice, thrice…

'That's why I don't go near them; drugs,' Elizabeth tells me quietly. 'I've seen what damage they can do.'

I place my hand on hers and squeeze. 'Oh, sweetie. I'm sorry!'

We reach a light.

'El?'

'Yes?'

'How did you find Jamie last night? Were you meeting him at his home?'

I look at the light, pretending to be intent on it turning green to bide me time on my reply.

'Not exactly,' I say, foraging for some decent reply. 'I wanted to talk to him about something. I'm just glad I was there at the right time. Why do you ask?'

'Well… how can I put it?'

The light turns green.

'It's just that, Jamie's never told anyone where he lives. I'm the only person who knows. And Nick, his best friend. And perhaps the postman… Not even Mum knows, or Dad.'

Heat rises to the tip of my cranium. It could have been either from the prospect that I would have to tell a big, fat lie in the very near future or – and I'm sorry if this sounds egotistical – a rush of delight at the fact that he's never shared his home with a girl, ergo, he's never had a serious relationship.

'And like I said, he never mentioned anything about you, so…' She tilts her head down. What on earth is she trying to say?

'Tell me, Elizabeth. Don't be afraid.'

'I don't mean to pry…'

'It's OK…'

'Well, I just thought maybe… if you and James were going out with one another, and he didn't have the chance to tell me… perhaps it's because that you are in the beginning of the relationship, and he didn't want to tell me of it, 'cos it's early days yet…'

I swerve, only slightly, as I feel blood singe my cheeks.

'We aren't like that,' I fumble. 'And I'm sure he would have told you, early days or not, if we were.'

She seems contented with this reply.

'He doesn't have any friends, you know, except Nick. And maybe a couple of friendly acquaintances at his gym. No one truly close… And here you are, like his guardian angel. You saved his life…'

She throws me off completely.

She's already crying by the time I take my eyes off the road to look at her. I feel the salty tears escape me too. She doesn't know the half of it…

We draw closer to his home – his garage *dash* storeroom – taking the street the ambulance took. I grate up the side handbrake, parking perpendicular to the alley, and take a breath. I am about to enter his home. His life. Everything he has. I feel a dreadful spasm in my gut, warning me that I'm not going to like what I see.

Elizabeth loses no time in getting to the corrugated-iron doors. I see she has already slotted a key in the padlock. I help her heave the door open. What a clang!

She rushes in, knowing exactly where to find things.

I step a toe. The first thing that hits me is the cold. The temperature is exactly the same as outside. Then the faint musty odour of mildew. Elizabeth hits a switch, and a dim lamp overhead lights the place to some extent. I am standing in an almost bare space, save a bed, bookcase and desk, and a makeshift kitchen. The bed is unmade, with a thick, grey blanket, which looks surprisingly cosy, and the desk – that which I had caught on my camera. There is carpet on the floor, almost fitted up to walls. It is soft and thick, with a subtle Versailles pattern, in a light shade of grey. It looks familiar. Where have I seen it? It isn't cheap… That's a Laura Ashley! Then I spot a burnt hole in a corner; someone had thrown it out. One man's trash…

The small bookcase is stacked with novels, tomes and volumes. Dostoyevsky, Hugo, Dickens, Shakespeare, Homer, Plato, Twain… Bronte – a *Jane Eyre* just like mine. Looking down, down, and then I read to my shock, the words "Ancient Greek" in Greek, no less. I huff, and shake my head, impressed, yet incredulous. *Ancient Greek? What on earth…*

I spot a gas stove with the propane tank underneath, a small stainless-steel sink with a plate and a bowl. A cereal box. A jam jar.

He's been living as a modern-day ascetic.

I sneak a peek at his desk. There is that chair. In the picture I took, I couldn't see it all. It was a proper office type; comfortable, anatomical – just the thing for not injuring your back if you have to sit for hours. There is that fat book, but his laptop is nowhere to be seen. I read the title of the book. *Computers and Engineering*. I look to the left and see a stack of more text books, all of which either had the word "Mechanics" or "Engineering" or "Computers" written on their spines. On the other side, a pile of sketch paper with mechanical designs of some sort, in axonometric 3D.

And then I see it – the UCL logo atop a formal piece of paper, half-wedged inside a book. I recognise it instantly. It is the print-out copy of the year's modules. Jesus. He *is* studying… and in UC bloody L! Of course! It's only logical; why sweep floors in a university other than your own? Bet he gets a reduction on fees too. I let out a small incredulous huff. Good for him. I tremble with sedate joy, as gram of guilt evaporates, assuaging the burden of wrongdoing a notch. At least his future isn't totally maimed.

I turn to Elizabeth, who is busily folding some light grey item of clothing and shoving it into a rucksack.

'What can I do?' I say.

'Toothbrush maybe. Towel…'

'On it!' I say, and walk, hesitantly, the five steps which take me to what can only be a bathroom area. The place is so small, there is nowhere else it could be.

Elizabeth is looking at me peculiarly. My hesitation sparks something new in her eyes – confusion? From the little I know of her so far, it's clear she's sharp; nobody's fool. I suppose I do seem a bit of a mystery to her, for there are signs that my friendship with James isn't quite above board. She's cottoned on to it. There I am, claiming I know him and where he lives, as I drove us without asking her for directions, and yet my behaviour has all the aspect of an imposter.

She says nothing. I say nothing. What's there to be said now? There are more important matters at hand.

The bathroom is pitiful. It isn't filthy or anything. In fact, it smells great. It's pitiful because it's in desperate need of replacement. The ceramics have reached that point where no matter how much bleach you put on them, they'll never sparkle white, tiles and all. The mirror looks new, cheap with a generic, plastic rim, but new. The shower has a plain, white curtain, half-way, drawn. I stare for a second and pick it between my fingers for closer inspection. I have the same curtain! Ikea; mid-season sale. There is a bundle of dark clothes in a corner, dwelling for laundry day.

I nab toothbrush and toothpaste from the cup, find couple of folded towels on a decrepit shelf, take one, and exit the bathroom.

I place the items by Elizabeth, and she puts them in the bag, her back to me.

I take it out from within my jacket and place it, surreptitiously, on the stack of books. I don't want her to see what I leave for James.

***

Elizabeth's body is taut on the seat of the Jag. She toys with her hair and searches for the hospital building, wide-eyed, out the rain-streaked window.

'Is it far?' she asks me.

'Not very. There's a bit of traffic.'

She doesn't seem appeased.

'Everything's going to be fine,' I say encouragingly. 'The doctors told me. Don't you worry.'

'I know… it's not that… I just hope he can patch things up with Dad, finally. I mean, after this, they have to see life's not worth it, you know? Being angry with one another.' She shakes her head, thinking. 'It's all pride. Male ego.'

She is opening up. My opportunity to fish for more details. 'But he was one foot out the door, wasn't he? Off to Oxford. What was the problem?'

'Oxford had heard of the arrest, and they let him attend, but he didn't go.'

'Why ever not?' I ask, angry, confused.

'Dad,' she says flatly.

I knew it. 'Your father?' She nods. I wait for her to elaborate.

'He refused to pay. He cut him off. He's a very, how can I put it…' she lets out a sigh. We enter the hospital parking, circling to find a space. I spy one.

'He,' Elizabeth continues. 'He was brought up in a very strict family with intense morals. I think he was hard on Jamie to teach him a lesson. I think that's why any mention of Jamie is stopped. It's too painful for him.' She pauses but isn't finished. I park in the space and wrench up the handbrake. I don't move a muscle. I don't even breathe.

'Dad…' She is choosing her words carefully, eyes downcast, searching. 'Dad regretted his… punishment… and at one point, he tried to get in touch with Jamie and apologise. Perhaps lend him some money to get his education done. Jamie refused, and Dad had come home and had a massive fight with Mum. I didn't hear much. I remember running up to my room and putting my pillow over my head.' She stops. There is more. My innards have become a knot.

'Mum had given Dad a right good bollocking that night. She said how he never should have acted in anger. His rage had got the better of him, and he'd lashed out harshly on poor Jamie, who'd never done anything bad in his life, mind you… just over that one skimpy joint!'

Elizabeth wipes her eyes. 'Of course, back then, Dad thought he'd raped that girl too 'cos the police were questioning him over it. Someone had pointed a finger at him.' Blood rises to my face. 'Anyway, it wasn't just over the spliff.

'All the parents had gone over to the house but not Dad. He couldn't have been more humiliated. He left Jamie to get picked up and taken to the station. But his pride didn't allow him to take back his words immediately. So, he left Jamie to find his own means. Then, three years ago, Dad had caught me secretly giving some of my pocket money to Jamie. Then he softened and got in touch, but as I said, Jamie refused. I suppose he has his own pride too…'

My eyes have fixed on a spot outside the windscreen, beyond the dusky, nimbostratus clouds. I am inert. I have just been handed the whole explanation – the gap is filled, and I cannot process it. It rings in my ears, like I've been given a death sentence.

Elizabeth gathers James's stuff and opens the door. She bites her lip and says, 'Dad doubled my pocket money after that.'

I stare, introspective.

'Are you coming?' she asks.

I shake my head. It dislodges a tear. 'No, I have to get going. Police are waiting…' I whisper. I have no voice.

'Right. Well. Thank you, El. You are a true friend. If he's awake, I'll give him your love.' And she shuts the door before I can react.

Back Then

'Kate! What's going on?' I hissed.

'Shhh!' she begged.

I looked right in her eyes, waiting for an explanation. They started to water, and she moved abruptly, walked to where she had flung her shoes earlier, and started to put them on.

She yanked her head to one side, *let's go.*

I found my shoes and followed her down the stairs.

She took my coat from the rack in the hall and handed it to me. Then she put hers on, grabbed her keys, some cash and her phone, and we were out of there.

It was a Saturday night, and we'd just come back from the shopping centre, spent, and massaging our feet. We had only sat in her room for twenty minutes when he'd come in. Now we were on the move again, in the dead of night, and in the dead of winter. We still had our work clothes on, the flimsy shirt and skirt but with thick tights on.

'Can we go to your place?' she asked, as we turned the corner that led us out onto the main street for the bus.

'Sure,' I said dubiously. 'Are your parents cool with it?'

She shot me a harsh look. 'Who gives a shit?!' she bit. 'They never cared about me. Besides, they'll see him, and they'll know why I'm not there.'

I felt a strange, nauseated misgiving wedged in the pit of my stomach.

'They're the reason I ran away in the first place!' she said, bursting into tears. 'They don't care about me, only their darling son!'

We froze are arses off waiting for the bus to take us to Edgware, as we sat in silence on the brutally-cold, metal bench.

'I'll call my mum to pick us up from the station,' I said, as I dialled my phone. Kate sat silently and scarcely nodded, staring into oblivion, her breaths: white gusts swirling in the night air, her eyes: red circles against her pale face.

Finally, the bus came. Kate, rigid in deep thought, barely able to beep her card, as she walked like a zombie to some seats. I reached her. She was almost catatonic. I sat us in a familiar place.

Whenever I got on a bus, I'd picture him. The memory was still so raw that it would surge into me like voltage, as soon as the ingrained surroundings awakened my subconscious. Even the smell of the bus did it for me. Over a year had passed since I last saw his face, and I always managed to conjure his presence whenever I entered one. Unfortunately, it didn't stop there. There were other remnants of the communion that once was. Other persistent reminders, sharp electroshocks, of the most vivid images that would find me unaware, whenever I saw, or heard, or felt, something associated with him. I'd be rinsing out my oil-painted hands in the Art-room sink, when I'd hear him say in that penetrant timbre, *is that paint on your hands.* I'd be watching television and there'd be a word or phrase spoken, which we had once shared, and I'd be spirited away to that particular conversation. It is why I had cut my hair – at least I wouldn't feel the sensation of fingers combing it all the way down. One less reminder.

But the worst – something I couldn't merely cut off – was when I found myself outside Milden Boys. *This is where he stood. This is where he asked my name and took my hand…* It had become sacred ground, but not the type you wandered onto for peace and comfort, but more like, the type you are not allowed to step on in fear you awaken the dead and forgotten.

I didn't want to – think of him, I mean – not after the way he'd blatantly proved he was a liar and had callously taken my heart and stepped on it. But my mind drifted to him, without my will. His image was seared for ever in my memory, like the deepest burn.

Mum, bless her, had the Jag running, and hot air welcomed us in the cabin, thawing our chilled skin.

She was happy to see Kate and tactful enough to understand the girl wasn't well. So she gave a quick, affable greeting and drove us home with no more words, just the occasional look in the rear-view mirror.

I vaguely remember the evening – not because of some lack of recollection, but because what followed after, just before we went to bed for the night, was so profound that everything else was inconsequential.

Up in my room, Kate uttered it in one horrifying sentence. Her secret. A horrible, sick feeling I had never felt before, gripped my innards like an immovable rock of obsidian in the depths of my solar plexus, pushing the bile higher.

She didn't elaborate. She didn't judge. She didn't cry. She sat, her eyes fixed on a sketch of mine on the carpet. A laconic explanation – short and to the point:

'Serious sexual assault.'

It was so repulsive, so vile, that I unwillingly felt as if it were happening to me. I had no words. Anything I would say didn't feel adequate enough. What *could* I say? How must I react? What words were there to help her?

'How could he do that?' I ended up saying, heart-wrenched. 'He's your brother!'

Kate shrugged helplessly, still looking at the sketch on the carpet.

'Don't your parents –'

'My parents are arseholes!' she snapped. 'They didn't lift one finger to help me. They act like nothing is wrong. They're in denial, like we are one big, happy family.'

Kate seemed more upset about this than about her brother.

'Rhys is ill. He should get checked. He should be on medication or something. He needs therapy, but oh no! Heavens forbid Mum and Dad ever admit it. No! Their idea of therapy is to stare stolidly at the telly and pretend their son isn't trying to stick his hand down their daughter's knickers, innit?'

The air went silent. We sat angry. Kate made a move to wipe an eye, then sniffed.

'But I don't let him. Oh, no. I bite, kick, anywhere I can... It's all right when he's away; life is bearable... but when he's home...' she shook her head. 'I can't be there.'

'I understand,' I said. 'How... how long has he been –?"

'A while. As soon as I became a B cup, I suppose,' she said. Kate was a C, like me. 'I don't know what happened. One minute everything was fine, and next minute...' Her face contorted to a sob, the bad memories taking hold.

I put my arm around her, hoping it would ease her pain, and at the same time thinking how I'd like to kick Rhys in the balls and tell her parents to get their act together... And secretly counting my blessings that nothing like that had ever happened to me.

Chapter Thirty

Now

I am left staring at the shut door of the Jag, and start to cry bitterly. All the repudiation of the past rips me asunder in a charge of heart-wrenching pain. For yes, I had denied it six years ago. I always knew there had to have been something I'd not seen. And because I never saw it clearly, I ignored it even existed. I was told there had been arrests, but I never took that extra step to follow up on it, always contented with touching the surface. Not daring to scratch deeper. Stupid, negligent searches online. They were never enough. I was fooling myself, thinking the internet had everything. I should have made sure everything was all right, personally. I should have found James, talked with him. Knocked on his parents' door, demanded they tell me where he was, where Nick was, anyone, and come face to face with the truth. Explain to his parents that it wasn't their son's fault. Now, I have come face to face with my offence, and it is a vile self-portrait.

'It is my fault. It's all my fault. I caused this…'

My phone call was what did it. Those 18 minutes from my phone call to the other girl's phone call had made the all difference. He'd told me he wasn't staying for long. I had got him into trouble by pointing him out and sic'ing the police on him. Then the inevitable events unfolded like an unstoppable cascade. If I had left it, not pass that Rubicon, James would have been in the clear – home and safe, and his parents none the wiser. If I had left it, his father would never have known, would never have cut his son off. James would have gone on to his predestined future and lived his rightful life. But this is the consequence, the impact, when one acts with ill will. It bombards a life into a scrapheap. Oh, what damage have I wreaked? For six years, this man has been living enslaved by my hard incursion. His father was merely his prison-warden. I was the condemning judge and jury.

'FUUUCK!' I scream, gripping tight on the steering wheel, bawling. I weep. I yell.

I rue.

I must give him his manumission. Free him… I have found out the truth, and now I must strive to make amends, hitherto, till I have atoned. Till I am absolved of my sin… by him.

I'll give him your love. What did she mean by it? What will *he* think of it? How will it be interpreted in his mind? Love? Give him my love? I harrumph cynically. I shut my eyes. No. I don't want her to give him my love. She can't; it's not her right – it's mine. And I'm not giving it to him. I'm not giving it to him because he doesn't need that burden. It would be unwelcoming. And, since I am forced to enter his life again, I don't want him to think of me, in any other light, than that of being his betrayer, his slanderer, the one who robbed him of a better future. Perhaps it's a blessing he already hates me.

I put the Jag in D and step on the gas.

Elizabeth's words reap through my mind. The part about her father cutting James off in the heat of rage, stunting his future, just to teach him a lesson. I can't believe it. But then again, families do incomprehensible things to their members, their loved-ones.

Then I think, yes, I can believe it, for didn't I act in rage myself? When I picked up that phone, didn't I want to punish him too?

There is that thought again. There is something that I've overlooked in all of this – not laid out properly in my mind. It toys with my senses as it loiters, cunningly, waiting to get caught.

'What are you?' I cry. 'What are you, you bugger?!'

I try to go over events, again and again, but get stuck. I can't concentrate. I'm too agitated. Too tired. Too starving.

***

I sit, staring up at the brick structure, the angle I am at, it touches the dark sky, half-covered in shadow. The same Victorian-style lamp hangs on the wall. Not all the windows are alight. It is late; people have gone home.

I don't want to go in.

I don't move, and I have visions of officers coming and dragging me in, screaming. I sigh, knowing it's futile; there is no way out; only through. Time to face the music.

I lock the car. The night is crisp, and I put my hood on, as I feed money to the metre. I walk up the stairs to the entrance and open the heavy, glass door to a gush of warmth, wrapping me, as I walk to the front desk.

I lower my hood, and the desk sergeant looks at me intently.

'Hi. I'm here to see Detective Inspector Archer?'

'Name, please,' he asks politely, his hand making its way to the receiver on his desk.

I tell him it, as he jabs some buttons for an internal phone call, mumbling something about me being there.

I stifle a yawn, putting my hand over my mouth, and my eye catches the movement. I see myself on a monitor, propped on a nearby desk. The camera is somewhere to my top, left corner, and I turn so that I can see my face full-on. How pale I have become. Deathly. A sallow, bloodless girl, I do not recognise.

I linger for some time; I don't know how long. Sounds have muted. Sight has blurred. People are figures of shade and movement around me.

I hear the desk sergeant say something to me, something about taking a seat. I move.

One pace, two paces, three…

'Ms Stephens?'

There is a man. His image indistinct. He comes closer, closer, and I see clearer, clearer. Tall, fit, dressed in civvies. He has that air of a man who sussed out his life years ago. He comes closer with his hand out. I give him my braced hand without thinking.

'DI Archer,' he tells me.

I blink, pulling myself out of the glaze.

'Good evening, Detective,' I say, wan. And remembering my cultured upbringing (as Kate puts it) add, 'I'm sorry for the delay.'

'That's quite all right. Is it broken?' he asks, referring to my wrist.

'I don't know.' What am I saying? Am I admitting to the police that I drove all this way with a broken hand? They'll have my guts for garters. 'I mean, I don't think so. I drove here all right.' My wrist *was* feeling better, admittedly.

'I see. Well, Ms Stephens, you've been rather difficult to find, do you know that?' It isn't a reprimand but it's the end of civilities.

'No,' I say spiritlessly.

'Please, come with me. There's a place where we can talk. We won't take up much of your time.'

We? His partner?

I'm led out of the commotion, through a corridor, and down, passed some offices and cubicles. There are a few people here, still on the job. The low, work-room banter, intermingled with phones ringing – landline and mobile – is heard. Sudden, shrill laughter fills the room, and I flinch.

DI Archer has taken me to the other side, away from the noise. He opens the door to an office and walks in, leaving the door wide open so that I may follow.

I enter, and, at first, I think I'm in the wrong place, because there at the other desk, is sat CI Daley.

'You know Chief Inspector Daley?' Archer says rhetorically. He is being pragmatic, business-like. No hiding. No beating around the bush. I panic. I know the only reason for Daley to be there is for the same reason I am there: James. I am going to hear it. I'm going to be chastised for not telling her of the assault this morning.

'Chief Inspector,' I say, with the startlement audible.

'Ms Stephens,' she acknowledges.

Something tickles my pharynx, and I cough reflexively, a good five seconds. 'Sorry,' I apologise, thoroughly embarrassed.

'Please take a seat,' Archer says to me. There is only one available, and I take it. Daley reaches out for a plastic cup, pours some water from the dispenser at her side, and rests it close to me. I sip. It does nothing to reduce the dryness stuck obstinately in my throat. Archer shuts the door and walks to his desk. Complete silence, just the soft ticking of the wall clock. They say nothing, and I look from one to the other. There is a heaviness cumbering the atmosphere, I do not like. I wait, tense, for someone to tell me what is going on.

'Ms Stephens, we would like you to answer some questions regarding the recent attack on James Laidlaw,' begins Archer. Daley makes a gesture. 'But before we do that, we'd like to know why you didn't report it?'

Nothing comes out of my mouth. I feel like a doe in the headlights.

'Ms Stephens,' Daley says, trying to get through to me. 'You left him before the ambulance arrived last night, and when you came to my office this morning, you still didn't say a word. Are you afraid of something?'

I look up at her abruptly, all this time transfixed to the floor. Something has jogged my memory, but I lose it.

'Whatever it is, you can tell us,' Archer says. There is trace of panic in his tone, even though he's trying to reassure me. He's afraid of losing me. 'Were not here to charge you with anything. We just need to be made aware of all the facts. Anything to help with the investigation.'

I rub my eyes. They are already wet. Finally, I speak. 'I-I know I should have stayed and talked to the paramedics, but to be honest, I panicked.' I take a breath, Archer is about to say something.

'But,' I blurt, stopping him, 'I didn't leave him. I stayed u-until I saw the lights of the ambulance come through the street. I'd even covered him with my coat so he wouldn't freeze to death.'

'Were you aware that the police were on their way, as well as the ambulance?' Archer asks.

'No.'

'Weren't you told on the phone?'

'I don't know. The woman could have said something, but I didn't hear. I was shouting, I was frantic. I was scared.'

Both officers glance at one another. Do they believe me? To their credit they're not blatantly doubting me with sneering grimaces.

'What about this morning?' Daley prods.

'I was going to, but the conversation had taken so many turns, I thought I'd come straight here; the police station responsible for the area.'

'It's almost a quarter to nine. You left my office at around ten a.m.,' Daley tells me. She's waiting for me to fill in the eleven-hour gap.

'I know. I know. I-I should have come.' I am full of remorse. 'But I wanted to see if he was all right first. That's when I learnt he had no ID. I don't know how many hospitals I called. I'm sorry... I hope I haven't impaired the investigation... Jesus! I had no idea there'd even *be* an investigation.'

'It's a serious crime, battery,' Archer tells me. 'If Laidlaw hadn't put up a fight, he'd have probably been beaten to death. Then that's murder.'

Silence.

They think James was the one who had put a stop to it.

'Good thing he's a boxer,' says Daley, guileless. She wants to stress James would have been a goner if he weren't.

Archer makes a clear intake of breath. 'Right,' he says. 'Let's take it from the top, shall we?' Another rhetorical. I tug at a cuticle, anticipating further unpleasant interrogation.

'How do you know Mr Laidlaw?' he asks.

I look questioningly at Daley. Hasn't she told him?

'In your own words, Ms Stephens,' she says, understanding me fully.

I nod and lick my lips. 'Um... Well. We met six years ago. He used to go to the boys' school, up the road from my school. We'd talked a few times.'

'And you've been in touch all this time?'

'No.'

'No? Did you meet recently then?'

'No.'

Archer quirks his head. 'So, how do you know where he lives?' How, indeed.

'I found out,' I say, and pray he doesn't ask me how again.

'How?'

I sigh, defeated. 'I hope you are good on your word, Detective.'

He raises a brow. I hear Daley shuffle.

'About not charging me,' I explain.

'Ms Stephens, if you've committed a serious offence, I can't promise you…'

'It's not serious. I followed him,' I tell him, straight. I feel a dab of relief admitting it, actually. I wait for reactions. Neither officers look angry. Mildly surprised, I would say.

'I thought so,' says Daley. 'When you asked me this morning on the subject, I knew there had to be a reason.'

The little I managed to read up on, in regards to following someone, is, generally, the seriousness of the crime comes down to intent. I hadn't harassed, bothered or come in contact with, the object of my pursuit. All I wanted was his own good. They can't charge me with *that*, can they?

'Why did you follow him? Why didn't you just speak to him?' Archer asks.

I glance at Daley again. I wish I could hand her the proverbial ball on this discussion as she's probably already surmised why I did it. But it has to be said in my own words.

'It was for good intention,' I tell Archer. 'I wanted to ascertain what happened to him before I approached him.'

'What happened to him?' Archer asks, puzzled.

'Yes. To ascertain why he was sweeping floors at my university. Not that that's bad or anything, but last thing I knew, he was going to Oxford. Do you see what I'm getting at? It made me wonder why he was sweeping floors, torn and dirty, and not making his way to some office in a suit. I know that sounds conceited and small-minded, like it's taken for granted you land a great job after a degree from a top university; I know it isn't always the case. But that's why I followed him. I needed to find out what happened.'

'Perhaps he failed all his courses. Dropped out?'

'I thought that, but no. It's because he never went,' I declare. 'He never went, Detective. His sister told me. And do you know why?' Archer is still. 'Because I got him into trouble.'

'Ms Stephens. Eleanora. You can't blame –'

'I can!' I cut Daley off. I start to tremble. 'You asked me what I was doing all day? I'll tell you. I have been running about half of London, trying to find out why he is impoverished. Gathering clues from anyone I could find. Do you know what I discovered? I ruined his life.'

Archer is showing scepticism. 'CI Daley sent me his file, and I read he got a full discharge. Nothing you did changed his life radically, Ms Stephens.'

'His father cut him off. Threw him out the house, penniless, because I had named him as a rapist.'

They both sit, mulling that over. Archer scratches his chin. Daley sits back in her chair.

I run my hands through my hair and wipe my eyes, fumbling for that tissue in my pocket.

'Do you know what, Eleanora?' Daley says. 'I think Mr Laidlaw's father overreacted. I don't think you're the one to blame for ruining his life. I think they are. Mr Laidlaw went to trial, was acquitted, and was a free man to continue his life. He was still young. Whatever feud they had, it should have been resolved. I mean, you can't be responsible for what he's done with his life for the past six years.'

'I don't know,' I say, despondent. 'All I know is, if I hadn't opened my big mouth…'

I hear my heart; it is drumming so hard; it's making my whole chest move.

'Let's continue with the matter at hand. The assault,' Archer says, seeing no need to continue the debate on who is to blame. I acquiesce with a quiet nod. 'We need to help Laidlaw now, as much as we can. Find the people who did this to him. Everything can help. We need you to tell us what you saw. We believe Laidlaw was ambushed by at least two men. They were lying in wait,' Archer says. 'Did you see anything?'

And then it hits me. It hits me so hard, it is as if I was walking in silence in a blinding mist, all this time, and suddenly the blaring shriek of a passing train pounds my ears, as it awakens me from my stupor.

Ambush… lying in wait.

Nobody knew where he lived.

Sometimes it takes one sentence, one *word,* just one – a spark which ignites the flame of synapsis, awakening our syllogism.

My whole body freezes as it succinctly challenges the only logical question: How on earth did those men find where James lived? They must have either hacked for details; paid someone to tell them; or… followed him.

I am suddenly very afraid. These men were ready to kill. If they ever found out there was an eyewitness, they wouldn't stop at harming me too. Before I speak, I need to eliminate information about myself, accessed on the internet. I am on no social media, except for my blog. I'll have to delete any personal information, or, even take it down. And what about my phone-number details? They could search my number; the time and place on the dispatch logs. There is the Data Protection Act; my rights to delete information – but that would need to be processed, and the red tape takes up to 21 days, so it said when I read the legislation online once. I need to be anonymous without delay. What if I am too late?

As for being followed? …Jesus… I'll have to be vigilant.

I need to get in touch with Sophie, yesterday.

Daley and Archer are waiting tensely. I must look like I need to be on medication. I don't talk. I don't move. My mind has drifted.

'Eleanora?' Daley asks. 'Are you all right? Any information would be great…' I hear her desperation.

Archer suddenly opens a big envelope, taking out its contents and spreading it on his desk. I see James's battered face, scaled 50% larger, all swollen and bruised, full of contusions. *That* strikes me brutally. The pictures are so high in resolution that even the hair's-width cut under his left eye is visible. I close my eyes. It takes a lot not to cry. Archer's trump-card to make me talk. I search for an excuse to leave.

'You see, we don't think this was some kind of random act. Laidlaw is a big man. If he were mugged by some, run-of-the-mill, street punk, I don't think the street punk would have got away with much unless he had some weapon to threaten his victim with. No. This was planned. They were lying in wait. They knew exactly where he lived. There were punches and, most likely, and the way some of the wounds showed on his face, brass knuckles.' I flinch.

'There'd have to have been at least two his size to pull that off. This was set up. It was attempted murder. Matters are very serious. We need your cooperation on this, Eleanora!'

I convulse. It is a reflex action. Nothing comes up; not even the drop of water I sipped. All I know is, in that moment, I want justice for James. The fury at what those men have done, unwavering my resolve.

'I have something,' I say abruptly, and get up. They both dart up, ready to halt any move I make to leave. The room fills with a vibe of alert silence. 'But please… I need a favour first, then I'll tell you what I saw.'

Archer gives a side-glance to Daley, apprehension chiselled on his face. Deep concern furrows in Daley's brow. She says, 'Are you afraid of something?' This woman is sharp.

'Chief Inspector. Detective,' I say turning to each. I shake. 'I know f-for a fact nobody knew where James lived. His sister told me that she, and James's best friend, were the only ones. Not even their parents knew! So, explain to me how they found him? H-how did they know exactly where he lives? All I want is to make sure I can't be found. If they found him by way of hacking or by following him, then they can find the person who made the emergency call. Just like you did.'

'They can't. It's extremely difficult. There are firewalls and everything. We have top technology on that,' Archer says. 'Is that what you're afraid of?'

'I am, yes, for my family, for my friends, anyone who is associated with me. My old address is on record for my present phone number. That's where you went to first, wasn't it? What if they get to my mum? My grandparents live there too. I want my information to be deleted now!'

They are thinking. They know I have the right.

CI Daley shrugs to Archer, 'We don't need to have her information online anymore. I suppose I could get data control to erase her number.'

'How long will it take?' I ask.

'If we inform the data processor of an emergency, I'd say within twenty-four hours –'

'What?' I say, panic-stricken. That isn't good enough. 'James is safe and sound in hospital. He is alive because someone had phoned, in time, for an ambulance. How long do you think it would take them to realise that that someone must have been there, ready, and had phoned for an ambulance mere seconds after they'd left? I don't know about you, but if I were them, I'd be getting extremely uneasy that this person who phoned might have seen something which may incriminate them.'

Archer stares, momentarily, at a loss for words. Then, 'So you *did* see something. Something …important?'

'I did!' I walk to the door. I wait for some reply, but both officers' inability to give me a plausible riposte is all it takes to convince me I am right in assuming I could be in some danger. I have no immediate aegis from them. Matters are thrust into my hands now.

I lift my braced palm, appeasing. 'Please… I'm not leaving. I just…'

I have to get in contact with Sophie, do that email exchange Kate told me. Open mobile data and write her a drafted email. But it has to be done covertly. 'Could I perhaps use the ladies?' I ask.

Archer nods resignedly. 'Of course. It's down the hall.'

I open a cubicle, slam it shut and lock. Data on, in a shaking hand. Email app. Sign in as different user. I punch in the new details, *franklymydearidontgiveadamn*, then the password; another quote from the same movie, and write the draft.

Need a favour. Please erase my phone call to 999 on 16ᵗʰ of this month at around 8:30 p.m. and other personal info on my blog, Eleanora Dishes. *Thanks.*

I sign out and wait five, nerve-wracking minutes, then sign in again.

Done. Break your phone and dispose SIM and Memory card. Use burner until safe. Good luck.

These people are quick. I do as told and take out the SIM, crack with my teeth, but the memory card, I tuck in my pocket. I'm not ready to part with the pictures of him. Then I slam my phone on the floor, and the screen cracks while other bits and pieces scatter out. I gather up whatever I can, and shove the remainders of my phone into three separate sanitary-towel bags and place them in three separate disposable bins. I wash my hands thoroughly, pad some water on my face as well, take in a breath to calm myself, and make my way back.

I enter the office, sit down and begin my story from the point in which I saw James at Camden Lock. I tell them how I had been in Camden to see him, have a talk, but heard him cry out. How I ran to the wall and saw two men beating him, one black one white, and I was afraid they were going to kill him –

'Why did you think they were going to kill him?' Archer already said they assumed this. I am going to provide him with evidence.

'I heard the sound of a gun, so I knew they meant business, especially when one of them said "nothing that can be traced". They didn't want to be found, ergo, they were going to do something far more serious than a mere beating.'

Archer rubs his chin. 'Possible…' he says, almost to himself. Daley agrees. 'It might just pass…'

He puts a hand through his hair. 'Then what happened, because they didn't use the gun obviously?'

'I think they continued throwing punches. I don't know. I had turned back, ran to a car, pushed and swayed it, so the alarm would go off, hopefully to scare them. To stop them. And when it did, I ran as fast as I could, so I could call nine, nine, nine and not be heard. I prayed it did the trick… After the call, I had to see if he was OK, so I walked back, and then I saw them turn into the street coming towards me, and I ran and hid. I was so scared. Then they got into an SUV and left.'

'Did you get a good look at them?' Archer asks.

'Good enough…'

'All right, we'll do a face composite. What about their SUV. What was it? Can you describe it to me?'

'It was van-like. Tinted windows. Black. It looked new, you know, the body? And I don't think I've seen that make before.'

'You didn't recognise the make?'

'No,' I say, disconcerted. 'I know my car, but that particular one is a mystery. It looked like it wasn't sold in the UK.'

Archer raises his brow. 'Is that so? If you saw it again, would you be able to recognise it?'

'I can do better than that. I'll sketch for you, and you can find out its make.'

Archer raises both his brows, waiting for the punchline.

'I have, what you might call, an eidetic memory,' I tell them.

'Oh, yeah?' Archer says with a note of fascination.

'Really?' says Daley, intrigued.

'All right, then. Let's see how good an artist you are.' He smiles. He knows I'm an art student. 'Perhaps you could sketch the assailants as well?' I meet his eyes and nod.

'Is there anything else you'd like to add?' he asks. I sit motionless, thinking over everything I've said. Have I left anything out?

'Detective,' I say. There is one thing I think prudent to mention. 'I heard one of the men say "did you get the stuff" and the other one said "yeah, let's get the fuck out". I think they took something from James.'

Archer takes this in, jots it down in one of those little note pads. 'Anything else?'

I shake my head. 'I can't think of anything else right now,' I say honestly.

He hands me a card. 'If you remember even the stupidest, most insignificant detail, don't hesitate in calling me, whatever the time.'

I take the card. 'I'd like something from you now,' I say, with tenacity that charges the room. *Leverage.* Archer is listening.

'Protect my family.' I tell them. It was no supplication, no plead. It was a demand.

He nods. 'Granted.'

Suddenly the office phone rings.

'Archer.'

I hear the voice on the other end say clearly, 'Laidlaw's awake.'

Chapter Thirty-One

Now

I look through the upstairs curtains and see a non-descript car at the edge of the drive. Archer told me it would be inconspicuous, so as not to rouse any suspicion amongst the neighbours, before he almost ran out the station to get to James; his priority now.

I had to return the Jag; Mum needs it for her weekly Sainsbury's. A mother who, as soon as she saw me, let out a cry and put her palm on my cheek. I must have looked wraithlike. It startled me, her touch. I haven't felt that in years.

'Tell Mum,' she urged.

'I'm tired…' I responded, distant. Then seeing her beseeching face, sighed and said, 'OK…'

'You look ill. Come to the kitchen, I'll make you a Welsh rarebit.'

Eating, I gave her the briefest account. I couldn't physically go through the whole shebang again. 'There was this guy I found beaten up outside his home, I happen to know.' She gasped. 'The police just wanted some information because it was a crime scene, that's all.'

'Oh, dear! Who is he? Do I know him?'

'No. He's some old friend of mine… you don't know him.'

'Will he be all right?'

'He will…'

***

I rest my head on the pillow in the spare room, eyes wide open. I know I won't sleep properly tonight; why try?

James…

Archer…

Daley…

My statement…

Those pictures of a wrecked face… If only. If only. If… I don't have the strength to dwell on the hypotheticals because all I gravitate around is the one incontrovertible fact. The one resounding conclusion to my condemnation.

I hear the hammer pound the nail through his palm. I am the one holding the hammer.

He is awake now. Archer is there, telling him all. He'll hear my name… And he'll know of what I'd done.

He'd been asleep earlier; Elizabeth didn't get the chance to *give him my love*. Good.

Despite having remembered what was eating at me at the police station, I feel that feeling again. Only this time, it is for something new. I know my eidetic memory is fading, but please, dear God, let me remember. For it is an image. Of that, I am sure. I try my hardest to think but my unrest, my bloody agitation makes it more elusive, difficult, so difficult to retrieve…

Back Then

I looked up the definition. *Serious sexual assault.* It meant, basically, all the sick things one could do to someone else without their permission, except for penetration.

'Ughh!' I groaned.

I didn't read on, I couldn't – it was too disturbing. Not only did a profligate storm rock my thoughts, this way and that, but I also felt it physically. I felt nausea. I felt sick. I wished I hadn't learnt of it. I wished Kate had never told me. I knew that sounded selfish, but I couldn't handle it. Going through the rest of my life in complete ignorance to Kate's personal torture would have suited me just fine! And last thing I needed was this to distract me from my homework. A Levels were around the bend, and I had to concentrate on my future. But I was me, and I had a friend who was dear. I had to, at least, lend an ear.

No sooner had I finished reading my notes on Plato's Republic, my phone rang. Kate. It was Monday evening, and she'd gone home, her brother having left for Liverpool again.

'Wassup?' I said.

'Mum was really pissed off with me for sleeping over at your place,' she said.

'So what? I thought she didn't care.'

'She thinks Rhys won't do it anymore, and we should all try to get along. "It was just a phase", she said and "there's no need to run off again". Silly woman!'

Rhys scared her. He taunted her whenever he was home. He'd creep up on her and get really close, touching her, and laugh when she shied away; only the touching wasn't exactly legit. She was afraid he'd totally crack one day and do her irrevocable damage.

'The woman is living in her own world, and you know what?'

'What?'

'Whenever I try and explain, she refuses to listen. She puts up this hand, like a bleedin' traffic warden, and says, "Catherine, I don't want to hear any more lies", in this pseudo-posh voice, like she just came out of Buckingham Palace's arse! Then she leaves the room, or puts the volume up on the telly. I swear I need to get out of here, like yesterday.'

I had understood why Kate had run away. It hadn't been because of what Rhys had done to her alone, it was because, without the support of her parents, she knew there was no one else to turn to, to save her. Rhys saw this, and knew he could get away with it. Kate had no other choice but to run, else face more of his wrath. He had taken sibling rivalry to a completely new level. A sadistic, vengeful level. It wasn't for sexual gratification – it was to implement sexual harassment to enforce his abuse.

'If he'd given me a black eye, or left me unconscious, I would have borne it,' she'd confided the night before. 'But taking it further, El? I don't know why he needs to incestualise. I don't know what I've done to provoke all this –'

'Don't you dare say it's your fault!' I'd hollered. 'Never say it's your fault! He has a problem. He needs help.'

'I know…'

'How many bags did you sell on Saturday, you sneaky, little cow?' I changed the subject.

I heard a crafty giggle. 'Why?'

''Cos the way you were selling I thought Megan would blow a fuse. You could see the fumes coming out her ears!'

I would drop these little bits of encouragement to Kate – a reminder of how well she was doing financially. Her parents had agreed to let her work under the condition she finished school. A Levels over, she was out of there. But this time she was going to do it right. Not live in the streets, never again; live like a human being, in a house, whatever shape or form.

'You, know? She makes the sell even more fun! Just to see that look on her face!' she said.

'Don't worry about your mum. You just focus on your life, and you'll be out of there soon. I'll always be here when you need me. And don't forget, when you get into uni, you'll be on campus far away from everyone, and you'll be getting a good education –'

'And I'll get a better job, therefore better money, therefore, better life and soon and so forth,' she said, not hiding how fed up she was of me telling her that.

'You'd better remember that, girl.'

Chapter Thirty-Two

Now

The gun-blast in my dream stuns me whole, forcing me awake with a paralysing gasp. I blink. I am stunned for some seconds. I feel tears trickle to my ears, as I lie leaden. *Breathe, slow… slow…* It is barely daybreak. A sky, slate grey, raw, cruel. I get up, dress, and slip silently downstairs, carefully avoiding all the spots where the floorboards creak. I use the downstairs loo so I don't wake anyone, and within minutes, I am at the door latch. I turn, as in habit, to the mirror. I see dead, bloodshot eyes, and almost do a double take.

I run to Edgware station, leaving the household in its fast sleep. Burnt Oak, Colindale, Hendon Central, Brent Cross, Golders Green – the train doesn't go fast enough. Off at Hampstead, practically on a sprint. Home. I need to sketch before I lose the intricate detail.

My spirit in want of peace in the seclusion of my own thoughts.

I sketch fine and true. Full realism. The men. The SUV. True to the last detail I can recall. True to every line, shade, characteristic and colour. I ignore the dull, persistent pain in my wrist and finish, finally. I photograph each sketch separately, using my professional camera, which is just as well, for I have neither mobile nor scanner, focusing the sharpest result as I can muster, and sending them via email to DI Archer at exactly 9:41 a.m. It's down to them now… and James. Now awake, I'm sure light will be made of all that preceded his attack, by him. The police will be off my back.

I stare, ruminating at the sketches now lying on my kitchen island. Those men so vivid in my memory. *Bastards*, I think bitterly. What gave them the right to do that to James? *What had he done to them?* A small utterance answers back. My breath hitches. Shit! What if he had done something and they were getting their own back? What if James is in over his head, caught up in dealings so deep, he'd have to get killed for them?

'Well, these sketches better bloody help with the investigation,' I say to myself. It is ironic – never has work of mine been of such importance, and all I want to do is burn it.

I have to get out of here.

Gym.

***

I pump and pump. Each intense burst of strength – leg muscles expanding and contracting as I drive them harder and harder. I can almost feel the lactic acid burn through each screaming cell.

With one final grind, I quit, panting. Post-workout satisfaction nestles in me. It feels good. Then I have a sudden thought.

'Yes, of course,' I say quietly to myself. 'Why hadn't I thought of that earlier?'

***

A flicker of light catches my eye. I squint to see. I take a few more steps. I notice an unmarked car is parked illegally on Gower Street, police light propped on the top; flickering blue light not making much of a difference in the sun; only I capture things like that. I am closer now, and I see him.

'How did you know I was here?' DI Archer steps out the car.

I had made my way down to UCL. I had to see if there was anything else I was missing in relation to James. If he was studying Computer Engineering, then Mallet was the place to glean for clues. Displays of people's work, inventions and publications of them, certifying the scientists' original ingenuity. Unfortunately, there was nothing in James's name, and I didn't have my mobile to search for past engineering articles online with his name on them. Perhaps that would harvest a result. I had left, disconsolate, but decided to fetch a painting from the Slade to finish up on whilst I was there.

Archer doesn't look happy. 'No thanks to you,' he says dryly. His manner is abrupt. I wonder what the matter is. Weren't my sketches up to scratch?

'What's the matter with your phone?' he asks.

'Oh,' I say and look away. 'It broke.'

'Broke?' he says, not trying to hide his disbelief. I look at him again. Why is he being mean?

'Yes!' I say, affronted. 'So, who told you I was here? I didn't tell anyone.'

He sighs. 'Your mother suggested you might be here, all right? We didn't find you in your building, so we asked a kid if they saw a tall, beautiful goth with short hair, anywhere around. OK? Easy-peasy detective work.'

Sarcasm? I blush despite myself, at his referring to me as beautiful.

'Sarcasm doesn't suit you,' I say, 'and I'm not a goth.' I add, a bit annoyed. Then I hear a harrumph. I look to see a man, I've never seen before, coming up to us.

'Right, well,' says Archer, flustered I dared retort. 'This is Detective Inspector Ferguson.'

I nod. 'Hello, Detective Inspector.' Another tall, lean figure. At least this bob smiles at me through his squinting, shamrock-green eyes.

'Ms Stephens,' he says with formality. They stand side by side, both looking down their noses at me, making me suddenly feel incredibly small. What is this? The intimidation game?

'We need to have a word,' Archer tells me, his tone lined with frustration.

'By all means.' I looked around. 'Here?'

'No. Let's go for a drive, shall we?'

They offer me the passenger seat. DI Ferguson sitting in the back. What is that, a tactic for me not to be afraid? Not to feel like some common criminal in the back? Soften me, to open up? Are they allowed to take witnesses for rides in cars?

'How's your wrist?' Archer asks me upon spying me rub it.

'Crap.'

He blinks. 'Right,' and turns on the ignition.

Just then, I catch a glimpse of the handle of the gun under his jacket. I've never seen a firearm before. Gun... something about a gun... There it is again; that pestering feeling that I've misplaced a thought. Omitted. There is something – it may not be important, but something – that might help with the investigation.

We drive for a bit, going south. The street is familiar. It is the same I had taken to go to the Met. I wonder if we're going to the station again.

Archer turns into a smaller street and parks just outside a public garden. Bloomsbury Square, if I'm not mistaken. What are we doing here? Am I right to feel a sudden brush of panic?

I sit, trying desperately to remove some dried ink from my forefinger; in vain.

Archer inhales a long breath. Then lets the air out, running his hand down the back of his thick, russet mane.

'We got a vehicle expert to identify the sketch you did of the SUV,' he begins.

'Really good job by the way,' says Ferguson, from behind.

I nod my thanks, turning, catching his beryl eye. I start to gnaw at my bottom lip.

'That particular SUV isn't sold in the UK and is rare in our parts. You were right,' continues Archer. 'In fact, it's so rare there are only two of them registered in London, making our job much easier.'

'That's good, isn't it?' I say, hopeful.

'That's good, yes…' He pauses, eyeing me. 'The one SUV owner is away and hasn't used his vehicle in over two weeks. He also has an iron-clad alibi.'

I nod. Panic waxing, as I sense by the pace of his words we're coming to the apex.

'The other owner claims his SUV was stolen but didn't know until yesterday, when he went to pick it up from his company's car park. Do you know the name of his company by any chance?'

I raise my brows. Why would he think I'd know? 'No.'

'It's a yachting company. A place called Golden Sea Yachts.'

My brain whirls. 'What?' I breathe. I shake my head, confused.

'We got talking to the secretary. Ever met her?' I don't like the almost cocky way he enunciates that.

'Yes, but what has that got to do –'

'She told us a couple of interesting things, didn't she, Detective?'

'She did, indeed,' replies Ferguson. They are doing that good cop-bad cop thing. All over-acting. What is that; a scare tactic?

'It seems the owner has an …obsession, you might say, with SUVs – a collector. He has quite a few. But he leaves one, a Chevrolet Tahoe, to be used by his employees in order to escort particular buyers or shareholders to wherever they want to go.'

I swallow.

'The secretary was very helpful…' says Archer, waiting for any sound to leave my lips. 'We asked her for a list of employees who had used the Tahoe recently. She told us only one employee, a chap called Nicholas Barton, had taken it.

'But you know what's strange?' Archer asks, over-doing it with the conspiratorial.

I shake my head slowly, dreading what I know I'm going to hear.

'She told us that one of Barton's friends had been in the day before, asking about him too.' Archer stops there, his eyes riveted to mine.

Ferguson then says purposefully. ' "Amazing, grey eyes", she said. "Tall, gothic-looking…" '

My pulse rate accelerates.

'Eleanora?!' Archer barks. I jump. 'Why didn't you tell me last night at the station?'

I'm thrown; lost for words. 'I…I don't know… I didn't know…' I stammer. 'H-how? What has Golden Sea Yachts got to do with… with… what happened to James?'

Archer glances at Ferguson, one eyebrow raised. 'So, you don't deny you went there asking about where Barton was?'

'I don't…'

'So, tell us how you came to be there then.' Blood rises to my temples, throbbing. I want to run. I don't know why I feel stifled, cornered.

'I followed James there,' I tell them. 'I-it was one of the places I'd followed him to that day. He didn't go straight home.' They both stare at me, like I'm telling pork pies.

'You mean to say you followed Laidlaw all the way to Canary Wharf?' Archer is incredulous. 'From where?'

'From Gower Street,' I say.

'Without him catching on?' asks Ferguson, almost impressed.

I nod tensely. 'I thought he would. I thought, every second, he'd turn around and see me, recognise me, even through my disguise; I'd be made. But… I don't know… he didn't. He just didn't. His mind was elsewhere. In his own world.'

I explain to them, in short, the ins and outs of how I followed him. Disguise, tactics. I carefully omit the part about taking pictures.

'You see, I saw the personalised plates on the Tahoe. GSY was written on them. I guessed it was a company car… I searched online and found Golden Sea Yachts. Then I clicked on anything that could give me information. I thought my best bet was to see who worked there, and I got a list of employees. Nicholas Barton's name was one of them. But it meant nothing to me at the time.'

'Please explain…'

'Well, you see, all this… personal investigation of mine, as it were, was to find out how James was living; why things hadn't panned out the way he'd wanted. That's why I followed him, as you already know, and I discovered his… his storeroom, and it verified my worst fear – he had next to nothing. So, it got me thinking. How did he pay for it? Who allowed him to stay there? Whose was it? I paid to get that information.'

'Paid?' Archer asks.

'Her Majesty's Land Registry,' I state.

'Good thinking,' Ferguson says. I forgo telling them it wasn't my idea.

'And what did you discover?' Archer is eager.

'It belongs to Nicholas's uncle. A Mr Tom Garner.'

'And how do you know that?' Ferguson queries.

'I searched Tom Garner's name and got a family-tree site. Nicholas Barton was there, but I didn't register that at first. It took me a while to realise his name was on both the GSY employee list and the family tree. Nicholas Barton is Tom Garner's nephew, on his mother's side.'

There is silence.

I take one breath, a second, a third… They need to let it sink in.

'Now we just need to know why Garner and, or Barton are helping Laidlaw,' Archer considers. 'Barton can't help us –'

'Oh that!' I say, interrupting him. 'I told you I didn't know who Nicholas Barton was *at the time*, but James had a good friend called Nick, back when he was at Milden Boys. His age fitted as well, but I never learnt his surname, even though he'd been a friend of mine too. Anyway, I needed to verify it because I had a strong feeling it was him. I couldn't find old school records online, so I went to Milden and they confirmed it. The Tahoe at Canary Wharf that had picked up James, Nick was driving it.'

'Seems they were still good friends,' murmurs Archer. He sends a glance to his partner. Something unspoken is said between them. 'He was helping him out.'

'Yes.' I nod.

'Eleanora, why did you go to see Nick?' Ferguson's voice comes from the back.

I shrug. 'I wanted to talk to him – face to face – about what happened in the past. I don't have his number, so…'

'Yes?' Archer wants me to expand. I don't want to go into it again but my hands are tied.

'I wanted to know what happened after James got arrested. His piece of the puzzle. That's all.'

James? Didn't they go to see him last night? I suddenly think. Why are they jabbing *me* for information?

I have a sudden aching to learn how he is. He's awake. Is everything all right? Is he lucid? Could they tell me? Will I be able to ask without sounding too maudlin?

'But what about James? Didn't you see him last night? Hasn't he told you anything?' I dare to ask. 'Why am I still being questioned? I thought you'd have got all the information you need from him.'

Archer is motionless, breathing hard. His jaw clamped tight.

'Detective?'

Archer sighs. 'Laidlaw claims he doesn't remember anything. It is early, I suppose. He needs to get his brain around the whole thing.'

'Nick?' I offer. 'I'm sure when he wakes from his coma…'

Archer shakes his head. He steals another look at Ferguson.

'What is it?' I hear the crack in my voice, feeling the air change. It's palpable. A dread.

They sit, inert.

'What?!' I demand.

'Barton,' Archer says solemnly. And the penny has dropped before he's even finished his sentence. It has just occurred to me that he used the past tense: *Were* still good friends. 'He didn't make it… We didn't know he was your friend too. We're very sorry.'

Bile reaches my throat as I lurch, swinging open the car door, in time for the contents from my stomach to splatter on the ground. I heave. I have no idea why I react with such passion to this news, but perhaps it's because I have an awful presentiment. I feel Nick's car crash isn't coincidental; how simple it is one can subtract a life. How easy it is to find me too.

I gasp and cry as I spit out the last drops. My diaphragm in pain. 'No! Not Nick… Not Nick…' *Not James … not me …*

The evanescent images of Nick's ridiculous, mirthful face fleet in front of me. His sly glimmer, always making us laugh, and when he'd always tried to make that effort to talk to me after James had stopped. Gone. Gone.

His last words to me: 'Eleanora, forgive me.' *For what, Nick? What had you meant?*

He got a death wish or something? I suddenly remember Bianca's words, and I want to find her and punch her.

'Eleanora?' Archer calls, his one hand on my back, the other, pulling me up by my upper arm. 'Come…' He hands me a tissue. I put it over my nose and mouth, squeezing the tears from my closed eyes.

'This wasn't an accident!' I cry. 'I know it wasn't!'

Archer assents with a bow of the head. 'We're looking into it, but we believe it was done by the same people that assaulted Laidlaw. We can't say more, but it seems Nick got mixed up in something over his head. We have no idea how Laidlaw is connected, however. We believe it has to do with what you overheard the two men say about "the stuff".'

I wipe my nose, say nothing.

'That's why we must be in this together, Eleanora,' Ferguson pleads. 'And if you remember anything or notice anything weird, don't hesitate to get in touch. This is manslaughter.'

'Did you tell James Nick is dead?' I ask.

'No. Unfortunately we found out about an hour ago. He passed earlier this morning. They had just informed his work while we were there making our inquiries.'

'Tell James. I'm sure if you tell him his best friend died, something might jog his memory.'

Back Then

A pounding came on my front door. Then the doorbell and more pounding. I heard Mum run out from the kitchen to ask, 'Who is it?' at the door in alarm.

'It's Kate!' came her voice from the other side.

I was half way down the stairs as Mum was opening the door, letting a ghostly, cold Kate in, and the night air.

'Katie, dear! What happened? Are you all right?'

'Shit, Kate!' I cried.

'Ell!' Mum said crossly.

I ignored her and took a shivering Kate upstairs.

'I'll bring some tea…' Mum called.

***

Kate rolled up her sleeve to show me the bruises. Then she lifted her hair to the side, revealing her right ear and a nasty cut all covered with dried blood.

'He grabbed me, then he threw me at the fireplace. You know how that marble juts out at the corner?'

'Yeah,' I said nodding, solicitous yet scared to hear.

'Yeah, well, it has my blood on it now.'

I left her sitting on the bed to get some antiseptic. I mulled over her words. She hadn't told me the whole story yet, and I was dreading to hear the rest. I wanted to postpone it for as long as I could. The repugnance swirled internally. I had no appetite to hear the latest, diseased account of her exchange with her brother. This had to stop. Not only for her but for me too. I pretended to be searching in the medical cabinet, all the while whispering that one verse which had the ability to calm me, '…For though I should walk in the midst of the shadow of death, I will fear no evil, for Thou art with me…'

She took the antiseptic from me, went to the mirror above my dressing table and started to apply with a trembling hand.

'He knocked me half unconscious,' she said, shaking.

'You can't let him get away with it!'

'I'm afraid to go to the police. What if they don't believe me? My parents would kill me if this ever got out. He needs help… going to prison won't help him.'

I didn't get that about Kate. On the one hand she'd protest for her parents to do something, yet on the other she supported their decision.

'Yes, but letting him continue doing this to you won't help *you*.'

She shook her head, ignoring me.

'I thought he'd kill me or something, and when he backed off a bit, I got up and ran out. Came straight here.'

Her story left me with that dreaded sinking feeling of unfinished business. For no doubt her brother had not given up. In the abyss of her soul and of mine, we both knew it – he'd try it again.

I couldn't see her go through that. What if he did worse? What if he caused grievous bodily harm? It was too painful to think. It wrenched at my thoughts.

Then the idea arose, offering a solution. Kate – in that instant – became that girl on the night of the party. And everything else fell into place.

Chapter Thirty-Three

Now

I walk in my front door to a lifeless flat.

Kate has been, and now is gone. Something's different; on the island are two, ancient mobile phones and a note.

They're from Sophie. One's for you and one's for a member of your family. We programmed some numbers. They're ready for use. XO.

I get a beer out the fridge, letting the cool, tart flavour refresh my mouth and take away the remnants of vomit. I close my eyes and take another swig. I have an empty stomach; the dulling will come soon.

Before I got home, Archer and Ferguson had taken me to the station to add to my statement and do an official face composite for court. They'd disappeared at one point, probably to have another chat with James, leaving me up to my own devises to find the nearest Tube station – a very busy Holborn – in order to get home. UCL was closed at any rate.

Before Archer left, he said it was just as well I hadn't written a formal apology on my misleading phone call six years ago, as the defence could use it against me in court – for I will be subpoenaed – claiming I may be an unreliable witness; known to lie.

That had stung. I'm not a liar. It was just once… No …twice.

I sit at my windowsill, alone amidst my desolate thoughts, as the mist descends. How has my life turned into this tumult of events? What is this inextricable mess I have been plunged into? What am I doing?

I may be home, but I don't feel safe. Where is my sanctuary; that *refuge* I thought I had?

Kate won't be around; most tangibly a good idea. I want to tell her to stay away for the time being. She doesn't need to get involved in even more of my shit. But I don't pick up the phone. There's no urgency. There's no need to tell her to stop, turn back. She'll be with her man, tucked up, safe and sound, like she always is when in a relationship. She's one of those girls that gets too enthusiastic, falling head over heels, before even getting to know the guy, always at his place, always doing stuff together. Then, suffice it to say, comes crashing down when the transient lust all fizzles out. But this is the one time I won't tell her to take it slow. This time I'm not giving her my advice, unwanted or not. Let her be with him. Let her be far from the madding crowd.

She told me she'd be spending Easter partly at Stuart's and then she'd pop over to her parents' house; Rhys isn't anywhere near. I told her to come over Edgware. She said she'd text.

I open my laptop and the family-tree site flickers on. I hadn't been bothered to click the browser off. Mother, Sadie Garner married Peter Barton. Brother, Tom Garner. Sons, Fredrick and Nicholas. *Now Deceased…* 'Murdered,' I whisper. My whole body spikes with goosebumps, chilling me.

I go to my room, sit on the floor on my thick Trellis rug, and face the window as dusk turns to night. I have no strength. I stay put, resting my head on a cushion I've knocked off the bed. The beer having that welcoming, soporific effect. My eyelids stay open no longer, and there I remain, silently, until night turns to dawn.

Back Then

It was over. A Levels were over. Summer holidays, and freedom beckoned.

That feeling of accomplishment that I had felt two years earlier, after GCSE's, flooded my senses again with elation. Only this time, it was for ever.

I left the main school building in the warm sunshine, thinking back on those past feelings in a diffusion of ebullience. Then *he* invaded my thoughts. It had been a while since the last time. They say time heals; I suppose they could be right. But today there was no preventing the memory; the image of his eyes, bright and clear in the sun; an exquisite Rayleigh scattering of light. There were too many series of events which triggered his appearance, unable for me to dodge. My heart sunk, knowing there would always be some point, or spot, or word, or deed that connect him to me. The warmth. The mist. The bus-stop. A particular street. A laugh. A gesture. Knowing that healing didn't necessarily mean forgetting. It was unfair. It would always follow me.

It's the last time you'll pass through here. No more Hilsmond. No more two-four-two… No more Milden.

Kate was to go on holiday to Devon, and then visit some family in Ireland. N&L didn't give us much holiday leave, and we'd see each other soon enough.

'I swear, if he comes, I'm running away again,' she'd said. I worried for her. I wished we would take her, but it wasn't my money and my mother wanted just family. Had she known what the poor girl was going through, I was sure she would tell her to come. But Kate emphatically insisted she not know; no one know. Besides, I was to stay only ten days in Greece because I had applied to do an intensive foundation course during the summer.

So thus, summer passed, and I was alone for almost three months and saw I liked it, perhaps, a little too much.

Chapter Thirty-Four

Now

It is the cries outside that awake me. Market day is (once again) here.

Market day. One whole week. One whole week since I saw him sweeping UCL floors that first time.

One whole week …and an age has passed.

I think back on how that week began. Assess each act; how it was executed and what the result was. What I had been meaning to do, concerning James, and how none of it happened the way I'd planned.

No statement of apology. No talking to James's parents. No confrontation. I have failed.

There is just one humble act I hope helps him in some small way.

All is quiet, that's why the cries are so distinct. There is no rain to interfere with the sonic reaching my ear, and at this time of morning, not a lot of traffic either.

I'm still on the floor. I crawl to my window, the plain net curtains hiding me from the outside. It feels warmer all of a sudden. Spring's decided to show herself, although there's not much sun. The clouds aren't thick – perhaps they'll relinquish their ungenerous attitude later on, and let us have a proper share of the sun's rays which they've been detaining for so long.

I need to let go for a bit, go out, unravel the thorns of torment that are perforating me, inch by inch. I need my friends. Oh, no, wait. They are off doing that last-minute getaway up north. Where did Suze say? I read the text swiftly before smashing my phone in. Something about Gretna Green and an Isle of White fest before going to Glastonbury.

I peer at the pre-paid burner on my bedside table, sourly. It feels portent to a future whose prospect has become cast in dark. Yes. That phone invokes a new standpoint in my life. Now, I'll have to think differently. I'll have to watch my back. In short, I'll have to be prepared for anything. There are no guarantees I am in the clear. Those men, or whoever they work for, may have found my number before Sophie erased it. Gretna Green sounds a great idea to vanish for a couple of days, but I can't go. Archer advised me not to leave London for now.

I pick up the device grudgingly, like it's going to snap my fingers off. No regular lines are permitted with these phones, otherwise my number will be compromised, and in consequence everybody else's. So, I have to buy a new one for communication with the rest of the world.

I take the Tube to Vic's work; I have to give her the other burner. The Northern Line rattling its way down, southbound to Tottenham Court Road. I'm trying my hardest to think back if I'd said anything incriminating on my regular line; some text or call. Can you tap mobiles? But my mind is too messy for any clear, coherent thinking and it's giving me a headache.

Victoria works in an advertising company. Her job is fun, as she claims, but the fun part isn't the position of employment she is in, but is when they allow her to test products and discuss her opinions on them to the company and to the manufacturers. Who else better than the honest opinion on some new, revolutionary strip wax, or the right texture of a frozen yoghurt, from the people who have as much to lose as the manufacturers if the product fails?

'We were given five different types of new, chocolate flavours from Cadbury's to try out… mmm… delish!' she'd said once. 'And they let us take home some packets! They were gone by next morning! Even Danny ate some and he's supposed to be kosher. Imagine!'

'Oh, my God, El, you wouldn't believe!' she'd said another time. 'We were given these amazing moisturizers, my cheeks were as soft as David's bottom!'

David is Victoria's boyfriend, whom she declares has softer bum cheeks than she has. Apparently, it's one of his best features.

'Too much information,' I'd said.

But David is a good sort. If he puts up with her shit, then he definitely loves her.

I enter the glass doorway and see my sister sitting at the front desk. It is early, and she isn't scurrying around ordering coffees for the higher echelons of the company. Plus, it is a Saturday and a day before Easter Sunday; not everyone is obliged to be in.

'EL!' She comes tottering, thrilled to see me, her tight pencil skit restricting quicker movement. She looks like a pinstriped penguin. But she is so pretty.

Always the pretty one. I remember Mum, her motherly pride bursting through whenever she introduced Vic as her daughter to anyone. That deliberate pause she'd take to let her words hang in the air, ready to receive the compliment she knew was coming, with grace. Vic's arms are open to embrace me. Embracing always means she hasn't seen me in a long time, and I am aware – at that moment – of how guilty I am for being the prodigal sister. The hard, unforgiving pang, hitting me, censuring me.

That split second before she hugs me, my eye goes to the telling scar across her nose. The token bequeathed upon her on the night of her accident. The mark which was left subsequent to her sojourn in hospital. How I had berated myself, cussed myself, for not trying to stop her that night. I was in anguish for days; the nightmares, dreaming of her death over and over, waking up in a cold sweat, fearful it was true. Mum had come rushing in my bedroom after the screams. She'd rocked me back to sleep, but I think she didn't do it just for me. It was the last time she held me. The first thing I said to Vic when she'd finally woken up was, 'I should have played the spoilt brat and made you not go back!' I'd cried and cried. 'Should have forced you to stay home…'

And all she did was smile and say weakly, 'What on earth have you done to your hair?'

'Mum called and told me, but you know Mum, you can never understand her. She probably got half the business mixed up. I wanted to talk to you but your phone's not with it. But you didn't have to come; we'll see you tonight. You're coming, aren't you?' She says while still hugging me. She lets go.

'Yeah, but I needed to get out a bit, so…' I say.

'You look awful, El. Totally knackered, child. Come and sit down and tell me what's going on in your life.'

She takes me to the small, plush couch with a coffee table stacked with magazines on one side, and a huge Yucca plant on the other, ready to poke anyone's eye out.

I put no embellishment, just the naked truth. I begin from the night of her accident – the phone call – right up to the present day, and within 10 minutes, she knows all.

She doesn't move, just gnaws the inside of her cheek.

'Hang on,' she says, like she's just had an epiphany. 'Is he the guy you had that fight over with Bianca? You know, when you asked me to pretend to be you on the phone?'

'Yeah, that's him. You remember that?'

'Could I ever forget? It was one of the best moments insofar as my acting career went.' The side of her mouth lifted, awaiting my reaction. She wants to lighten the mood, but…

I try to smile. 'I did an unforgivable thing to him, Vic. Absolutely disgraceful… I despise myself.'

'Oh, El,' she says, and is about to say something when the phone rings. She goes to answer it.

I look down at my hands, across the room, through the glass wall to the outside.

'Hang on, boss wants some coffee,' my sister calls to me, dialling some coffee shop and placing an order.

I get up. 'I'll leave you to it,' I say to her, as a couple employees enter. 'For now, you'll be able to find me on this number.' I give her the burner. Then I say in my broken Greek so the others won't understand, 'Be careful. Keep your door bolted… and I'll see you tonight.'

'El?' she says in our native English, taking the phone from my hand mechanically, not giving much heed to it. 'You did right to help him, even after the way he treated you.'

I find a café, actually it finds me; its aroma reaches my olfactory nerves yards away. I need some kind of breakfast, even if it's more like *brunch*time. I sit at a window seat, watching the street outside. The distinct piquancy of the cappuccino taking me places I love. My village, family and friends. The vista of soft, yellow sunset over the ancient verdant hills. I miss that smell of sage and oregano. The zing of the hesperidin. The tang of rich, vinegar-sharp olives and delicious grilled octopus. The pot plant of sweet basil, warding off mosquitoes. The fights with my cousins around the family table, about who got first ten points on The Settlers of Catan. The evening cicadas' droning buzz. I feel the nostalgia. When will I go again? It has been far too long… The prodigal native.

Thinking over what Vic said, I can't help but smile. Of course, I did right to help him. The truth is, looking in retrospect, James's words had stung my ego rather than leave me traumatized in any way. It had been the impulse of a smote, naïve teenager wanting to sting back, but not thinking of the consequences. His only crime (poor choice of word, I know) is that he'd lied to me. It had all been an act. He was young, immature, probably. And I'll forgive him that. Yes. I forgive him for his touch, for his look, for his kind words. I've grown in mind and body since then; nothing like how I was. Grown those bloody butterfly wings, as they say. I have moved on; up on a high plain where a gamut of life's opportunities is laid before me. There is no need to even hover on the past anymore.

There is a newspaper someone has left on the opposite bench and I take it. I haven't read the news in so long, and I am curious to see if anything had been mentioned on Nick – it was a hit and run with a bad end. That would have made the papers, wouldn't it?

I turn each page carefully, and there it is. One small column, squashed between other headlines.

Police are investigating the death of a hit and run after the victim, Nicholas Barton, succumbed to his wounds early yesterday morning. Detective Inspector William Archer of the Metropolitan Police, who is in charge of the case, says we could well be looking at murder by intent and says the case is linked to drug trafficking. The victim had been hit by an SUV earlier this week and, according to witnesses, the SUV impacted into the victim's Ford Fiesta "on purpose" leaving him for dead. Family of the victim are deeply saddened and hope the criminals be brought to justice soon. The funeral service is to be held at Highgate Cemetery at noon, Monday.

Drugs. I flip the paper in half, sip the rest of my coffee, and wonder if James had been in possession of drugs the night the thugs got to him. The *stuff*. The taste of the coffee goes mawkish in my mouth. Would he have turned to the one thing that had got him into so much trouble? I sigh and look meditatively at the folded newspaper on my lap. My eyes wander over something familiar, then they stop. There, on the back, is the same ad I saw on the McAdam's site. The boxing tournament. And then I remember what I told, what's her name, Siobhan about wanting information. I *do* want to learn how to – suddenly, it all comes back to me. One great wave of recollection. Back to the time I had started in secret to learn how to box. Yes, I remember… I'd stumbled across a book on it in the school library and I'd taken it home. I thought I'd teach myself; the basics at least. I thought to surprise Dad.

I never got to surprise him.

I must have been only a month into it, when it was so abruptly nipped at the bud. I probably blacked the whole incident out. I must have deposited it somewhere in my mind where I wanted to forget it; it was too profoundly connected with Dad. I rub my temples. 'Of course… how did I forget?' I whisper. It must have been the trauma of losing him.

I feel now, as though I need to fulfil the past. I feel there's a missing part. I am like a mechanism; I'll run but not run well. In that instant I know, learning to box; finishing what I'd started, would be the part to complete the mechanism. I want to live it, breathe it. To be part of a group, a people, a team that love what you love. I didn't want to be a passive observer anymore. I wanted to know how it was to actually get into the ring and physically fight. The punch. The force. The passion. The exhilaration.

That.

Chapter Thirty-Five

Back Then

'You got in!'
'I got in!'
'Oh, my God!'
'Oh, my God!'
Kate; she'd got into LSE, and we were shouting down the line to one
another in silly merriment. In a way, I was more excited for her than I had
been for myself the year previous. She was freed from the household which
had manacled her in its depths, drowning her with sour disappointment.
She had kept her promise to finish school, and her parents had kept their
end of the bargain; she was free to walk out the door whenever she wanted.
They laid no objection, no protestation. To their credit, they did look hurt
and saddened after observing Kate's eagerness, her unrestrained enthusiasm
to leave; never look back. Kate, being the most kind-hearted person ever to
roam this earth, immediately felt sorry for them, and had hastily reassured
them she loved them, but they needed understand *her* need to be by herself.
'We are going to club till we drop!' she declared. 'The N and L gang and a
couple of friends from school. Bring Vic if she wants… oh, and Padma.
Gerry told me she could get us in Ice for free 'cos she knows one of the
DJs on the second floor. It's one of the best clubs in London!'
We went – all of us. Enthusiasm and stupid glee saturated the atmosphere,
as we all took the tube ride to get there. All dressed up to the nines for a
night out in town.
The music, the people, the laughs… We went on each floor and danced to
whatever they were playing. Padma, Vic and I danced to a track we'd heard
two summers back, when we'd all met up in Athens. Vic and I had taken
her and her sister to a club on the coast, and the fun we'd had all came back
to us as soon as the DJ spun that particular vinyl on the turn table. We all
shrieked with delight and ran to the dancefloor.
It had been a wonderful night… up until Kate got home to an ugly
surprise.

Now

I rush market. I shop quickly for the various foods needed for the blog,
greeting farmers, producers and traders with a smile, but without lingering

for a chat as I usually do. I don't stay and savour the fresh, whole-grain bread, the scent of ground coffee, the creaminess of the cheese. I quickly test the firmness of the mushrooms and the cherry tomatoes, though, buying a good quantity of both. I leave the happy vibe; it is sunny. People are instinctively in a good mood.

I try to be, but for another reason. I want to get home and search for a boxing club. Unfortunately, the gym I go to isn't equipped for it.

After placing the produce from the market on the little kitchen isle, I rev up my sleepy laptop while starting to make lunch. I bought ingredients for a week; olive oil, cheese, fresh butter and eggs, but what I want to prepare for the blog today is something for Easter. Lamb chops with lemon and oregano. A traditional Easter menu in Greece, but the touch that makes it authentically mine is the sprig of rosemary and cooked in clay baker. I prepare my camera – on the ready for the now-clean-from-all-personal-information blog. I have a living to tend to, and I'd promised my readers I'd make this dish in time for Easter Sunday lunch.

I pull up the search engine and type for any boxing clubs near my area. I find loads, but one in specific looks extremely encouraging for girls who have never boxed before. As soon as I finish with the blog, I'll go.

Of course, cooking in a clay baker takes its time, and after having placed it in the oven, I decide to pop out and quickly buy a new phone. I go to my local electronics shop and am almost harassed – but in a sweet way – by the salesperson, who is a very persuasive young man, to buy the latest in mobile technology. I tell him I want the cheapest smartphone for now and he humbly obliges, still not quite believing I haven't fallen for his best vending moves. *Been there, done that*, I think.

Upon returning, I smell the delicious aroma of the slowly cooking lamb, as I run up the stairs. It is almost done. Another ten minutes without the lid on, to roast the meat and potatoes to a light crisp.

I choose a plate with a cornflower-blue meander on the rim, and I place a sizable portion of the chops on it, making sure to make it look chef-style, with the sprig of fresh rosemary delicately placed on top. I position it on the windowsill, whose window pane doesn't budge, where the basil hangs. I photograph, upload but don't eat. I keep lent.

The trainer I speak to, a girl a few years older than me, who boasts a few titles in the bantamweight category, tells me to make sure my wrist isn't broken first and she'll have no problem in getting me started with the basics. I haven't felt this kind of enthusiasm in years. I'm eager to begin. I have to get the x-ray done. I go privately; anxiety in wanting to know *now*, settles the decision.

It shows my articular disc has suffered a bad strain, trying to absorb the shock of the impact when I had fallen to the ground. It caused a hairline fracture, which probably started healing up nicely days ago, because it is barely visible on the X-ray. The only way to be sure is to get an MRI. The treatment is the same in any case. Rest. I am to give it another week or two and the brace can come off, but no heavy duty for at least another month.

Bugger!

I get dressed, it's approaching 11 o'clock at night. One hour till the biggest feast in the ancient church is to be celebrated. A holy communion where even sinners are allowed to partake.

Back Then

It had been almost a year since the last time. I remembered what idea had come to mind, and I had said to myself that if he ever touched her again...

She'd come to the flat where I was lodging, about a couple of hours after I'd said goodnight to her outside Ice. Trains ran at 5, and she'd gone home, braved her brother's attack, and had come straight back to me.

I'd wrapped her up in my bed as she told me, stuttering with gasps of tears, her ordeal. She'd got away last second. He would have done more... I had never seen her in such a battered shape of attrition. She was turning into another person. I was scared. The Kate I knew was losing the battle. The Kate I knew was dying.

She'd finally fallen asleep. I kissed her temple, swiping the tears from my cheeks, and crept quietly out of bed. I hastily shuffled on jeans, top and plimsolls, and left the building. I had to be quick.

Not again. Never again.

Chapter Thirty-Six

Now

The doorbell rings and I'm lifted out of my daze. I've been quiet at the table, staring through my tall-stemmed glass of Moscato, watching as each shift of light changes the liquid, refracting a pale shade of yellow on the white tablecloth.

It was a long night in the old, stone Anglican church; its external neo-gothic façade belying what it really is inside – a modest, Byzantine-rite church. The hymns canted were about light and glory, of joy and salvation.

A resurrection; the trampling of death, the bestowal of life. I tried to feel it. I did. I was taken, briefly moved. For all that may be lost may be found again, only for me, I'm not so sure. I feel to be in purgatory. Stuck. And I will either move up or down when I finally reach one port of call – my complete confession to James. Then I shall await my comeuppance.

David has made his (belated) arrival, and is instantly surrounded by all the hot-blooded females of the clan, kissing and hugging him, grandad shouting, 'Leave the lad alone!' Grandad has been taciturn, not meeting my eye, and this is the first full, convivial sentence he's made all day.

David smiles awkwardly, as usual, and goes red as a lobster. It has to do with his more reserved upbringing. It had been the same with Dad, after all, bless him. Mum would always tease him on that, always overdoing her public displays of affection just to see him squirm. She'd turn and face him, pucker her lips fun-lovingly. He'd always laugh uncomfortably and say, 'Oh, Alexia,' a little reproachfully, but then stop and give her a kiss on the lips, won over. He never got mad, never told her to stop, like some winger. They'd never had a bad word between them. Not once did I hear them fight. Not once.

David is implanted in his seat at the table, between my sister and me. Gran comes with his plate, proud grin moulded on her face; the classic, Greek grandmother showing how much she loves you in proportion to the amount of food she gives you. David's face has turned lobster again. His plate is stacked.

' "What do you mean he don't eat no meat?" ' quotes Vic, heavy Greek accent. ' "I'll make lamb!" ' we say together.

The mood is instantly lifted to a more celebratory footing, glasses chinking, toasts encumbered with profound, ancient meaning. Greeks have a billion blessings for everything and can't be explained perfectly; something is always lost in translation.

As I'm sipping back my aromatic libation, letting the balm of somnolence sooth me, I almost miss what David's just said.

'What? What was that?' I ask, through the stress of exigency. I've caught key phrases: *car accident, died* and *computer engineering*.

'Yeah, it's sad,' he says. 'He died. And it was only a few days ago he'd put on Grapevine that he and his partner made an excellent way of retrieving and storing images. I won't go into details 'cos you won't understand, but he's designed the component which will enable –'

'How? How did he die?' I press, not wanting to hear techie stuff that will go completely over my head. David, who is an IT consultant himself, gets extremely enthusiastic when something new and exciting happens in the cyber cosmos, explained once that Grapevine is a forum where every geek around the world communicates. It's where deals are made, proof of patents are released, and general information is shared. Anyone looking for anything worth investing in looks there first.

'Well, last night, his partner announced he'd died from a car accident. Sad…' David tells again.

'Do you know his name?' I ask.

'No. You don't really put personal information up front. If anybody's interested or serious in getting in touch with you, then you're DM'ed. His username is, was, Anarchist Oblon-dot-G, making it sound oblong. I think it's an anagram.'

'Anarchist Oblong? He had a sense of humour,' Vic says.

'What about his partner's username?' I push.

'Hmm, let me think. He joined recently to inform us of the tragic news. It's something generic, no originality to it,' David informs me. He takes a couple of swallows from his wine, thinking. 'Hang on,' and gets out his phone from the back of his jeans. One minute later. 'Here it is. Jboy.'

'Jboy,' I repeat. *Jamie boy*?

'OK. I've had enough of tiptoeing around what we all really want to know,' bursts Grandad. He's staring darkly at me. I know that look. The storm in his eyes was gathering, and now it rains on me. 'Care to tell your family what's going on in your life for once?'

Everyone is silent around the table. I feel heat rise to my cheeks. Gran pretends to be cutting a loin, all demure. Mum shrugs at me.

'Could you please drop the estranged-daughter act before we all enter the next life?' Grandad snaps.

'Hasn't Vic told you what's been going on?' I look at my sister, not believing she hasn't told anyone. 'And I was here Thursday…'

'Thursday?' he says, miffed. 'You came while me and your gran were asleep in the dead of night, and then left like a thief at the crack of dawn. I hardly think that's visiting!'

I swallow back my shame, unable to utter a word in my defence, because he is right.

'But it's not about visiting,' chimes in Vic. 'It's the fact that you don't talk to us.'

'I talk –'

'It took you days to come to me.' She stops me.

'It's not *only* that, Victoria,' grandad says, his temper holding its momentum. 'This goes far deeper, El. It's as if we don't exist. It's been months.'

'Months?' I cry.

'Months. Since Christmas.'

I stare, mouth open. Jesus, he's right.

'I've got a lot on my plate this year.' I hear my voice become tiny, and sense the agony of remorse quaver within. 'I'm sorry. I didn't mean it…'

'Not even a phone call? Not even to see how we are? One minute of your time is all we ask.' He is so hurt. I've wounded him. Wounded them all.

'Dad, leave her alone,' says Mum. 'It's not her fault. We've been through this. I was never there when she needed me.' Mum's mouth trembles. She's holding the floodgates back with effort.

'Mum…' Victoria tries to console. David clears his throat uncomfortably.

'No, Mum. Grandad's right,' I say quietly. 'It's been entirely my fault. How you were in the past has nothing to do with me acting like an idiot. I'm sorry. I'm sorry, Grandad,' I tell him. Then I suddenly hear Daley's words. *I don't think you're the one to blame for ruining his life. I mean, you can't be responsible for what he's done with his life for the past six years.* If I believe what I just said to my mother, then accordingly, I ought to agree with Daley. But just as Mum admitted it, feeling the guilt, so must I, even more. For my guilt has one extra layer: I literally hindered James's future. Mum didn't do that to me. I'm fine. He's not.

Grandad's expression eases, and he sits back, folding his arms. Then I admit to all of them, 'I'm going through a lot right now. I'm in my last year. I've got that bloody thesis to finish. You know, I hardly speak to Kate, and we're flatmates! And to top it all off, I'm most likely to be summoned as a witness to an intent-to-murder charge, and the criminals haven't even been caught.' I look at my sister. 'That's what you should all be focusing on right now.' Then I turn back to my grandfather. 'Not me not phoning. Things are so much more serious right now.' His grey eyes gleam. 'Do you know, I asked Detective Archer to send a patrol car here, because I was afraid the assailants might come looking for me at my old address?'

They all cry out simultaneously.

'What do you mean?'

'Are you in danger?'

'El. Why didn't you tell us?'

I put my palms up. 'I'm just saying… just bear with me!' I look into grandad's eyes, which hold my own shade. 'Sorry, grandad.' I lean and kiss his cheek.

Suddenly, my phone vibrates intrusively on the table. My new device. I look at the screen. Kate. I read that she won't make it and to send her love. Rather a brusque text which I find odd. I get up from the table with a, ''Scuse me,' sensing their gaze on me, and dial Kate's number out in the front hall. It rings then goes onto voicemail. I hate talking to those things so I hang up.

I stick through the next hour or so. I fumble through answers, find ways to avoid grandad George's clever questioning on the assault, so he won't worry. I joke about as best I can with David, who has an uncanny way of making me laugh, and finally, quietly, leave.

'You're going to leave without saying goodbye?'

It's Mum; her voice peremptory but hand in hand with suffering. I haven't heard her speak like that in years. I'm overwhelmed with emotion; that spark of her old self; the erstwhile mother I used to know prior Dad's passing. I turn sharply around, and embrace her. 'Bye, Mum. Love you,' is all I say, as I feel oncoming tears.

***

I return to my stark, bleak flat. I knew it would be, but for some reason the desolation hits me worse. Why? Did I expect something to happen?

I turn on the shower and put myself under the hot water. And cry.

For once, I do not want to be alone with my thoughts. I dress and go for a stroll.

I stop outside the pub Kate and I frequent, or used to. The awnings and flower pots encircle the exterior, and the din which emanates proclaims it is open. After quick deliberation, I decide to sit for a quick drink.

I find a seat, sequestered in a dim corner, half my G and T left in front of me. Soon I'll get the fix in my bloodstream.

I wonder what Aiden, Suze and Juliet are all doing right now. Probably arguing on the motorway; who is to blame for taking a wrong turn, and then laughing as they crack jokes on comparing the journey to an egg hunt. I bite my lip, whimsical. I wish I were with them. Then I wander to Kate. Where is she? Not bodily, I mean, but her substance. We don't talk like we used to. I thought she could have been a recourse in my hour of need, but not now. No. She has a life. She has no need of me, really. Why? Why am I alone? I always seem to be alone.

I'm not an introvert; I never reject company but never seek it either. But the truth is, I never fight for it. I have always waited for others to make the first move. If they want to be my friend, they are welcome. Aidan, Suze and Juliet had all made that move, as did Kate. But with Kate there was, is, an indescribable rapport between us. We had hit it off in the very first seconds of knowing one another. Kate is an exception and, even if I have no other friends like her, she would be enough. But I don't want to be afraid to make the first move. I know I'm not hard-wired that way. I'm not. It's not that I lack courage. I found courage years ago. It's more like something, stupid as is may be, is stopping me.

Patrons of the pub have doubled in number. It's peculiar on a day as this; so many people. The pub has gigs on occasion, and I think maybe tonight is one of them. A fact that is verified when a bunch of girls sit around the sofa I'm on and start chatting about the "hotness" of the vocalist we'll be hearing tonight. Only then do I notice the flyer of the band stuck to the notice board.

The Crashers playing tonight at 9.

The girls are tipsy, as am I, and somehow, I get included in their conversation. The main topic is, of course, men.

'Can't live with 'em, can't live without 'em!' one declares, and we all raise our glasses to that. We buy another round and talk until the band walks on the little stage to the other side of us. They are handed a strong, encouraging applause, whistles and hoots. The lead singer indeed exudes a sexuality, what with his deliberate gruff hairstyle and skinny jeans, but it comes with the territory, I guess. I'm sure if I saw him walking down the street on an ordinary morning, I wouldn't look twice. Well, perhaps; if he had a nice arse. I have a flash-image of James's half-bare arse from the photo I'd taken of him, and blush hard. But I don't care – it is dim and I am drunk. Somewhere along the way, I did a pencil sketch of it, now stowed away in one of my many sketchpads; the image of it now in a vault of my mind, however long that lasts for. I haven't heard any news of him. He had awakened the day before yesterday. Spoke to the detectives… Is he home now?

I gulp another mouthful, trying not to think about him. But no sooner have the band started the riff than I find myself thrust back in time, when I once used to listen to the very song, riding the bus to and from school. The morose plucking of the bass guitar; the sweet, sad pulse of the melody. Like a heartbeat of sorrow. It is Placebo's poignant rendition of *Running Up That Hill* pillaging my very synthesis.

I see my seat on lower deck. ' "It doesn't hurt me",' he sings, and my lip trembles.

The streets I'd pass. The warmth the bus gave on those freezing winter days. The electric guitar sadly strums. The bass guitar resonating pain.

I see Bianca, her snide smile and dirty look. ' "And if I only could…" '

The time I'd been fooled and missed the bus. ' "I'd make a deal with God" '

And his look. His face through the glass. He was sorry. I could see he had been sorry. The guitar thrashes, the bass vibrates through me, reaching the crescendo.

The tears come down slowly but the music continues, relentless. ' "Keep running up that road. Keep running up that hill…" '

I can't keep it together. I can't. I succumb to the memory. I have lost all self-control. I feel my mascara sting my eyes as it is seeped by my tears.

I vaguely feel my phone vibrating in my pocket. It takes me some seconds to pull myself out of the abyss. The phosphorescent word is warped through the blur in my eyes, but I can still construe it. Kate.

'Hey, Kate!' I shout so she can hear me over the vocalist. I'm happy she's called. My friend. My sister. She says something but I can't hear, so I tell her to hang on a second, as I grab my jacket and unsteadily make my way through the crowd and outside. I totter to the other side of the street, distancing myself from the hubbub.

'Kate! Wha's up?' I slur to the receiver.

'YOU DECEIVED ME! YOU LIED!' she shouts down the line.

'Whah?' I say, bewildered – too drunk to catch. 'Wha' are you talking abou'?'

'I told you not to get involved, and you did! I told you not to say anything, and you did!' She sounds like she's crying.

It takes me a second and then I freeze, rooted to the street. She can only be talking about one thing; the only thing she ever asked me to do.

And I betrayed her.

Back Then

I lied.

I lied over and over again. But they believed me. The purpose of the call was true, the rest – who I was and how I knew – were lies. It was enough to convince them and, hearing an account on it two days later, was told that within the hour they'd pounded on his door.

He hadn't resisted. In fact, when his mother had frantically tried to deny the "allegations", he'd stopped her, telling her it was about time someone had done something, leaving her to collapse to the floor.

I had taken Kate to the police station late that evening, after she'd received a call from her father. She didn't want to go, then after some persuasion by me, said she was going to deny everything; still convinced there was a better way to get her brother help. I hadn't said a word; let the police do their job.

He had appealed for psychiatric evaluation; it was denied. After hearing that, my heart had slumped, stricken – for that, *that* was what he needed. Therapy. Medication. A considerate ear to loan him understanding, then a wise mouth to offer solutions to mend his bent mind.

In the end, the court didn't do their job.

His sentence: Incarceration for up to 5 years.

There was one tiny fraction inside me that thought perhaps I shouldn't have done it; find a different route to help him. But it was too late now.

PART THREE

Chapter Thirty-Seven

Now

I phone Kate but she doesn't pick up. I knew she wouldn't, but still…
I wonder how she found out. After all these years, why now?
I send her a text with simple yet honest words:

I'm sorry for never telling you.

I don't push it further; she needs time, and I need… what *do* I need?
I want to go far, far away.

***

Monday comes through a shroud of tenebrous unrest. It's Nick's funeral.
Although he may have gone out of his way to talk to me back in the day, I
hadn't known him that well, and thought not to go, but no sooner had that
thought sprung, when another, more dominant thought, overran it. *Of course
you must go; it's Nick. You got him into trouble too. He had asked for your
forgiveness… the least you could do is ask for his.*
   I can't stop shaking as I get dressed in the dark attire fitting for the dark
day. Incessant tears that wash my face, sting hotly. *Stop! Stop! Just stop!* My
attention is on Kate. On James. How I am held accountable for them, for
myself. My own devastation. I brought it upon myself the moment I'd
stabbed them in the back. I am the shipwrecked, marooned on the isle of
my soul. Afraid. Alone. Heartbroken.
   'But I'm not sorry for helping you, Kate,' I cry to the bathroom mirror.
'Say what you want, I'm not sorry. You benefitted so much from it, and you
know it!' Then I scream. I am at the verge of losing my mind. I throw my

boot that stubbornly refuses to fit my foot across the other side of the bathroom. It hits the mirror, a bursting shatter, as shards fall into the basin. I wail. I don't want any more of this! I hit, punch, and kick whatever I find…

I'm trembling. I wipe my face and draw in one big, stuttered breath. 'Get your act together!' I command.

The throbbing in my wounded hand, though, substantiating that pain is constant.

I take the Tube – six stops to Archway Station, crossing at Camden Town. Camden… how many more times will I have to pass through this place until I stop *associating* it with him? Infinite…

I exit and head west, cutting through each street, having ample time to make it on foot.

I spot the church's spire first, and as I get closer, make out some people gathered at the entrance. Their faces downcast, bereaved.

I enter the solemn, almost full, church, and sit in a back pew, passing a couple of photo-reporters. I suppose they do have a story to follow up on.

Ice runs down my spine at the ubiquitous feeling of sadness one is enveloped with upon entering a realm of mourning. But there is something else; some other apprehension, I can't quite put my finger on.

I don't know a soul, but I feel someone's eyes on me. I turn to my right and scan some pews. She is concentrating a little bit too much on what is going on in front of her. GSY's secretary. She snitched on me, now she can't meet my eye.

I feel another sudden chill; the vast, yawning structure not helping to make my mind at ease, as each movement drives a breath of icy air around me, and each sound, each hushed murmur resonating, like a hundred spirits whispering secret messages to one another from the vault to the nave… Shhh… Shhh…

Just then, a dissonant, blood-curdling wail reverberates all around the cavernous space. Everyone turns in the direction of the plangent cry. Nick's mother is losing it, her husband and other son trying to calm her; inconsolably.

On my part, the sound alone has made me burst into tears. The force of her pain stabbing me through. I wipe at my eyes, try to calm myself. I then catch a sudden movement of long, blonde hair being flicked back two rows further in front of me. Elizabeth? Yes. Unmistakable – the shade, the texture… She turns slightly to her left to talk to the person next to her. Seeing her profile, I am left with no doubt it's her.

I shift in my seat to see who she is talking to. My heart stops. I almost don't recognise him, and blink the tears from my eyes in case I'm not seeing right through the blur. His long hair is gone! It's now short enough for me to see his nape. That's why I didn't spot him when I walked in; the marker wasn't there. His long, illustrious hair – gone!

But he is up. He is well. A warmth kindles my centre. He is a breath away. I want to run to him and caress him, show my happiness he is in health… but of course I don't. Not because this is neither the time nor place, or because I don't have the guts. The sad truth is, if I did embrace him in any way, he'd probably shove me off him in disgust.

The service starts with a homily from the minister, a soft soliloquy replete with platitudes one hears at funerals. I don't pay much attention – I don't think anyone can; the pained sobs coming from the front are enough to distract even the most attentive audience.

My eyes fill with salty tears again, but I don't wipe them away this time; there's no point – there'll be more.

James moves. He turns his face to the right. I am dead-still. His jaw has a fresh strip of bandage stuck to it. He is wearing a neat, white nose brace, holding the bridge of his nose in position. I remember how bloodied it was. So… they'd broken it? That wonderful, proportioned nose… But his wounds are healing. His face is mottled with faint, yellowish-blue bruises and small incisions, all in the process of diminishing.

I notice some faces turn my way. To all appearances, wondering who I am. Wondering if Nick had any tall, goth-like (yes, I admit it) girlfriends. A teenaged boy, in fact, hasn't stopped looking over his shoulder. He is a row in front of James. The boy catches something on James's face and suddenly turns to the front. Then James makes a hesitant motion to the side again; the teenaged boy must have stirred his curiosity. I don't move. I don't breathe.

And before I know it, he and I are face to face.

Chapter Thirty-Eight

Now

For one precipitous moment, he does it again; studies me the way he had done when we were supposed friends. A light, Cox-Pomona red dapples his cheeks, and I again feel that crazy burning blush rise, regardless of my tears, as though I am sixteen all over again. How does he do that to me? His eyes, however, are a cold scorch. They say the eyes are the windows to the soul, but his are a window to mine. What they hold is my perfidious handiwork; my damage to his life.

So, that's how he feels about me. *Of course that's how he feels about you, you idiot! Didn't you get the message, loud and clear, that night? Why should he have changed his opinion of you, just because you saved his life?*
Does he know I saved him?

If anything, he hates my guts even more, now that DI Archer has probably told him, in fine detail, just *how* exactly I am involved in his assault. I cringe. I am ashamed he knows I followed him. I half-think he's going to get up, march straight to me, and tell me to get out of his sight! But his back is rigid. Motionless. Too motionless. Have I surprised him by being here?

I close my eyes and see his. Irises – the shade of the morning sea after a thunderstorm. So clear. How many times have I secretly painted them, secretly sketched his countenance while pretending to jot down notes back in Hilsmond? Each time the iridescence formed a new light. A minuscular difference of luminosity and depth. Today they are a cornflower blue with a dab of cerulean and streaks of baby blue and yes, the smallest hint of celadon. There is the arc of a brown shade around his pupil – the remnants of a distant relative who had dark eyes; the light copper flecks mixed with tan and a tinge of burnt sienna.

I open my eyes. I see Elizabeth looking at me. She smiles sadly. I return the gesture. James takes this in with a sudden jerk of the head. Hasn't Elizabeth told him we met?

Just then, someone sits invasively next to me; his arm touching mine. And I look to see Detective Inspector Archer, himself, looking straight at me. I turn back just in time to see James's face form a constrained scowl at Archer, before turning to the front again.

'How are you, Eleanora?' Archer whispers. I looked at him, deadpan; in no mood to talk. Let him see the tears.

We say nothing till the end of the service, watching as the coffin is ceremoniously lifted on sturdy shoulders and walked out of the church. Nick's bother is one of the pallbearers. He looks like he's going to fall apart; crumple to the floor. Nick's immediate family follows – his mother barely able – and everyone else right behind them, on their way to the burial ground. A sonorous, dim chatter resonates as the church empties.

James and Elizabeth get up, striding slowly to the door, and I see James has an arm-sling on his left arm, under his leather jacket. I don't see plaster; it isn't broken. Is it to immobilize his shoulder? Had those men dislocated it? What else? What else had they done?

James is quietly greeted by Nick's father, who gently man-hugs him, patting him on the back. I don't see James's face but his shoulders give a quick judder. It is a movement you make when you're about to cry.

I let them leave, let everyone go first. I want to be the last person out.

DI Archer doesn't budge. Why is he here? Hasn't he cut that bloody Gordian knot yet? Unless… James hasn't told all…

I get up to follow the procession, Archer on tow. He wants something – I can sense an exuding exigence; a burning to solve the case, and fast. We walk to the door and step outside into an inclement sky. That grey overshadow is closing in on us. I button up my coat as high as it goes, feeling the chill of the damp, descending zephyr.

Archer squints, peeved, at the sky. 'Looks like rain…' he begins feebly.

'Hmm,' I agree listlessly, and walk on.

'Eleanora?' he says, coming up to me. This is it. He can contain it no longer. I hear the desperation in his voice. 'I need your help.'

I whip my head towards him, incredulous. 'Here?' I hiss. 'This is no place to discuss –'

'I know, Eleanora, and I'm sorry, but I don't have much time. Please… For the good of the case.'

I bite my lip. I know he's right, only, what more have I to tell?

'Just tell me anything you can on Barton. What kind of person was he?'

I am disgusted. Shocked. 'We're about to bury him!'

'I'm sorry. I know. It seems really base of me, but it's for him too. So that he may rest in peace.'

Rest in peace. Archer hits home, sharp-shooting me in the centre of my breast. I give in with a sigh. 'I didn't know him very well. I saw him last, six years ago…'

'What was he like?'

'A normal teenage kid…'

'Define "normal teenage kid".'

'I don't know… he was funny. He was a bit reckless but on purpose, you know, to make people laugh. I remember he made fun of his teachers all the time… played tricks on them. He… he was computer savvy. He knew how to hack. He'd hacked their system on more than one occasion.'

'Drugs?' Archer asks. I stop short. 'I know he took drugs at that party six years ago, but that's not what I'm asking,' he continues. 'Everyone takes something or other at a party. But what I want to know is if he was a habitual user. An addict. Do you know if he had a dealer?'

I stare at him not believing my ears. 'How on earth would I know that? We weren't *that* close!' I exclaim. 'I mean, OK, he did always look half ill and stuff; he smoked a lot, but that's just an opinion… circumstantial… that's not evidence.'

Archer lets out a breath and strokes his hand through his hair.

'Detective,' I say, frustrated, 'why are you asking me all this? Haven't you got this information from his parents?'

'They aren't saying anything, are they?' He's upset. 'Doctors' records are private unless I have a warrant to search files… but I need proof. Someone's statement. By the time his body was sent to the coroner – and I shouldn't be telling you this – all traces of drugs were gone from his blood stream because he was in a coma for so many days, attached to a drip, cleaning everything out.'

We turn a grassy corner, the mourners are at a distance, still slowly making their way around old tombstones. The dominant grave of Carl Marx looms in front of us and, soon, we leave it behind and into the path that leads deeper into the cemetery.

'I read an article the other day about the case. It mentioned your name,' I say. He glances to me. 'You believe it's drug related?'

'Yeah.'

I mull that over, pacing on. In the distance I espy *him*, one head above the rest.

Suddenly, something tight grabs my arm and I am swung back around at a jerk, letting out a short yell: Archer, bringing me to a painful halt. Anger, impatience streaks his face. *What the…?*

'I'm getting tired of this, Eleanora. Stop hiding information!'

'What do you mean?' I say, bewildered, my heart full throttle. I can't believe Archer has such a short fuse. And now he's hurting me.

'Drugs!' he states. 'You know something, and you're not telling me!'

I search desperately. 'Do you think that James had drugs on him the night he was assaulted? That that was the "stuff"? Because I refuse to believe that. I refuse to believe he's a dealer. He can't be –'

'Why?' he bellows, his face getting very close to mine. Everyone can hear him. The mourners may be far off, but I know Archer's voice has definitely carried in the silence of our surroundings. But there's something going on; he's never shown signs of being a complete bastard. I would say it was feigned if my arm wasn't hurting so much.

I stare, frantically, at him. 'You're causing a sce –'

'Tell me!' he hisses, shaking me roughly. 'Why don't you believe it? Do you know how much cash you can make selling drugs? This could have been his ticket.'

For one sickening moment I remember what Kate and I had hypothesized. How we both thought it was drugs as well. Then another reasoning comes to mind. 'Why suddenly sell drugs now? He's known Nick all his life. Why now? No. Do you think he doesn't know how much money can be made? Why didn't he start years ago and live better, have that chance to go to Oxford?'

'You tell me.'

'Because it's not who he is!'

He grunts scathingly, sarcastically. He squeezes a little more.

'Let go!' I cry.

'I could arrest you, right now, for withholding evidence,' he snarls. 'Don't make me do it!'

'Detective Archer!'

We instantly turn to see who's spoken. James is standing three feet away, dislike plain on his face.

'Leave her alone,' he tells Archer quietly yet firmly, looking straight down at him. The boxer stands a good few inches taller than the detective. Unfazed, Archer glares at him, his lip curving in a gloat.

'Please,' James says, with a tone of forewarning, not hiding his distain. I raise my braced-up hand to try and remove Archer's grip on my arm. That is going to leave a bruise…

'Do you have something to say, Mr Laidlaw?' Archer asks, giving him a feral look.

James notices my bound wrist, and furrows his brows, then sees me looking at him, and something passes his eyes.

'Mr Laidlaw?' Archer calls, deliberately menacing. James grinds his jaw in defeat. He gets closer to the other man. Closer to me.

'After I have finished burying my best friend, Detective,' he says, spitting the word "detective" out. 'I will… have a talk with you. Until then, please refrain from harassing Miss Stephens.'

Miss Stephens. No *Eleanora.* The proof of dissociation.

Archer gives an arrogant smile of satisfaction, 'Good,' and lets go of my arm with a shove, sending me tottering two steps back, still utterly confused as to why he is being so gruff. I rub the spot where he's just manhandled me. James, disgusted at him, then disgusted at me, turns his back and walks to the burial site.

I stand there stunned, blinking, unable to believe it all. What just happened? Did he just come to my rescue? What is going on? Why come to my rescue when you find me disgusting? It reminds me when he intervened that time on the bus with Sarah. He'd stuck up for me. Could he be doing it again, now, like some kind of duty for saving him? Or is it simply that he is chivalrous to the core? I am stumped.

I turn to Archer, who has morphed back into his old, calm self, and it suddenly hits me what he's just done.

'You did that on purpose!' I tell him, seething.

Archer gives me an unpretentious, arid wink, 'Had to,' and walks away. I can almost see him mentally rubbing his hands together in delight. He'd planned it. He knew James would react this way. He figured out James's cavalier temperament, and played him, using me as bait. I want to give him what for, demand an apology, but I have no time.

I jog to catch up, and enter the bleak row of mossy graves surrounded by rich, emerald underbrush and scraggly trees. I walk on in silence, passing the monuments propped on each grave. The angels, the Celtic crosses, each a tribute in memorandum. There beyond, is George Eliot's grave; a tall Cleopatra's needle. I pause, briefly, to look at her tomb; it isn't every day I come to these parts. The least I can do is to pay my respects to someone who has given me solace in her prose.

Of those immortal dead who live again in minds made better by their presence, I read. *Thank you…*

The procession has come to a halt and is gathering around the site of burial. The background noise of strained whimpers of a mentally collapsing mother never ceasing.

I look around me. There are his eyes again, fixed on mine, wan, and hollow as the grave in front of us.

I can feel the chill. I can feel whatever happens now, there is no turning back, as sure as the grave awaits us all. I am here now, in his life whether he likes it or not. And only when I have talked, have confessed, will I disappear from it. He will never need to know me again.

'Ashes to ashes, dust to dust…'

All guard is down now. James is statue still, the only sign of movement are the tears. Tears that fall freely, quietly. As do mine.

I forgive you, Nick…Whatever it was, I forgive you. Rest in peace.

Chapter Thirty-Nine

Now

I am running.

The rain, coming on fast, torrential. I'm just in time, through Archway Station's shelter, before I'm completely soaked to the bone. I run my fingers through my drenched hair, noticing how long it has become. After years of pixie cuts, I feel like Rapunzel.

'El!' I hear a voice shout through the crowd. People who foolishly left home this morning without an umbrella have piled in, leaving the place crammed and puddled. Me, one of them.

'El!' she calls again. I see her. Elizabeth. We both look ridiculous, like two drowned cats. We give each other sedate grins while wiping off the water from our faces.

'As if crying wasn't enough,' she says. 'I've worn my cheeks out from all the wiping today.'

'Tell me about it,' I reply.

'Jamie had to leave with that annoying detective. I didn't want to go to the Barton house alone,' she informs me. We swipe our cards and find our way to the escalators. 'Let's hope it's stopped raining by the time we reach Edgware.'

'We? I don't live in Edgware,' I tell her.

'No?'

'It's Hampstead Village for me!'

'Hampstead? Really? Oh!' She sounds disconcerted.

'What's up?' *Now what?*

'Nothing, just Jamie told me to go home with you. I was running to catch up with you. We thought you lived in Edgware. I thought…' Elizabeth looks utterly bewildered. 'I thought he would have known where you live since you *are* friends…'

I don't know what to make of that. He entrusts his sister to me?

I land on the first concourse and jog to the platform, hearing the far-off rumble vibrate under my feet. Elizabeth is next to me, and within a few seconds, the train whooshes by, clamouring away with its ostentatious presence. We say nothing, knowing it's futile to be heard over the racket. We wait for the train to settle and the doors to open, people to alight onto the platform, vacating as much space as possible. We get in and find a couple of seats. She is quiet but I know she's waiting. She hasn't got the courage to prompt me. The train judders on, onto its next stop: Tufnell Park.

I wet my lips and say, 'Elizabeth. I don't know what James has told you of me. Obviously not a lot…'

Her face is lined with curiosity, patiently waiting for any salient points I might throw her way.

'We don't have, what you might say, a typical friendship,' I say, knowing if I go into detail, she'll want to know more. It is best I not say much, besides, they are her brother's secrets too, not only mine.

'I'm sure James will tell you in his own good time what… how we know one another,' I say, smiling reassuringly. Her face drops in disappointment.

'Nobody tells me anything,' she says, hurt.

'He will tell you, I'm sure of it. Just give him time. He's had a lot on his plate this week.'

She bows her head. 'Yeah… you're right…'

We get off at Camden Town and cross over for Edgware branch.

'I wish they hadn't taken the vending machines away,' Elizabeth says. 'I'm famished.'

'Would you like to come over to my flat?' I suggest. 'You can eat with me.'

She beams.

***

Elizabeth adores my place, declaring how she wants the same when she leaves home. She flips all my canvases lying upright around the place, exclaiming her awe at my talent. 'No way! That's a photograph,' she says, adamant I didn't paint it.

'Come on, Elizabeth,' I say, making light of it. 'You can see the brushstrokes, surely!'

'They're beautiful! Can I buy one?'

I blink, stunned. 'Of course, but not now. I need them for my exhibition. Which one do you like?'

'That one!' she points, straight out. 'The boxer. It looks like he's about to punch through the canvas. It's so real…'

I heat some of yesterday's succulent lamb, and make her some Greek Mountain tea (Ironwort) with thyme honey, to sooth her.

'This is delicious, by the way. Where did you get it? It definitely isn't Marks and Sparks. And this tea? What is it?' She sniffs. 'It smells… different.'

'I made the lamb. And the tea is hand-picked from my Gran's village in Greece.'

'What?! I don't believe it!' she cries with her mouth full. 'You're such a good cook! And you're *Greek*?'

I laugh. 'Only about an eighth. But it's a very strong eighth!' Then I inform her that I write a blog on food and tell her the name.

'*Eleanora Dishes*,' I say, scrunching my nose. 'It's silly but I like the way it has a double meaning. Literal and metaphorical.'

'Actually, it sounds cool! I'm gonna check it out. I love feta cheese! And, oh, I'm taking Classics for GCSE. I am absolutely in love with Odysseus. I can totally understand why Penelope is loyal to him. If I had a man like that…' She sways her head dreamily, making me laugh, and I go the fridge and bring her some feta.

The rain turns into a pitter patter, as Elizabeth stares out the window.

'I should get going,' she says reluctantly. 'Jamie might be home now.'

'Home?' I ask, curious. Elizabeth, I've gathered by now, has a very tractable nature.

'Yes, he's back home,' she declares with a wide smile. 'He came home the day before yesterday. Mum insisted. Dad too. He's trying to make things up to him. Practically got down on his knees and begged Jamie to come and rest back home, 'cos Jamie was insisting he go back to his garage. But Dad grabbed him tight, and heaved Jamie into his car.' She trails off for a pause to hold back the tears. I feel the weight of her words too and am overwhelmed with what they imply. I feel my eyes well. 'That's wonderful news…' I say.

'Yeah, it's been great… I'm so happy. Mum is a different person; she hasn't stopped baking something or other for him, always humming a tune. Dad's taken time off from work to be around him as much as he can. He's back in his old bed, for the time being, but it's as if he isn't home, 'cos he's been on his feet, non-stop, since he got out of hospital. Even on Easter he had some important, online call. He's got some kind of solicitor, I don't know… Anyway, I've barely spoken to him all this time. I didn't even get a chance in the hospital. I want to be around him as much as possible.'

'I understand… I'm awfully glad they've reconciled.'

'Yeah…' she says, looking straight at me with her child-like eyes. 'I think all this was a blessing in disguise. Albeit a horrid disguise, but sometimes an extreme has to be reached in order for people to find common ground. Those are Jamie's words…' she adds sheepishly.

'I agree…' I smile.

'I mean, Dad's been helping Jamie get dressed and shave and stuff; Jamie can't move his arm just yet. It's nothing short of a miracle…'

'What's the matter with his arm? Is it dislocated?'

She nods solemnly.

'What else did they do to him?' I ask quietly. I fear to hear the extent of abuse.

'Well, you saw his face today. They broke his nose and fractured his jaw. He's eating from a straw. He has a bruised ribcage, lacerations everywhere… he was lucky he didn't get a punctured lung.'

'Jesus.'

'The doctors say he'll be good in a couple of weeks. He needs rest, but he isn't resting. I mean, the way he ran when he saw that bloody detective grab you like that…'

I hold my breath.

'I thought Jamie was going to kill him! He was shaking you like a ragdoll!' Elizabeth shrieks.

I open my mouth to say something, but find I can't. I smile awkwardly, as I try to slot the day's events into some order. He came to my rescue, yes, but it doesn't make sense.

She is waiting for a response. I give her the only reason I believe.

'Your brother has always been a gentleman, and I thank him for it.' I am sincere.

***

I take Elizabeth back to Edgware. She insists she's old enough to go home by herself, which I agree, but also remind her that her brother wanted her to travel with *me*. 'Complaints to the manager,' I tell her wryly.

The stretch between Hampstead and Edgware is overground, and as we roll past patches of land, police training grounds, schools, office buildings, houses of worship, Elizabeth speaks.

'He *is* a gentleman, you know. I think you summed him up perfectly. He's always been good. He's never cheated. He's never lied. He always obeyed. He was diligent in his schoolwork. He helped Dad fix things. Cleaned the car. Set the table for dinner…' She stops. She can't say more because now she's crying. I put my arm around her to comfort. I chew over her words. I know I must beg to differ on a couple of her points, but I can't deny the *eunoia* of her brother's mind. I feel she's absolutely right.

Elizabeth hugs me and squeezes before we round into her drive. I have stopped walking, indicating no wish to go further, saying, 'Well, here we are!'

'Thanks again for everything, El!'

'Come by anytime,' I say. 'You have my number.' I give her a smile.

'Please come in. Say hi. If Jamie isn't home, then to Mum –'

'No, no. I have to be off,' I say hurriedly. I am already walking away. 'Tell him another time. Soon. I'll speak to him soon.'

Chapter Forty

Now

I sit, inert, staring at the cup of tea I've been given, as I try to assimilate what's just happened. The only element I sense are the tears rolling down my face. One day after the funeral, and I almost had mine. I don't know how much more I can take. My life has become a landslide, and I can't see the bottom.

I wasn't caught totally unaware. There had been something out of place, off-kilter. A shift. A different odour. A different aspect. My sofa. I hadn't noticed it right away; only after I had come back from my first day at the boxing club and was about to get some water, did I stop short to inspect.

I was on a high when I came home. Stacy, from the club, had rung me up and said I could start some training without my wrist coming in any physical contact. She would show me how to fight air. I had jumped for the chance to get out the flat. I had been writing on my thesis all that morning, and it seemed like a good opportunity to unwind.

I had been about to open the fridge when I saw one side of my sofa had been pushed forwards ever so slightly. I am OCD when it comes to furniture symmetry, and my sofa wasn't parallel to the coffee table. Sure, I could have left it like that from the day before, but I knew that wasn't the case, for I had just straightened it that very morning and hadn't touched it since. Or had I? For a minute I thought was going crazy, but that's when I looked around the place to check if there were other objects where they shouldn't be. And my heart seized. One of the sketches I'd done for the police was on the floor.

Primarily, I thought Kate had come to get something, but that felt off. She wouldn't just come and go, and at the exact point I had popped out. She'd make known her arrival. Of course, under the circumstances of our tenuous friendship… who knew?

I rang Victoria on the burner.

'Is Mum OK?' I'd asked her.

'Yeah. Why?'

'I think someone was in my flat.'

'What do you mean? Where's Kate?' She was frantic.

'Kate's…' I hesitated. 'Kate's away.'

There was a pause.

'Call the police! They told you to call if you see anything weird. If you don't, I will!'

'OK, OK!'

We hung up. I didn't want to stay in my flat. I didn't feel like my own anymore. I put on my jacket, grabbed the essentials and was out my front door, bounding onto Heath Street at a jog, up towards the tube station. I'd phone the police from there.

And then it happened. The sounds came first. Wild revving of a large engine – the menacing, threatening growl so close, and then the shrill screech of a tyre burning on the tarmac, in a sudden torque. I jumped at the sound but didn't stop running, instinctively looking behind me. A broad grille of a Range Rover was charging my way, veering onto the pavement, seconds behind me. I bolted to a sprint as fast as my legs could carry me, every muscle ripping as my lungs screamed for more oxygen, heart thumping, like someone's actual fist was punching my sternum from the inside. Last second, I skidded tightly around a corner, into the street where great iron bollards are welded to the ground hindering entrance to cars. I heard the shrieking of brakes and shouts from all over. Few pedestrians were out, but I could hear enraged shouts and curses clearly.

I didn't look back, just ran as far away as I could. Trembling, gasping, renting the air with my cries.

They had been a tick too late. The momentum of my jogging saved me, as I had sped up just in time.

I didn't know where they had gone… they could come back around the other end and find me…

Where to hide?

I ducked into a tiny restaurant, hidden inconspicuously under a tall Georgian building, an awning shading half of it, new phone in hand, and dialling to Archer. The restaurant was empty; too early for customers. A woman came out from behind, annoyed. She opened her mouth ready to speak but stopped when I yelled, 'THEY ALMOST KILLED ME!' I was shaking so hard I couldn't hold my phone steadily to my ear.

'Eleanora?!' Archer said, bewildered.

'It was a R-Range Rover. It c-came up right b-behind me. It almost r-ran me down! Oh, God!'

It took him a fraction to realise what I was saying, then he shouted, 'Where are they heading?'

'Up, towards the Tube.'

He hollered, 'All units to Hampstead Tube. Range Rover, northbound. Vicinity of Heath Street…' He was in his car. I could hear the siren come to life. Then he said some codes and, '…victim is key witness to an assault…'

A moment later, 'Eleanora, where are you?' he demanded. I told him where.

'W-what should I do? What if they come looking for me?' I was terror-stricken.

The woman let out a gasp and darted to the door and locked it, rattling the glass panels.

Archer shouted some orders – a dispatch of some kind.

'Eleanora, we're sending an officer to the restaurant. Stay put, OK?' he ordered.

'K…'

'Now, tell me whatever you can on the Range Rover. Colour.'

Trembling, I tried to get my mind to rewind, back through the panic.

'I-it…was a dark green… that pine colour…'

'Number plate?'

'No… I was running away from it, I had no time… Wait!' I remembered. 'The writing in front… the letters… s-some were missing. It must have been the two thousand-two model.'

Archer clearly enunciated this information on the CB.

I thought of all the people, all my loved ones, and how those men who were after me could get to them.

'Archer,' I called down the line, 'they found me! They could find my mother, my sister…'

'We'll get a patrol car to them,' he answered decisively. As he was sending the orders, I phoned Kate on the pre-paid. Grudge or not, she'd have to suck it up.

She didn't answer, I knew she wouldn't, so I left a message.

They know where I live. Don't go to the flat. It's not safe.

The phone shook so hard in my hands that it dropped. I was shaking profusely. I picked it up and pressed *send*. Archer, on my other phone, went dead.

I sat and waited, on edge. The restaurant owner said absolutely nothing; she, like me, heard the faraway sirens. My agitation should have abated, instead it got worse.

'ELEANORA?!' An officer was at the door, knocking, a few minutes later. The owner got up and unlocked immediately upon seeing it was the authorities.

'Eleanora Stephens?' the officer said, looking inside the shaded space and spotting me. 'I'm Police Constable Jane Hawkes. Detective Archer asked me to assist you as he is currently pursuing what seems to be the Range Rover you described –'

Her walkie-talkie bellowed something incoherent through bad static just then. Then two very distinct gunshots sounded and we all jumped. PC Jane Hawkes went pale and turned to go outside again, her walkie-talkie continuing to broadcast distorted words I couldn't understand.

I thanked the owner of the establishment for her shelter with a panicked nod, and stepped outside warily, only to hear another gunshot. This time, it wasn't from the walkie-talkie.

Chapter Forty-One

Now

Police have apprehended two men said to be responsible for a hit-and-run earlier this week, leaving their victim, Nicholas Barton, severely wounded and succumbing days later. After a pursuit and an exchange of fire, leaving one police officer lightly wounded and both felons severely injured, they were taken into custody and are under stringent security in hospital pending trial. The men had been apprehended after being pursued in Hampstead where they had almost run down and killed a key witness who had seen them beat a man, in connection with Barton, outside his home 8 days ago. Investigations are ongoing as witnesses are being questioned so as to shed light as the reasons why all three victims were wanted dead. – The evening news, four days earlier.

Mens rea. That was what I was told happened in my case. *Guilty mind.* They were thinking to do me harm but didn't. There was no actus reus. *Guilty act.* Archer was explaining to me.

'But the car chase?' I had cried indignant. My hands couldn't stop trembling, the tea spilled over the sides of the mug I was holding. I placed it down at his desk. DI Archer had already put his palms up to calm me.

'Let me finish, Eleanora. I wanted to say prosecution agrees with you. They have the evidence, that had it not been for the bollards, you would have been run over. So, it was actus reus indeed, but with obstruction to complete the act. The crime goes from recklessness to intent.

'The same goes for Laidlaw,' he said. 'The defence is contending these accusations; they want to plead guilty to grievous bodily harm but prosecution is not backing down; seems we have a strong case, thanks to you.'

I sat quietly listening. There was still that feeling, something I had missed; forgotten to say.

'What about Nick's case?' I asked him, in the hope I'd hear something that might jog my memory.

'As for Nick's, they were charged on involuntary manslaughter and pleaded guilty; there wasn't as much evidence to prove more in his case.'

'Except for Nick lying dead because of it,' I said, infuriated. Archer, harrumphed in agreement.

'Yes. It's ironic, isn't it? But that's the law. If there isn't enough proof…'

'…Even prosecution know they won't win,' I ended, despondent. Archer had affirmed with a nod.

'You will be summoned,' he said. 'But it won't be for a while yet, I'm guessing. They were both badly injured, and we have to wait until they can both attend trial.'

'Do you admit they found me from hacking the phone call I made that night?'

Archer shook his head. 'I doubt it. There was no breech in the system when we checked.'

I blinked, confused. What had Sophie actually done then? But the more worrying thought was, 'So how did they find me?'

'Apparently, one of the nurses at the hospital described you to them. You've got very distinct characteristics, do you know that?'

I tutted, irritated. He smiled, tongue in cheek.

'You were right in thinking they'd find out you were there to ID him. Then it was a matter of luck you were at the funeral. They must have followed you home.'

My hair stood on end.

'What?' I breathed. But I would have recognised them. Two large men would have stood out. I expressed this thought to Archer.

'They had an accomplice. Remember GSY's secretary?' I nodded, feeling her cold eyes on me at the funeral. 'She was going out with one of them. She claims she doesn't know anything. She's still being interrogated. Don't worry about it; they're all going down.'

I sat silent for some moments, absorbing the information.

'I'm… um, sorry about the funeral thing.'

I raised my brows and blinked. It felt peculiar; uncharacteristic of him to be …*sorry*.

'But I had to act fast… I wanted him to see me ruffle you up, so he would talk. I mean, not even after learning his best friend had died, did he say a word. Do you believe that? My last resort was you, Eleanora. Chief Inspector Daley had told me what had happened in the past between you and Laidlaw, and I had to risk it, otherwise we'd still be on square one. I hope you understand. …And I'm sorry if I hurt you. Did I?'

'No… I'll live,' I said quietly. We glanced at each other, realising just how black my humour had become at that moment.

But I understood why Archer had done it – why he had gone to such straights. To physically use my body to get his way. I didn't know what deontology he patterned himself to when faced with desperation, but I gave him kudos, albeit reluctantly, for using me, since it culminated to his desired outcome. I couldn't judge… look at me; look at what I had done to reach my goal. I could have been arrested, handcuffed and charged… and that was only for stalking. I dreaded to think what the penalty was for prohibited photography.

But that aside, it begged the question as to why James *hadn't* talked. What could have been more important than not giving crucial information to the police? Again, I expressed this thought aloud to Archer.

'The trial will answer that,' he told me, 'all in good time.'

'Well, you're lucky your plan worked, Detective. I thought he would have left me to the lions… unless he wants to throttle me himself,' I said dryly. 'Do you know …he called me a fucking ugly, anorexic bitch, that night I called the police? I suppose Chief Inspector Daley mentioned?' Archer heeded this with a pout of the lip and downcast eyes. 'I can't explain James's actions – he doesn't like me. He is a mystery. I have no idea what goes through his mind.'

'Eleanora…' He held a thought for a second, then resumed. 'When we're young we do stupid things. Sometimes we say things we don't mean, act in ways we don't understand ourselves… especially boys. Boys are total asses at that age. Really immature. Apart from myself, of course,' he added as a joke, which provoked an unhappy smile in me.

'Girls do stupid things too,' I said, fairly dolorous. He nodded solemnly. I lowered my eyes, rubbed at them. I stared at the mug.

'Detective? Did you tell him it was me?' I looked up at him. He blinked, trying to decipher what I meant. 'And by *it* you mean?' He was right. There were so many *its*.

'The phone call I made six years ago.'

He fixed his gaze on me, ruminating on his answer. 'No. It's irrelevant to the case. All he knows is that you followed him the night he got beaten. That you were the one that called the ambulance.'

So, I'll have to tell him. Tell him all…

'How did he take it, when he heard he was followed?'

'He was upset, but I don't think he'll press charges because, after all, if you hadn't been there, he would have died, if not from their fists, then from exposure.'

'Did he ask why I followed him?'

'He did. I told him it had been for good intent, that's why we hadn't pressed charges… but if he wanted details, then he'd have to ask you. Then he can deem for himself if it's worth suing. But I didn't tell him that last bit.' He grinned.

'Thanks, but he has a solicitor. He knows his rights,' I told him. Then I pulled a lengthy breath and let it out with a push. 'Well, detective,' I said, as got up to leave. 'Thank you, for everything. I hope… I hope everything turns out well…'

Archer nodded and followed me to the door. 'I hope so too.' He gave me his hand. 'And I hope I didn't leave a bruise.' He paused, then let go of my hand. 'I'll see you at the trial.'

***

Exhausted. I now feel the honest meaning to that word. The true, literal substance of it. I am mentally, spiritually exhausted on the past four-day's reflections, no longer having the capacity to think with clarity as the quagmire of jumbled thoughts block any sound reasoning.

Not having helped James as I initially planned, all I can do, now, is prime my apology. I know it will be soon. Every chance has been hindered so far, but I am under the impression it won't be long, forthwith. I'll find him. I will. I know where he lives…

And betraying my dearest friend? Her unyielding absence marking how deep my treachery has gone. She had sent me an arid text, *Are you OK?* after the Range Rover incident, and after responding in the affirmative, nothing else.

And almost getting killed? Isn't my torture enough? The nightmares are worse, on top of it. Waking up, gasping, on the cusp of fantasizing my demise. My house – the tiny flat, which I have grown to love, has been invaded and doesn't feel like home anymore. Where is the warmth and safety? My haven? Ripped. Violated. Vulnerable.

And my dissertation? How am I to get it done, alongside my final project; my exhibition? They have all been relegated to last place in my list of priorities. They should be first. My degree should be first. My life should be first…

I prepare, methodically, no heart into it, more as though I am putting on every-day clothes rather than this lovely dress.

The hand brace, heretofore, off (wrist with only the smallest remnant of pain) as the sleeves of the oxblood bodycon are short. I look in the full-length mirror. The outfit is a startling contrast against my pale skin, but admittedly, it looks like it was made for me. Perfect fit, even round the bust. Comfortable, soft. I don't do much to my hair; just blow-dry it into neater, slicker, curly ends and smooth my fringe to one side, holding it back with a dainty hair-grip, which has tiny diamantes on the top. I apply makeup. I enhance my eyes and rosy-up my pale cheeks. Kate had insisted I put on plenty of my crimson, matte lipstick, which I do. I think of her back then. That night when I had been trying to put lip liner on her. That night when I first saw her brother, and she'd told me all. Poor girl. If it weren't for me, she'd be here, and I'd be helping her with her makeup. I wonder how she's faring with that.

I slip on my four-and-three-quarter-inch black, satin, N&L stilettos. I am apprehensive else I sprain an ankle. I haven't worn heels this high in a while. They're going to kill my feet; I can see it coming. I move closer to the mirror, wobbling a bit.

I let out a sigh. Ready.

I have a wedding to attend, and, allegedly, life is continuing. Four days earlier, I'd thought different.

I don't particularly want to go; my frame of mind lingers on the terror, unable to calm, but it would be awful of me to back out now. I simply can't do that to Melanie – not on her special day.

The car toots, and I grab my light, black evening coat. The day is mild, but you never know – this is London; spring London.

I step downstairs, stilettos not giving me too much hardship. I think of that cynical Greek saying: What is pain compared to beauty?

Suze has come as arranged and is waiting for me in her old Mini.

'Where's Juliet?' I ask, as I cram myself in. 'I thought you were going to get her first.'

'Where's Kate?' she asks back.

'She's made other arrangements,' I say, disguising any hurt I feel regarding that situation.

Suze pauses. 'Oh,' she says, and puts the car in first.

'Juliet?'

'Oh, yeah,' Suze says evasively, as she glides the car into the street. 'She's, er, ill.' Her voice sounds strange, restrained.

'Ill?' I say, surprised. 'Is she ok?'

She lets out a long sigh. 'Don't tell her I told you.' I brace, always having hated that precursor to a bad secret. 'But it's morning sickness.' Suze looks at me, eyebrows raised, awaiting my reaction.

'What?!' I squeal. 'You're kidding?!'

'Nope.' Suze is trying to suppress a grin.

'She's pregnant?!' I say, stating the obvious.

'Yep!'

'Whose is it?' is all I can think to say, although it's definitely none of my business and neither Suze's. But then again, if Juliet told her of her pregnancy, then she probably told her who the father was.

Suze grabs her lips between her teeth, stifling a laugh. 'Sam's,' she says, and bursts out in her familiar wicked laugh.

'Sam's?!' I almost shout, absolutely shocked. Well, that explains her reaction when we were shopping in the West End. Suze is in fits; a husky chuckle that sets me off too.

'I mean, can you imagine Sam as a dad?' she says, snorting each word through her laughter.

I burst out anew.

'Stop! Stop! My mascara's going to run!'

***

Suze and I make as quiet an entrance as possible in the church, considering what we're wearing on our feet. We're late, we heard the organ strike its last notes just as we were parking the car.

'Hope we don't come in on that part where the minister says that thing about forever holding our peace!' whispers Suze.

'Shut up! You're going to make me laugh again,' I tell her under my breath.

The place is filled with baby's-breath bouquets, not only along the aisle, but on big floral stands, here and there. I smile; so Melanie. And, looking in, there is a rather large display of pink roses, intermingled with more baby's breath at the altar. But the real beauty is Melanie, herself, and Harry standing solemnly in the centre, heads bowed, listening to the minister.

Suze and I scamper to a couple of seats Aidan has kept for us, towards the back. A column blocks my direct vision of the alter. I move left and right to capture whatever I can.

'What? No posies for the Knights Templar?' whispers Aidan, with a cheeky grin. I smile back at him, trying to picture how the recumbent effigies at the nave would look with some of the flowers placed benevolently on them.

'You're gorgeous by the way,' he tells me. 'Every guy is staring at you…'

'No, they're not. Don't be silly.' I feel my face redden, and hide behind the column.

'Yes, they are!' says another voice from behind. Kate. She sits a little way off, not quite smiling, but her eyes are soft. That is consoling; it means we'll talk soon.

The vows start, and I crane my neck, wanting to witness such a significant juncture in one's life. Both bride and groom glow, they are in a happy dream, holding hands and proclaiming their troth. Harry sheds tears.

222

Melanie's voice trembles, and I think she's going to cry with the intensity. I ponder, right then, on how nerve-wracking it must all be – to pledge an oath so profound, the bonds tie you for ever. A promise eternal. Now husband and wife. Two bodies, now one, united.

The organ fills the air with a thrill tune, giving me goosebumps. Guests throw confetti and holler a load of hurrahs to the newlyweds as they exit the church. The happy couple, elated, big smiles, photographer snapping away.

Just then, a visual snags my eye. It's apprehended something familiar in my peripheral. I strain to look better through the haze of tulle and confetti. But it has gone. I stare. I stare beyond. Blond. *His* blond.

'Hate this part,' Suze says, giving me a nudge. 'For the next half hour, the photographer is going to be barking orders to everyone. Let's go.'

We leave them to it, making our way to the Mini. I spot Kate, she's alone… and taciturn. That isn't like her. She's usually full of life at weddings.

'Where's Stuart?' I ask her. She avoids my eye and pouts, trying to sustain composure. I know that look. I've seen it too many times.

'Kate…'

'Broke up days ago,' she whispers.

'Shit! I'm so sorry…' I'm actually peeved. I wonder what it was this time. And if she broke up, where has she been staying all this time? I put my arm around her, as she sniffs back the tears. I spit out some obscenities.

'Right. You're coming with us,' I say, and lead her to the Mini where Suze is warming it up. Suze, sensing Kate isn't quite with it, shoots the bull about the ceremony and all the hot guys she spotted, trying to lighten the mood. 'Did you see that blond, fit piece of hotness sitting on the other side of us? He was hidden behind a column from where you were sitting, but I could see him perfectly.' She's all enthused. 'He was like a Greek god…' She babbles on. I join in, even though I didn't pay much attention to anyone in the pews. I try to lift the cloud of depression. Kate sits, melancholic, in the back, as we wind through the streets of London to get to the upscale, City-of-Westminster hotel where the reception will take place.

So, there we have it. Kate. Another failed relationship. She must be feeling like shit. First me keeping my deceit a secret from her for so many years, and now Stuart, over. OK, I know she's lived through her fair share of breakups, and always comes out a winner, but even water erodes the rock.

We are shown into a grand, floral-bedecked hall and are told where our seats are. We make our way through the labyrinth of baby's-breath-festooned, round tables to number 12; ours. Soft, Balearic music blending in with crystal glasses chinking, alongside the hum of voices. The place is filling rapidly, and is plain to see everyone has downed a glass or two of the complimentary, pink champagne we were offered at the door.

The high-pitched, happy chatter resounds all around. The occasional burst of laughter and giggling, children cantering here and there, all help to lift the burden of my prolonged dispiritedness for the time being. I feel myself ease up.

There is a sudden, loud guffawing behind me by, and judging from the sound, a group of men in the throes of laughter.

'Eleanora!' It's Kate. My heart stops – she sounds terrified. She never uses my full name; only when there is something I need to be made aware of immediately. I peer at her, affright. Her poor face; a mark of concern.

'Eleanora,' she says again, just quiet enough for me to hear. Her eyes fleet to something behind me. The group of men? What has she seen? I am frozen to the spot, thinking it's them – those men who wanted me dead. *But Kate's never seen them,* my mind shouts rationally. *And they're locked up.*

'What?' I say. She nods to whatever is behind me. 'Is that him?' she asks under her breath. I frown and turn, preparing myself.

His tall, athletic frame, now clothed in a dapper suit, champagne glass in hand, is what I see first. He is still laughing, head tilted back, in the remaining throes. Kate has seen my sketches of him countless times. Now without nose guard and skin all healed up, she knows who he is all right.

'James,' I utter, startled. It *had* been his hair; I was right.

One of his friends gives a nod in my direction, and he turns to see who his friend is indicating to. The smile on his face drops, as if someone just slapped it off him, the second he sees me, and his jaw locks.

Dear God, how he hates me. Kate's hand grips my arm.

'Come on!' she says, coming to my defence, and takes me the last few steps to our table, making sure my back is to him. I sit myself down, plonking my glass on the table clumsily. Then I look at it, take it again and down the champagne in two gulps.

What is he doing here? How does he know Harry and Melanie? My brain seeks the answer. UCL is the most plausible. Harry is in Engineering, post grad …Oh, my God… Of course…

Kate gazes persistently into my eyes, trying to ascertain what is going on in my brain. She's not going to leave it alone. So Kate. I want to cry, if nothing else, happy I know I have my friend back. Her searching, sapphire-blue irises always ready to comfort and console me.

'Why was he looking at you like that?' she asks, irked. 'Doesn't he know how you saved him?'

What am I to say? Where on earth can I begin? I shake my head. 'He doesn't know everything –'

Just then music blasts the room, as the happy couple enter amongst the shouts and applause of all their guests. They are given a standing ovation, and plenty of wolf whistling, as they make their way to the dancefloor for their first dance as husband and wife. I mechanically join in, stiffly clapping.

The lights dim, and there is a quick double tap of drums through the speakers, and then the flow of the soft synthesizer, gliding into the dulcet melody I savoured so many times when I was young. 'Love,' Martika croons silvery, 'thy will be done.' The melodiously filling the room, tingling my spine. More cheering and whistling ensues, as Harry twirls his wife in his arms and starts to sway under the spotlight; the disco ball shedding coruscations of light around the whole expanse.

We are all standing, and right opposite the dancefloor, there I see him. I make out his shape in the nominal darkness. The dots of light glide over him, and I catch his face. He spots me then, and looks me in the eye, harsh, like he is rebuking me; a scowl. I do not like it. It scares me… It grieves me. Why such an unequivocal dislike for me? Even before all this crap. Am I that abhorrent? I think of my nocent act and remember I must come clean. It had been the initial plan, after all. *I should have started with that then none of this would have happened*… But then I stop myself. If I had done that, then who would have stopped the thugs? I shiver. Gran says God always enlightens us, it's just sometimes we chose to ignore Him. I don't know what it was, but I supplicate a small thanks for the decision I made to follow him. Fire with fire.

…And he is alive.

Come clean. Now. Here. Today. Today must be the day. 'I can no longer run, I can no longer hide,' states Martika.

I turn to the girl I call my sister, who now has worry lines carved on her forehead. I squeeze her hand and leave the hall.

Chapter Forty-Two

Now

I breathe in the flowers in Covent Garden. Nothing can take the feeling away of how woebegone I am, I know, but I have jumped this hurdle. It may be behind me, but its aftermath is still present.

I had gone to the Ladies' room to calm down, prepare what I was going to say. How to phrase everything. Only, I couldn't calm. Not with what was then, so close at hand.

I ran the water and washed my hands, arms and neck, letting the coolth help me. What I really wanted to do was throw water all over me, scream and leave.

There was a window in the powder room overlooking London, but not quite high enough. I suddenly got the urge to go higher up and have a better look. Perhaps be able to find some peace to think clearer. He wasn't going anywhere in the immediate future. I'd find him a little later. So, instead of turning right to go back to the reception, I turned left to the wide, carpeted staircase.

Up and up as far as I could go, I reached the last landing and looked out of the large bow window, the sun, passed the meridian, reaching my face; warmth lingering on me.

London; my birthplace and home. The grey-white brick against a sky struggling to be bluer. I could just about discern the peak of the Shard and, across the Thames' rippling, khaki-green current, the tip of the Gherkin and the wedge of the Sky Garden.

All was still; a stagnant peace.

Silence.

Silence.

Silence… –

'You shouldn't have done it!'

My spine went rigid, as each hair bristled instantaneously, right to the top vertebra. My heart hammered as I breathed in a gasp. The voice was stern and extremely pissed off.

So, he found me first.

I turned. He was standing a few yards away, hands deep in his navy trouser-pockets, no jacket, just his white shirt and slim, blue tie, matching the colour of his limpid eyes. So handsome it hurt. It hurt because it was hopelessly unrequited.

I felt my nostrils singe, the sign of tears. The time had come. *Be Strong. Be true.*

'Which one?' I whispered, not daring to raise my voice lest it broke in half. He started, not expecting an admission, and I continued, contrite. 'I've done so many. Which one do you mean?'

He took his hands out of his pockets and came closer, incredulity on his stricken face. That face which had borne so much, broken and battered. I could feel his heat. I wanted to put my arms around his waist, rest my head on this chest and will everything to go away, except us…

But I looked down, unable to look at him directly. I was too ashamed. 'You admit it?' he bit.

'Yes,' I breathed. 'Could you tell me, specifically, what I shouldn't have done, so I can explain? I've done so many things…'

He harrumphed sadly. 'So many things,' he repeated. He shook his head. 'Well explain this, why were you following me? Tell me that!'

226

I looked up at him then, and winced. The anger in his hurt face hit me bad. His eyes ransacking mine for an explanation.

'I'm sorry. I'm so sorry,' I said beseechingly, between hitched gasps, as tears fell. I wiped them away. 'I'm sorry for ruining your life!'

He didn't move, just his chest rose and fell, vehemently inhaling.

'What do you mean?' he demanded. What? He never found out? But of course he didn't; nobody found out. It had been my dirty, dark secret. I took a breath, finding the right words. Everything had to be said.

'I don't know how much detail Archer has told you – it doesn't have much to do with the case – but I had to tell him the truth why I was following you. How I happened to be there when you got …beaten…'

'And why was that?' he asked in an unsteady voice. He took another step closer. He was almost touching me. This time I looked him straight in the eye. That blue, so sharp. He was heated, the pink spread across his cheeks. I could see all the details of his face. That indistinct freckle just resting on his left cheek bone.

I gathered all the courage I could muster.

'I wanted… I wanted to see why you w-were sweeping floors in tattered overalls i-instead of going to some office in a nice suit!' I let it all out. He looked down, clenching his jaw, but I didn't stop.

'I thought nothing had happened to you after th-that party six years ago, and you'd be off to Oxford as planned. I was never told of what really happened, so I left it. I left it right until I saw you at the Slade, bent over a fucking broom! I-I had to know! I had to know what happened. And I found it was all my fault!' I was losing control, wiping fresh tears and readying myself for the final blow which would hurt me as much as it would hurt him, if not more.

'*I* was the one who called the police that night. *I* got you arrested. I had said your name deliberately, so they would come for you.'

I shook, holding in the convulsions. I didn't want to cry hysterically in front of him. I brought my hand to my face; hide my shame.

'What?' he said. His eyebrows had drawn together like he hadn't understood. He stepped back as if I had struck him physically. I nodded slowly.

'I went to the police to take back the false report, but they wouldn't let me…' I tried to explain, but it seemed he was still trying to fit his head around all the new information.

'It was you? Why? What had I done?' His eyes were glistening, torn with agony.

'Nothing! Nothing compared to my…' I tried to find the right word, 'totally puerile… act… I was hurt by what you'd said, but that still doesn't excuse me from doing you so much damage!'

He wasn't listening. He took more steps away from me, turning his back, running his hands through his hair. I wasn't done. I had to tell all. I had to tell all to free my conscience.

'And the worst of it all, is when I went to the police station, Chief Inspector Daley told me there had been another call from the house that night a-about eighteen minutes after mine. You see, due to my lie, your life altered. I was the catalyst that caused that alteration, b-because if I hadn't called, you would have left long before any police came…' His back stiffened. 'And none of this would have happened to you.' I ended on a whisper.

There was silence. A static reticence for some moments.

'I know I'm not fit for your forgiveness, James. But please believe how sorry I am –'

'Fuck you!' he blurted, bitter, wounded.

I took in a sharp breath, recoiling, as the laceration tore me. I had said I would accept any reaction, but saying and doing were two, far different things. I couldn't… I couldn't stand it. I took a step back, wanting to leave. Wanting to get out of there fast. Wanting all this to end.

'I don't want you to ever follow me again,' he declared, still with his back to me.

'Never…' I promised.

'And I came looking for you now, to tell you you shouldn't have left me money. I'm not a charity case, and you insult me.' His words were wrought with suffering even though he articulated them with a clear affront. 'I thought my father had left the envelope, and when he denied giving it to me, Lizzy told me you had been there, in my home…'

I stared at his back. One hand was back in his pocket the other rubbing his face, downcast.

What I had left on the pile of books in his garage was close to £3,000. I had asked my mother to loan me some of the amount when I had gone to get the Jaguar in Edgware, as I know she keeps cash in the house, and I had withdrawn the rest from my account, just before I had gone to pick up Elizabeth.

I knew there could have been a chance he'd take it as an insult. The thought *had* crossed my mind, but it was the only thing I could think of to atone on such short notice.

'I'll return you the money as soon as possible. If I'd known you'd be here, I would have given it to you today.' His tone was curt, rough. Cold.

'I never meant to insult you, James,' I said, my throat scraping. 'Do what you like with the money –'

'Guilt money!' he burst angrily.

'Yes. Guilt money!' I answered just as angry. He turned around abruptly, no doubt startled at my admission again. His eyes were red. I felt torment looking at his eyes; something ripping my heart out. He was close to tears.

'I don't deny it!' I said. 'I wanted to help! I just wanted to make amends. Especially after I saw the way you were living…'

His back straightened, indignant I should antagonise him again. I didn't continue; the man had his pride.

'I'm not your pity project, Eleanora! I don't want your money,' he bit. 'Just go!'

I walked slowly to the staircase, took a step down and saw Kate half way up. She looked enraged. She'd been there for God knew how long. She must have heard quite a bit by the look on her face.

She came running up, and before I knew what she was about to do, she went passed me and stopped in front of James, who now looked extremely wan yet puzzled by her presence. She held up a finger at him, pointing, and said in a fierce whisper, 'Don't you forget, if it weren't for her, you'd be dead. She stopped them from cracking open your skull. She saved your fucking life, you bastard!'

'No, Kate,' I said, turning back. 'If it weren't for me, he wouldn't have been there in the first place.'

James glanced my way sharply, but with something unclear in his mind. Kate was by my side in a few strides. She clasped my forearm for one heartbeat, 'I'm sorry,' she quietly said, and took the stairs down.

I turned, locked eyes with his, and trembling, said, 'I know you've always hated me, and now you probably loath me, want to spit in my face; I deserve it.' Anger, consternation showed prominent between his eyes. He kept silent, however.

'But it's been killing me, knowing I am to blame, knowing I've caused you so much misfortune. All I can hope is one day you'll forgive me, but not for my sake, James, for yours.'

I didn't wait for a reply, just turned and went hurriedly down the stairs.

Chapter Forty-Three

Now

I throw a punch. It feels good.

I throw a second and third, more and more.

Thanks to the vigorous inculcations by my coach, Stacy, I have made quick progress enabling me to get on with my conditioning on my own.

'Not too much weight today, El,' she warns, walking off to help another girl with her head gear. I over-did it the other day, and we don't want to burn my muscles too much … again. It reminds me of the time I had gone hiking up the peaks in Cumbria – Suze's last-minute revelation – and the next day couldn't walk for shit.

I have been at the gym for over a fortnight, every day, without fail. I didn't wait the full month I was told to do in order to start training – I was too eager, and Stacy suggested I start with something light first, not taking me to the punchbag straight away. So, I began rigorous calisthenics and anaerobic strengthening, earning myself some encomiums from the other girls in the gym. Legs, torso, upper arms, shoulders and backside, easing my way into a more fit physique, quicker than I had been doing at my former gym. Stacy has shown me how to punch the air and various stances I can use until I find my style.

'And tie your hair back!' she calls to me over her shoulder. 'Do you know how to do a French plat, cornrows?'

'No,' I pant, without pausing the punches, my breaths short from the exertion, and also on the fact that my mind is filled to the brim with so much trial and tribulation.

Today is my second day using the punchbag.

Punch!

Fuck you! His caustic words reverberate vividly in my mind, as each strike brings alarming clarity. I punch again and again.

Just go!

Punch! Punch!

Fuck you!

Punch! Punch! Punch!

I throw another jab, and I see his laugh. That soft second before he saw me. Before he clenched his jaw like he'd tasted something vile and wanted to spit it out.

Punch!

'Fuck me?' I growl under my breath. 'I saved your life, motherfucker!'

Much has happened since the wedding, and all recollection comes hurtling, paradoxically more intensified, as I labour at my conditioning. I was hoping the workout would clear my mind, but so far, nothing. I would have borne the hardship better if at least, during training, I'd be rid of all bad thought. Perhaps time would blunt the edge off; it won't disappear entirely, that's for sure.

I was served a summons to appear in court first thing Monday morning – the trial was afoot. Apparently, my affidavit wasn't enough; they want to have my evidence viva voce.

But that is unimportant in relation to what went down with Kate.

Arguing over every-day, insignificant matters never harmed a friendship, but the fight we had over the subject of her brother was something far more volatile.

I hadn't stayed for long at the wedding after my confrontation with James – being in the same room with him put me in an awful strait. Through my slight monachopsis, I didn't want to pretend to be having a wonderful time for Melanie and Harry's sake. I really did want to be having a wonderful time. I tried. I didn't do too badly. I really was joyous for them. I danced – more like being dragged to my feet and forced by Suze, but boogeyed all the same. 'That's the Greek god I was telling you about,' she'd yelled in my ear, over the music, gazing beyond my shoulder. I didn't turn.

'Let me guess,' I'd said, unenthused but still side stepping to the beat. 'He's tall, blond, with a slim, blue tie.'

'How did *you* know?'

I chatted politely to anyone who went out of his way to approach me, no matter how stupid the chat-up line was, all the while consuming quite a bit of whatever alcohol I was being offered, mostly from a rather intoxicated Aidan. I danced with Aidan if you could call it dancing, that is.

I had stolen side-glances at James who seemed to be putting it on too. There was an undeniable constraint in his manner, and I knew it had to do with our earlier "talk". He was tipping back tumbler after tumbler. He had caught my eye and I, his. We had both turned away quickly on each occasion.

I had eventually slipped away, after having informed Suze I would be going home by myself, and giving Melanie and Harry two great, big hugs goodbye, wishing them all the best. I inconspicuously exited the foyer, out into the warm (for a change) evening.

As for Kate, she was dancing the night away; she usually partied hard after a breakup, clubbing. So, I left her to it.

Into the mild evening, with the sun on its dusky descent, I started to walk to the nearest Tube Station; Covent Garden.

Aware I was still extremely light-headed from the booze, I breathed in the warm London air, a mixture of humid stone and cooked food, as I wound through the cobbled streets, meandering to a stroll through the waning thoroughfare, passing the neo-classical piazza. The quaint flower displays besprinkled here and there, an avowal to summer. I stopped to smell some roses. Some people were gathered round a band that had just finished with their song, clapping and taking pictures. A juggling unicyclist prepared for his act. I remembered Dad taking us to down here to see one once. I must have been around ten. I had a funny feeling it was the same juggler. I remembered the eyes.

For those small moments I had forgotten my woe, and smiled wistfully to myself. I turned back. I wanted to go browse the piazza. How could I walk passed indifferently, to the beckoning pulse of London encapsulated in this one place?

Hearing a few wolf whistles on my way and a cringey, 'Sexy babe!' called out to me, I realised I wasn't exactly wearing attire suited for a casual stroll, and my high heels were an instant attraction to any hot-blooded male. I was about to start my stringent regime of feigned obliviousness, which was, basically, to keep my head down, as I guessed there would be more cajoling to come, but then reminded myself how I'd said I'd have to change my mentality; be more out-going. So, I looked up, let whatever come my way. If I didn't like it, I'd turn it down. If I *did…*

Making my way deeper into the market, I felt a sudden tug at my arm, caught tight. I gasped from fright, but looked to see it was Kate.

'You scared the living shit out of me!' I said, holding my hand to my chest.

'Listen,' she said, ignoring me. 'We need to talk.'

'What now? Can't it wait for later?' I was weary and fed up.

'I'm not coming back.' It was said so deadpan, I'd been unable to comprehend it at first.

I stared at her, momentarily speechless. The buzz I had from the drinks I'd consumed earlier wasn't helping much either.

'What do you mean?' I asked warily.

'I think it's time I moved out.'

Again, my brain struggled to believe what it was being told. 'What…?' I uttered, frowning.

'Look,' she continued. 'The past few days have been shit…' Her lip wobbled then. I felt my eyes sting.

'I've had time to think. Time to think about a lot of things,' she said, swallowing. 'It's been difficult knowing my best friend betrayed me.' The space went still as her words lingered. She was right. But I was right too.

'How did you find out?'

'Sophie,' she said. 'I was over at her house, and I saw how easy she could get information at a click of a button… so I got curious. I had always wondered who it could have been. I thought maybe some neighbour had heard… I asked her to trace back, starting with the police, the phone call. She found it was made from a phonebox along your old building. The time fitted… I knew it was you…'

'Kate… I had to!' I cried. 'You know I had to!'

Her tears flowed. 'I didn't want you to, and you went and did it, like what I said was a motherlode of bullshit.' Her voice was raised. We got stares from Londoners around us.

I loved Kate but she was frustrating. Stupid. Ignorant when it came to this. I got defensive. I couldn't keep up acting like I was a consoling buffer. Someone had to get it through her thick skull.

'Are you sure?' I said, a little scathing. 'Are you sure you didn't want me to?'

She bit her lip. She knew deep down I was right. God knew how her life would have ended up if it hadn't been for me.

Then I couldn't help it; I had been so furious with her conduct, I had to lay it to her. It was a long time coming, and I felt a release with every single trenchant word.

'Are you telling me you wanted him to continue? Is that what you're saying? Because I didn't exactly see you or your family do something about it. And *you* know as well as I do, if I hadn't phoned, it would have gone from serious sexual assault to downright rape!'

She slapped me so hard across my face, I saw a white flash. The blood dropped from my left nostril; the sensitive one. Someone's, 'Ooo!' in the distance was vaguely heard. We were making a scene.

'Right,' I said sarcastically, tasting the metallic tang of blood. She cried and breathed with difficulty, hitched stutters for inhalation.

'That's not the point!' she wailed. 'The point was you didn't respect my wish. You didn't keep your promise!'

I let out an incredulous huff. 'I'm sorry I didn't respect you. I am! But you can't see the forest for the trees!' I shouted, immense annoyance charging through me. 'And I never promised you anything.'

She blinked, looking back into the past, trying to remember.

'And even if I had,' I continued in the same tone, 'keeping a promise like that; to not tell a soul that my friend is being sexually abused over and over again, is just as bad as if I'd assaulted you myself!'

Kate stood motionless, her incessant sniffing the only sound coming from her.

'You were the one that hated your parents' indifference, and now you have the gall to question why I *wasn't* indifferent?' I said, the exasperated strain grating in my voice.

She breathed in a small breath, wiping her eyes. I wiped my nose, the blood streaking the back of my hand. This time, I had no tissue in my pocket.

'You expected me to stand by and let him do all those things to you?' I hissed, hurt, indignant. 'What kind of a friend does that? Remember I told you about the girl who got raped at the party, the party where I had accused James of raping her? Her friend phoned the police the very same night! I should have done the same, as soon as you'd told me what Rhys had been doing to you!'

She'd looked straight at me then, pained and pitiful.

'This isn't a game, Kate! This is your life, your sanity… *your* body. He was destroying you!'

I gazed in, beyond her to the juggler, flinging his knives in the air, as the kids watching him squealed with delight, bright round faces looking up in awe.

'It's funny,' I said, bleakly. 'I think about those two phone calls – yours and James's. I compare their result.' She turned her eyes down. 'He has a right to be angry at me; I screwed his life up. But you… you flew! You were liberated.'

She regarded me then. I gave her one last saddened look. 'I've had enough shit for one day, Kate. Do whatever you want. If you need me, you know where to find me…' And I left her there with her tears …and the truth.

Kate didn't come home that night either. Not even making her see the blatant fact of her past didn't change her stubborn mind. Where on earth was she staying? Stuart's place was off the list. Maybe some other friend. Her parents'? I cringed at the thought.

***

I do a good 20 minutes on the punchbag, and feel the rivulets of sweat run down on my temples and between my breasts. I skip, do push-ups and sit-ups. I get in the ring and do some padding time. *Let them throw their punches. Him. Her. Whoever!*

'So, who's coming to the superheavyweights on Saturday?' Stacy calls out to all of us. 'It's going to be one hellova night!'

***

I walk in through my front door, the quiet greeting me. No more Kate to keep me company; I have got used to the unchanging ambience of my flat.

So, when I shut the door behind me and turn on the light, I feel that shift again. My mind goes back instantly to when I had found my sofa crooked and the sketch on the floor, and I panic.

They are in jail, I reason.

My spine feels a chill and I freeze, as the bloodstream of sheer shock darts through me, causing me to drop my gear bag.

There, on my little kitchen island, is the same envelope I'd left on James's desk.

How on earth did that get in here? Kate and Mum are the only two people with a key, and I highly doubt they have anything to do with it.

I move surreptitiously towards the island.

The A5-sized tan, manila envelope, lies squarely on the centre of the island, puffed with its contents. Doubtless, the money I'd given James. Only, it looks puffier. I'd given James less notes, making the envelope thinner. That means he used the money and put back other notes to make up for it, I surmise.

Good. I'm glad he used it, even as loan status. But how did he get in my flat?

I take out the wad of cash and a piece of paper falls out. It is a note. In strong capitals it reads,

ALWAYS LOCK YOUR DOOR.

I flush. How embarrassing; I left the bloody door unlocked. How careless and totally irresponsible of me. Now he'll think me a fool. *He already thinks you a fool, you idiot!*

But still, you can't really open the door from the outside, unless I left it ajar...Oh, Shit! I try to think; recount my steps. Did I? Jesus!

I look back at the door. I missed him for minutes. At least he had the decency to close it behind him.

Just then, a more embarrassing thought crosses my mind. He saw my flat! I'd better not have left any stray knickers lying on the floor, or anything. I run to my room, spying each corner of the carpet. Nothing, thank goodness, except for the puddle of clothes I'd worn the day before.

So, he's seen where I live, just as I had seen his home. Thence we are even on that score, at least.

Chapter Forty-Four

Now

Boxing is perhaps the only sport with so many different titles and categories, under a whole bunch of varying rules, that it takes some research to understand, fully, what is going on – which rules apply to which title and so on and so forth. Therefore, in the beginning, I was confused.

The competition I am going to is for amateur boxers that are aspiring to make it to the Olympics or the Pros, thus upping the bar on the competitive scale. Novices and intermediates, these under the age of 17, and the older fighters or Open Boxers mostly having reached a point in their career which will lead them to further glory. And as the flyer had said, the last Saturday of the tournament was for heavyweight and super heavyweight, both men and women.

I don't know if James is competing; there is nothing online. Certainly, the club he goes to promotes the competition, but that doesn't mean all the boxers will be fighting. In my club, only one girl in the Light Welterweights competed the week previous, and now we are all going as spectators.

Stacy told me I was a hard worker and my potential was great, but I needed to put more muscle on and make it to Lightweight, which would be preferable for my height.

'You need to show your opponent you mean business!' she said. 'And you can't do that if you look like you've just stepped off a runway and afraid you'll break a nail!'

Stacy has given me a diet. Protein and carbohydrate rich, most of whose recipes I have uploaded for my blog and have received plenty of positive feedback, which has spiked my income.

I had taken a picture of myself in front of the mirror in only my training shorts and training bra before I started training as a boxer, so as to check my "before and after" photo at the end of it all, to see how my body has progressed.

The boxing venue is at York Hall in Bethnal Green. I've never been there before, and learning of that gem in east London – boasting neo-Georgian splendour *and* notoriety for one of the world's top boxing venues. I got a titillating rush.

I step off at Bethnal Green Underground, where only the silent whisper of the 173 souls who tragically died in World War II had left their last breath. The rush of panic as the throngs of bodies ran into the subway to take shelter from a Nazi air-raid, only to meet their doom from the crush.

'Rest in peace,' I whisper, as a chill runs down my spine, passing one of the cream tiles in frieze, specifically placed on the wall in memorial to the tragedy.

I ascend the stairs from the subway. A sudden shift from its harrowing, heart-breaking past to a polar-opposite sensation. I can almost feel the buzz of excitement draw me closer and closer with each stride, to the heart of it all. There is a rhythmical movement on the pavement, all in unison to the beat. I personally am late, and rush by the high-pitched voices that are chatting about some boxer, with a nervous thrill.

And upon entering the main hall, I understand why. The structure is perfect. The spectator has no problem viewing the match no matter where he or she sits. The intimacy of that alone induces more enthusiasm, like you are almost in the ring yourself.

The lights are ablaze as is the atmosphere. Cheers and hoots and jeering. There are cameras; it's being televised. The slight whiff of melting plastic from the stage lights and the pungent smell of hops and sweat drift upwards, intermingled with some over-abundant perfume some girl is wearing. I take off a layer of clothing as the warmth engulfs me. I am in casual, almost grungy, chic – dark grey, skinny jeans (yes, finally), a shimmery, black, three-quarter-sleeved top and high-heeled ankle-boot sandals, bought with my 75% discount from N&L. *My* look for the occasion. *This* is Eleanora. *Not* gothic (not in the strict sense). *Not* mainstream either. And *not* hidden under baggy clothes.

Stacy signals to me with a wave. We have seats on the front row of the left balcony, if we are to be facing the stage from the door. My point of vision is at a 40° angle, give or take, just above the ring. I couldn't have asked for a better place.

I am being given quick updates of the other matches I missed, with much enthusiasm, from my fellow boxing-club mates. I am just in time to see the referee name the winner of the fight I have just caught at the end.

We're into the heavyweights. This match and then the super heavyweights. There are no women in these categories.

The bell sounds loudly, *DING! DING!*

I gnaw on my cuticle. The fighters go right at each other, each in orthodox stance in the beginning, but then calculating which'll make a better throw. Their coaches blasting a word or two from their respective corners, aiding their prodigies, the audience blasting more… The fighters are tall but leaner than James. If James is fighting tonight, I'm guessing he'll be in the super heavyweights, and I have a funny feeling he is. I see how the coaches are passionate, urging with vehemence their advice, and I remember Brian's rage. How he'd looked; just like these coaches. His anxiety. His passion. That's why he'd been so mad when James hadn't gone to his training on time. Now I understand; he had been under a strict regime for an important event – this one.

I spot, two seats to my left, an unclaimed card of the evening's events, and am about to lean over to get it, when a voice above me says, 'Oh, hello!' I look up startled, caught red-handed.

At first, I don't recognise her. Well, I do, but not from *where*. Then, all of a sudden, I do. By account of us having interacted, it comes to me quickly. It's the highlighted-blonde mother who lives behind James. She has the biggest grin I've ever seen stretched across someone's face. What is she doing here? And then I answer my own question. This isn't some impromptu appearance – She knows James, and not just as a casual neighbour.

'Hello!' I say, not hiding my astonishment. She sits down next to me, taking the card.

'You here to see Jamie?'

OK; confirmed.

'I thought you said you didn't know him.' I say, raising my brows in that way you do when demanding answers. I have a smile though, just feigning to be miffed. 'And how do *you* know I know him?' I cry, suddenly baffled. Her smile broadens – if that's possible.

'I don't,' she says. 'I just saw you here and thought this can't be a coincidence.'

'What's a coincidence?' says a voice behind her. There, standing, is a cheery-faced, swarthy-skinned bloke. He places himself in the seat by the blonde mum, beer in hand. Her husband; they both wear same wedding bands.

'Nothing, darl,' she tells him. 'We were just talking about Jamie.' She jerks her head my way. He smiles at me, giving me his hand.

'Dean Hayes,' he says affably. 'How do you do?'

'Eleanora Stephens,' I tell him, as he shakes my hand vigorously. 'How do you do? You can call me El.'

'And I'm Imogen,' puts in the blonde mum.

'So, you here to watch Jamie then?' asks Dean Hayes.

'No!' I blurt. Both husband and wife look taken aback.

'I mean, I didn't know he was fighting,' I explain. They look confused.

'I came because I box and my gym got some tickets…' I clarify.

'Ah!' says Dean. 'You box?' To his credit, he sounds intrigued, not eyeing me suspiciously like I'm pulling his leg. Imogen mirrors her husband. I thought just then, what they say about old married couples – as the years go by you end up looking like each other. They may have had different characteristics but their mannerisms and gestures were as if they were twins.

'Come on, Fitzroy!' someone shouts, and we all rotate our heads to the ring, as the fighter named Fitzroy rams some good hooks into his opponent, causing the referee to stop the round. The crowd is in an uproar, fulminating the call.

'I can't just go around answering questions about my friends to total strangers. You can understand that?' Imogen says leaning into my ear. Ah, the explanation.

I nod slightly. She was right. 'Yes…Yes, I understand perfectly.'

'Nothing against you, dear,' she adds, patting my arm.

'I know. You did right. I would have done the same,' I reassure her. True, I must have looked like a deranged fool that night, knocking on her door to ask about storage space. Of all the things I could have said!

DING! DING! DING!

The round is over.

'I suppose I did come on a bit strange that night,' I admit to her. She raises her brows. 'Come to think of it, I'm surprised you didn't shut the door in my face.'

Imogen giggles. 'Well, yeah…' she says. 'I wanted to at first, but you looked harmless and I felt sorry for you. Plus, your excuse was so funny! Storage space!' She lets out a full laugh. I feel embarrassed. Can people read me so well? Do I have, what they call, a glass face?

'What are we laughing about, darl?' Dean asks his wife.

DING! DING!

'Nothing. I'll tell you later,' she says, shooing him with her hand. Great, I think; I am going to be the laughing stock of their pillow talk. Then I think, *my excuse?* Yes, I had gone under the pretext of inquiring about storage space, so what does she think the real reason is? My face burns with what she might have speculated on. Shit! Does she think I… with James…?

238

Just then the crowd goes crazy. I turn and see one of the boxers jabbing his opponent with a combination of punches, unyielding. I bite my lip at his stamina, his strength. Amazing… The referee puts an end to it, however, as the boxer who is eating the punches, seems he's had enough, and has started to fall on the canvas. There is cheering and clapping, whistling and shouting from the outcome – a KO.

'The fans are wild!' I say to no one in particular, mesmerised at all the over-charged enthusiasm. Stacy concurs.

'Wait till you see the super heavyweights,' Dean calls over to me. 'This is nothing!' Jesus! What are people going to do? Jump off the rafters?!

'WINNER… JARED FIIIITZROYYYY!' the voice in the loudspeaker over-pronounces.

Cameras, reporters, all find the winner for a statement. We settle back in our seats waiting for the last fight to begin, as the turbulence wanes. People get up from their seats hurriedly, moving about, either off to refresh themselves or pop out to relieve their bladder. Dean gets up to get a drink, and Stacy goes to powder her nose.

'Imogen?' I say quietly. She's already looking at me. 'I don't want you to think that I…' My words aren't right. I huff, trying to find better. I take a different route. 'It's true I had come to ask you about storage space under false pretences, but it wasn't for the reason you think.'

She considers for a second. 'Just so I get this straight,' she says, all of a sudden serious. 'You think that I think you did it because you fancy Jamie?' Stating it so bluntly, I blush.

'Are you telepathic?' I say sardonically. She laughs. I giggle.

'But it wasn't because of that,' I persist, all fun aside. 'Just so we're clear. I had come because I wanted to help him'

She sees the look on my face and something flits her eyes. She places her hand on my arm and tilts her face aslant. I continue, having no idea why I need to explain myself to this woman, but her openness towards me was impetus. 'I used to know James. When I saw where he was living, I couldn't ignore it. It was such a far cry from what I thought his future would have been. So, I searched for anything I could in order to help him. That's why I'd gone to your house – to double-check if he was really living in a garage…'

She jerks abruptly, an "O" of astonishment shaping her mouth. 'Oh, my God! Oh, my good God!' she utters. 'It was you! You! Of course! Why didn't I realise earlier? He told us it was a girl he once knew who found him. We didn't hear a thing that night! The telly was on, I don't know what… all we heard was a car alarm, but nobody really cares about that if it's not theirs!'

Right then, lights dim dramatically, and the electric guitar from Puff Daddy's "Come with me" resonates through the hall, as rhythmical floodlights flash around the walls. Each strum, charging my body.

And there he is.

He comes in first, under an eruption of applause. The boisterous cheers escorting him along his walk to the ring. He does none of that familiar skipping, swaggering movement boxers make to intimidate opponents. No. He is subtle. Alert. Focused. A kind of brooding walk. He punches the air a couple of times, and that is it – the two swift hooks are enough to send the crowd into a frenzy. But what really takes my notice is that his head down, humble, and perhaps abashed with all the attention. He's always been modest; he never bragged when I'd asked him of his popularity. No arrogance. Not up himself.

He is in black. No shimmer, no glitz-and-glam satin like most boxers wear. It reminds me of the simple black T-shirt Tyson had worn in the match against Botha in 1999 – a match I had seen with Dad. Only James's isn't a T-shirt. It is the regulation shirt; the loose vest. His broad shoulders and shaped arms on display; that place where the deltoid meets the rounded, sinewy bicep, creamy white, contrasted against the black. His regulation protective headwear, black also, with strands of his rich, honey-coloured hair jutting through. Gone is his stubble – that is another rule; clean-shaven jaw.

He reaches the ring and slides in between the ropes, makes his way to the centre and lifts his left hand in thanks. Again, the crowd goes wild. Left hand? Is James left-handed? I think back quickly to see if I'd ever seen him write. I can't remember. Then the memory hits me so hard, I hold my breath. The hand that had stroked my hair on that night was his left. Then another flash: the boxing stance he had taken to demonstrate to his friends earlier that night was southpaw. *Dad's been helping him shave* – Elizabeth. His left arm was in the sling.

I have no idea what I am doing. My movements are mechanical. Do I clap? Do I hoot? Am I standing? Probably all three. All I know is how I feel. Proud. I realise this must be a dream come true. Through the toil of his life, he's accomplished this. I wipe an involuntary tear streaming down my cheek; a movement Imogen sees. Still clapping she asks me if I'm all right. I nod.

James's opponent walks in, or rather, jumps in, escorted by some death-metal song, whose vocalist is screaming at us.

Dean comes, hands a beer to his wife and another to me.

'Oh! Thanks!' I exclaim, surprised, taking it eagerly, the ice crispness beckoning to my taste buds. 'It's so hot in here, you read my mind!'

'Cheers!' we say, and chink our bottles. I take a few satisfactory chugs, letting the stuff do its work. What nice people these Hayes's are.

'In the blue corner,' the presenter booms on the mic. 'We have a newcomer fighting his first official match here with us tonight. Wearing the black shorts, from Camden Town, JAMIEEE LLLAIDLLAAAWWW!' The announcer blasts James's name in a monotone.

We all get up instantly and cheer. I'm not afraid he'll see me. I'm too high up, plus the place is packed. James puts his left hand up again in recognition of the crowd's support. Seems he's very popular, especially to the female populous, as they howl and wolf-whistle at him.

I see his team in his corner. Brian and the other three cornermen, or "seconds", on the ready, all wearing *Laidlaw* on their simple black T shirts.

'COME ON, JAMIE!' Imogen hollers down at him, her two hands on either side of her mouth. He looks up. I didn't think Imogen could be heard over the commotion, but apparently, I am wrong. I want to move; get out of there! He'll see me now! Shit! Why did Imogen have to shout his name?! I don't want to distress him before his big fight. He'd made his feelings clear with that elegant *fuck you* of his, and my presence will throw his equilibrium off. I'm blocked between Stacy and Imogen. Thwarted.

'JAMIE!' Imogen shouts again. He sees her now, smile on his face. But his eyes suddenly flicker to me, and that's that; too late! He freezes, an imperceptible frown across his eyes. His hand suddenly comes down. I am persona non grata. He probably thinks I followed him as well… *bloody hell!*

I shrug apologetically, shake my head, 'I didn't…' I mouth. He blinks unexpectedly, then his features take a look I've never seen before on him, a reticence, I cannot deduce. He gives one more thanking wave and turns to his corner, head up, eyes down, jaw tight.

Oi! Last time I checked, it was a free country. I can say whatever I want and go wherever I want. Well, except the men's toilets – Vic. It's true; I have a right to be here.

Let them throw their punches.

'And in the red corner we have two-time super heavyweight champion with nine wins, and three draws, in the red shorts, from Clapham, GRRREGORYYY MMMOLLOOOYYY!'

Molloy receives a warm reception also, as he is the favourite to win, and better known.

A pin-up-shaped girl, wearing only a tank top, fishnet tights, high-platform pumps and what looks like her personal pair of boyshorts pants, struts around the ring holding up a rectangular sign with the number "1" written on it. I see James glance at her arse – what man wouldn't? – and continue, indifferent, listening to Brian and co. Not his type?

My eye catches a movement, something I've seen before. The hair. Yes. It is Elizabeth. She is ringside at a table, with what can only be her parents. I have never seen them before, but one look confirms they are definitely from the same gene pool. Unmistakable; the large frame of the man and the colouring of the woman. But the beautiful thought that overpowers all is the fact that his father is beatifically smiling at his son.

'Could they make them any sluttier?' harrumphs Imogen sardonically.

'You have a pair of those knickers, don't ya?' says Dean in jest. They both burst out laughing.

Round one; the bell reverberates loudly.

Southpaw stance; he is up and ready.

The fighters dance around for some seconds, measuring each other out, then Molloy throws a quick jab but James avoids it, bobbing his head. Molloy throws another and James avoids that too, but serves a sharp left hook on Molloy's ear just as Molloy's right arm is descending. Molloy takes two steps back, his wide, muscled shoulders, slightly hunched in defence mode, gloves in front of his face, covering up. There are jeers and calls from the crowd.

James prepares for another attack, on his toes, edging towards his opponent. Both fighters punch; long, vigorous limbs, flexing. Molloy, a cross punch, but James gets him with an upper cut, sending Molloy back. Both men are big. Battle of the Titans.

'COME ON, JAMIE!' I hear Elizabeth shout. The boxers find themselves in a clinch and are broken up by the ref. He says something to them but no boxer reacts – they don't dare take their eyes off one another, always on the ready, calculating. They come charging at each other again, sending throws in each direction. James lashes out on Molloy, releasing two, sudden blows on him and the crowd goes wild with delight as Molloy stumbles back.

DING! DING!

First round is over and the boxers are back in their corners. I see the vast rise and fall of James's chest, breathing hard from the effort, every inch of his skin covered in a light gloss of perspiration. He nods, listening to Brian as they take out his mouth-guard and give him some water through a straw, cameramen getting a close-up of him.

Imogen and Dean are praising James, but I can only think on what Imogen said earlier; about knowing I had saved James. When Kate had spoken to James at the wedding, he had looked puzzled as to how exactly I had saved him. Then I remember Archer's words precisely. He knows I followed him and called the ambulance. But did he tell James about the car alarm – the real reason why James isn't dead?

'Imogen?'

'Yes, El?'

'What exactly did James tell you of that night?'

She studies me, wondering if I suddenly forgot the details myself.

'Well, where should I begin…?'

DING! Round two.

Imogen's attention is drawn back to the match, as is mine.

James's and Molloy's aggression seem to have intensified. Their brief respite having given them fuel. There is visible energy to each punch, more potent than before, causing the audience to get more and more excited, as the comments shouted to the ring multiply.

Suddenly Molloy gives everything he got and lands three hooks on James. James takes the first on the jaw but holds up his arms in defence from the other two, just in time to block them. James's team shouts something at him and he moves. Back in his southpaw stance, knees squatted, he waits for Molloy to bring it on. Sure enough, Molloy's bounding body makes its move and swings a hook. James bobs and weaves, slipping a sly jab straight to Molloy's face. Molloy draws back, teetering for a second, as the blow catches him unaware.

The place goes frantic, unable to contain the gratification of such a spectacular match.

'What a show!' Dean cries. 'WELL DONE, JAMIE!' he shouts. Imogen chimes in, and even Stacy and the others from my club. I clap and clap. I want to shout *well done* too but I don't dare. Just think it. Thoughts are secret…

James doesn't stop there; he moves on Molloy, one left hook, then another, driving Molloy back, onto the ropes.

DING! DING!

James doesn't seem to hear the sound that signalizes the round is over, and the referee has to ply the two fighters apart, pointing an angry finger at James, giving him a warning. James nods in compliance and goes to his corner.

His frame expands and contracts fast, the sweat sheening his skin. His cheeks flushed with exertion. Brian and the team are at work again.

'If he keeps this up, he'll win for sure!' Dean tells us, excited.

'Yeah,' says Imogen. 'He's bloody good, isn't he?'

Here, Stacy decides to join the conversation. 'It's amazing when you see talent like that out of nowhere. Lord knows how many more hidden fighters there are out there,' she declares. Dean, Imogen and I all look at her. 'I heard Laidlaw isn't intending to make a career out of it though, which is a shame, and he only wanted to compete to see where he's at. A colleague said he was doing all of this for the love of it!'

'Yes. He told us that too,' Imogen says. 'He's a friend of ours,' she clarifies.

'Well, tell him he's got talent and he should keep it up. He shouldn't waste it!' Stacy states.

There are a few seconds left before the next bout. The urge to know if I'm right, is killing me.

'Imogen?' I say, feigning composure while inside there is total amok. She looks at me and her smile abandons her face. 'What is it, dear?'

'Did James explain to you about the car alarm you heard that night?'

'No…' she says, nonplussed.

'So, he doesn't know where the car alarm fits in, in all of this?'

She heeds me, uncomprehending.

'I don't know… all I know is he never mentioned anything about a car alarm… mind you, we didn't get to talk much because the day he came over to give us the tickets for tonight's match he was moving out, and had boxes to load in his car…'

'He was?'

'He's found a place –'

DING, the bell tolls for the next bout, cutting Imogen off, and again our attention is diverted to the ring.

With eyes riveted on these defining moments, the two mighty bodies combat with formidable energy. The power of each prevailing punch hit with precision for the best possible outcome – for amateur boxing isn't about knocking your opponent down by sheer brute force, as it often is in professional boxing, it's about technique and technical points.

Both fighters are strong but one is stronger. He jabs, finding an open opportunity. The other boxer shows signs of tiring. Still, he perseveres, more in defence rather than attack.

The stronger fighter carefully judges another blow. A thrashing left hook, making his opponent's head swing back, causing him to stumble but not fall. He finds himself on the ropes as his opponent whales on him with a volley of punches.

The crowd understands the weaker man can handle no more, and goes insane with the inevitable outcome.

The referee waves his hands vehemently, indicating the fight is over. Technical Knock Out.

The cheers and yells of ecstatic delight reverberate through each inch of the place, filling us with a thrill. Lights flash, and music vibrates as the place is lit in joyous commotion.

Everyone cheers, their half-crazed apotheosis, as James's hand is raised and is named winner.

Now I shout. I shout and clap and cry, and I don't care if he doesn't like it!

Imogen hugs me, then Dean hugs me, then they hugged each other as the rush of merriment takes hold.

James droops his head, abashed, unable to believe it. Then he looks up and grins, face bright and truly happy, both hands in the air. He is the winner! He is the winner!

'Let's go down and congratulate him!' cries Imogen. 'Coming?' she asks me.

'No, you go,' I say. And, holding two thumbs up to me, she and her husband descend.

Brian and the team step onto the canvas, taking off James's head gear, revealing sweat-drenched strands, congratulating him and embracing him, pats on the back, ecstatic with the win.

Suddenly, a sheet of long, platinum-blonde hair catches my eye, and before I know it, a girl has plastered her body up against James's. Her arms wrap around his neck in a tight, intimate hug, whereupon she lands him a kiss, squarely, on the lips.

Have you ever wished you never saw something? The pain of witnessing it so insurmountable, you want to escape it, turn the clock back, and carry on life unwittingly, ignorant of the fact? Because I confess it punched me in the gut, having to see that affection. And what's worse, I will remember it for ever, eidetic memory or not.

Siobhan. I recognise the biceps. My mind drifts back to when it had been Bianca who had… taken him away…

This, however, doesn't make me stop clapping, believe it or not; just with less enthusiasm. I have a spasmodic urge to run but don't. No. I will stick this through. It wrenches me, yes. Stabs deep to see her touch him like that… and to see him return the kiss, twists the knife deeper. It is clear he's with her. And even clearer, in my mind, that I can never be.

I hear Vic: *Be above circumstance. Chin up, sis. You can do this!* No. I won't run like a coward.

He pulls away from the kiss – it was quick, thank goodness – and all of a sudden, looks up… at me! The heat in my cheeks burns – he's caught me – but I keep on clapping, resolute. *I can do this! I can do this!* I clear my throat, force away tears, and shout straight at him, 'WELL DONE, JAMES! WELL DONE!'

He suddenly lets go of Siobhan, and blinks; he wasn't expecting that. I see that strange look, I saw before, come over him. Siobhan turns to see what has caused her abrupt release. But I don't see her face – my eyes are fixed directly on his, defiant, as he meets my gaze, fast.

One beat, two beats, three…

He's thinking again, analysing me, doing that thing with his jaw. *What does she mean by this?* I can hear him say. Finally, he shakes his head, like he can't fathom my manner. He turns his back on me to continue his laudations; he has more pressing matters to tend to.

Lights on him, cameras flashing, people whirling left and right, calling his name. His mother? His father? Elizabeth? Brian? I don't know.

The interviewer approaches him vying for his attention, microphone in hand. He has stuff to do; a role to fulfil. He faces his duties and prepares for the camera.

The place is still ablaze with the exalting mood of the entertaining night, and I have nothing left to do but go home.

Just go…

I look around me. The balcony is half-empty, people taking some last pictures of the venue and uploading them. Stacy is gone. I vaguely remember her saying goodnight to me. Some of my clubmates are still hanging around, discussing something or other.

I take one last look below, I see Elizabeth's face; a reflection of pure happiness… her parent's wear it too; radiant with joy and pride for their son. A caress of fervour envelops me, I sense his existence changing for the better; a gradual restoration of a life I had bulldozed. Elizabeth has spotted me and waves. His mother glances up at me then, catching me wipe my damp cheek. She knows who I am. *You've got very distinct features…* Elizabeth,

I am willing to bet, has described me to her family with meticulous precision. I want to run to the woman, get on my knees and beg to be forgiven for turning her family upside down. But I can't.

'El?' I turn. It's Kevin from my boxing club. 'Bunch of us are going for a drink. Want to come?'

I go. I'm glad I do; I don't think I can face being alone just now.

I sip on a pink concoction the barman insisted he make for me, my anodyne for the night – I didn't have the power to argue – and listen with agreeable contentedness to my friends, Martha, Lorraine, Kevin and Joseph – the team; the part of a whole I belong to, break down a detailed analysis of the matches, rehashing each highlight with endearing enthusiasm. The DJ plays various genres of rock music, accompanying our banter, in the dimly-lit, industrial-vintage barroom.

I am facing the bar, and every so often the barman gives me a thumbs up, trying to cheer me up, as I'd entered rather downcast. He is being funny and flirtatious, pouring the contents of bottles into a shaker from over his shoulder, all show-offy. I find his gesture singular for a bartender. The breed usually have an air of indifference after they've handed you your drink. I find his tattoos fascinating, however. Although, I could have done a better job. Not to blow my own whistle... Jeez, what has the man put in this libation?

'Stacy's begging me to compete in that charity fight-night in August. I don't know if I'll be ready by then,' says Lorraine.

'Why not?' Joseph asks.

'It's right after my holidays. My diet will be all wrong and I'll've put on weight for sure – the flabby kind,' she explains.

'Come back earlier to condition,' Kevin recommends.

'Can't. Kieran has been given leave on those dates; it's the only time we can go... and quite frankly, I can't wait to see Santorini.' She rubs her hands, goodie!

'Oh, yeah? You're going to my gran's homeland then?' I say smiling, the gesture of Greece always there to brighten my mood.

'What? You Greek?' Martha asks, surprised.

'No... Yes... I'm English; part Greek.'

'Cool!' Lorraine declares.

'Yeah,' says Martha. 'Greece is so cool. I had such a great time when we went to Crete. The beaches were the best! Oh, my God, I have to go again.'

'I thought there was something about you,' puts in Kevin. I think Kevin likes me. I sensed something the first day I started at the club. He *is* a sweet guy, in all fairness. Should I go for it? Is this my chance to *live it up*? No more procrastinating?

'Oh, yeah?' I say coquettishly. 'Good or bad?'

'Bad. Really bad,' he says, scrunching his nose, feigning to be disgusted.

'Yeah, bloody awful. Look at you!' Joseph joins. I feign to be shocked, and smile. I'm so crap at this flirting shite.

'Shame though,' whines Martha. 'It would have been good practice, Lorraine. Charity events are great for beginners. El, what about you? Are you thinking of taking part? I think you'll be up to it by August, the rate you're going!'

There are chuckles. I shrug. 'If Stacy thinks I'm ready, then yeah. Why not?'

'I don't think *you'll* put on any flabby weight by then!' says Kevin, lifting his glass for a toast. They all giggle at that, I too. My skinny-complex has shrunk to insignificance, and share their jest sincerely, sipping on my cocktail, which is actually bloody fantastic, then almost choke on it when *he* walks in.

Chapter Forty-Five

Now

'ELEANORA STEPHENS!'

I jolt out of my half-stupor by the deep, stentorian command. My heart thuds deafeningly through my ears, as the rush of undesired adrenaline jacks up my every nerve, not only from being startled, but from the split second it takes for me to realise where I am and what is about to ensue.

I blink up at the courtroom clerk, trying to arrange my thoughts.

I had been dreaming of his face; that look, the moment he'd spotted me at the bar in Bethnal Green. Trying to figure it out…

He'd sauntered in. Out of all the bloody bars in that side-street, which was a long, well-known strip full of nightlife, he happened to choose the one *I* was in.

Everything is done for a reason – Gran. I was dreading this reason…

Accompanied by his team and, I was guessing, some other members of his club… and Siobhan – with no sign of his family, though, or of the Haze's – they made their way to the bar in a boisterous cluster. They made no effort to hide their rejoicing, obvious they'd come to celebrate James's title.

247

He was right opposite me. I looked away, trying to act as lackadaisical as I could, hoping he wouldn't see me. I didn't want my presence to upset him, and I didn't want to leave, needing this much desired reprieve. So, I crouched into a position so his line of vision to me was obstructed by bodies. Much like when I had been following him...

Heads turned in their direction, as James's band of merry men praised him in rowdy cavorting, high above the music. Toast after toast in his name. Good; getting sloshed would take the edge off things.

'I'm going to congratulate him,' Kevin said all enthused, after about twenty minutes. I could tell he'd wanted to go the second James had walked in, but thought to wait a bit. 'Anyone else coming?'

They all got up except me, and gave me a questioning glance. 'You go, I'll guard our table,' I said, thankful I had that pretext.

I watched as they went up to him through the crowd, and my heart thumped. He could turn any moment.

Joseph and Kevin had reached James first, holding out their hands, big smiles. James shook their hands heartily, one by one, and although I couldn't hear what they were saying, I gathered all four of my friends were telling him that they had seen the match, and he was accepting their good wishes.

I guzzled down the last of my cocktail, taking in a long breath, struggling to go with the flow. I took out my phone, and pretended to be doing I-didn't-know-what with it. I had mounted my old memory card on this new phone, and only just remembering, I ought to delete those illicit pictures; for I had infringed a privacy law... and an ethical one.

I had just begun to delete the first one when movement caught my eye. I looked up from my phone, and jumped upon seeing his eye riveted to mine. There were no words to describe his expression; I didn't even think I could draw it. Apart from the clear resentment he had for me – probably thinking I'd somehow found out he was going to come to this bar, there was that something else intermingled. That indecipherable look. I have never seen that look on anyone before. What was it? What was he conveying to me?

The guys were making their way back to the table, only this time, en mass with the whole McAdam's team. They invited them to our table.

Panicked, I looked around me; wanting to find a crevice and hide. Could I make a run for it? I had to leave. There was Siobhan, glossy-cheeked, drunkenly smiling at me; face lit up in recognition of who I was. She was walking unsteadily towards me in some very precarious heels. *I could have sold her something better...* it was too late to do anything; I'd look a complete fool if I made a dash for it, like some half-mental Cinderella at the stroke of midnight.

James was lingering behind, pensive; he didn't want to come any closer than was necessary to his betrayer. *She saved your fucking life,* I heard Kate's words resound in me. *Yes, I bloody-well did*, I thought. Didn't that account for something?

I got up, unsteadily, making like I was planning where everyone should sit as a pre-emptive to forestall the inevitable. My machinations were short-lived.

'Hello,' Siobhan said in her broad east-end accent, grinning up at me. 'I thought it was you.'

'Hi,' I cooed. I was tipsy but reciprocated amicably. 'Nice to see you again.' People were shuffling around us, bringing chairs and arranging them.

'Well, isn't this a coincidence?' Brian said genially to me, the air of a man satisfied with his day's work shone on him – kind of reminded me of Dad. 'I remember you!'

'Hi,' I said, giving him a smile. 'Congratulations! The match was fantastic.' James; he was close now and could overhear. I could envision his face with this new blow. I stole a look, and my breath caught. I would have thrown myself at his feet, had we been alone, and pleaded for forgiveness, only to save him from that wounded expression. *Yes,* I wanted to say. *I also found out where you box, and I'm sorry for intruding in your life. I'm sorry! I am! But my intruding saved you, and I don't regret that!*

But I only felt the aperture between us widening even more, a chasm dividing us, the abyss at our feet. I wanted to go...

'I suppose not, Brian... Boxing night, an' all...half the clubs in London were here tonight,' Siobhan was saying. 'She boxes... I'm sorry,' she said turning to me, 'but I didn't catch your name.'

'Eleanora,' I said, bluffing my way through the conversation.

'I didn't think you were serious when you came to our club. I thought what's a pretty, swish girl like you doing here. But you proved me wrong. Serves me right for thinking double standard. Ha, ha! Jeez, I'm so drunk! Well, nice to see you found a club. Shame it couldn't have been ours.'

'Yeah,' I said. 'It's a little too far from home.' I took my jacket from the seat, fumbling to find an excuse to leave.

'Take a seat,' Kevin called, and Siobhan slotted herself, but almost falling off, in one of the three last seats; she was right plastered. All were in deep conversation now, and were ordering a fresh round of drinks.

There was no way I could ignore him; he was tonight's hero, and I hadn't even said a word. I had to express some sort of compliment, even if he did hate every inch of my being. But he owed me, because I saved his life. *You can do it...*

'C-congratulations, Jamie,' I stammered, straightening my backbone, or trying to. I lifted my hand and offered it to him. It had crossed my mind that he might turn away, averse to touch, but I knew he was too much of a gentleman to do that. He did, however, hesitate for a millisecond, not expecting my token. He looked at it, then took it in his own. I gave a quick convulsive huff. How long had it been, that touch? The contact of our skin? His hand, strong and warm against my dreadfully cold one?

'It was an amazing match,' I said, and felt the tremble seize me.

He looked oddly at me. 'You always called me James,' he said, rapt …or tipsy. Then realising what a stupid thing to say, said, 'Thank you, El,' and let go of my hand.

'You always called me Eleanora,' I retorted. He blinked, and yes! – he gave me his coy side-smile. I could have cried.

Siobhan heard all that; she gave a wee jerk of the head. Good; she ought to know about James's past if they were to be together.

'Do you two know one another?' she asked. She didn't sound jealous. She merely sounded inquisitive. James turned to her, a quick, 'Yeah,' then he turned back to me. The conversation wasn't over.

'I didn't know you were boxing tonight,' I continued, apologetic. 'I'm sorry if I upset you, James. I promise I didn't follow you. We had tickets…'

He nodded slowly. 'I know. I gathered…' Then that unidentifiable, reticent countenance emerged again. Now it was my turn to scrutinize him; try and analyse what those deep blues were saying. *What? What?*

'Come on, you two,' Siobhan cried. 'Sit down!'

James sat next to her, but looked up at me, wondering why I was still standing.

'Actually, I have to get going,' I said.

'Oh, no, El!' cried Kevin. 'It's early.'

'I've got an exhibition to prepare for; my thesis, ya' know…' I shrugged.

'Oh, come on, El!' said Lorraine. 'What, you gonna paint now?' she laughed.

'Might do,' I said tartly. 'I do my best paintings in the middle of the night!' That made everyone titter. James failed to hide his smile too.

'Seriously, I need to get an early start. It's been a busy couple of weeks,' I said. James folded his arms; he knew what I meant by "busy". He was making an effort, but I could tell he'd be more at ease if I left. I didn't want to wreck his night… as well.

I made for my phone sloppily, and it slipped from grasp, falling on my foot and then sliding onto the floor at James's feet. The screen lit up, and James picked it up before I could reach it. His whole body froze, eyes glued on the image in front of him.

I felt my skull boil… *Shit! Oh, shit!*

My heart thrashed – the shame of what I had done; how I had rudely violated his privacy, and now he knew!

He got up abruptly, scraping his chair back, startling everyone. He grabbed hold of my hand, and yanked me out of the crowd of the bar, in long, angry strides, onto the street, now filled with inebriated revellers. He let go of me, making me face him first. He was livid. I was shaking hard, eyes uncontrollably welling in distress; a cataclysm tearing me apart.

'What the fuck is this, Eleanora?' he roared, holding up the image of him where his tracksuit bottoms had rolled a little down his waist. 'I can't believe it! I can't believe what you've done!'

I bent, doubled over, wanting to be sick.

'This is illegal!' he shouted. 'You invaded my privacy! You could be charged for that!'

'You're right! You're right! Delete it… You can s-sue me, but I was going to delete it!' I made a quick move, grabbed my phone from his hand before he could do anything, and punched at the screen, trying frantically to remove all evidence. Stupid thing wasn't even dual core; the screen was moving too slow! Too slow!

'Eleanora, stop!' he said, and snatched the phone back from me as fast as I had taken it from him. He was breathing hard. 'I don't want to bloody sue you!'

A touch of time passed, as we looked painfully in each other's eyes, my breath getting caught. He started to shake his head slowly, eyebrows drawn down, and the disappointment set in his eye. An eye which had become watery. He wiped at it.

'Who are you, Eleanora?' he uttered. 'I don't know who you are anymore…'

That ripped me to shreds.

'James, I've been so stupid,' I wailed. 'I've made so m-many mistakes… right from the start… right from that fucking phone call… But these pictures… I-I didn't take them for anything… underhand. You have to believe that! It was wrong of me, I know, but it was only to… confirm… to know how things were… I'm sorry for invading your privacy. I'm sorry… How many more times do I have to say that to make you believe me? Yes, I'm a liar… I wronged you… a-and I will be eternally sorry for that…'

He brushed his hand on his face, then through his hair, and breathed out. He came closer to me, the pain sculpted in his face.

'Why *did* you make that phone call?' he said, quietly. 'You mentioned something at the wedding about *nothing compared to what I'd said*. What did you mean?'

I wiped my eye, and stared at him dubiously. He honestly had no idea. It had never occurred to me that he might not remember.

'You don't remember?' I asked.

He shook his head. 'What did I do to you?'

***

I look up. The court usher is staring at me, one eyebrow raised.

9 a.m., the summons had said, and a quick glance at my watch shows a quarter to twelve. I'd nodded off – half-dazed with weariness – as I sat outside courtroom 1 waiting… waiting.

251

All of what the barrister discussed with me earlier is a gap in my memory, and I feel I'm going to screw this all up.

I get up hastily, feeling a head-rush dizzying me. I have eaten next to no breakfast, and can feel the result of that bad decision as anxiety, made worse by hunger, rakes through my belly. Trying not to take heed of it and, straightening my jacket, I take a look at the usher in his black robe – *Charon; ready to guide me through the river Styx*, I think dryly, and step forward where the courtroom is waiting. I am a secondary witness and wasn't allowed to hear court proceedings before I testify. Now, it's my turn.

All is hushed, save some swishing of paper being flipped, a crinkling and another swish. The faint, musty smell of old, polished oak attenuated with varying odours, ranging from perfume to a redolence of the dusty outdoors. Someone clears his throat while I am led to the witness box; a long walk passed the row of jurors. The wood creaks under my feet as I face the court, and I feel a chill despite the insulation of wooden panelling surrounding the place and the weather forecast's hope for a mild day.

I am at a corner of the chamber. I sense, more than see, the judge to my left, perched up high, and… *him* somewhere seated near, towards the centre, behind his solicitor.

What did I do to you?

The defendants are in an elevated box to my far right, guards posted next to them. I don't feel like meeting their eyes – the horrid darkness that another human being wants you dead raises a swirling in my stomach.

I know Vic and Mum are seated in the visitor's gallery. And Kate; true friends never stop being that. All three of them a harbour to lay anchor in this tempest. I know his family are there too, but I am unable to look – my eyes refuse to move.

A Bible is thrust before me. The movement sends off particles of dust hovering in the air, caught in the sunbeam which reaches the bench in front of me, hitting the wood wainscoting. It is the exact same colour as the soft glow of the noon sun seeping through a jar of thyme honey. Rich, deep. Burnt sienna. The image of the descending summer on the veranda of our village cottage.

I am told to repeat, and I snap out of my reverie.

'I do solemnly, sincerely and truly declare and affirm that the evidence I shall give shall be the truth, the whole truth and nothing but the truth…'

I swallow; my throat has gone bone dry.

'For the benefit of the court, could you please state your name?' The voice comes from my right.

I see the friendly barrister who talked to me earlier, standing and addressing me, eyes round and sincere.

'Eleanora Stephens,' I say.

'A little louder, please.'

'Eleanora Stephens,' I call.

'Ms Stephens,' says the barrister – what's his name? He mentioned it earlier. 'I know I will be the one asking the questions, but would you please direct your answers to the jury?' Rhetorical question. I nod and turn instinctively more to the right where the jury sits. Unfortunately, this movement puts my line of vision directly to James. Fantastic. He is sitting, arms folded and face slanted towards me. His eyes are down.

You called me a fucking-ugly, anorexic bitch.

'Could you please tell the court where you were on the sixteenth of April, of this year, at around eight o'clock in the evening?'

'I was in Camden Town, near the Lock,' I say, loud and clear.

'And what were you doing there?'

'Waiting for James – Mr Laidlaw,' I correct myself, and feel extremely uncomfortable speaking his name. I sense him stir.

It had been all a ploy to lead me on…You wanted to make me look a fool.

'Why was that?'

'I wanted to talk to him,' I tell the jurors.

'Did he come?'

'He did.'

'Did you speak to him?'

'No.'

'Why was that?'

'Well,' I fumble for words. 'I, um… thought it would be better to talk back at his place, not in the middle of the street.'

'I see. So, he didn't know you were there?'

'No.'

'Did anybody else see you?'

'Not that I know of.'

'Then what happened?'

I bite my bottom lip, feeling it quiver. All memories coalescing in one great, lucid semblance.

'As I was reaching his, er, place, I heard a loud shout.' I swallow again and breathe. 'It was guttural. It came from behind the wall which divides the street from Mr Laidlaw's home, so I couldn't see. There were noises. A bin got knocked over. It was like a scuffle…, and then I heard another shout, and I ran towards the wall. I looked around the side, careful so… I wouldn't be seen.' It feels like everyone is holding their breath. Abject palpability fills the room.

'And what did you see?'

253

'He – Mr Laidlaw – was being beaten up badly. By the time I got there, he had already been rendered to the ground. He wasn't moving.' I tremble. James looks at me now, attentive yet not hiding the impact of my words. This is the part where he has probably no memory of. His eyes are welling, and mine too.

You'd planned it with… Bianca and Trisha, and you were all making fun of me… I heard everything you said, up in the bedroom.

'They were punching his face, relentlessly, into the ground,' I say, as I look painstakingly into his eyes. There is a gasp from the visitor's gallery. Probably his mother.

'Both men were beating Mr Laidlaw?'

'Yes.'

'One wasn't casually looking on, as the other did all the work?'

'No, they were both on top of him.'

He nods. 'Please continue.'

'Then one of them got out a gun and was about –'

'My Lord!' Someone bursts out, and I jump. It is the defending barrister. 'The witness claims she never saw a gun in her affidavit. She only *guessed* it was.'

The courtroom fills with murmurs and movement.

'I understand, Mr Boyd,' says the judge. Right Honourable Mr Justice Holt, I read on his plaque. 'But I'd like to hear Ms Stephens' testimony and her reasons why she believes it was a gun.'

Boyd looks helplessly back at the solicitor behind him. She whispers something, and he sits.

'Mr Sharpe, please continue with your questioning,' Justice Holt says to my barrister. Sharpe – that was it.

'Thank you, My Lord.' And to me, 'You say one of the men got out a gun. How do you know it was a gun?'

'I heard that metal sound when you… prepare it to shoot.'

'When you arm it?'

'Yes.'

'Mr Laidlaw wasn't shot. What did they do with it?'

'One must have been about to shoot.' I paused, trying to find the words. 'But the other man said "no, nothing that can be traced", and that's when I ran. I had to find some way to stop them, because I knew they wanted to…' My throat gets caught. And a blessed tear finally finds its way down my cheek.

'To?'

'To …kill him…'

254

It takes one heartbeat, then the shockwave reverberates. Gasps, murmurs. James's eyes transfix on mine, like he wants to envision what I had seen, through them.

I didn't mean it… I was stoned, Eleanora… you shouldn't have believed it! You shouldn't! oh, Jesus!

'Order!' is hailed. 'Order in the court!'

The murmurs reduce slightly.

'Then what did you do?' Sharpe asks me, ignoring the tumult. The court goes instantly quiet again.

'I found a car on the other side of the wall and rocked it, setting the alarm off. I wanted to scare them. Make them stop what they were about to do to Mr Laidlaw.'

James sits inert, only the heat on his cheeks and his hard breathing are signs he's with us. This is the part he was never told.

'And the car alarm went off?'

'Yes.'

'And this had done the trick, obviously, as Mr Laidlaw is alive and well as we can all see?'

'Well, yes. But I didn't know that then. I thought I'd find him… dead.' It is getting hard for me to breathe. James flashes a pained glance my way. His lips are a pink line, severe, distressed.

'I see.' Sharpe bends his head gravely. 'Tell us what happened next?'

'I ran… I ran up the street. I was so scared… I thought they were going to pull the gun on me. I turned into another street as fast as I could, and prayed they hadn't seen me, and I phoned for an ambulance… I waited. Then I started to walk back… to see if he was alive.' I am trembling now. My hands are ice-cold.

'Weren't you afraid the men might still have been there?'

'I was, but I didn't think. My mind was confused, distraught – I just w-wanted to see if Mr Laidlaw was alive. When I turned into the street which led to the wall, I saw the men coming towards me. I quickly ran to hide.' My lips pout involuntarily, as tears are flowing. I'm shaking all over. 'It was dark… I had my hood on and kept my head down, and hoped I hadn't roused suspicion. I remained hidden until they left.'

The jury looks sympathetic towards me.

'I see. And did you get to see their faces?'

'I did,' I say repressing the urge to glance towards the defendants.

'And can you point them out in this courtroom?'

My heart starts to pound. The one thing I don't want to do. I wish I could say no, but take in a breath and sway my head in the defendants' direction. I lift my shaking finger and quickly point at them. I make sure I don't find their eyes.

255

'Let it be known on record that Eleanora Stephens has pointed to the defendants in the dock. Thank you, Ms Stephens. Now, did the defendants say or do anything while you were walking in the street?'

'Yes. One said, "Did you get the stuff", and the other replied, "Yeah let's get the… fuck out of here".' Saying the F-word in such formal circumstances makes me feel a bit thorny.

'Did you see the so-called *stuff*?'

'No.'

'My Lord,' interjects Boyd. 'Mr Orme and Mr Jackson have already confessed and have pleaded guilty to stealing Mr Laidlaw's prototype. What more does my learned friend wish to hear?'

I heard their names. Orme. Jackson. Now the ghosts of my caliginous dreams have names. But what is that about a prototype? Then I remember the conversation with David on Easter Sunday, and am convinced my conjecture had been right.

The judge agrees with Boyd, and Sharpe stops that particular line of questioning.

Sharpe then opens a file where I instantly see my sketches of the two assailants photocopied to a slightly larger scale. He hands them to the usher saying, 'If your Lordship pleases.' The usher then brings them to the Judge. Justice Holt looks at them, then looks directly in front of him at the defendants.

'These sketches, My Lord, were drawn by Ms Stephens herself,' declares Sharpe. His Lordship peeks over his glasses at me. 'The likeness is excellent. Do you have an eidetic memory, Miss Stephens?' he asks.

'Um. Yes, My Lord,' I say, with gross reluctance. I am stuck between a rock and a hard place. I can't prevaricate my way around this, like I do with everyone else. James stirs. He is looking down, biting his lip, trying to hold… a grin? For one instant I wonder why, then sudden recollection springs to the forefront of my mind, and I see the portrait of the bus driver I had so vehemently denied sketching from memory to James. Heat rises to my face. He remembers. He bloody remembers. Is that a sarcastic, resentful grin then? Another brick in my wall of lies?

Well, I did. Why shouldn't have I believed it? You'd ignored me for so long all those months previous. I was young and impressionable, and you wiped your feet on my heart. But you know what? My sister almost died in a car crash that very night, and I didn't care about you or anything else after that. It showed me your shit wasn't worth it, James. It's ironic, because you were the one who'd taught me how to measure what's important and what's not, remember? None of you were important. Or worth my time, or my pain…

'Ms Stephens, how did you find Mr Laidlaw after Mr Orme and Mr Jackson had left, what was his condition?' Sharpe asks, bringing me back.

I breathe deep. 'Wounded badly. Cut. Bleeding all over the place.'

'Did you apply any first aid?'

'No. It was dark, and blood was everywhere. I couldn't tell where I needed to clean, and I was afraid I might infect him. I just put my coat on his chest and placed my jumper, very carefully, under his head – the ground was cold and wet – and waited for the ambulance.'

'Was Mr Laidlaw unconscious?'

'Yes, but he… moaned faintly at one point. He must have been in a lot of pain…' James makes a move like I've nudged a memory, and wipes his palm over his face taking a long breath.

'Could you ascertain if anything was broken?'

'No.'

Sharpe nods briskly, draws breath through his teeth and says, 'Now, Ms Stephens, let us skip forward to the twenty-second of last month; twenty days ago. In your statement you say you took a quick look at your pursuers in Heath Street. What do you mean by that?'

It takes me a second to register the abrupt change of subject.

'Well, I mean I turned reflexively around when I heard the engine of the Range Rover coming up behind me.'

'Did you see the faces of your pursuers?'

'No. It was very quick. I turned back almost instantly; there was no time. If I had lingered, it would have been the last thing I ever did.' Hairs prickle all over my body. *He* is still, and staring straight at me, horrified. I wonder if he learnt of these details.

'There is a CCTV video which captures the scene on Heath Street. I would like the ladies and gentlemen of the jury to ascertain for themselves the extent of potential grievous bodily harm, which could have been afflicted on the witness, had the vehicle touched her.'

A video? That takes me surprise, and I waver and lurch as if I'm suddenly on a rocking boat, oscillating through bad tides. I have quietly become aware that I am coming down with something.

I large-screened monitor to one wall is switched on, and lights are dimmed, and within half a minute, a not too blurry image of me running up Heath Street can be observed from an angle, I judge at being as high as the two-storey building opposite. Then a dark, rectangular shape materialises from nowhere, and rushes headlong, obliterating me from view, then it makes an abrupt deflection, sideswiping whatever is in its way, and disappearing from the screen. It is over so soon, I am left blinking.

'Now, let's see that again in slow motion, shall we?' suggests Sharpe, devising nobody caught the whole thing, and presses the remote.

And there it is, frame by frame. It is easy to see just how close the bumper of the Range Rover has come to the heels of my running legs, and for a moment I think I'm actually going to get run over. I turn the corner, literally, last fraction of a second, as the next frame shows the Rover completely covering that spot. The Rover then swerves, knocking down

257

shop stands and parked bicycles – barely missing passers-by – in order to avoid crashing into the iron bollards. Those things are impenetrable.

The screen goes blank. The lights are back on. Everybody's face looks sombre through the hushed whispers.

'Statistics say, death caused by a car crashing into a body at over forty-five miles per hour is a near-conclusive ninety-five per cent. And that's with an average, small car. In our case, we are talking about a whopping SUV.' Sharpe pauses, his eyes fix on the jury. 'Do you know what speed this Range Rover was doing?' They say nothing. A couple gesture a "no" with their heads. He holds up an official paper – the speedometer reading, I suspect.

'Ms Stephens?' The question is now directed to me.

'No,' I say, voice cracking.

'Forty-seven point three.'

I do not move. I feel the blood palpitate around my cranium. My mother has made some motion; I cannot tell. James has his gaze pinned to something on the floor. I see his jaw-muscle contract.

If my shit wasn't worth it, why bother helping me now? Why come to my rescue? Why, Eleanora?

'Forty-seven point three miles an hour,' Sharpe reiterates, enunciating it slowly; letting his words sink in. 'My Lord, I have no further questions.' Sharpe seats himself with an air of composed satisfaction.

Mr Boyd gets up. He had been shuffling through the file in front of him all the while I was being questioned by Sharpe. Boyd's poise induces a prescient fear that slithers within my psyche.

'Ms Stephens, please explain why your statement to the police, on the events involving Mr Laidlaw's assault, was one day late?'

The boom of my pulse thunders in my ears. I instantly know what he's trying to do: ruin my name, ruin my credibility. Prove to everyone I'm not to be trusted.

'Because I told them the next day,' I say, tense. Some find humour in my answer. I didn't mean it to be funny.

'Why was that?' he asks. Then before I can reply, 'Because in cases where a criminal offense has been made, police arrive at the scene as well as the ambulance. They found no trace of you. Why had you left before talking to the police?'

Sharpe springs to his feet. 'My Lord, where is the relevancy? The witness is here for us to ascertain what happened on the night of Mr Laidlaw's assault. It is of little matter *when* the statement was written. Ms Stephens is not on trial here.'

'Mr Boyd?' asks His Lordship, turning to Boyd.

'I want to establish how unreliable this witness is, My Lord. Who can trust her if she fled from the scene? Why didn't she stay and help the police? Why should I – *we* – believe her statement?'

The judge is convinced. 'Ms Stephens?'

Each and every eye penetrates my mortal soul, chastising me. Guilty before even being proven as such.

'I… I didn't know the police were going to be there…' I sound pathetic, even if it is the truth. It's plausible, though. Where is it written that the police come when you call for an ambulance? Had I ever been taught that? No. Did dispatch say? I couldn't tell.

Boyd gives an exaggerated chagrin, feigning to disbelieve me. 'You didn't know?' He's almost mocking.

'If I was told, I didn't hear it. That's the truth. I-I can't remember if the woman on the other end said something… All I remember was shouting at her, telling her to get an ambulance there fast. Giving her the name of the street. That was it…'

Boyd rubs his chin. 'But why didn't you stay anyway? Usually, a person stays until they see the wounded off. Why leave?'

I stare at Boyd. *Why are you torturing me?* 'I was scared,' I tell him.

'Why were you scared? What were the paramedics going to do to you?'

The build-up of consternation sinuously passes through me. 'I panicked. I freaked out… I don't know what was going through my mind.'

I'm not a liar! I want to shout.

Because I own up to my shit, James. Because as soon as I realised that it was me responsible for how you ended up, I did my utmost to… to try and make amends. To atone for the harm I caused you, and to beg for your forgiveness, actually. I fractured my wrist because I fell running, not to lose you. I risked my life to get to you, to make sure you were safe, and not freeze to death on that street. All because I want to make it up to you!

'Didn't you stop to think a crime had been committed, and that entailed speaking to the authorities?' Boyd doesn't give up.

I stare at him, devoid of anything but anger. 'All I thought that night, Mr Boyd, was for James not to die!' The intensity of those words cloak the room in a nimbus of silence. My heart thrums. Heat consumes me but I'm shivering. I feel James's eyes seer through me.

Boyd coughs, clearly seeing I've convinced the jury, and takes a new direction to his cross examination.

'It says in your statement that you waited in Camden for three hours for Mr Laidlaw to arrive. Why didn't you just call him?'

'I don't have his number.'

'But you are friends, are you not?' He is surprised.

'No.'

'No?'

259

'No.'

Boyd pauses. He looks up, drafting the right question in his mind. 'So, what was so important that you had to wait for Mr Laidlaw for three hours to tell him?'

'I-I…' I look at James, through bleary eyes. He looks back, a questioning look in his eyes. 'I wanted to talk about something that happened between us in the past. It was something I needed to get off my chest.'

'It wouldn't happen to have been about a phone call you'd placed to the police six years ago?' I close my eyes, ready to topple forward in my seat. I hold onto something to make the giddiness stop. 'A phone call, where you blatantly lied to the police, claiming Mr Laidlaw had raped some girl? A *lie*, Ms Stephens?'

I don't know how he found out, but he is desperate to drag me through the mud. I am the only eyewitness, and he wants to rip me to shreds with the blade of my own condemning words. Archer had said it was just as well I hadn't written an official apology so they wouldn't use it against me, but they found out, done their homework, nonetheless.

James has whispered something to his solicitor, and Sharpe is up. 'My Lord, this is entirely irrelevant. What Ms Stephens did, six whole years ago, has absolutely nothing to do with her testimony here today. It is like saying, when she was five she stole a biscuit from a jar, and is now being asked whether she likes to ballet dance! It pertains to nothing in this tribunal.'

'Mr Boyd,' Judge Holt says, tired, 'where are you going with this?'

'My Lord, I am going in the same place as before with this. I want to show the jury that Ms Stephens is a liar. That we should not take her testimony into account.'

'What was this great lie you said Ms Stephens?' the judge asks me, a tad melodramatic.

I stare blankly at him for a second. I shake my head and swallow dry air. This is a gauntlet I must pass. There is no way out. And even if there were, I would not take it. Confess, now, before man and God. 'It is what Mr Boyd said.' There is stirring at my confirmation. 'I had called the police… claiming Mr Laidlaw had …raped a girl. It was a nocent falsehood, I admit, and I had no idea of the ramifications it would bring, especially with the police and with his family, and consequently with his life. I'm very sorry. That was why I wanted to talk to him in Camden. I only found out recently just how much trouble he got into with that lie of mine. I had no idea of the repercussions.' I shake my head, feeling the intensity of my next words flow forth with flame. 'I was sixteen and stupid, my Lord. I admit I did a very stupid thing. But, am I to be defined as a liar for the rest of my life?' I bite my lip as it trembles, wiping the rolling tears from my face. Now Elizabeth knows of my treachery, his mother and father. Mum… Vic… and the whole world. I start to shiver, the tears are unremitting. I look up, and find Archer in the gallery. He grins, giving me props, nodding his head. I look down; I don't deserve that. I don't. My eye drifts to James involuntarily. His eyes are brooding, despondent, as they hold my own. His cheeks suddenly suffuse that beautiful, gentle pink, and then he softly, slowly …smiles.

'Mr Boyd, I'm afraid Mr Sharpe is right. This has nothing to do with the case,' Judge Holt adjudicates. 'Do you have any other questions?' Boyd is composed even though his plan has backfired.

'Just a few more, My Lord.' He turns to me. 'You claim, Ms Stephens, you knew the defendants were going to kill Mr Laidlaw. You never saw a gun, just presumed it was from a metal sound. Had you ever seen a gun before that night, Ms Stephens?'

'No.'

'So, how can you be so sure it was?'

I look at Sharpe for help. He gives me a nod in support. Useless.

'You didn't see a gun, and there is no gunshot wound on Mr Laidlaw,' Boyd drills, trying to convince the jury with a feeble refute.

I shrug, stumped for a moment. 'Well, they were holding something over Mr Laidlaw's head. At the angle I was at, I couldn't see what, but that, and with the sound of metal, and what they said about not wanting something that can be traced… Oh!' I stop abruptly. *Traced.* A trace. There was a trace. I gasp as each hippocampal neuron explodes the image before my eyes. 'Oh! That's it!' I cry. That image… a revelation… dear God! How on earth had I forgotten that? Me, with that bloody memory of mine? I must have shielded it from the forefront of my anamnesis; not wanting it to torture me. I had been agitated. Or maybe I'm at the pedestal of losing my gift.

Boyd is looking at me quizzically. There is an ounce of fear behind his eyes. James is suddenly intently staring my way. I meet his scrutiny, eyes searching once more. *What? What?* they are saying. If my eidetic memory is worth its salt, this is where I must prove it.

I clear my throat and state, 'There is a mark where the blood on Mr Laidlaw's forehead has been smudged, ever so slightly. That's where the gun touched him.' I say with such marked assurance that Boyd's mouth hangs.

I hear a deliberate cough from someone in the gallery. My eyes dart straight in the trajectory of the sound. Archer. He folds his arms, amused. At the corner of my eye, I discern movement from Mum and Vic.

'Excuse me, Ms Stephens? A smudge?' Boyd asks at a loss.

'Yes.'

'Do elucidate.' He is cocky but apprehensive.

'Detective Inspector Archer,' I glance at him in the gallery, 'showed me the forensics photographs taken at the scene. In one of them, the blood on his – Mr Laidlaw's – forehead has a circular imprint, I strongly believe was forged from the shape of the barrel. It is just above the right eyebrow.' I put my finger to my brow to indicate. 'The arc of the circle is approximately twelve millimetres away, I'd say, from the highest brow hair. Judging by the arc, I place the diameter of the barrel at around eight millimetres, give or take some tenths.'

In all my 22 years, I have never voiced the extent of my gift. I have only drawn it. I have never orally described the fathomless detail in which I perceive things. The depth of it is recondite even to my inner-most circle. I dare look at my mother. I'm sorry for never letting her in on that, all these years. All these years, begrudging her that part of me. I glance at her. I don't think I have ever seen a prouder smile on a mother's face. She is pleased I have finally disclosed my mind to the world; that I haven't denied who I am. I know she has been waiting so long for this moment. Little does she know it won't be for much more. I'm glad, at least, she got to live this one experience. I owed her it.

Vic is grinning like an idiot. Kate too.

Boyd maintains his poise despite the apparent unease lining his own forehead.

'You can't see it initially,' I continue. 'But it's a high-resolution image. I'm sure if you zoom in… I don't know what else to say to prove it was a gun… 'But there is no doubt,' I add.

My eyes pass quickly over to James. He is already looking at me. He has that face again; the one I don't understand.

'Gentlemen!' His Lordship booms from on high. The barristers stand. 'I have heard enough.' Here His Lordship angles his face down at a robed man with a stack of papers in front of him. 'Mr Farris?'

Farris faces the judge. They confirm under their breaths. Then His Lordship looks up. 'I see no evidence to refute what our eye witness has said. And in light of her… her eidetic memory, I suggest forensics be done again for the benefit of the jury. Are there any more witnesses?'

'No, My Lord,' both barristers say.

'Very well. I want forensics again and your closing statements, gentlemen.'

Here the judge utters something to Farris again, and nods. 'The court is adjourned for the day after tomorrow, at nine,' he declares. I think he is going to thwack a gabble, but apparently, English crown courts don't use them.

Then Judge Holt is up, and everyone rises in unison. I sway a little and grab onto something. Then I sense his gaze, and find his eyes.

You weren't the one responsible, Eleanora. I was.

Chapter Forty-Six

Now

I hurry past St Paul's Cathedral, feeling a cold shiver all over me, as I walk straight through a flock of pigeons, causing them to bluster up in a profusion of feathers. Blossoms are out, harkening London to warmth and beauty.

I had left the Old Bailey hurriedly, but not before I had interrogated Vic on what the court said about this "prototype".

Kate came close to our huddle. I gave her my hand, and she took it and squeezed.

'Well, apparently, those two men thought James had their drug money, but the package had nothing to do with drugs,' explained Vic. 'They saw Nick hand over a package to James one day. What with James's appearance they thought he was a dealer or something, and they followed him. That's how they knew where he lived. But they didn't attack him then.'

'They waited,' put in Kate.

'The thing is, the first package was official papers on what James and Nick were working on –'

'Some amazing computer component which James has invented, that they were getting patented, signed and sealed by a solicitor, so no one could steal the idea,' Kate said enthusiastically. She grabbed me, big smile. 'It wasn't drugs like we'd thought!'

'Do you remember David telling us about Anarchist Oblong at Easter?' Vic asked. I nodded. 'That was Nick, but I think you already knew it, right?'

I nodded again. 'I wasn't sure though.'

'If you take the G out, you get an anagram, which when sorted spells Nicholas Barton.'

'James explained everything in court,' Kate said. 'How he and Nick were creating this amazing software, how he was apprehensive someone might steal it…'

I looked around, finding James. He was afar, in deep conversation with Sharpe. Moved, I smiled. He invented something worth stealing. Was it that valuable?

'I understand,' I said. 'So, they just mistook it for drug money.'

'Yeah,' they both said.

'And the second time?'

'The second time, Nick had funded James to make the actual prototype, and that's what they had stolen,' Kate told me.

'After that they connected the assailants to a vehicle, which is owned by some ultra-rich magnate, who also owns the yachting company Nick worked for. They happened to be his bodyguards. The magnate is probably mafia, but they had nothing to pin on him, 'cos the assailants said they had taken the vehicle without the owner's knowledge that night…' my sister clarified.

'Which is all a bit dodgy, but the police can't prove anything,' said Kate.

'But why kill?' I asked.

'That's where you come in. They needed to prove intent,' said Kate.

'That's not the motive,' I said. We each mulled that over for a second.

'Let's leave that up to the jury,' Vic resolved.

'Guys, it's organised crime, innit?' Kate blurted. 'Cross them, and they'll kill you for nothing! Nick owed them money, and they didn't have the patience, so they made an example of him.' We stood, motionless. A chill shot down my spine. I closed my eyes feeling dizzy again. The ominous symptoms of some virus were at the threshold.

'But why hadn't James told Archer about the invention from the start?' I said, tired.

'He was bound to secrecy. The buying computer company had made it a proviso in their contract because they wanted to sell it as their own invention. He had to keep *mum*. The name of the company was only told to the judge,' Vic revealed. 'David believes it's one of the biggies.'

'El! He's bloody rich!' Kate confided under her breath. ' "Well-to-do entrepreneur…" '

I stared, as my eyes filled. Kate's did too.

'Shall we go and get something to eat?' Mum said, suddenly beside us.

I told them I just wanted to go home and sleep. I must have looked like death itself, for they hadn't argued. Vic, sensing something was up with me and Kate, took Mum and left.

'Where have you been staying?' I asked my friend of friends. She looked tired but seemed all right, like she'd accepted her lot.

'With Mum and Dad,' she said.

I raised my brows. 'Really? Everything OK there then?'

'Yeah… Things are… good, funnily enough,' she said, grinning.

'I'm happy for you…'

Then, she gave me a hug, surprising me. 'I'm sorry for… slapping…' Her voice wavered, and my tears dropped. 'Forgive me, El…' And unfolding me from her embrace said, 'Now go and get some sleep. You look shattered. And we'll talk soon, OK?' She walked to the exit and turned, happy. 'Gotta dash. I've got a job interview!'

'I'm proud of you!' I called as she went through the glass doors, smiling back at me.

Elizabeth came running up to me, just as I was about to exit myself, and gave me a tender *abrazo*. She looked back at her brother who was still conversing with Sharpe, then back at me, smiling. Her face showed signs of crying in spite of it, like the first time I'd seen her.

'El, I can't thank you enough. You saved his life… I – we – he had no idea…' She shook her head. 'He didn't know… we spoke the other day…'

I had no idea what she was trying to say. I was too off-balance; she wasn't making sense… or was it me?

'When I came home after the funeral, he had been frantic – I'd switched off my mobile to save some battery and forgot to turn it on – anyway, I told him you didn't live in Edgware anymore, and he asked for your address. He said he wanted to give something back to you.'

'Yes…' I confirmed, too tired to say more.

'We hadn't said anything else until the other day, after York Hall. He was full of questions. We talked about everything, from me telling you about Dad, to your being bullied. How you helped me. How you took me to the hospital even when your hand was …obviously hurt. About you telling me you had been the one to call the ambulance…' She stopped. A fresh tear rolled down her face.

I tilted my head, wondering what she wanted to say. Wondering why she was being so nice. Didn't she hear my confession in court? Didn't she hear how I'd deprived her brother of his future? I wanted to leave. I didn't know how much longer I could stand. 'Tell me. What is it?' I urged.

'He told me about the wedding. What he said to you, and I'm so sorry he treated you like that. And after what you told us today in court; how close he came to dying… Mum told me to thank you from the bottom of her heart. A big thank you from all of us. She would have come herself, but she isn't feeling too well.'

I couldn't believe what I was hearing. 'Elizabeth, I wrecked his life! You ought to be upbraiding me, giving me a piece of your mind, not thanking me!'

'No! If it weren't for you…' She sniffed, shaking her head. 'Please forgive him. He didn't know… Archer didn't reveal much to him. His interrogation was rather one-sided, so Jamie says.'

I took her hand, grasping hard. 'There is nothing to forgive,' I said. 'It is you who ought to be demanding my apology. I should be asking for your forgiveness, not the other way round.'

She stared at me, stunned. 'No…'

'Listen, I have to go, I don't feel very well…' I gave her a hug, then releasing her, said, 'I want you to tell your family that I'm sorry. I'm sorry for causing the rift between James and your father, and everything else. Do you hear me?' She nodded solemnly. 'Take care, Elizabeth.'

As I got to St Paul's, I heard my name being called. *It sounds like James*, I remembered thinking. *It can't be…* and didn't stop.

***

I unlock my flimsy door and run for the medical cabinet. My skin is crawling with goosebumps, and a ripple of shivers brushes my skin. I am raising a temperature; cold at the tips, head on fire.

The underground had been stifling. A clammy residue of humidity brought by a foul brew of unfiltered air and body odour. What a fug! I had alighted feeling like puking.

I get the Panadol, reprimanding myself for not taking up Mum and Vic's offer. I would have been taken care of now, instead of going through this illness alone. And it feels fierce.

I swallow the pill, almost to the point of convulsing, and put on a warm pair of tracksuit bottoms, barely able to find where to put my legs in – I am shaking so much. I get my grey fleece robe, wear it and put the hood up, find my thickest socks and shove them on my feet.

The bloody antipyretic is taking too long; either that, or it wasn't a big-enough dose. I can't get up, I have to text Mum. I do so with great effort.

I lie down on my bed curled up, putting my hands between my thighs to warm them and close my eyes, as the shivers continue, teeth chatting.

***

I don't know how long I've been asleep for, but the chill of another bout of fever is upon me. I hear a knock on the door. *Mum has a key*, I think dazedly. *Unless she came straight from London, as soon as she saw the text, and didn't have it on her. Yes, that was it…*

It is still light outside, a sky of soft afternoon blue. I move to get up; it is with difficulty, as a throbbing headache is crushing my cranium. Still, I manage to get my feet on the floor, holding onto walls and furniture, as I reach out for the latch on my door.

'Mum –' I say, but stop. Because it isn't Mum; it's James.

'Wha?' I breathe, and close my eyes, feeling my knees give, as a heavy convulsion shudders my body. I hear a, 'Jesus!' and next thing I know, I am being carried, effortlessly, to my bedroom.

'I'm all righ'…' I whisper, exhausted, to his chest. He's warm.

'I can see,' he says with soft sarcasm, and places me on my bed, pulling the cover over me. I turn to my left, facing my window, bringing my knees up again. The bed vibrates with my writhing. Why is he here? He is baffling me again. Is he going to leave me now? I want to say something; tell him I want him to stay. I do. I do, even though I shouldn't, but the fever has other plans. It snatches any strength I have with rapid, agonizing breaths, rendering me a helpless body of torment.

Then the bed rocks me back a bit; he's sat on it. There is movement. I can't tell what he is doing, but I hear a muffled thud. Was that a shoe dropping to the floor? And suddenly he is under the cover, pressing the heat of his body along the entire expanse of my back, as his enormous right arm wraps around my waist, bringing me flat against him. He positions himself to fit the same shape I am, gathering up his knees so they slot below mine. He isn't wearing jeans. He is still in his courtroom clothes. Some softer fabric on his thighs, as the heat of his body emanates through to me. The shivering reduces instantly, and gradually my breathing eases.

I feel his breath on my ear, a faint, 'Mmm,' as he rests his cheek near the top of my head amongst my hair. I vaguely think how glad I am I washed it that morning. His hand searches for mine. Finding it, he weaves his fingers urgently through, and holds tight, trying to expel the icicles they have become.

'Your hands are always cold,' he whispers into my ear.

I don't know where I find the energy, but whisper back, labouredly, 'Cold hands, warm heart, says m'gran.'

He huffs, 'That gran of yours…' I can hear the smile in his voice. He brings our hands to my chest, making small motions of reassurance with his thumb on my knuckles, brushing the side of my breast lightly by accident, once… twice…

We are there, locked, for some time – I do not know how long; I drift in and out. It seems endless. I do believe he has fallen asleep and woken up, each time, with me. He must be exhausted too from today's long, weary trial. At one point, I wake again, and hear his heavy breathing of slumber near my ear. The sun has set. The vesper of a remaining luminance lingering through my curtain. He starts to stir, moving his hand right on my breast, cupping it, and then I feel him. A slight but distinct hardness pressing against me, separate from the rest of him. But I've started to doze away again, with that old, much-missed feeling I am home. Safe. The seafarer finding anchorage, finally… finally. The tumult has faded into a ripple.

'Eleanora…'

But I am gone.

Chapter Forty-Seven

Now

I move. I am… wet. *What?*

'Eww!' My whole body is covered in sweat-drenched clothes, stuck to me. 'Yachh!'

'You up?' Comes Mum's voice, giving me a fright.

'Ma?' I say loudly, causing my head to rattle. It is better, but still sensitive.

'How are you feeling?' She pops her head around the entrance of my room. I want to tell her I don't need her now; she can leave… but say, 'Better…'

'Oh, sweetie pie, you look dreadful. Sorry for not coming sooner. I left my mobile home 'cos they said mobiles weren't permitted in court, and we got back late, and by the time I saw your message…'

''S all right…' I say, and proceed to take off my robe. 'I need to get changed.'

'Here, let me.' She walks to the chest of draws, and hands me some crumpled underwear and a pair of wrinkled but fresh pyjamas. 'I'll make you another cuppa,' she says, and leaves me to it.

I look around me as I take off my wet stuff. There is a febrifuge, a cup on the bedside table. A bowl of water with a flannel in it. A thermometer.

Fragments of the night come to me; flowing in and out like calm waves on a beach. A soft, strong hand lifting my head. A sip; something medicinal. A voice coaxing gently, to lift my head and drink. The *plip, plip, plip* of droplets into water, and the coolness of the compress on my forehead. Large fingers smoothing my cheek. A face silhouetted against the window. That face coming nearer, nearer. I had called his name – I know I had. I had begged to be forgiven. It was a plea driven by the force of nightmarish delirium.

I gasp, remembering his reply; the soft, fervent utterance, 'No. It is you that must forgive me, Eleanora. Please…'

He'd held my hands tight – I remember the pressure. He'd bent over, his head bowed low, something moist touching my knuckles; he'd been crying… he'd been crying.

I cry too.

I stare blankly at the mirror in my bathroom, stupefied. *That wasn't there yesterday.*

'Mum?' I call, weakly walking towards the kitchen.

'Mm?'

'Did you… get me a mirror?'

'What? Mirror? What mirror?' she says, the *clink, clink, clink* of the spoon stirring the tea. 'I'm so glad you got that window fixed. 'Bout time.'

Window?

A warm breeze touches my skin as I gawk upon seeing the window panel all the way up; the problematic one. That thing wouldn't budge no matter how hard I'd tried. Now it is gaping open.

Mum hands me my tea, heedless of my puzzlement.

'Go lie down. You don't look well enough to be up. Come on.' And she puts her arm around me, taking the cup, and walks me back to bed.

I rest my head back on my pillow, now alone in my room, and my thoughts wander back.

Bethnal Green… I close my eyes, wanting to blot out all the grim atrocities.

You're not the one responsible, Eleanora. I am.

I had been unable to believe it; this confession. It was incorrect. I had been about to contradict him, but before I could say a word, he'd taken my hand and placed my phone in it, closing my fingers around it firmly.

'Yes, I am,' he'd stated, reading my mind. Then, taking a step closer, had surprised me when he rested his palm to my cheek, gently stroking a tear away with his thumb. A second later, he'd turned and strode back into the bar.

I think of Court… all those questions. That gun print. The prototype. What will the outcome be?

Him…

Him carrying me, holding me. Firm. Tender. Close. …Hard?

The sudden frisson of recollection collides into my thoughts. What did *that* mean? Isn't he with Siobhan?

And if Mum isn't the one who changed my mirror and fixed my window… Jesus. What is going on?

I look at my mobile. The time is 12:08. If he stayed with me all night, then I suppose he had ample time to mend my window. As for my mirror? Did he actually go out and buy one for me?

'MA!'

'What?'

'What time did you come?'

'Oh, about an hour ago, I'd say. Why?'

'Nothing…'

'I'm going to make you some soup, and then I'm off. Will you be all right?'

No.

'Yeah. Thanks, Ma…'

I awake this time to the grating of keys in my keyhole. I blink in the gloaming. I must have slept all afternoon. Thankfully, feverless. I punch on my phone. 8:26. Who on earth is at my door?

'El?'

'Kate?'

PART FOUR

Chapter Forty-Eight

Back When

The painting halts me mid-stride. I've seen that hand somewhere before. Two years ago? No – almost three now. Have almost three years really gone by since then? I'm no art expert, but I know it is hers. The unmistakable undulations and tones; that beautiful saturation of light. That sharp detail which strikes the observer right to the soul...

So, she is here... of all the places. Here. Close. So close. Funny, I never ran into her... It would be, what, her first year then, and this would be her end-of-year exhibition? There is a little signature in the corner, I stoop closer. *ES* is scrawled in a calligraphic hand. *Eleanora Stephens* – the stamp of authentication.

They asked me to clean up in here before I leave. I never turn down overtime; I need the money... Poor Lizzy made up her mind to give me her pocket money, and I, the rake I am, didn't make much of an effort to talk her out of it.

Nick is helping as much as he can, but there are times when he relapses, and ends up in so much debt, it takes him months to get finances out of the gutter. I've told him, time and time again, to get his arse into rehab, but he insists he owes me and wants to get me on my feet, and by doing that, he has to work. He claims it had been his fault; forcing me to take his dope that night, dragging me away from… her embrace… that look in her beautiful, grey eyes; an image I'll never forget…

If it weren't for me, Jamie boy…

I go over and over that it my mind, to the point of going insane. Because no matter how I was arrested, nobody is to blame but myself.

Now

It is as if I am 18 again. That abhorrent sensation lodging itself in the depths of my stomach.

Five years they had said. It is only four and a bit. They let him out early, and he hadn't told a soul. Nobody in the Ward family had been informed.

Kate came walking through my door, that ineluctable, piteous look stamped on her face, and I felt the spasm strike me where I have been wounded before, making it twice as painful.

Kate had been working on her thesis, her back to him, unaware, when he came in the front door.

I hold her now, on my bed. The only comfort I can offer.

I cleaned up her wounds (the external ones), brushed her dishevelled hair, and made us both tea.

'I should be the one making you tea…' she'd said meekly.

'I feel much better.'

She got her pillow from her room; we lie, listless, in the silence.

'You were right, El,' she says, crying afresh.

'Shut up,' I rasp. 'Just shut up.'

She lets out a stuttered sigh. 'He didn't know Dad was upstairs, just assumed I was alone; the car wasn't parked outside. In a way, I'm glad he… tried again; only so at least one of my parents got to see… finally.'

'Kate…'

'Broke my laptop…' She wipes her eyes.

'Shit…'

She harrumphs bitterly. 'Never seen Dad do that in all my life; lash out like… like someone had turned on a switch in his brain. He was all over Rhys within seconds.' She offers a cynical smile. 'I screamed this time. I never used to; I was always too scared, but now… I was screaming the house down. That's when I heard Dad rush to me, and pulled him off. He told him he needed help. Therapy. That this wasn't normal. Wrong.'

I close my eyes, making the water gathered there flow over.

'Called John.'

'John?' I ask.

'Detective Inspector Ferguson.'

I blink, confused. 'How do you know Ferguson?'

271

She smiles softly, 'He was the young, over-eager officer.' She pauses deliberately for it to strike a note.

'Oh, my God!' I say, suddenly recollecting. 'Green eyes!'

She assents.

'What a coincidence,' I say, and chuckle weakly.

'You know, I'm starting to believe your gran; all that talk about nothing being coincidental.'

'I think she means that we are given choices, and it's up to us to select the right one.'

'Well, whatever it is, I'm glad I was offered John as a choice.'

I look up at my ceiling in silence.

'Saw him in court. He didn't know who I was at first, then I told him. You should have seen the look on his face... I suppose I clean up rather well.' She grins wearily. 'Anyway, he gave me his card. Told me to call if ever I needed anything. And so, I did. I told him that was the reason I'd run away back then. I told him everything. I've never told any man my past.'

I raise my brows and sip my tea. 'Really? You've never told any of your relationships?'

'No. It's too embarrassing. Bloody humiliating. With John it's different. I feel he's been a part of it from the beginning.'

'Plus, you aren't in a relationship.'

'Not yet.' I can hear the cheeky grin.

'Where is he now; Rhys?'

'Down at the station. He's being charged as we speak. John came when they took him. He said he came as a friend, 'cos it wasn't in his jurisdiction. Rhys went willingly. He knows there's something wrong with him. He cried and hit his head on the wall again and again; he was half-mad. So tired and bitter from prison... They are requesting psychiatric evaluation. I think he'll get it this time.'

'That's good. He'll get help. Proper help.'

'Yeah... When they put the handcuffs on him, he looked so sad, crying. I don't think he could handle any more prison time.' She sits up from her pillow and bows her head.

'I told him I forgave him, and he looked at me, like... like the way he used to, before he ...did that shit to me. And he said, "I'm sorry, Cathy". That's how he'd call me when we were little.'

Back When

I asked to clean anywhere but there. I don't want her to see me like this. It is a miracle our paths haven't met, and I want to keep it that way. Not that I am embarrassed, well…; it's an honest job, more like, I'd have to explain why. Why for so many things. Why I never went to Oxford. Why I'd left her in the lurch that night, if I can remember all the details myself, that is… I know I owe her that, at the very least.

Everyone has gone home for the day. I browse her work, unhindered, again. *ES* whirled in the corner; this is hers. Such amazing talent. It's preternatural; my mind cannot encompass. I look deeply into each colour, each brushstroke. That fragmentation of light. The harmony of the whole composition. It is a three-canvased parallax of the same prospect. That place – is it real, or something she conceived from her own imagination? Those heavenly crepuscular rays that transcend into another realm. Where is such a place? That sky has the colour of my eyes…

It's strange how she could see so much beauty but never saw it in her face. How it had never crossed her mind that she was being bullied because of that beauty. Beauty is subjective, I know, but still; couldn't she see how far above the rest she was? I recall I had been about to tell her, but never got the chance because I had been ensnared by the others. No, that's not fair; I was equally to blame. Why had I been such an immature, weak fool and done their every bidding? Even Nick's. I had left her… alone, to fend for herself. I like the way I'd been so mad with what the bullies had done to her, and there I was, doing it to her myself… indirectly, perhaps, but… no; there is no excuse. It wasn't indirect if I were accomplice and not lifting a finger to stop it. I'm a total hypocrite.

I'll never forget the look on her face as she was running up that hill to catch the bus. There was blood on her face; I'd made her bleed.

I wish I could go back… run back to her, and hold her tight in my arms; make everything bad go away. Tell her I was sorry for being such a bastard. Never let her go again.

Dad, you were right; I'd done wrong, but it wasn't because of the one drag I had pulled on that joint – it was because of Eleanora…

I will never deserve your help.

I take one more look at the painting and smile, reminiscing on that time she'd insisted she didn't have an eidetic memory. Why would she deny something like that? A gift like –

My brain halts! *Eidetic memory*; from the Greek *eidos*: that which is seen. A stimuli of visual sensory. Yes! That is it! The fragmentation; its eidos. My mind goes into overdrive, as I figure out the sequence of components I'd have to put to create *my* eidos. It would take money to invent… shit. But it would be worth it in the end. Things could change. Things would take a turn for the better… I feel it.

I can't have run home faster. I unlock those corrugated iron hunks of crap and fling them open, get to my desk and draw an axonometric projection of an archetype in a speed of exhilarating enthusiasm. I need to get a state-of-the-art PC, like they have in the science engineering labs; only the best…

273

***

It is ready, in theory. I've been up all night completing the final, important touches. Now all that's left is to build it and test; do all the trial and errors necessary to make it perfect…

Chapter Forty-Nine

Now

'There is no doubt the defendants, Mr Henry Orme and Mr Liam Jackson, were intending to inflict grievous bodily harm on the victims: James Laidlaw and Eleanora Stephens.
'There is no doubt that the defendants knew where both would be, and they were lying in wait. They had, in short, conspired to cause serious wounding to the point of killing. For in the case of James Laidlaw, we are now in no doubt a gun had been pointed on his head, as forensics found an imprint of that said gun on the high-definition photograph taken of James Laidlaw's forehead at the scene of the crime. An imprint of which dimensions could fit a point-three-eighty calibre, semi-automatic pistol. It is true: the pistol was never shot, but that was only because they didn't want *anything that could be traced*. This doesn't annul Mr Orme's and Mr Jackson's intentions, however, which was to finish the job by other means: relentless beating.
'As for the victim, Eleanora Stephens, they had followed her, and found where she lived, and waited for the perfect time to run her down. Thankfully, their timing *wasn't* perfect…
'So, I put to you, ladies and gentlemen of the jury, what would have happened to James Laidlaw if our eye-witness, Eleanora Stephens, hadn't intervened? How far do you think the defendants were willing to go? And what if there weren't bollards in the street Eleanora Stephens had turned into? The indisputable fact that a car, travelling over forty miles an hour, will kill a human being on impact.' I shiver. I would have been dead for sure… James meets my eye then. He flinches. 'I think we all know the answer to those questions.'

Sharpe sits, arms folded, knowing his evidence is beyond a reasonable doubt.

Mr Boyd, gets up to deliver his closing statement. I am motionless in the backrow of the visitor's gallery, exhausted from my recent illness, but ears alert to hear the outcome. Kate wouldn't let me go without her, and now I have my head resting on her shoulder. She'd informed Aidan, Suze and Juliet; filled them in on everything. They are here, with me, a mixture of awe, anger and curiosity etched on their faces. I shut my eyes. The less I see, the better.

'My Lord, Ladies and Gentlemen of the jury,' Boyd begins. I keep my eyes shut, head throbbing with pain. I am by no means fully recovered. I need ibuprofen.

Boyd's rebuttal is weak. He grabs at straws, saying why should the defendants lie, when they'd already pleaded guilty to everything else? About how, if they really wanted James dead, they'd have done it. And if they really wanted to run me down, they would have, since a car is faster than a human running.

Kate snorts loudly, without volition. I open my eyes just in time to see her slap her palm over her mouth, mortified the judge has given her a dirty look. Ferguson fails to hide a stifled smile. James's mother and father turn to us, Elizabeth too. And most of the court, even James. Jackson looks straight at me, my heart speeds up erratically. I didn't want to meet their eyes, but now it's too late. It surprises me how forlorn he looks; if the jury find them guilty, it would be double attempted murder – a double, life-time sentence, on top of involuntary manslaughter.

My head, still resting on Kate's shoulder, feels a soft movement of air shifting; the tendrils of my hair swaying. I open my eyes again, to see James's mother looking sympathetically at me. She takes my hand and presses gently. For a small moment I want to tell her, in full detail, second by second, of what had transpired at Lara and Robert's party. She is here, in front of me; this is my chance, my opportunity…

'Thank you,' she whispers, 'for my son. Whatever the outcome, I know you saved him, and I will be eternally grateful.'

I shake my head. She is too kind; I don't deserve it. 'Mrs Laidlaw… I'm so sorry…' I breakdown in a sudden torrent of silent tears. She takes me in her arms, hushing me, patting my back, as I quietly sob in her shoulder. 'My dear girl… My dear, dear girl…' she whispers in my ear. 'It is not your fault. It is *not* your fault.'

Chapter Fifty

Back When

It is her…
She's cut her hair. All those lovely, long locks – gone!
Same smile; same smooth, milky skin; same lissome body; same beautiful eyes – they don't change, thank God.

I wonder if she still stammers. First time I heard it, I wanted to kiss her right then on the lips. I'd stopped myself last second, playing it cool.

We are well into winter now, and I was just finished with my rounds and making my way out, all wrapped up warm, hidden under a beanie and jacket, (which is just as well, otherwise she would have recognised me – if she remembers who I am at all) when she exited the Slade building, not having put her woolly on, and I saw to what extent she's done away with her hair. It is one of those really short, girly dos. That thing where they leave tufts of hair jutting out here and there. Pixie cut – that's it! It suits her; she has a great jawline, and those lips…

I let her walk on, chatting to her friends. I don't like the way one of those blokes is in her space. He looks like a prick. I can see how she avoids him; good girl. They're going down to The Crown for a bite to eat. I'll have to avoid that one…

I look at her. How happy she is. Looks like she finally found friends, true friends. She isn't unpopular here; they love her. I'm glad. It's what she deserves.

I turn towards the science-technology building; there are a few things I need to tweak on my inchoate mechanism. Carter allowed me to use some of the equipment, and I have been dying to test things out. It's progressing slowly and money is running out again; buying and shipping all the suitable alloys and silica has taken much from my meagre savings. Nick wants to help, he says. I tell him he needs to pull his shit together. No more dealers.

When he starts to regurgitate his affairs in the underworld, I cut him off; I don't want to know. No names, no places, nothing. His parents don't know. All they know of is his addiction, but they aren't much of a help; they're in denial. I talk to them about Nick whenever I get the chance, but they are at their wit's end and have given up telling him what to do. And his brother is doing some post-grad in Scotland, too far away to even be of any practical help, if not moral.

He said this dealer owed him. I have no idea what he is talking about, but the upside is: he'll have some cash to fund me, now he is back on his feet financially. I told him I didn't want drug money, and he reassured me it wasn't – this was pure honest bread. I gave him the benefit of the doubt and said nothing else. I have to make the most of whatever I am given and ration everything else, even training. Brian won't like that.

***

It is a success! My calculations and system, modulated to the right point. Now it is a question of complying with all motherboards and be more compact, and the lens; they are both far too large. They have to come down to pocket size.

There is still a lot of work to do, but I'm getting there. I'm bloody getting there.

Now

I lie down on my bed and cry; droplets of relief. The day has taken the last atom out of me, and I am prostrate with weariness. It seems like I have been sieved through an hourglass and have finally squeezed through the other end, battered, broken, abused. But alive.

It had been all rather anti-climactic actually; there had been no verdict from the jury – no nerve-wracking *how do you find the defendant?* And that moment's silence just before the juror opens his lips to announce the earth-shattering answer. No. As we had all been loitering in those grand hallways awaiting the outcome, Sharpe had come rushing out of some chamber, black cloak fluttering, with a grin on his face, heading for James. James is always easy to spot; head above the rest. Sharpe'd stopped, looked around searching, found me, and seeing I wasn't fit to get up from the chair, he gestured to James to approach me. As he did, he looked at me from top to bottom to ascertain I was on the mend. When his gaze reached my eyes, I showed him my gratitude for all he'd done to nurse me back to health with a timid smile. He smiled back.

All started to gather round, sensing the tenor of Sharpe's actions. Archer was there too. Ferguson mumbled something to him, and he gave a nod. I looked into Archer's eyes. They knew what was going on; they'd probably seen it a hundred times before.

'They've pleaded guilty,' Sharpe declared, 'for a reduced sentence.' Archer, then, gave me a wink, and I smiled.

277

There was an overwhelming rush of relief. That instance when you can finally breathe normally; let that blessed release flow in you like a cool surf after being too long under the sun.

James's family embraced him, the cries of joy reverberating all around.
I glanced at him, and he, me. It was all over.

***

I open the draw to my side table, and fumble for the notebook and pen. It is to be full disclosure; from day one. It is the last thing I have to do. No more tarrying.

Dear Mr and Mrs Laidlaw…

Chapter Fifty-One

Back When

It blew a fuse, and there were some persistent bugs in the code.
Nick got to it. He cleaned up after the summer and is now on some better plain. We've always worked well as a team; from day one: the day he invited me to his house when we were nine and showed me, with a well-chuffed face, his Linux OS. He is one of the best; that's what keeps him going: that intrinsic skill to blindly proceed like nobody's business. He got his degree early and all… I, on the other hand, have one more year. I can't complain though. I had to scrounge for almost three years before I could apply and pay for fees. But that is water under the bridge; my penance, I suppose.
'Bloody entrepreneurs,' Nick says, tickled with the idea, while bending over the keyboard, tapping at it, like some impassioned Amadeus. 'We'll make a bundle. I think I'll buy a yacht…' he muses.
'Mate. If you get this thing running,' I say to him, '*I'll* buy you a bloody yacht!'

***

There is little cash left. I broke Brian the news the other day: I'd have to quit. For the three years I've been fighting at his club, I've had to scrimp. Boxing had been the one thing I couldn't let go back then. I've kept at it because it keeps *me* going. Brian wouldn't hear of it, though. I told him things were tight, and he insisted I continue, and we'd find a solution. I told him I didn't want hand-outs.

''Oo said anyfing abou' 'and-outs?' he growled kindly. 'I said we'll find a solution, o'ight?'

'Don't leave us, Jamie.' It was Siobhan; the new girl. She'd overheard the conversation. I think she has a thing for me but …she isn't really my type. There's only one type for me.

***

We are close, very close. Just a few months, perhaps weeks, if funds will keep…

Maybe after Christmas…

She is in her last year as well. Then she'll be gone, and I won't see her again. I have to get this done fast; make some decent money, so I can move out of that shithole and find somewhere more… presentable. Perhaps then I could dare face her.

Now

I stare at the door. I blink… nothing changes.

I drop my gym bag to the side and stand, still unable to believe. What is going on? A fixed door? The peephole has a cap on it, and it's freshly painted in an odour-free titanium white. All signs of peeling gone. There is a bigger bolt too. What's the meaning of it? Has Mr Jones suddenly decided to fix the place? But without telling me he entered my premises? Unlikely… he would have told me; he is very explicit about things like that.

Kate? No… with her dissertation deadline around the corner, where would she have found the time?

That leaves my mother, sister and …James. And everybody knows both my mother and sister would never do something like that without the whole world knowing about it beforehand.

I pour myself some water and sit at my window seat, rest my head on the cool windowpane and listen to the welcoming cries. Market day.

My mind travels back; the prelapsarian of childhood years before poor Dad left us so unexpectedly. And there is a sudden yearning, a gaping hole, in much need to be filled. My body and my mind have felt the absence for too long, and now it is even more emphatic as *he* too is no longer part of my life… again. I feel a nostalgia to breath in that aroma, to observe that hue and to touch that pure aestival embrace, worse than Odysseus's nostos.

'August, right after the match, I'll go,' I ruminate.

I enter my bathroom and halt. *His* mirror. Whenever I look at it, my mind goes to him. And each time I feel that heart-wrenching gut-punch… All the memories of the past weeks are too vivid. I'll have to replace it…

I get under the shower, and no sooner have I begun to scrub – *Hang on… James?* Was it he who had come and fixed my door? Had he obtained my key somehow? Did I leave it open again? I am at a loss. No matter how he entered, I have a mind to give him some of my lip; tell him it is illegal. He can't just come in and… This is worse than what I had done with the bloody photographs. I must tell him to stop. I don't want his help. He needn't feel as though he has some sort of obligation.

As I get out the tub, something clicks. The window. The mirror. The door… it's my fix-it list. What is next?

I go to the kitchen, locate the little piece of paper with all the jobs needed around the flat from the message board.

Things to fix.
Door: peephole, bolt, paint.
Window
PC
My life, or a vertical garden for now!!!

What's he going to do next, buy me a PC? He'd better bloody not!

Chapter Fifty-Two

Back When

It works! It bloody works!

We tested, over and over, making sure nothing was wrong. All seems good. Of course, we used images from stock online, and now the only thing left is to feed images through the specialised lens, straight to the component and the software. There is nothing stopping us to announce it through Grapevine, however. Even at this stage, it is a very delectable and profitable piece of computing. The prototype is ready for use, and let the highest bidder win.

I think on how things will change. It could be mere hours until I stop sweeping floors!

But they say never count you chickens, and they are right. I am getting way ahead of myself.

'Hannah's got her girl in hospital, Jamie,' Janet phones to say. 'We'll be needing you to fill in at the Slade, at least for this week...'

'What's the matter?' I ask.

Janet sighs. 'They fear it's Leukaemia...'

'Shit...'

I have to go. What's one more week? Besides, they've been so good to me all these years, it would be crass of me not to help. I can't leave them in the lurch... no one, ever again.

Nick has found himself a job at some yachting company – his inside joke – to get a loan from the bank, that final monetary push to culminate our innovation. Have one or two prototypes more, on the ready. He arranged a notary to patent everything, somewhere near where he works in Canary Wharf, and now it is ready. I am to go this coming Monday, as soon as I get off.

Now

My exhibition went well. I can't say fantastic, but at least I got that degree I never thought I'd get.

The trail over, court adjourned, I'd gathered strength, and had all but glued my arse to my desk chair in order to focus on whatever I could for my thesis: *The Real Iconomachy*. I think I must have read every single publication circumferencing the historical issue, to the point of me not knowing whether it was night or day, as the hours passed. Professors were happy with my artwork but disappointed I hadn't strived for that extra substance they knew I had within me.

I sold all the landscape collection to some young, wealthy guy I knew I'd seen somewhere... but banged my palm on my forehead not being able to place where. He loved the parallax of the Thessalian plains I painted two years ago so much, he insisted he offer me more as a guarantee. I was sad to see them go, but I supposed I could always recapture them before I forgot entirely.

281

I searched for *him*, I won't deny it. Apart from a video of his fight posted online and his interview after, there was nothing else.

I click *Replay* on the video for the umpteenth time. 'I'd like to dedicate this win to my best friend,' he tells the camera, his face gleaming, but something sad passes over his eyes. He hesitates for an infinitesimal moment before saying Nick's name, then proceeds to acquaint the rest of the world on where, precisely, Nick is.

He graduated too, so I learnt from Harry, but I didn't see him at the ceremony. I only went… for him… and Mum, who insisted she wanted to see me in that stupid square hat.

My phone announces a caller. Withheld number.

'Hello?'

'Eleanora? This is Chief Inspector Daley.'

Chapter Fifty-Three

Back When

It is Saturday, I tell myself, and *Easter holidays*. There should be no reason for her to be there…

Just until Monday… at worst, till next Monday, depending on Hannah's daughter. Poor thing. Sometimes this world is too cruel.

I am early, wanting to finish on time. I want to try out the lens, and I know the perfect place.

I sweep carefully around easels and sculptures, admiring the work. I enter one of the classrooms and recognise her work instantly, and smile. It is propped up on a shelf on the wall amongst other crafts and paraphernalia for display.

They'd been doing some kind of figure, life-drawing piece; a naked guy, and by the looks of it, a rather seasoned one. Thank goodness it wasn't full frontal!

Time I finish up.

Ten or twelve students have accumulated throughout this morning, probably there to finish up something or other before everything closes for Easter. I pass them carefully, just in case she might be there, down the last stretch of corridor. The sun suddenly bursts through the window, and I idle for a minute to catch the warmth. I close my eyes and let it shine on me…

A door bangs, startling me out of my reverie. I turn to see who it is, but no one is there; just the hermetically-shut door staring back at me.

Get on with it, I scold myself. I am famished and need a bite to eat desperately.

One hour later, I plunge a bite of the mouth-watering burger. *Count Dracula with a succulent neck,* I think wryly. I'm at the pub I've been avoiding. Can't be bothered to avoid it today. I want to eat and eat well! I've almost forgotten how delicious the food is in here. It must take me two minutes flat to finish the rest.

As I am washing my hands in the men's, my phone buzzes: Nick.

'Get your arse over here now!' he says, enthusiasm dancing in his voice.

'What's happened?' I demand, a ripple of excitement knowing I'm about to hear good news.

'We've got a buyer, and you're not going to believe who it is! I'll come with the Tahoe. Don't be late!'

I run out, passing swiftly through the throngs of people now gathered in the pub, safe from the rain. Out through the swinging doors, headlong into the torrent of pelting water, feeling the coolness cleanse me, and head straight for Warren Street Station. I have to be quick; Nick wants me there as soon as can be, and I don't want to waste time; I need to put the lens to the test. If it works to the degree I hope it does, then we'll be selling my invention for a great deal more.

I take Victoria Line and change at Green Park, Jubilee Line. I let it transport me to the perfect paradigm of British heritage. Perfect because of what it symbolises. Perfect because it will be recognised worldwide.

I ascend at Westminster; Big Ben is towering above me. The rain has made it all the more perfect, as it stands stalwart and majestic, defiant to today's clime. I know "perfect" is already a superlative; you can't add "more" or "less" – something is either perfect or it's not. But allow me philosophise, and dub this an exception.

Quickly I prepare, scooting further down the bridge so my camera lens can scope the whole of the Houses of Parliament. I point it and let the eidetic image formulate. *One, two, three, four,* I count in my head. Finished, I make hasty tracks and run to the south bank, crossing over, diverging from puddles. I process the image of the London Eye too. Why not? Since I'm here…

That's it. I'm done. Off I run to Waterloo, my mission now accomplished here. Nick is waiting.

Now

And there it is: the PC.

What is he up to? Why is he doing this? The dichotomy if his actions are disorientating. Totally enigmatic. I tut and huff at his gall. Now I'm well pissed off. He didn't want my guilt money? I don't want his guilt gifts. He just wants to appease his conscience after telling me to fuck off. Say sorry because I *did* happen to save his life. And I suppose, no matter how much we may despise a person, if they've saved your life, you say thank you. *How can he despise you after what you felt when he held you in your bed?* my mind asks. I have been told that that particular organ of the male anatomy has a mind of its own…

I approach my little kitchen island where the box lies. The partly-bitten apple looking back at me, beguiling me to bite. No. Way.

I am back from the police station. CI Daley wanted to disclose the developments in the rape case. Foremost being, Robert Simmonds is currently in prison for a second account of ABH. Furthermore, that the girl – Tracy Gascoigne is her name – admitted she'd been assaulted, raped, off the record, and is still fixed upon not pressing charges. She is a happily-married mother now and has no wish to dredge up the murky waters of the unwanted past. Quite frankly, I don't blame her. Without warning, I see Lara's face loom before my eyes. I wonder if she ever found out about her half-brother.

I receive a text from Stacy as I stand contemplatively, still glaring at the PC. The 2nd of August is the charity fight, and she wants me to get my wrist checked, once again, before she goes through with any formal paperwork.

So, I think to go down to UCL, pick up some remaining art stuff, say goodbye to some people I never got to see at graduation and pop in the hospital around the corner for an X-ray. Kill two birds…

The temperature has risen to mid-twenties today, and everyone is donning the summer look. I've put on shorts. I haven't put on shorts in for ever. My legs have filled out, somewhat, with all that pumping of iron. I'm aware my self-confidence is amplifying. I took a picture of myself last night and compared it to the one I'd taken when I first started at the boxing club. There is a marked difference, and even that humble amount is enough for me to feel good about my body for once in my life.

(I had also flicked through the remaining pictures of him; the same memory card is still mounted on my phone – I never got to delete them all, and I don't want to).

***

I am sitting in the outpatients' waiting area. I am finished with Uni; collected some bits and bobs left from projects and said farewell to whomever I found.

I think of my parallax while I gaze out the glass wall, onto the street. I need to make more of those since they were so popular. Now that Kate is not paying half the rent, I have to find somewhere else to stay if I am ever to save enough money for a down payment on – I freeze. My heart leaps, as if seeing a revenant.

It is him! It is him walking in the street…

T-shirt, cargo shorts and that sandy-blond hair, now up in a scruffy man bun. I breathe out. Oh, how that beauty never falters. I feel his body wrapped around mine, the sensation of that night when he drove out the fear. His closeness, his protection, his discretion to stay and help. He needn't have done it… he needn't have continued his presence in my life – fixing my flat and the PC offering. It calls to mind that time when he'd acted the same way after he'd been sucked in by Bianca. He'd never severed our link. He had taken care never to ignore me. But he is under no obligation now. He needn't, *mustn't* continue this link. Our lives are no longer side by side. I have to tell him.

I get up, heart full-throttle to follow him, but come to a sudden halt. I remember what I promised. *Never…* I stay put.

I watch him carefully. Seems he's coming in. Yes. He saunters towards the hospital entrance, up the small flight of stairs. He is holding something. What is that? A bar of chocolate? Should I speak to him now? – No. Not here. Somewhere quieter, and where I can give him back his PC. I crouch a little, watching, as within a few strides, he reaches the lift, pressing the button to summon it. I move surreptitiously closer, his back to me. He turns his head to the side. Can he feel my stare? The doors open just then, and he gets on. I've just about seen his hand reach pretty high to hit the button; he's going way up, when he turns to the front, and I quickly swing behind the wall. I hear the doors slide shut and bend my head around the wall again.

1st floor, 2nd floor, 3rd… up and up to the 11th floor. Then the lift comes down again, without him. He could have got off on any of those floors, true, but it is a slow day (summer holidays), and the lift seems not to have made a stop; it ascended swiftly, and I am willing to bet he is there – on the 11th floor.

What is on that floor? *Who* is on that floor?

I check the hospital guide map. It is a children's ward. I instantly think of Elizabeth, but calm when I see it's for kids up to the age of 12.

My name is called just then and have no other choice but to go for my X-ray, curiosity filling my every nerve.

It's none of your bloody business, I reprimand myself.

My X-ray takes under five minutes to complete, and I wait for the radiograph to be given to me, and the findings. Fifteen minutes go by, I am given my X-ray and can leave, but don't. I sit down again, in the waiting area, this time behind my X-ray envelope and wait, eyes riveted to the lift. It is over ¾ of an hour when the doors to the lift open, and he paces out behind some others, head above the rest. I place the whole envelope in front of my face and shrink behind the counter of the reception desk. He exits the hospital, and I bounce to my feet, making a bee-line for the lift. Inside, I hit 11.

I'm not following him, not in the literal sense… I pick at my nail. I should have been a bloody litigator. I could talk my way out of being guilty of murder. I think Kate's extremities have rubbed off on me. Gee whiz.

The doors roll open and I step out, not having a clue what I am looking for.

I walk along the corridor, peeping furtively into some rooms. Children of all sizes, either up or asleep in their cots, parents encircling them, and smiling, friendly nurses, adjusting tubes and chatting along. They are keeping a cheery mood in spite of the harsh reality of their surroundings. There is distant crying; some infant in pain. My breath hitches. I don't know how nurses do it sometimes. Day in, day out, witnessing the suffering… and of children. It takes a special kind of person to choose that line of work.

I pass a door, then stop. The face. I recognise the face. I turn back and look through the door again. Yes; I've seen that face before… and anathematise inwardly, as once again, not knowing where.

She is in her thirties. Medium build, long, light-brown hair, round brown eyes, and a countenance like she's been dragged through the streets of London on a rope.

'Can I help you?'

I blink; I was staring obtrusively and didn't realise. And without thinking I say, 'I'm sorry, but I think I've seen you somewhere before, but I can't remember where.'

She pulls her head back at this non sequitur.

'Sorry,' I apologise again. 'That sounded a bit –'

'Mummy?'

We both turn. A little girl is lying on a bed to the woman's side. What a darling cherub she is, but a cherub with no hair to speak of. I bite my lip, suppressing a convulsion to cry.

'What is it, Millie?' her mother asks.

'I want some more chocolate. Jamie said I could have as much as I wanted.'

'Oh, all right. Have another bite.'

And there, on the bed-side table, is the same bar of chocolate I saw James carry earlier. And in a flash, it comes to me. For once in my worthless life, I remember where I've seen her. UCL; she is one of the other cleaners.

'I'm sorry for disturbing you,' I utter stupidly, suddenly feeling totally out of place. Both mother and daughter look at me questioningly. 'Is there anything I can do?' I ask out of politeness… and genuine concern. The mother stares at me for a second, obviously wondering why I am still there.

'I'm a student at UCL,' I inform her quickly. 'Well, former student.' And she instantly smiles and settles. 'That's where I've seen you, right?' I add.

'Yeah,' she confirms. 'Unfortunately, I haven't been there in a while.' She glances at her daughter. 'It's been difficult, what with Millie's dad stationed in Cyprus. They are preparing to be deployed to Syria.'

'Oh, I see.' I do. I understand what she is saying. Not only is her daughter floating precariously between life and death, soon, so will her husband be.

'But friends and family have been a great help. Can't complain. Jamie, for example – the friend who gave Millie that bar of chocolate – has insisted he pay for any expenses…' She swallows, wiping her eyes. 'He's been so kind…'

'Mummy. Stop crying!' says Millie, her little face cross. 'The doctors say I'm going to be fine.'

'I know, darling,' the woman says, caressing her daughter and giving her a kiss on her small, bald head. 'I know.'

'And Jamie said I could go to his house, as soon as I leave here, and explore the back of his garden. He told me it's along the canal, and I am welcome to search for hedgehogs under the brambles,' Millie declares with innocent enthusiasm to me.

'That's lovely,' I say, echoing her enthusiasm. 'Brambles are a great place to find hedgehogs.'

'I love hedgehogs,' she states, then yawns.

'And how are we doing here?' calls a nurse, bustling into the room just then. She has a *shufti* at Millie's chart and prepares to take her blood pressure.

It is my cue to exit. I nod a *goodbye* at the mother and leave quietly.

Chapter Fifty-Four

Back When

My whole body seizes in excited anticipation.

I feel the vibration first, then the rumble... it coincides with my senses. I jump off the escalator and run.

The rolling stock blusters through the tunnel and decelerates noisily to a stop. Both platform doors and train doors yawn wide. Hordes of people get off, a stampede scattering left and right. But even more get on. I'm wedged by the door, but I don't care. I couldn't care less if I were practically folded in two. All I care is for me to be there already!

The doors shut, and we are finally on the move. The train's going slow; too heavy. *I want to get out and give it a heaving push*, I think musingly, as I stare out the window into nowhere.

But... what's that? *Who* is that? Is it... *her*?

Those were her eyes... Now they're gone!

Gone...

It couldn't have been.

Now

HM Land Registry. Enter.

So, he has a house by the canal, does he? Right!

***

It is afternoon, I am on the Tube with a big box on my lap, hidden within a large toy-shop bag. I acquired the toy-shop bag when I went to buy Millie a big, fluffy hedgehog that morning, and had popped by to give it to her. The delight on her wee face was indescribable, as was her mother's. Hannah, she'd said, giving me a warm hand. *He* hadn't been there, thank goodness. I want to be armed with his gift before I confront him; shove it back in his face. It had crossed my mind to give it to Kate, but that would mean I accept it. No. I do not accept it. If gifts aren't from the heart, I don't want them.

I am on my way to his home; a house. There are no other James Laidlaws residing near a waterfront; it has to be his. I am nervous, I have to admit, on what might be said or done, but the stronger sense of anger, dignity, eclipses everything else. I am determined. Ready.

***

This is definitely no storeroom.

I stand opposite, agog. At this vantage point, I can just about see all the way through the Georgian-styled, brick detached, right out onto the first shrubs of the back garden. The evening sun shines directly through the front door, sending a spectrum of dazzling brightness straight to my retinas, like dancing fluorescent fairies, rendering all other objects into shadow. It shines directly through the front door because the front door is wide open, showing an open plan all the way to the back of the house, where the wall is one great opening. In fact, the whole place is open; under renovation.

The house is full of movement; builders moving in and out of rooms, hardhats on and tool belts hanging from hips, the fuss and commotion emanating from within. A thwack of a hammer. An electrical grating of a power tool.

I move my arms, adjusting the box which holds the PC, distributing the weight differently, as my right arm is getting numb. I have done away with the bag; I want to give it back to him in the exact same way he gave it to me. Only now, it is going to be difficult. How can I go in and confront him with all these people around?

I should go, are my thoughts, and am about to, when I hear someone shout in a deep Dublin accent, 'Hey, Boss. Dere's a damsel in distress standin' outside your house,' he says teasingly. 'I t'ink she may be lost.' There are some laughs.

'Is she beautiful, O'Connell?' Comes his answer from within, keeping up the fun. He thinks O'Connell is pulling his leg.

'She's flammin' gorgeous!'

I blink.

'You been inhaling the adhesive spray again, O'Connell?' calls another builder. I hear laughs.

'If she's flammin' gorgeous,' says another man's voice, 'then I t'ink I'll go out and point her in the right direction, eh?' More laughing, and what seems to be Gaelic skylarking.

'Boss? You'd better take a look. She's carryin' somethin' heavy,' O'Connell tells him, the jesting gone. He can probably see the unease I wear. And before I know it, James is already a shaded silhouette in his front door. Light rays resting on the top of his head, like a golden halo. I can't tell his expression because he has his back to the setting sun, and the beams are in my eyes. He doesn't move though; probably stunned I am there, and wondering how I found out where he lived.

I cross the quiet street, PC jutting out like a dish tray in my arms, and reach his front gate mere yards from him. Without a word, he paces towards me, now shielding the sun from my irises. In overalls and holding a hammer; I can see him better. He is hot; heated from his toil, helping the builders. His cheeks are rubicund. But I am disheartened by his expression, though; the disappointment of me being there – I can tell. Does he think I followed him again? Why, oh why, does he dislike me so much?

'I didn't follow you,' I say, no preamble. 'Just want to make that clear. I came to return this.' He stares at the box and shakes his head slowly. He opens his mouth to say something but just harrumphs, incredulous. 'How did you find me? How… Here, give it to me,' he says, slotting the hammer in his belt and taking the PC off my hands, correctly figuring it is getting too heavy, and places it on a ledge. 'I'm not taking it by the way; it's yours. But tell me how you found me.'

I blink at his absoluteness and harrumph myself. 'I don't want it –'

'We're not having this argument now.'

'Yes, we are, James. We have to.'

He takes in a breath.

'You can't just come to my flat and –'

'And what?'

'And fix things like that… without asking… a-and buy things… I mean, how did you get in? Did you get a key cut while I was ill in bed?'

'No,' he says, looking away. I search his face for a clue.

'Well, how then, James? I'm waiting…'

'Kate.'

I raise my brows, flabbergasted. 'Kate?!'

'I found where she works and asked her to give me a key.'

'She never told me…' I mumble, hurt. We never keep secrets like that from each other.

'I asked her not to tell you,' he admits. I stand inept for some moments.

'Why?' I ask. 'I-I don't understand. Why are you doing this? Is it because I saved your life? I don't want anything in return for that.'

'No,' he says quietly. 'Not just because of that…' He is being cryptic, but I want to know. I want to know where I stand.

'Is it because you feel sorry for me?'

He is puzzled. 'No. Why would I feel sorry for you? You have a good life, good friends, you're independent; I'm proud of you, not sorry for you.'

'Then why? I'm confused.'

'I just wanted to help you, all right? It was the least I could do.' There is vehemence and irritation in his answer.

'Well… thank you,' I say a bit sheepishly. 'But please don't go buying me a vertical garden. If you do, I'll bring it right back to you,' I warn him.

He grins slightly. 'OK. I won't… but the PC is yours.'

'No! I cannot accept it! Please understand…'

'Understand what?'

I try to calm the quake within, as I am about to throw his words back at him, and say silently without umbrage, 'I don't want your guilt gifts.'

Something paves its way over his eyes, and he looks down. He has the decency to look sorry, demeaned.

'Do you understand now? It's against my principles to accept a gift like this.'

He lets out a sigh. 'Eleanora,' he says under some control. 'It is not a guilt gift.'

I open my mouth to protest, but I don't get a word out.

'If you ever need it, it'll be here waiting for you,' he tells me. I look directly into his eyes, and can't stop mine from welling. I hold back the tears, though, hard as that is just then, and look away. Why is he so bent on it?

'Eleanora?' His voice is hushed. 'How did you find me?'

'Luck.'

'Luck?' He folds his arms, somewhat diverted. 'Don't really believe in luck…'

'Me either, really,' I say, thinking about Gran's philosophy on that.

No such thing as luck. Why do we say good luck *when someone is sitting for a test? It's like we're saying it's OK if you haven't read because luck will make you pass – which is wrong. Luck in Greek is also fate… and we are all masters of our own… that's why we must always read for tests; never rely on chance. And that's why Greeks don't say* good luck, *we say* good success.

'BOSS!' booms a builder from a glassless window. 'We'll be needin' you a sec, in the kitchen. Just some last adjustments, and we'll need to finish up with the windows before we leave. It'll be dark in a couple of hours.'

'I'll be right there,' James calls back. Then he squints inside, then back at me, something on his mind. 'Come with me. We'll talk in the garden,' he suggests. 'Let me see what they need first.'

He takes the PC and guides me inside, placing it on a chair. I can't stop myself staring at the lovely interior and think how good it is he has this; that after so many years of a dingy, mildewed garage, he is finally living the way he ought. James sees me looking around and gazes at me intently. Does he want to know what I think? What does he care what I think? I smile awkwardly, nonetheless. I *am* happy for him, I can't deny.

The kitchen is at the back and its door, or whole glass wall, leads to the garden. It is almost finished; a utopia for any chef. I stumble in awe at the vast island and the pots and pans hanging from the ceiling rail above it, and feel a sudden, small pang of… what is it? Loss? Can you feel loss for something you've never had? Yes. I think you can. You can empathise with limitless ability. I feel like everything is unobtainable. Unreachable. The shipwrecked man watching a boat sail in the distance and knowing, without a shadow of a doubt, that no matter how hard he cries for it to come, it never will. Denied. I guess Siobhan will have that *obtainability* now.

A house with a garden, preferably near a waterway, someday with someone, I think and lighten my dispirited heart. I will have my house one day. I will not deny myself my own happiness.

I walk on through, leaving James to discuss whatever with the builder, and pad down the long lush tussocks of grass of a much-in-need-of-a-mow lawn. I continue to walk down towards the weeping willow at the end of the garden, curious to see why it hangs so low. And upon reaching its side, I discover its trunk is rooted on a lower level of ground; on the embankment of the canal. Regents Canal. Jesus… he has his own private landing, giving him direct access to the water. How beautiful.

I close my eyes for I don't know how long, and listen to the breeze stir the curtains of leaves, breathing life into them. A glorious psithurism, like a distant waterfall, causing my spine to shiver.

'Where were we?' he says, making me jump. I turn around. He is holding two glasses of lemon juice, offering me one.

'I'm all right, thanks,' I tell him, refusing it.

'What? Don't you want to see if Lizzy followed your recipe faithfully?'

Heat singes my cheeks; he knows of my blog. Of course, he does – Elizabeth said she'd told him. I suddenly remember – I promised her a painting.

'Oh,' I say, fazed. I extend my hand and take the proffered glass. It is straight from the fridge, the condensation already apparent. It is cold to the touch and welcoming; it has been a hot day. 'Cheers!' I mumble and bring it to my lips, feeling his eyes on me, and take a sip. He sips too. It is very well done. The sharp, refreshing lemon and the sweet blend of sugar are well balanced. I make a sound of surprise and smile, licking my lips. 'This is pretty good. In fact, I think it's better than mine!'

He laughs then, and I almost want to cry. Laugh, James, laugh. Be happy. It's your time now. I am keeping it together though. I keep it together…

'I'll tell her that. She'll be happy to know.'

'Yes. I suppose the student must surpass the teacher,' I say placidly.

I want to ask him how she is. How his mother is, his father. Does he know of my letter? But the purport of this meeting has no air of blithe discourse, even if he had laughed but seconds ago.

I put the glass down on a small, round garden table and swallow, clearing my throat. I throw back my fringe and my now very long strands of hair that have blown in my eye, and answer his question.

'You want to know how I found you?'

'Please.'

'I went to University College Hospital the other day –'

'Ah!' he says, cutting me off. 'You saw me there?'

'Yes.'

'And what? Did you follow me home?'

'No!' I cry, affronted. 'I told you I didn't! I'll never do that again. I gave you my word.'

'Sorry,' he says, disconcerted, shifting his weight on his other leg. 'Carry on.'

'I saw you walk in with a bar of chocolate in your hand and go to the eleventh floor… well, I presumed.' And I explain to him how I remembered Hannah's face from somewhere, and saw the bar of chocolate on the table beside Millie's cot. 'I never forget images, like the time I'd drawn the bus driver, but couldn't place him. Do you remember that bus ride, back then, when you saw my sketch?'

'Yeah.' He smiles, but it doesn't reach his eyes.

'But this time, for the first time, I remembered where I'd seen her, and then little Millie started talking about you, where you lived and, well, Her Majesty's Land Registry did the rest.'

He is silent, thinking.

'You were so adamant about that,' he says softly.

I blink. 'About what?'

'About not having an eidetic memory… Why? Why did you hide it?'

A sparrow flutters to my glass on the table, jouncing its head, measuring my drink up for size. 'Because I was bullied for it, James,' I voice clearly. A declaration. A fact.

'What?' He's appalled.

'Yes. Every time I'd open my sketchbook I was taunted and smacked and kicked, the pages ripped from my hands and thrown into puddles…' I shrug and calmly continue. 'And so, I learnt to hide it. To draw in secret. That's when I realised I had the gift of remembering everything I'd seen around me, and I thanked God for it. Drawing was my only *querencia* back then. Sorry. That's Spanish for –'

'I know what it means.' His eyes pierce mine. 'It was your source of mental strength. To be your most authentic.'

'Yes.' I smile remembering his cleverness. 'If I didn't have that… I don't know where I would have been. The upside was, I didn't have to draw in front of the bullies anymore, and I was heartened. Because of course, it didn't stop the bullying entirely, but at least it was one less thing to badger me about, to make fun of me. I suppose …I *was* a little bit weird.' I hear leaves rustle behind me, then the breeze drifts to us, stroking our hair. He is silent.

'But,' I continue, 'who cares? I don't think about things like that anymore. They're so unimportant, so childish. We were young. We were stupid. Life goes on, eh?' I end in a non-smile. James, however, doesn't find this light, and disagrees with a gesture of the head.

'Eleanora, I…' he begins, and stops. He looks away, not wanting to meet my eyes, as his jaw grinds. I know that action. I know why. He is feeling guilty. He had been a part of that bullying. It may have been brief in comparison to the years I had endured, but if he feels remorse over it, then I know he can't despise me. It proves he cares. But I don't want him to think it hurts me still. It doesn't! My life doesn't even compare to it in the least, and it actually insults me he thinks so. He himself said I was independent, had a good life. Proud of me… What did he mean by that?

'James?' He is rock-still. 'Look at me.'

He does, then he takes in a breath, and closes his eyes. A tear falls. A tear! I feel a tremor take hold of me.

'No, James, don't! It doesn't matter; what you did… It doesn't!' I cry, the emotion strong. He remains downcast.

'James.' I take a step towards him. I put a hand on his. Will he accept it? He locks his hand in mine, fast. Then, turning to me, bringing my hand closer, he twists my forearm a degree, finding the faint scar from my brush with death, stroking it with his thumb. He knows where it is; Elizabeth has told him. He looks so sorry. I don't want to cry, but the tears are on their way. He needs to know I'm OK. 'I heard you, you know, the night you nursed me. I never got to thank you for that. And I accept your apology… but please, don't think about it any longer. I don't care about silly things like that; I'm OK. Everything's fine. You're fine. Look at you! Look at this beautiful house! Your invention, *your* mind made this happen. This would have come to you, no matter what had transpired six years ago. You leave that behind now, everything behind; be happy.'

He squeezes my hand and says gently, 'No. No, Eleanora… If it weren't for you, I wouldn't have thought of it.'

'What –' I have no time to finish my sentence, as he takes me hurriedly into the house by our locked hands. Turning a corner, into a small, fully-renovated study, he stops and faces me in front of a fireplace.

'Oh, my God!' I gasp. There, atop the mantelpiece, hangs my triple-canvased parallax. My Thessalian plains.

'I bought them,' he states.

'But I sold them to some guy…'

'I asked him to buy them for me, make the best offer so you wouldn't give them to anyone else. Luke is a good friend of mine.'

'Thought he looked familiar…'

'He was at the wedding.'

'Ah, yes. That's where; the group of guys you were with.'

'Yes, that's right… Well, it was when I saw these paintings, I was inspired. The idea came to me for my archetype.'

I frown in confusion. 'But I exhibited them years ago,' I say. 'What do you mean?'

'Do you think I never saw you at UCL?'

I breathe suddenly in. He saw me? Good God. My heart pumps violently, sending the blood straight to my face in a fierce blush. 'What…?'

'I saw your work, and I knew you were there. You'd started to sign your canvases too. E S; there was no mistaking them. It must have been when you were in your second year when I saw you one day, coming out of the Slade with some friends. It took me a moment to realise it was you because you'd cut your hair so short… Anyway, about two years ago, as I was cleaning, I saw these canvases and thought about you. I was amazed you could capture all that expanse, all that ineluctable beauty, and remembered how you'd tried to hide your eidetic memory, and no sooner had I thought "eidetic", than it hit me. Eidos. That's when my invention came to life in my mind. Right there, looking at that.' He indicates to Thessaly.

I am breathing hard. All this information… He'd seen me? He'd seen my work? His idea came from my parallax?

'I don't know what to say…' I am quiet, my brain racking. 'What do you mean you saw my work and knew I was there? E S could have stood for anything.'

'I recognised it.'

'You recognised it?' I am both astonished and incredulous. 'How?'

He looks at the parallax and blinks a couple of times, pondering. 'I remembered your style.'

'Remembered?' I don't hide my confusion.

'I'd seen your work on the Hilsmond website,' he says, now turning his eyes to me. 'You'd been given merit. They were praising your paintings. They had uploaded a few, and that's how I knew.'

I stare at him dumbfounded, and all at once remembering how I'd done the same to see if Milden had any information on him. I remember finding his A-Level results. Two A starred and one A.

I am still looking into those beautiful eyes. How he knows me so well. How he knows every delineation. How can I not have him in my heart, even knowing he is with another? I am lost.

'I'm sorry, Eleanora. I'm sorry for being a hypocritical bastard. Telling you the bullies had to stop, and then becoming one myself. I'm sorry for leaving you, deserting you. I was an idiot.' His eyes brim, glistening at the edges. His cheeks are on fire.

I shake my head emphatically. 'I told you it doesn't matter,' I whisper, afraid to raise my voice else it crumbles.

'It does! I have to say what happened, why. You told me everything at the wedding, now let *me* confess.'

I feel my tear ducts tingle, my eyes seep in moisture.

'I'm not trying to make an excuse for myself; there is no excuse for my behaviour.' He droops his head and inhales slowly. 'It started when Nick asked me to help him with the girls. He'd no experience, and in the beginning, I did it for him. I had no intention of getting myself involved with them. I was quite happy chatting with you on the bus. I shouldn't have continued, that was my mistake; for not turning away when I should have. Nick pleaded, "one more day, Jamie boy, please, one more day", and I did it for him.' James swallows. 'Nick was the best friend I ever had…'

'James…' A tear drips from my jaw.

'I tried to talk to you, but you'd become distant, so I thought I'd better leave it. Perhaps I was too spineless to say I was sorry. I was young and stupid, as you say… There were only two months left of school, and I'd be gone anyway, and thought it was for the best. But as time went by, I couldn't stop thinking about you; the injustice. It heckled me, you know. It wasn't me! That's why I'd try to catch your eye. I'd even started to call Elizabeth, El at one point. I had to see you, to talk to you. I thought at the party would be a good opportunity; to explain, to apologise. One last time to see you. To be with you. I couldn't go away without that.

'I'd only said those words to those bitches so I could indulge them, and then leave as quickly as I could to find you... but you'd left by then. So, I thought to leave too, but I couldn't go without Nick; not in the state he was. I had to drive him home. As I was luging him down the stairs, I heard the sirens...'

My heart bleeds; a horrendous undercurrent of grief. 'I'm so sorry...' I whisper. I want to hold him, put my arms around him tight, prove to him how sorry I am, profess it was always him I cared for. I love. But I don't. I can't. There is a solid wall blocking me, barricading me in each direction, and her name is Siobhan. 'Will you ever forgive me?' I whisper. I look up at him. I beg. My heart will crack.

'Eleanora...' he begins reproachfully.

'Please James. Don't tell me it wasn't my fault when we both know it was. I need to know if you forgive me.'

One heartbeat, two heartbeats – 'Yes,' he says gently, coming towards me. 'I forgive you.'

We stand in silence; even the builders seem to have laid their tools to rest, conscious of our torment. Then I convulse, uncontrollable tears fall from my eyes. 'Thank you, James.' And before I know it, he has me in a soft embrace, as I cry into his chest. A chest, a body, a soul I crave to be near me always. I hear his heart beat and cry more knowing it will never be so. 'I forgive you. Shhh... I forgive you...' He rocks us unperceptively, hushing our pain. 'Forgive me... Forgive me too, Eleanora... I'm sorry for hurting you. So sorry for saying those things.' I nod my answer. I cannot speak. 'And... thank you for saving my life.'

The words ring deep, permeating through me, right to my nucleus. I exhale with a sob. 'You're welcome, James,' I answer, barely audible. He slowly releases his arms, and I behold those beautiful eyes for a second. Then he moves to a corner of the room, reaches for something, and hands it to me. My cashmere jumper – the one I used to protect his head. It has been cleaned. 'I owe you my life,' he whispers, and there is that look again. I shake my head. 'You don't owe me anything.' He is going to say something more but stops himself.

'I'd best get going,' I mutter. There is nothing more to be said. Explanations have been given. It is over. It is all over. There is no reason for me to be in his life any longer.

James walks me to the door. O'Connell and his team are shuffling about, trying to be polite about it as possible.

Suddenly, I have a query. 'James? Why had Nick asked for my forgiveness? Do you know?'

He pauses, thinking back. 'We'd had a fight over the girls at one point. I told him I'd had enough; their company was boring, and wanted to focus on A Levels. At first, he begged me to not back out, but after a while understood how much better your company would have been, for me, at least. Then he realised he had been to blame for depriving me of your company, and I suppose, you of mine.'

'Poor Nick,' I say, almost to myself. 'You know, he never stopped talking to me those remaining months at Milden.'

James nods. 'I know… He was a good kid.'

I walk out into the sun, mellowed, silent.

'Eleanora?' James calls to me, as I am about to reach the gate. 'Why were you at the hospital, if you don't mind me asking?'

'X-ray. For my wrist. They need to see if I'm all right to box.'

'Are you?'

'They say I am.'

He bites down on his jaw; something is bothering him.

'What is it?' I ask.

'Make sure your hand is well rested. Do your training a week before the fight if needs be. You don't want to injure it again.'

I open the gate and walk out onto the pavement. I look up at his house and declare, 'She'll love it.'

He blinks. 'What –'

'BOSS!' O'Connell shouts, stopping him. 'We need you upstairs! The bleedin' door won't open in the guestroom!'

'Goodbye, James,' I say. I don't wait for his reply. I'm running far, far away.

Chapter Fifty-Five

Back When

I am lying in my bed, half excited, half wary. I should be happy, rejoicing still, but something is off. All the paperwork is done; it is officially ours. Nick and I are full and rightful owners, signed and sealed. An amazing,

297

enthralling sense of accomplishment has nestled within me. So, why am I feeling paranoid? It's true, if anyone got their hands on the component and software they'd come into a fine fortune. But the only way they'd attain my creation, without my permission, would be over my dead body. And they would easily kill for this kind of money.

We told the notary we'd got an offer already, and he said he'd get the papers ready for the transaction. I can't wait to get the component off my hands. Let it be someone else's responsibility. Nick and I had jumped with joy, high-fiving and hooting with happiness, like a couple of hooligan school kids on a football-match win, as we left the solicitor's office.

I left him and went home with one of the fragile components, swaddled safely in bubble wrap; a nice, tight parcel, and Nick went home with the other we'd made for safe keeping. The buyers were to come from America in a few days. Everything was set.

I sprinted down the escalators at Canary Wharf Tube Station, mind rejoicing with the day's events. I had the most precious object I'd ever owned in my jacket, and all I could think was to hide it in that secret nook in the garage, fast. My mind was guarded, I mustn't lose it, I must conceal it, until I could hand it over, with great joy, for the perfect price.

It felt strange, like eyes were already on me, but I brushed off that thought. Who could know it was me? My face wasn't in circulation anywhere, nor my personal details. Nick had been the front, the rep, on public domain, not me.

At Camden I wanted to bolt out of the station; get home as fast as my legs could carry me. I walked briskly, in and out of people, avoiding any contact. Quick…

One more turn, I got my keys ready. I slammed shut the iron door and padlocked inside. In the darkness, I found the nook and safely placed the parcel in there. I let out a breath I had no idea I had been keeping in for so long. I got changed; put my tracksuit bottoms on and lit the laptop. I had my thesis to finish.

I typed for a bit, retouching some phrases that didn't quite make sense, and got up for a stretch. My muscles were aching.

My phone rang: a withheld number. It was the fourth one today. I answered it, but again, no one replied.

'Shit!' I shouted. 'Fuck!' I didn't like it. Who was hounding me, taunting me? *No, Laidlaw, get a grip! It's impossible. Nobody knows who you are.* I was being illogical. They could simply have a wrong number.

I made sure everything was secure, turned off all lights and laid in the eerie silence.

***

I cannot sleep. I phone Nick. He doesn't answer; his phone is unobtainable. I get up, tiptoe to the sink and find that chef's knife. I put it under my pillow, and lie down again. I turn left side, then right. I can't find a position to relax me, let me sleep. It's futile; I'm too restless. What was that *she'd* said once? *From your mouth to God's ear?* Yes, that's it. And for the first time in years, I pray. I actually pray in silence.

Dear God, help me… It takes me a short while, but my lids get heavy.

***

I wake to the sound of my phone's annoying vibration next to my ear, squinting at the first hints of sunrise that are seeping through my curtain. Freddy? What could Nick's brother – Shit!

'Freddy? What's happened? Is Nick all right?' I demand. I shiver at the premonitory silence.

'He was in an accident last night.' I hear the tears in Freddy's voice. 'He's in a coma, Jamie.'

Now

I stare at my fix-it list and pluck it from the board. Then I crumple it, and am about to throw it on the floor in vexation, when I notice writing on the other side. I flip over the piece of paper, and to my horror, for I'd forgotten what I'd written, gaze at the words in front of me:

Secret wish-list:
 House with garden, preferably near a waterway, with someone, someday…

I grunt ironically. *He stole my idea…* then on a sardonic note, *perhaps we might become neighbours!*

I walk to the window and pull it up. Altostratus wisps ornament the fair blue, as heat wafts in. I turn to the few paintings I have left and find the one she wanted. I bought bubble wrap, heavy-duty postal packaging paper and duct tape. I proceed to cover *The Boxer* up carefully. I write the name and address, and half an hour later, hand it over to the courier. It will be delivered to her doorstep tomorrow morning.

***

The match is in two weeks. I am getting a bit anxious to tell the truth. Not about winning or losing, more like, for not making a complete arse of myself in front of hundreds of people.

Stacy had told us details weeks earlier. It is to raise money for breast-cancer treatment, and the boxers are only women, some recovered breast-cancer patients themselves. There are to be five matches in random order, the weights being; lightweight, light welterweight, welterweight, middleweight and light heavyweight, and we are to be told, in the beginning of the event, who would be fighting first, second, third, and so forth. It isn't going to be amateur-boxing rules, but professional, in other words, longer bouts and no head protection. You could sponsor the boxers online or at the event itself.

Boxers and their teams are allowed to invite a plus-one for free, but everyone else has to pay the staggering ticket price. This doesn't hinder the event being almost sold out a week before it starts. Who can turn down an opportunity to experience London from so high up, and donate to cancer research at the same time?

It is to be a fun event, everyone dressed in boxing attire, or whatever they have near to it. It's summer anyway, so, I reckon it wouldn't be far from what we wear this time of year anyhow. Better than a stuffy suit.

There are to be articles written in women's fashion magazines, boxing magazines and the like, and anywhere else affiliated with the event. It is a magnanimous cause, and I feel honoured to be a part of it despite the stifling pressure from all the media hype centred on it. I'm not used to this type of attention or social media. Writing a food blog, you are unseen, concealed, behind pictures of food and recipes. This boxing match? My face, my body, my actions will be recorded; I'll be known. I don't want to get caught cold.

You'd better put on a good show, then. Can't back out now…

As I am having a bout in the ring with the other girl in our club, who is also lightweight, Chloe, I have a sudden itching to know just how Sophie had done her magic. Out of the blue, I get these total lucid moments when conditioning, or in the middle of a bout, and today is no different. My mind goes to Archer too, as I give an upper hook to Chloe's jaw. I think of the trial, the pumping of questions by the barristers, Nick's burial rites, Kate and Ferguson – they are seeing one another now. Kate had called him her angel and he'd blushed, when they came round a fortnight ago. I've never seen a copper blush, and it was obvious what they meant to each other. Then I drift to *him*. Saving him. My parallax hanging on his mantelpiece. He will always have a part of me in his house. His words; he *had* wanted to be with me on the night of the party. Chloe almost knocks me one, but I bob and weave, the action snapping me back to the ring. Then I land her a combination, and it sends her tottering back, receiving praise from Stacy, who has a short monologue saying how I am a natural, and if I keep it up, I'll make it to the pros. Of course, that is OTT.

But Sophie. How did she do it? Bit late in the day, I know, but still...
curiosity is killing me.

*Archer told me no one had hacked the system. How did you
do it? I know it's been weeks, but I just got
ridiculously curious. Thanks again. El.*

I decide to take a shower before I refresh my email again.

*Simple. It's a dormant virus. It's only activated when
a foreign computer hacks into the system. If Archer told
you they weren't hacked then it means two things. Either
they really weren't hacked, or someone from the inside
got the information. As far as I can see, no one has
bothered your phone number, hence...*

I "send" Sophie a link to the match. *Hope to see you there.*

*Are you kidding? The Sky Garden? I'll be there with bells
on!*

Chapter Fifty-Six

Back When

I am afraid. How could this have happened? A hit and run? My mind is in
chaos with this harsh vicissitude.
Nick is lying attached to tubes, fighting for his life. The first 24 hours are
the most critical they say, and we are all praying he makes it. His parents,
Freddy, are all in a state of forlorn listlessness. Paralyzed, unable to do, say
or think; much like their Nick.
The doctors aren't optimistic; the MRI showed too much damage.
I sit stunned, torpid. I am without the ability to form a rational thought of
how this came to be. Is it a coincidence? I hate that word.
Freddy is saying something. I didn't hear.

'What did you say?' I ask him.

'I said the police are looking into it. They procured the CCTV recording of the street, and it shows some van crashing into Nick's car. They believe it was deliberate.'

My ears pound. The police… Deliberate crash… What has Nick done now? Who has he pissed off? What does he owe? It has to be a dealer. Shit! He has always been such a reckless kid. This time he played with fire for too long. I suddenly remember the other prototype was in his car.

My phone rings, and I see *withheld number* flashing on the screen and punch decline. Screw whoever it is.

I make my leave, offering encouraging words to Nick's parents, but they can tell I am trying to believe them myself.

I leave the Royal Free and its heart-wrenching ICU. I go home, thoughts drill my brain; it's like finding myself against a blizzard. I open the last beer can in my pathetic fridge and gulp and gulp, anything to subdue the bedlam pounding my mind. I crush the can in my hand and throw it hard at the wall.

I write an email to Croft, my solicitor, explaining the situation, and ask what will entail, now that Nick is… I can barely think it; things are too grim. He writes back and tells me that if anything *happens* to one party, all assets will be transferred automatically to the other.

My God, Nick! What the fuck have you got yourself into this time?

Two hours later, Croft calls me back. 'They're sending a representative. He's coming Wednesday, noon.' And then he tells me the amount, and I drop my phone. I close my eyes and see …hers.

***

Wednesday, Nick is no better. I have to go to the gym; I am running late, and it tries on Brian's nerves, especially so close to an important match. Match… I have no appetite to fight; there are more pressing matters. But I owe him; he'd been so understanding in my moment of need. Siobhan called, and before she could say anything, I told her I was on my way. Brian is probably fuming.

I was detained till late at Canary Wharf last night, that's why I am late for my session today. I had to finish what I started, with or without Nick, so it had taken me a bit longer without him, to set things up, ready to show how my *Eidos* works to the rep from the American company. Edwards, my notary, offered his office for the presentation. After hearing *that* sum, I'm sure he would have offered his body.

I train, readying for the big fight. I will do this for the people who've supported me all these years. I can feel the nervous excitement in the air. I train like a good pupil, obey Brian's program for me for that day, not uttering a word of disagreement. He even looks at me peculiarly, at one point.

''As everyone gone mad today? First, that peculiar goth girl earlier, and now you. You feeling o'righ', son?'

I leave Brian in a rush. Hardly dressed, I run to the Tube. Northern Line, southbound, change at London Bridge. I have twenty minutes till noon, and my heart thrashes, straining to get me there on time.

I enter Edwards' office, gasping for air. The rep is already there with a big grin latched to his face. Croft is also present, suit and tie, creased to perfection. I didn't have time to dress in something better, but I see neither has the rep. Plain jeans and a top. I've been told that computer companies in America have a more laidback mentality about clothing. I feel settled; at least I don't have to impress him with my appearance.

We get down to business after the preliminary how-do-you-dos and firm handshakes. He is speechless as soon as I get it working. The computer has transformed into a different machine before his eyes, and in no time, we are engrossed in my new discovery. I go through the motions of the code, but he's already grasped it. I can see why the company sent him. I hand him all necessary backup with all the software Nick and I have ever used. Then I proudly hand him the component and the lens, like I am handing him a part of me, but also, with great relief. It is a strange mixture of feelings.

'We'll need you to sign a confidentiality contract,' he says, that American drawl becoming more pronounced the more he is animated. *I'll bloody sign anything you want, mate*, I think. *I'll bloody sign your arse!*

Croft presents the new contract, which was drawn up by the notary, on standby if Nick hadn't pulled through in time for the signing. Which he hasn't. *Nick will be so happy. I'll go and tell him…*

I sign with trembling hand for both of us, and then the rep clicks a button on his laptop, and I see the transfer of funds cross from their bank account to mine. I am speechless, trembling, unable to grasp the reality. Is that amount really mine?

The rep slaps me on the back. 'Congratulations, Mr Laidlaw! Nice doin' business with you.'

I find an ATM and withdraw the limit for the first time in my life. I stutter a sob – the sheer, overwhelming relief upon hearing the machine count notes, and not blink some message of me being some unauthorized user. I shake excited, scared, pulling the money out like it might evaporate in my hands. *Jesus, thank you!*

I go to find Hannah and her girl – someone also fighting for her life. My first deed will go to her.

Done with the one hospital, I go to the next. Nick has to know of the news.

***

His mother is there; won't leave his side. Her face has become ashen. Literally the colour of ash. She sees me through the window and gets up, bends to pick up something and comes out with a box. It's the second prototype. I inwardly heave a sigh of relief.

'It has your name on it, Jamie,' she says. She's exhausted. She can barely speak. 'They found it in Nicky's car.' I take it, the package is undamaged – cardboard and bubble wrap are both shock-proof, I suppose. The component should be intact.

'Could you tell him something for me?' They don't let non-members of the family in, and I ask her to convey him the good news. 'Tell him we did it! Tell him …he can choose his yacht.'

The woman looks at me like I've lost my mind, but does my bidding, trusting this must be something that can help her Nicky. Anything to help…

I watch as she speaks to him. Nothing changes. Damn it! They say people in a coma are supposed to be able to hear things, feel things. His mother hasn't said it loud enough, enthusiastically enough. I bang the glass and shout through it, 'WE DID IT NICKY! WE FUCKING DID IT, YOU HEAR ME?! WE DID IT! …WAKE UP! WAKE UP!' I bang and bang and bang. His mother is crying. I feel the tears of frustration sting my eyes. I've caused an upset. The nurse on duty comes and tells me to leave. I notice the security guy making his way towards me.

I leave. I don't want to, but I've been shown the door and… it *is* getting late. I'm half dead.

I take Northern Line at Belsize Park; two stops to home.

On the train, I drift. I think of the hole I live in. I should start looking for another place, yes; first thing next day. To buy a car, no; a sports car… Thoughts percolate; extravagant material goods I have missed out on all these years. Which shops to go to, which deals to make. Realty estate, car dealerships, electronics… a big, plush sofa… the best super-king-sized bed! But suddenly I stop. What am I talking about? *Calm down, Laidlaw. Everything will happen in its own good time.* I ground myself, as my train of thought leads me to the fundamentals: people I love and can now help. An amount is for Nick and his family, first and foremost, then to those who have always stood by my side. To those who have always had my back.

I pace out Camden Town Station. It has already got dark, and the chill bites through. I sway my gym bag over my shoulder and walk briskly on. I still have the other prototype hidden in my jacket and want to quickly bury it in my wall. It is over; all my problems, over. I turn into the street, not seeing where I am going, and almost bump straight into a girl. She has her height… My next move will be her. It is time. Time to own up; have the balls to apologise for the way I treated her.

I turn into the alley. A sharp pain hits my back. I let out a cry as it sends me sprawling to the ground. *What the...* A kick in the stomach, I groan. I cannot breathe. Another blow on my face. Another...

I hear her voice. But how is she here? Am I already dead, and her voice a remnant from my soul?
Then I feel the pain knife me viciously, and I groan. I am alive all right; this aguish could only be of this world.
I dream her voice... *Don't move, James.* Only she has ever called me James. I am not dreaming. 'The ambulance is coming. You're safe now.'

Chapter Fifty-Seven

Now

I twine the wrap firmly around my knuckles, thinking of Dad. He'd have loved all this. I could just picture the smile on his face, like the smiles he'd give us coming home on those bitter winter evenings. *Who'd have thought, eh, Dad? Did it for you...*
I weave the protection around, extra tight, especially on my right-hand wrist. The doctor said I was good to go, but I haven't abided faithfully to the healing process. I haven't relaxed my hand for the required amount of weeks, and I feel a furtive misgiving linger at the back of my mind. I remember James's advice. I didn't listen to that either.
I wear black and the mandatory pink ribbon – the breast-cancer-awareness symbol – sewn securely on the breast of my tank top. I taught myself how to make a French plat; my hair now long enough. I've taken out the six studs that decorate my ears, and I am ready, physically. Mentally, is a whole different story.
The organisers picked out the order in which we are to fight, from a glass bowl. As "luck" would have it, I am to fight last with, one, Maria Guerra, from a club in Hammersmith. She comes from a long line of boxers in her family, back in Mexico, and is brimming with experience. She'd offered to fight because she'd been diagnosed with a tumour in the breast some months back. It turned out to be benign, but the fright she'd got had called her to duty to help others. She told me this herself, as we were having a

friendly chat, waiting for our turn to fight. I told her this was my first
official match.

'Don't pulverise me and knock me out too soon,' I told her. 'Let's give
them a bit of a show first!'

'Uh, ah!' she voiced, serious. 'Doesn't work that way. The crowd will know.
Besides, I don't want to fight a pussy. You put your heart into it, you hear?
It's the only way you'll know your own strength. You'll enjoy it more too.
Literally, put up a fight, and they'll have a great show!'

I've never put up a fight in my life.

Time is upon us. Stacy had appointed Joseph and Martha as my
cornermen, and all are giving me last minute advice on my weak spots.

'You have to be quicker when you weave…'

'Put more force in your back…'

'Got it, yep,' I say. I adjust my gloves and skip, readying myself. I breathe
deep and exhale. Jesus, I am a nervous wreck. Especially after what *he* had
said.

I had mingled a little earlier before confining myself in the room
designated for the boxers to change. Everyone is here except Padma and
Suze. They're both on holiday. Padma is in Mumbai. 'My dad's arranging
my marriage,' she'd shouted over the phone.

'What! You're having an arranged marriage?!' I'd cried.

'Ha, ha. That's not even funny, El,' she'd said, unimpressed. 'No, he's
arranging the logistics of the family 'cos Raj and I are getting married in
London, and we've both got such big families.'

'Can't wait! Bollywood wedding, here I come!'

I'd approached the tables they were sitting at. Mum, Vic, David, Gran,
Grandad, and next to them, Kate, Ferguson, Aidan, Sophie. Sophie, a
stunning cyber-geek, who was really wearing bells – two, dangling from her
ears – had given me a sage titter.

And… Archer.

I had given him my plus one. He deserved it. Getting in the line of fire,
vigilant to get the case solved. He needed a (free) break. He stood to
embrace me, and I returned the gesture. *In another life*, I thought…

He was looking very debonair, and I told him so. He guffawed, going a bit
rosy in the cheeks. I'm sure it was the booze. When I saw he was placed
next to Sophie, I bit my lip. I could just imagine their conversation. 'And
what do *you* do for a living?' But when I glanced at them from afar, I
smiled. Opposites attracted, I supposed.

Stacy had called me to get ready, and I wended my way through the tables
to the changing area. Something had caught hold of my arm. It was gentle.

'Eleanora,' the voice I knew so well said. I closed my eyes and shook my
head. No, no, no. What was he doing here? Why couldn't he just leave me
alone, let me forget him in peace?

'James, please,' I begged. 'I-I can't…'

'What is it?' He was confused. I stared at his translucent, blue eyes. Could he not see my plight?

'What are you doing here?' I asked, perhaps a bit sharply.

He looked taken aback, befuddled. 'I came to see you fight.'

'Why?'

'What do you mean why?'

'I said goodbye. Please leave me alone.'

He let go of my arm, as if electrocuted.

'There is nothing else we need to say. There is no reason for you to be here,' I continued, heated, tortured. 'Don't prolong this. We've been over it. I forgive you, you forgive me… it's done. You're free to go and live your life, James. You don't have to feel like it's your duty to help me out anymore, to sponsor me, or whatever. Our paths are separate now. You don't ever have to see me again. So, you can go back to your house, your garden, your engineering and live a beautiful life with her… Just go!' Hearing myself speak, it made me wince the way I ranted so bitterly. I never thought I'd voice my reproof to him (albeit six years too late), but I couldn't stand him being in my life knowing it would amount to nothing. I couldn't compromise with being just friends.

He stood, as if I'd punched him in the face. He was stunned, hurt …and angry.

'*Her*?' He tilted his head. 'Who –'

'Eleanora! Get a move on, girl!' Stacy's voice came from around the corner. I had to leave; I was running late. I stepped away from him. 'I've got to go.'

'Eleanora?'

I held his eyes. I was shaking. I felt awful, wretched, but it was the only way. All or nothing. I had to be cruel to be kind, to myself.

He looked aggrieved, dismayed. I had no idea why. Then, embittered, he said, 'You know? For all your paintings and pictures, your unmitigated perception of everything around you,' he said vehemently. 'You are so blind!'

Silence. Deafening silence.

One heartbeat, two heartbeats, three…

Martha came, and all but carried me inside, shutting the door on James.

***

I hear my name. I breathe in with a prayer. Going through the motions, walking in slowly under a spotlight and some bad-ass tune escorting me to the ring. I am given an encouraging round of applause. My odds are probably a million to one, and they're feeling sorry for me.

I hold my gloves before my face in orthodox but am too shy to make any fancy moves. I manoeuvre myself between the ropes, onto the canvas.

London is all around me. I'm perched high and am able to watch the Thames turn the colour of the sky. A chromatic spectrum of blues, constantly changing idiosyncrasy with the help of the city's atmospheric ambience. What an evening. I put one glove in the air in thanks, and see him. He hasn't left. He comes closer, moving in and out of people. It is a buzzing atmosphere, activity, commotion, excitement. It is open bar.

James is close. The man is going to ruin me. His presence is throwing me off.

Maria is now being announced. She comes in like a pro. I find myself punching my gloves together, clapping and grinning through my mouthguard, feeling like Jaws in *Moonraker*. She bows through the ropes and comes onto the ring, jumping and brandishing her hand in the air in salute to her ovation. She grins at me through her mouthguard.

It's going to be difficult fighting someone I like. That's why when fighters meet in weigh-ins and interviews before the match, they throw each other threats to psyche themselves up, create an animosity towards their opponent. Enough to beat the living shit out of them, next time they meet.

The referee brings us together to tell us her quick advice. She wants a clean fight and to keep our faces guarded. We nod, and she lets go of our arms so we may go to our corners. People are already hyper, calling and whistling. Tense excitement is heightening.

I know he is analysing my every move, but I mustn't have him in my sub-conscious. I must converge all my attention on me and Maria.

The bell tolls loudly, and my adrenaline goes insane. I prepare instantly, putting fists up in my stance. I have no idea what type of boxer Maria is, so I have to be quick to anticipate her moves. She's coming closer to me and measures how good I am at blocking her jabs, throwing me a few. I'm taller so they don't reach my jaw quite that well. I cross punch and pull back, away.

'Come on, Eleanora!' I hear him, but Maria is lunging for me. She is clearly the one with more power, but I'm the one with bigger reach and agility, and I hook her in the ear. She bounces back a bit, creating some distance. There are whistles and clapping, praise yelled my way. The voices all blend, however, now I'm in the heat of things.

I am gaining more confidence with each throw. Maria finds me with a cross and a hook, and I manage to throw a cross back at her, before I teeter back. I need more strength from my waist downwards. We approach again, toe to toe. She punches, uppercut then hook, a combination taking me back ringside. I parry her right arm with my left, and finding an opening, jab her, I think, in the eye. She's away, stunned with the jab. I think I hurt her. The referee holds her, checks if she's OK. She nods and is released to continue with the fight. We each throw combinations and find ourselves in a clinch. Before the referee breaks us, the bell sounds for the end of the first round.

I am breathing wildly. I sit in my corner, ridiculously enthralled I haven't made an utter fool of myself. They take out my mouthguard, and I'm given water through a straw. My face is cleaned and arms and neck towelled. Stacy is rambling some advice to me, but all I hear is: *you are so blind*. Why am I blind? What have I overlooked, not understood? What has been my error, my misinterpretation?

'She's vulnerable on the chin!'

My heart comes to a standstill. He is at my corner, beyond the ropes, giving advice. Stacy makes no bones about her annoyance, but when she looks to see who it is, is pleasantly surprised.

'You're Jamie Laidlaw?' she says.

'May I come up?' he asks. *No, no, no,* I scream inside me. Martha and Joseph make no objections, on the contrary, they exchange some friendly words. Of course; they'd become all chummy at Bethnal Green.

'I'd be honoured,' is Stacy's answer. The shouts are instant, calls coming from the crowd all around, as he enters the ring, but I don't hear what they say, for he is right in front of me, kneeling, his face level to mine.

He takes the right side of my face in his left palm hastily (there is little time) and brings his left cheekbone to my left temple, the sensation making me close my eyes, and whispers in my ear, 'I'm sorry for upsetting you. I beg you to ignore it all; focus on the match, all right? You can do it.'

I nod. His hair has fallen on my face and I breathe it in. I want him. Oh, how I want him!

'Try to get her on the chin –' The bell dings, forcing us to finish, and he quickly tells me to, 'Be strategic about it, find your opportunity.' And then releases me. Mouthguard in, I am up and all *seconds* leave the ring. Just Maria, the ref and me on the canvas. A canvas painting its own picture.

Maria is at me, being first to punch. I don't like to be in the defensive, I fight better when I attack first. I make it clear by giving her a check-hook and continue with a jab and uppercut, placing my legs firmly in position. She pulls back a bit, rearranging some legwork, but I don't let her charge first. I'm at her with a one-two, finding her chin. She covers up, but it's too late. Now I'm punching her arms and whatever lands near her face, as she backs up to the ropes. She paws but is trapped. The referee has to stop me. Maria moves around the ring, measuring her next move. I've cut her somewhere; blood trickles to the side of her eye. She is told to go to her corner. A qualified cutman tends to her, giving me a breather.

I go to my corner where Stacy quickly slaps an icepack on my cheek and presses hard. I look around tentatively at James. He is still perched on the back of my corner, solicitude delineated on his features. He moves his head slightly, flicking back some hair, and suddenly that look, that look which has bemused me for so long. And it hits me! I remember where I've seen it. Dear God, I remember! The combination of the two movements. Seeing that combination – the flick then the look – fires my recollection. That! It was at the party. He'd been about to kiss me.

You are so blind. I feel the shivers feather their way over my skin, as, at long last, I get the picture. I finally get the blessed picture! I know what he means, and my heart leaps, breathless.

I am no longer blind, I tell him with glistening eyes. I see.

Chapter Fifty-Eight

Now

I am alone inside a neoteric, glass oblong. I've shut the door behind me, the noise has blotted out. I breathe hard, my heart not wanting to settle. How can it settle? I still have too much energy inside.

The rufescent sun is setting over a twinkling London. Those oranges, pinks and violets. I am so high up I can see the world. My world.

It was a great match. We'd given the audience a fantastic show. In the fourth and final round, we fought hard at each other until one of us gave.

Maria, after realising I knew her weak spot, covered her jaw unceasingly. I found her in other places, mostly at her with quick combinations, but they exhausted me, and I had to slow down. She found me on my nose, and I bled. My vulnerable area. If I didn't stop bleeding then Maria would win with a technical knockout. I was taken to the corner, let the cutman shove a swab in my nose to staunch the wound fast, which stung my nostril, sending tears to my eyes. I breathed through my mouth. I was up again, focused, biding my time for the perfect swing.

I bobbed and weaved and ducked, so she wouldn't find my nose again. I swayed away from her short punches and jabbed at her to ward her off.

Maria was showing signs of tiring, as was I. We found ourselves in a clinch. Once, then twice. I twisted out of her clutch and gave her a sudden, hard uppercut, catching her off guard. She toppled back, falling, her knees, giving. People howled, going berserk. I heard my name, lights flashing. The referee was starting the count. But I felt something wrong, and it was in my wrist.

'Are you all right, Eleanora?' James called over the shouts. He'd caught my distress, my pain. I shook my head. I saw it in his eyes; they drew to a worried sadness.

If Maria was unable to get up, I'd win. But if she got up, I wouldn't be able to continue with a damaged wrist. I'd have to forfeit.

Maria got up on six. Dazedly, but up.

My blood pulsed rapidly, as my heart sank. I knew I'd lost. The tears were already in my eyes, yet I smiled warmly at James. He smiled back and gave me a nod. He knew what I had to do.

I bowed my head and knelt; threw in my towel.

There was a second of silence, confusion, then the place erupted into a frenzy. What was I doing? What was wrong? Where had Guerra found me? What? What? But all I knew was, if I continued, I wouldn't be able to draw ever again. I felt it. Felt it the first time I'd tried to sketch after falling on the wet ground at Warren Street Station.

The referee waved her arms. The match was over. Technical knockout.

I felt arms pull me up. It was Maria. She was shaking her head fiercely. 'No! No, Eleanora! Estúpida! What are you doing? Get up! Get up!'

The referee took us by our gloves, stood between us in the middle of the ring, and lifted Maria's hand up. There was ongoing clapping, hoots and cheering. But Maria grabbed my arm and lifted it. 'No!' she shouted to everyone. 'Eleanora's the real winner, not me!' In the distance I heard my family and friends holler in agreement, and the cheering got louder.

Maria and I hugged one another, and I thanked her for her kind words. 'Niña loca!' she said kindly, and I knew in that instant Spanish would no longer be despised.

I left the ring, jumped down, cradling my arm. Photographers were taking pictures, and the organisers were talking into the mic. 'Thank you, ladies and gentlemen, for your amazing donations tonight…'

My wrist was starting to throb. I looked to see where he was, and saw Vic in conversation with him. She caught my eye and grinned. *I can see what all the fuss is about…* I felt my wrist screaming to be released from the glove and quickly left the blare of the tumult behind me, seeking quiet to nurse my wound.

Back When

I hear her voice in my dream. James, she whispers. She tells me to get better soon…

'Do you know a girl called Eleanora Stephens?'

I look at the detective, bewildered. I've been awake for just over an hour, barely coming to terms with finding myself half beaten to death, lying in hospital. And now this fuzz is saying her name?
I don't answer.
'She found you,' he says. 'You were assaulted, Mr Laidlaw. Can you remember anything?'
I'm silent. I have a splitting headache.
'Anything at all, which can help us find your attackers?'
I close my eyes, I'm tired. Plus, I don't remember… I have no memory.
'Sorry,' I whisper huskily. And fall asleep.

***

I wake to darkness and the bleep of soft machinery. I see my vitals on the monitor. A little heart shape showing my pulse.
I think of the detective saying her name, and the bleeping grows rapid. She found me? How? Where?
Eleanora! God! This is no fluke, no accidental occurrence. I am being given another chance, and this time I'm not going to defile it.

Now

I teethe at my left glove, loosening out the strings, placing it under my wing and pulling it off. The tape on my hand has unstuck in some places. I wipe some sweat off my forehead then I undo my right glove, careful not to hurt myself. I take a look. The swelling has begun.
I don't cry; I have no reason. I fought well, everyone saw I was going to win, only my over-worked wrist couldn't take any more.
I sit on a chair near those gigantic glass slabs that make the wall, and stare at that glorious horizon, letting my heart slow. It is so beautiful up here. I close my eyes. Will I remember it tomorrow?
The door opens and closes. It is him. I made out his reflection. I look down at my hands, my mind devoid of all thought… save him, here.
I hear his footsteps come closer. Then his shoes are before my eyes. I blink. And suddenly, he kneels in front of me, head bowed, his blond hair, falling on my hands. He takes my right, and slowly, tenderly pulls off the tape.
I don't speak; my mouth won't move. I gaze at his beautiful, soft complexion, tinted with that light pink on his cheek. I have painted it so many times, he being my anonymous muse, but I have never touched it. My hand goes to his face – it must! – and strokes his cheekbone, his jaw, over

the scar left there… He closes his eyes for an instant, then opening them, beholds me, and I see that look which I now know its meaning.

'I was never with her,' he whispers. 'It was the heat of the moment. I think I would have kissed anyone at that point. Even Brian!' He smiles gently. 'You thought I was with her?'

I nod. I stroke a strand of hair off his temple. His eyes shut at the sensation, dark gold eyelashes swooping down.

'Do you remember, back when we were riding once on the two-four-two, I'd told you I thought I knew the reason why they were bullying you?' I'm silent. He looks at me. 'I told you it wasn't a problem –'

'And I couldn't fix it,' I end for him. 'Yes, I remember.'

He regards me with that look, eyes bright blue, searching. 'My theory proved true…' He lifts a hand to stroke my cheek. 'It was because of your appearance, Eleanora. They wanted to bring you down, punish you for being who you are, for looking the way you do.' His gaze is steadfast. 'More beautiful than anything I've ever seen.'

Tears come to my eyes; how can they not? He moves closer to me, on his knees, between my legs. Those long, muscled hands have found their way around my neck, through my hair. He brings his face up to mine, his lips touch me, finding my right eye, then my left, with light kisses. I shiver. Those wonderful lips kissing me – dear God. My temple, my cheek, the corner of my mouth. Softly… softly… warm… Kisses which leave me breathless. 'So beautiful within,' he whispers 'So beautiful…'

I lift my hand and stroke my thumb across the side of those lips, which have just kissed me, wordless. All I see, all I know is that look.

'Eleanora? I haven't apologised for one more thing.' I stop. There is remorse in his eyes. He bites down on his jaw, looking downward between our warm bodies. I place my injured hand around his waist and my other on the curve of his neck. Then I find his eyes. 'Tell me,' I whisper.

'The way I spoke to you at the wedding. It was…' He stops. Seeks what to say. He takes my hand from his collar and brings it to his heart, grasping tight.

'Do you know what it's like to find out the only person you've ever loved betray you?'

I draw a quick breath. More tears gather as my whole body vibrates from the pounding in my heart. *I know what it's like,* I want to tell him but cannot answer; the admission of his love has transcended over everything.

'I'm sorry for being so harsh; it was the shock. I never expected, never dreamt, you'd do such a thing, and when you told me, my heart ripped in two.'

'I know…' I say, as tears fall. 'I know how you felt. Didn't I act harsh when I had picked up that phone?'

'Yes, but it was my fault. My fault for everything. I didn't accept my father's money, not because of pride, as Lizzy presumed, but because I didn't deserve it. I didn't deserve it, Eleanora, because I had wronged you. I had deserted you. In the end, *I* was the one that betrayed *you*, right from the start.'

I shake my head. 'No, James… we've been through this –'

He moves abruptly and takes me in his embrace, one arm around me; lifting me up from the chair. His other hand goes to the small scar I have above my temple. He strokes it with his thumb.

'I'm sorry for making you bleed when you were running to catch the bus.' He is trembling. 'I knew they were planning to hide your coat, and I didn't do anything about it. I wanted to get out and run back to you so fast, make everything up to you, hold you in my arms… I'm so sorry… Could you ever forgive me for that?' A tear flows from his eye, and I move my hand from his chest to wipe it. 'Nick,' he swallows. 'Nick carried on talking to you, not only because he was a good kid, but for me. He knew how I felt for you, even though I never told him. But I'd changed. He could see it in the choices I made, my reaction to things. How conflicted I had become. He became something like my envoy, keeping a connection. He told me years later. He felt bad for making me stick with his stupid girl plan…'

I blink, but James isn't over.

'When I saw you were at UCL, I asked to clean anywhere but the Slade. I didn't want you to see me like that –'

'James…' I try, but end in a stuttered sob.

'Then when I knew things would change, when I got the idea to build my component, I knew I could face you then; I could dare be in your life.'

'Stop it, James!' I can stand it no more; he is tearing me asunder. I wrap my arms around his waist, close, and don't care of the dull pain in my wrist.

'The house,' he continues, putting his palms to my cheeks. 'I wasn't upset you came. I could see it in your eyes I'd hurt you. I just didn't want you to see the place before it was finished, because I bought it, having you in mind. Everything I did was for you; to be worthy of your forgiveness.'

I lose all composure and cry, and cry. 'James, James…' I manage, after a while, then take a breath. 'I don't know what I would have done if you'd died. I love you so much… from the moment I saw you… I've never stopped!' I gasp my breath in. It is too much!

He searches my eyes as another tear escapes him. 'I wanted to get up in that courtroom and crush those bastards after seeing what they did to you.' He brings his face closer and whispers fiercely to my lips, 'I love you. I've always loved you, Eleanora. You are my life!' Then he touches his beautiful lips to mine and all thought, all sensation, is him. Those soft, full lips kissing me hard and passionate. I take his mouth; I cannot get enough. My heart is pounding, my loins arousing. He holds me higher and tighter, bringing his hand under my nape and through my hair, loosening, freeing those ebony locks I thought he once despised. But he didn't. He doesn't. He has me up against the glass wall, his body flush on mine, as I wrap my legs around him, letting me feel every part of him and he, every part of me, roaming, discovering. My fingers intertwine that beautiful blond mane, finally, and I let out a groan of joy. He takes my lips harder then. His glorious, powerful body, positioning even stronger on me, his beating heart thudding through his chest, touching mine. But those lips, oh, those lips; soft, hot, needing, searching, tasting. The release of all pain and suffering in each fervent motion, dissolving all our woes, absolving each other of our wrongdoings; eliminating the bad and spurring on the good, henceforth as one body, one soul and one heart, as all of London, below us, bears witness to our testimony.

Epilogue

Friend Request: Bianca Matthews. 'Uch!' I say. I read the first sentence of her message.

'I see you married James Laidlaw…,' I read inwardly, in that snobbish annunciation of hers.

I slam the laptop shut. 'Eff off, bitch,' I say, and instantly feel better with myself.

Gran says, if someone is meant to be in your life then they will come again and again. Not if I can help it, Gran. Not if I can help it!

I finish up on my latest parallax and exit my studio. A studio filled with every single sketch, every single depiction, even the one where I'd sketched James's half-naked backside from my phone. James is my obedient muse now. He's posed for me in every position humanly possible. The full frontal is the best, though. Even Gibbons would agree. I blush.

My eidetic memory has finally given up the ghost, but I still remember the light, the hidden beauty, the realism and romanticism, and my ability to paint never wanes. I am grateful. So very grateful.

I pass the landing where our wedding pictures hang, and stop. I pause every time to glance at them. It still feels unreal sometimes. It still feels like it wasn't me. My Ophelia dress. My beautiful groom. A church full of friends and family. Father Athanasius smiling through his white beard. The way James is looking at me as I smile to the camera. That look.

I had taken him to my village. I had held his hand as the sun set… He'd taken in a big breath, awed, and I'd reached over to him and kissed him on our veranda, under the vines, overlooking the undulating hills, as the dwindling summer sun melted into a fabulous magenta spread across the horizon. I'd whispered it was a dream come true, and he kissed me deeper.

I go to the kitchen and check my ingredients. Homemade souvlaki – Gran's recipe.

Then I stop and watch them out in the garden, and my breath hitches. His little, blond head just peeping through atop his father's supine body on the picnic rug. I can't stop the tears coming. My heart is bursting with gratitude; just how inconceivable it had all felt, and now look!

I pour some lemon juice from the fridge – Elizabeth's recipe – and take it out to James. My James. My husband. It's scorching today. He sits up at seeing me, and I sit down next to him, handing him the glass. He sets it aside and kisses me fervently, stroking my hair down to my back, as he usually likes to do. Then strokes the bulging mound on my abdomen, with a contented smile.

'How's Nicky?' I say. 'He been a good boy?'

Nicky turns on hearing me and babbles something to me. I laugh, 'Only you know what you're saying, little man!'

'Eleanora?' James says tensely.

I'm startled. 'What is it?'

'Say that again.'

'What? "Only you know what you're saying, little man"?'

'Yeah…'

'Why?'

'I think I've just come up with a new idea…'

I smile.

'I think I'll sell it as an app.'

***

I sign in later that evening. Nicky has dropped off in James's arms, and he takes him up to bed. Moments later, he is downstairs again with the baby monitor on. There is peace as we both sit in each other's embrace in the living room, TV on low.

I click on to her friend request again on my laptop, which is resting in my lap, as James watches, curious. He jerks when he sees who it is. 'No, Eleanora. I don't want –'

'Don't worry. I'm not,' I reassure him.

There *is* one thing I would like to tell her in response to her inquisitiveness. I type.

'If it weren't for you…'

The End

Apologia.

Although I have done my best to be as accurate as possible in my assertions involving the elements of this book, I know, however, I have made a few mistakes here and there. In regards to the judiciary system in England, UCL policies, UCH policies, boxing regulations, Inland Registry Service, and other minor details, such as Highgate Cemetery, St Dunstan's-in-the-East, Temple church, York Hall, let me be the first to say it was unintentional. But with every work of fiction, there are always some unavoidable depictions that must be put in, in order to make the story work. I did as much research as I could, having had practically no first-hand experience in either the judiciary system, nor UCL, boxing, etc. to bring Eleanora's narrative to life. It was purely to make this book more enjoyable. I do not know, for example, if a singer busks in London Bridge Underground, or if three cleaners work in UCL, or if police officers can be invited to other police stations, but you understand why I wrote it in, right?

Acknowledgements.

Many, many thanks to Vassia Sarri who has paved the way to this self-publication. Your enthusiasm alone has not only brought me great assistance but hope and confidence. Keep up the good work!

To my sister, Christina, after whom Eleanora's sister, Victoria, was inspired, and for once being a goth herself and taking me with her to those nightclubs... Thank you, to both you and Stuart, for helping me in proofreading this book and offering your advice on improvements.

To Mum, Helen, who unknowingly was helping me in her own way so that I could write. Thanks for all the ironing and cooking of food.

To my dear friend Pru, much like what Padma was to Eleanora, who helped with her advice, too.

Much thanks to Kate Bush's *Running Up That Hill,* which, with Placebo's melancholy rendition, encapsulates Eleanora's feelings perfectly.

The quote from the film *My big Fat Greek Wedding*, many thanks.

Prince's, *You Sexy MF,* and Mariah Carey's *We Belong Together*, again, many thanks.

Martika's *Love Thy Will Be Done*, one of my favourite love songs, thank you.

And to Nikos, Irene, Helen, Eleutheria-Skepi, Philothei and Panteleimon for your incredible patience and support. I thought you'd all get sick and tired of me typing avidly on my laptop every free second I got, but no, on the contrary, your smiles were my biggest encouragement. Your comments, such as, 'Finished yet?' spurred me on! This is dedicated to you, and so is my love.

About the author.

Dorothea Neamonitos worked as an ESL teacher for over seventeen years before turning to fiction writing. Born and raised in London, Dorothea moved to Athens when she married Nick. Together they raise their five children. If it weren't for you is her first completed novel.

You can follow and support Dorothea on:

@dorothea_author

Made in the USA
Las Vegas, NV
21 December 2021

39104338R10184